THE EXECUTED

CRIMSON DAWN CHRONICLES

INTERNATIONAL BESTSELLING AUTHOR

YD LA MAR

Uncharted Territory
Eastern Wastelands
Clan Lekim
Ashborne
Human Resistance
Silverforge
Clan Cirse
The Steel Fang
Clan Sira
Clan Sae
Black Hollow
Western Wastelands
CIRLITICA

PROLOGUE

"HAVE HER EXECUTED BY THE END OF TOMORROW." HER commanding voice was devoid of emotion—as if the conversation was merely a continuation of inquiring about what the dinner menu consisted of.

The beings before me weren't normal. These menaces of Clan Cirse were of the many nightmares told around the fire to ward off children from being tempted to stray too far from home.

In this fallen world, it became easy to blame the mutations in genetic code because of some unknown virus from the past. Humans easily became divided into those who evolved and those who remained the same. At least, that was what the rumors were along my journey away from home.

They considered themselves the elite in this world, developing a hunger for the blood of their own kind. Four major clans branched off, each one against the next—and every one of them hungry to use humans as chattel for their own pleasures and feedings.

Memories of my father's warning of Clan Cirse ran through my mind. I missed my father, my own home... the way my mother used to comfort me. But the smell of his blood continued to linger in my nostrils... or was it my own?

My muscles ached as I hung here, a prisoner of war, if one could call it that. Clan Cirse happened upon me during my travels through some of the dilapidated, heavily human areas. I looked around my torture chamber and noted the abundance of tools they had, and how much we lacked out there. Humans were left to live in wastelands, looking for scraps, trying to hold life together through small communities while the clans lived like royalty.

With another stuttering breath, I took in the scent of blood and decay, along with the chill from the outside. It didn't make any sense why a northern clan would be so far south.

Growling to myself, I hung my head. I wanted it to be over. I was tired of it all. I should have never crossed the path to the East. The last human encampment with burning bodies on crucifixes drove me into a fight or flight response. I never witnessed anything as horrendous as the cooked bodies of vampires shrieking in agony while flames continued to come to life, consuming everything in its wake. Their suffering burrowed itself under my pores until it became a part of me—as if I were one of them, charred for the pleasures of men and their 'retribution'.

Hung on this wall by the shackles at my wrist, I pondered the stupid probabilities of my past decisions. Running seemed easier at the time, but now, I wasn't sure which was the better choice—if death was imminent no matter the chosen path.

Like a horrible aftertaste that refused to wash away, the smell of charred flesh buried itself into my memories.

"You still alive?"

The voice of one of my tormentors broke me from the recollection. The images of skin peeling off bone faded into the background, now replaced by his wicked smile.

"Darius, don't play too much. The queen wishes for an audience in her final hours, if you please." As if it was a request and not a requirement, her voice lingered in the air like the devil's advocate. "Remember that she will be used for Queen Isabella's peace treaty with Clan Sira."

"Yes, of course, Mistress Tyre."

Tyre. The vampire with short grey hair, eyes as blue as ice, and pale skin gave me one last glance before she exited the torture chambers without another word. Her air of superiority revealed she was one of the few close to the Queen's side.

Purebreds were all alike, I quickly came to find. The chosen among the elite in a world that was beneath them, and they wished to eliminate the unworthy.

Purity, indeed. More like a holocaust among a pathetic excuse for existence, a world already brought to its knees. Was there no mercy to ever be found again in this wretched place? Life should have been obsolete for *all* of us.

Clan Cirse was everything I heard it to be, down to the gritty fact that they were barbaric in their agenda to find *peace.* It was just my bad luck that I ran across the wrong group on my way to ask for water.

The ache in my shoulders made me moan, igniting interest in Darius who stood by watching me with a wicked smile.

Peace was for fools who still believed it existed. Hope was an infection that didn't discriminate.

My torture master sliced my ribs once more to bring my attention back to him. My skin itched from healing itself. His corrupt smile made my gut churn with bile that threatened to spew in his face.

Perhaps I should let it.

I watched as he licked his lips in anticipation of the 'fun' he'd be privy to before the night ended— the night before my final execution per the orders of the Queen.

It was always going to come down to this, wasn't it?

"Pretty little thing, aren't ya? What were you doing out on the streets, hmm? Were you playing bait for Clan Sira?"

His mouth hovered around my neck, then down to my naked breast—his eyes that of a devil who waited to devour the soul brought forth before him. Little did he know that Clan Sira knew nothing about my existence, so their offer of a peace treaty would be for nothing. I made sure to keep that little tidbit to myself.

With a harsh inhale, he pulled back and gathered himself. "Your lack of enthusiasm bores me, hybrid. Good riddance. We don't need abominations like yourself running around, anyhow. At least you will prove your purpose in a larger plan now."

His fingers brushed my skin with a false sense of reverie. He teased my flesh until I wanted to claw my own skin off to rid myself of his touch.

Unable to help myself, I spat blood in his face, smiling with crimson-coated teeth. *If I am to die this day, let it be known to the world that I died with my pride still intact.*

Right at that moment, the image of my father's eyes haunted me. He would have blamed me for this, told me I should have prepared for the possibility. Soon, a different kind of hate lurched in my gut. If hiding me wasn't enough, his disapproval for my own downfall would have killed me anyway.

I lifted my head with a smirk, watching my undertaker wipe his face off with the back of his hand. He smiled back and undid his buckle, and I lifted a brow in challenge. It didn't matter anymore. Nothing did.

He brought it down in rapid successions

against my chest, drawing my hisses through gritted teeth.

I felt my skin fileted off bone by the time Mistress Tyre came back with the intention of escorting me into the court before the Queen.

"Darius. Really?" she grumbled.

Grabbing my arms, she broke my wrists with an audible crack to slip them out of the shackles. I pressed my lips tightly together to stifle a moan. My body was tossed onto the floor and kicked one last time for good measure.

Clan Cirse can burn in the depths of hell.

Groaning, I buried my face and hands away from her lest they see how quickly I heal. It was something that led to my troubles back home, back in Silverforge. The community turned against me the more I began to change. I had never compared the extent of my healing abilities to a normal vampire, but today was not the day. No, I'd rather take *all* my secrets to the grave.

Father would at least be proud of that... if he knew what I was capable of.

Hard hands grabbed my body and lifted me. My legs dragged behind me over concrete and carpeted flooring as the one called Tyre continued to pull me toward a room I had never seen.

She threw me a few feet in front of her. My arms automatically extended to cushion the fall and I instantly knew my mistake as the wind was knocked out of me. Hopefully, no one else noticed.

A boot landed on my back the same moment I

tried to push myself up. Darius stomped on me again, slamming my face on the floor, rattling my brain.

"So this is she?" came an unfamiliar feminine voice in a bored tone.

My anger rose with every breath. What was with these Clan Cirse members? If they were so bored of everything, they should exterminate themselves to rid themselves of their misery.

I should cool it. I shouldn't lose my temper but these vampires were testing me.

"Not much of a hybrid, is she?" Tyre scoffed.

The adrenaline in my body morphed into something that overtook my senses, a phenomenon that had only happened a few times in the past—my exponential increase in strength. The moment my father found out was the moment everyone else in the community did, much to my dismay. The smell of their blood still lingered in my nose to this day.

I didn't understand it myself, but at this moment, I let it take over.

With a quick twist of my body, I grabbed Darius' ankle and broke it with a loud crunch that echoed in the room. He howled in pain and the smile grew wider. The others in the room pulled him back when he lunged at me, screaming profanities. I looked over my shoulder and blew him a bloody kiss.

Queen Isabella stood from her throne, her long grey hair played behind her and stepped forward from her dais. I wondered if this was a common trait of the northern vampire clan or if she was merely related to Tyre by blood. As she took each step, she looked down at me with disgust. With a knee on the ground, I glared back at her. The feeling was mutual.

"Deliver her at nightfall," she snapped. "Make sure you drop her right at their doorstep and they see your face, so they know *who* calls for them. Tyre, you will accompany Darius to make sure the proposition of the peace treaty is articulated correctly and effectively to Clan Sira."

"Yes, my Queen," Tyre replied. Her continual calmness irked me.

The vampire queen bent down, grabbed my chin, and forced my face toward her. Her eyes bored into mine with such internal hatred that I could not help but reciprocate the same energy. My body buzzed with the need for bloodshed, but my mind knew I was outnumbered amidst this horde.

The room suddenly dropped in temperature, goosebumps prickling my skin. Isabella's other hand shot out toward me, her claws piercing the side of my throat as she lifted me up. The warmth of my blood seeped down my sides as I struggled to spew my hate in her face.

The queen's eyes flickered before she bore her fangs. "Fool. You are *nothing* to me! A mere hybrid piece of scum amidst a world led by the elite. The others will come to accept the fact that I was destined to rule this world. Clan Sae, is only the first and they will be destroyed by my hand."

Her grip tightened, the sound of blood squelching overshadowing my gargles as my eyes began to roll back.

"They think to offer *me* a truce?" She laughed humorlessly. "Pathetic. The only thing they could offer me is a knee as they bow before my throne, worshiping me as a God."

Another set of nails dug into my neck, ripping away at my flesh as my consciousness began to fade, my soul trying to leave my body.

The queen's growls echoed in the room and bounced in the back of my skull right before she pulled her arms outward, and everything turned into darkness.

I

ELISEO

"We're organizing the next group. You in?"

I gave the kid a look. He must be new to have asked me such a stupid question. I was usually the one who led the scavenge groups here in Ashborne.

"Yeah," I grumbled while looking him over. "I'm in."

I gave him the benefit of the doubt. He might just be *that* stupid.

Over the past few years, Ashborne accumulated a multitude of new arrivals. The mass increase in unfamiliar faces made me uneasy but that was the way of the world. Humans were all trying to survive and the best way to do that was to inject yourself in established communities like this one.

The last hunt we organized ran us into a small human encampment, threatened to be overtaken by new, rogue vampires. My eyes zoned out before me as I went over the information we had accumulated over the years through our experience. Newly created vampires were stronger than usual, nasty and had a brutal hunger for sex and death. Knowing this, we couldn't allow the human group we came upon to be slaughtered like a buffet—and we couldn't leave them to fend for themselves after most of their fighters were taken down in bloodshed.

Blinking a few times to rid myself of the memories, I realized the kid was still standing there as if waiting for more words from me. I got to my feet, dusted myself off and walked away, ending the conversation. He could find me when they were ready. I didn't need to babysit his ass.

Making my way past the center of Ashborne, I headed toward Samuel's residence and knocked on his doorway. "Fucker! Are you up?"

"Shit, with you banging on my door, I'm up now." A groan floated past his hung curtain—a makeshift door and barrier. Samuel had a tiff with someone's husband, ending up shattering the original wooden door that came with his place right off the hinges. Why he chose to never find a replacement after that incident, I would never understand. This fucker was just *asking* for trouble.

Samuel popped his head out from behind the fabric with his hair all over the place and his dick out, glistening for all to see. I scowled. This was what happened when the world went to shit—respect and decorum went out the damn window.

Ignoring what was in front of me, I continued. "We got a group rounding up."

He rubbed his face and threaded back his hair with his fingers. A feminine groan floated out through the curtain, and I raised an eyebrow. Samuel smirked and clasped his hands behind his head, shrugging.

"Look, you should know this by now." His dick rose halfway when the next feminine moan came out, causing him to turn his head over his shoulder as if by an invisible force.

I punched him in the arm to get his attention back. "Asshole. Tell your pussy to leave. Get ready. We head out in a few. I don't trust this new kid they got going around gathering folks. Too young, too stupid, and I ain't dying today."

Samuel's face sobered as he crossed his arms over his chest. "Fuck. Why are they letting the newbies go out? Didn't we just save them from themselves?"

I wondered the same thing. But I was simply another soldier in this place, just like Samuel was. They needed us for our muscle and our survival instincts, nothing more.

"I don't know, and I honestly don't care. I'm sure it has something to do with making everyone feel 'welcomed'. I just want to come back alive, you feel me?" In a world gone to shit, we had to watch out for ourselves first and foremost.

"Yeah, I feel you." Samuel turned around and yelled out, "Hannah! Get your ass out of here. I need to leave."

"You asshole!" came a feminine screech.

He smirked and tilted his head in acknowledgment before heading back inside. The sound of arguments grew louder and louder, but I refused to stand and listen. Samuel and his girl went through this every time he had to leave. I honestly began to conclude that it was her weird way of showing him she was afraid he wouldn't return.

He should be grateful someone wanted his ass to come back at all.

I left his porch and looked over the sea of heads that had accumulated during my short talk with Samuel. Ashborne was lively during this time of the day. I walked past the next few homes, keeping my eyes out for my usual crew. We always scavenged together and we always came back fruitful. Every time we tried different groupings, the men always came back complaining about someone wrecking the mission, or someone didn't come back at all.

A dark, familiar head crossed my line of sight and I focused in. With two fingers in my mouth, I put out a whistle over the growing crowd around the center of the town. Reed's head turned, over a block down, and whistled back.

"We got a group heading out?" he hollered over everyone, making a few turn and scowl.

We ignored them as we continued to communicate loudly. "Yeah, go find Gunner, and tell him to meet me behind the market."

We used to have one more to our crew, Khalil, but he was a lone wolf, and couldn't handle the rapid growth this place brought. That scary fucker was a force to be reckoned with, but his nightmares always got the better of him—a past he never spoke about. I hoped wherever he ended up, he was still surviving. We needed more men like him in this world.

Reed threw a thumbs up in acknowledgement and I turned to leave the center neighborhood streets, trudging back toward my own residence on the outskirts of town, closer to the wall. Socializing was something I could only take in doses.

A few paces away from my house, I heard her voice and inwardly groaned.

"Hi, Eliseo." Mrs. Reyes from three doors down quickly walked toward me, trying to flag me down the way she usually did when she could catch me outside of my home. She was one of the many reasons why I didn't hang around back here much.

I gave her a courtesy wave and continued through my front door without looking back. These women and their false sense of security behind the community walls. Didn't they know that life was not promised to anyone? She could take her plate of alternative cookies to someone else.

Locking the door behind me, I gave my humble home a look over. Ashborne was lucky to be able to build the collective over a former gated community. Most of the homes were still sturdy and worked for the most part. Walking down the hall, I turned to look for my weapons cache. We had been able to collect a lot on our last run, increasing the ammunition supply. Grabbing the shotgun and pistol, I checked everything else in the house to make sure nothing was out of place.

Sure, it was nice to be within a walled community, but that didn't stop thieves from being who they were. I would know. I'd thieved plenty in my time.

Strapping up, I went around inside my home to secure the house. I had lived alone here for a good handful of years, left the previous encampment behind with bad memories of a past I wished to forget.

I could still see her face, coated with blood and fear as I watched her choke and gurgle until her last breath. I should have never left on the hunt that day. I should have stayed and protected her.

Gritting my teeth at the flashbacks, I walked out my front door and looked left and right to make sure Mrs. Reyes wasn't waiting for me. I appreciated the good neighbor sentiment, but there were things to be done and I didn't have time for stupid little trysts with women who would only end up clinging to a man like me—a man with no commitment to offer.

Locking the door behind me, I quickly made my way toward the main building on the other side of Ashborne. My team and I liked to strategize and split into groups before we left the premises. It was good practice to have a plan of attack in a timely manner in order to keep our numbers up when we made it back. Despite the influx of new community members, it wasn't good to lose the ones who were already established here.

"Fucker, hold up!" Samuel's voice called out behind me, making me stop in my tracks.

I turned and saw he was finally dressed in cargo pants and a henley that had seen better days. At least his dick wasn't swinging about.

"Where's Hannah?" I asked.

"Pfft. Off somewhere cursing my name, I'm sure. Don't worry about her. She'll be fine. She knows I'll come back."

Did she? Let's hope his good luck streak doesn't run out any time soon.

"Oi!" Another familiar voice came toward us. We both turned to find Reed walking beside Gunner who was fully strapped with a crossbow and bolts. It was smart to have quiet long range weaponory in case we ran into trouble.

"Hey, wassup man?" Gunner tilted his head in acknowledgement as we all walked toward the meet spot at the front center of town.

"Looks like they rounded up a good number this time," Reed added.

I turned my head to find at least a good sixteen people milling about with weapons. Most of them looked around the age of my crew while some of them looked like boys, making my shoulders tense.

"Gentlemen, so glad you could join us," Sergio's, our makeshift governor, snarked. Always one with something to say, yet never had the balls to go out there to get his hands dirty.

I ignored his statement and chose instead to look over the crew. My eyes narrowed on a smaller fellow that looked to be the size of a young teenager. *This won't go well at all. We don't have the luxury of losing people. Why were they desperate for numbers on this trip?*

Sergio cleared his throat in an attempt to get my attention. I couldn't care less. The only thing that ran through my mind was how far I could carry this kid in front of me if he were to go down in a fight and we had to retreat to home base.

"Eliseo. Glad you and your men could join us," Sergio tried again.

I ignored him and took a step forward.

"Kid, we don't need any casualties today. Why don't you stay back and protect the people back home while we go out and fight the good fight, eh?"

The boy I addressed turned. He had a baseball cap covering most of his face. His oversized clothes didn't help his case whatsoever, it only made him look younger, drowning in layers of fabric.

He didn't respond, instead just turned around and walked to the other side of the group, putting distance between us. *Asshole.* He would definitely be a liability. Couldn't even take a command when he heard it.

"Reed, keep an eye out on that one," I instructed.

Reed came up behind me and scanned the people. Once he saw where my sights landed, he answered, "You got it."

Sergio cleared his throat again and I finally turned to face him with a scowl. *What the hell is up his authoritative ass?*

When he saw my expression, he backed up with both hands held up, palms out. I didn't like asshole politicians who thought they knew better than the troops. He needed to know his place, *and stay there.*

With a curl of my lip, I turned to address the people gathered with Samuel snickering behind me. "Look, this ain't our first rodeo and if it *is* your first, then you're shit out of luck, because I'm not here to teach you a damn thing. Keep your eyes peeled for bloodsuckers, stay alive, and gather as much useful supplies as we can. Stick together. Don't go trying to be a damn hero on your own because heroes die, ya feel me? That doesn't help us one damn bit."

Some of the newbies squirmed where they stood. *Figured.*

I whistled to my guys and they started to number people off. Samuel's jovial voice boomed loud enough for everyone to hear. He knew my temper was short for stupidity.

"Alright, we're splitting into three groups. Gather around, everybody." Samuel pulled a map from one of his cargo pockets and walked toward the wall of the closest building, spreading it out. "Team A, you will be heading east. Team B, you hit up the north area. Team C will scour the west. We meet back in this spot in two point five hours. Any questions?"

"I don't have a watch. How will I know two point five hours have passed?" The question came from the kid who announced the group was gathering this morning. Was he shitting me?

Samuel chuckled. "That's exactly why I split you all up the way I did. Each team will have a time keeper. Stay alive, or we're leaving you behind. We're not about to harbor the infected, got it? We've got too much at stake."

I stared at the kid who spoke, emphasizing everything Samuel pointed out with a look. When he caught my eye, he audibly swallowed and turned away from my ire. We had yet to leave and I was already tired of this nonsense.

"Alright, let's gather the vehicles," Gunner continued, his voice loud and clear.

As everyone began to move into position, my temper slowly died down, knowing that I would get some action today. Living in a walled community was nice, but it made a person too lax. Some days, as much as I hated to admit it, I missed living on the run, hopping from abandoned building to abandoned building. It kept my skills up and my mind sharp. And in a world where bloodsuckers were out to devour you, it was a necessity.

We needed to be on our P's and Q's in this life. Bloodsuckers continuously grew in number, and for all we knew, we'd be surrounded and taken as cattle for their blood farms. Rumors about people going missing gave most people nightmares but I wasn't going to let that happen. We survived too long to become mindless blood banks.

Having a crazy doctor in the camp was enough.

"Gunner, take the jeep," I ordered.

He nodded at my command and moved toward our outer garages.

"Samuel, you're going to be with me." The fucker saluted me like an imbecile, but I ignored it.

My prior military background would go with me to my grave. I hated to let people know what I was capable of, because expectations were then placed on you. No. These days, it was everyone for themselves. We did what we had to to survive. *I'd* done what I had to to survive—from thieving to murdering.

I didn't regret a thing.

I made my way toward the vehicles and caught the small kid in my periphery, following me with a few others. Crap, was he on my team?

Samuel, the asshole, laughed and walked toward one of the other teams, pretending he knew nothing of what occurred.

Gunner started the first jeep while Reed grabbed the only Humvee we had. Looking at the crew cab truck, I wondered if I should just chuck the kid with Reed for more protection.

I unlocked the driver's side door, rolled my shoulders, and turned to address my designated group. "Team A, get your asses in the truck so I can do a headcount!"

A few people followed Samuel with the kid a few paces behind. I counted the heads around me and spotted Reed with the other team of five.

"Alright, are we all strapped up?" I asked, scrutinizing everyone. "What kind of weapons are you all carrying?"

"Everyone's got at least a pistol on them," Samuel supplied. "I'm strapped with a few extra knives."

At least a pistol... I wasn't feeling good about this.

"Anyone with a quiet, long-range weapon? Silencers? Anything at all?" I looked over the men to see how they would fare in hand-to-hand combat based on their build.

The kid I was uncertain about cleared his throat but didn't say anything. His baseball cap was tilted down, hiding his face. *Let's just get this outing over with,* I inwardly groaned.

"Alright, everyone in the car," I commanded.

Samuel snickered again, and I slapped him upside the head. He flinched and scowled at me. It was his fault I got this group. What the hell kind of division was that? He couldn't get me anyone reliable at all.

"Damn, Eliseo, don't be such an ass," he complained as if knowing my thoughts. "You still have me."

"That doesn't make me feel better whatsoever." I was lying. It did, but he didn't need to know that.

The other two teams had already left the garage and were headed toward the gates. Once the last man got in and shut the door, I pulled out after them, thinking over all our strategies to make sure we made it back alive.

Let's hope we didn't run into any other bandit groups or bloodsuckers. I really didn't feel like saving another group of humans if I was being honest. My mood soured as I thought of the group that was with me now.

Hopelessness was stifling. I opened the window, leaned my elbow out, and rubbed my head.

The air already felt different on the other side of the gates. The ominous sound of the wall shutting us out, reverberated in my skull as we drove down the desolate streets right outside the community. Rusted-out, abandoned vehicles littered our view as we trekked toward our destination. This outing would lead us a third of the way north towards the Clan Lekim's territory.

Looking at the rearview mirror, I cataloged what we wore. It got colder the further north we traveled, but it wouldn't be freezing like Clan Cirse's territory.

Gunner drove off the road on the next right and led us toward the last town we'd ransacked. When we crossed into the town's limits, the scenery was desolate and rundown, the same as it was the last time. Windows were shattered and some buildings had been decimated for ages. Despite the uninhabited area, something was off.

My eyes narrowed in suspicion. "Samuel, when was the last time we came this way?"

Samuel looked around and answered me with his face toward the passenger side window. "Two months."

"The corner store. That's new," I pointed out.

Samuel turned his head to look at the location I indicated. "Yeah. That wasn't there before."

He grabbed the radio and it crackled to life before he pressed down the button. "Keep your eyes peeled. Looks like recent activity."

"Roger that," Gunner's voice clearly came over.

An hour on the road, and the scenery went from city buildings to vast areas of farmland. There hasn't been a time I remembered it looking like anything else. What was the world like before the change? Before we mutated and became two different types of people. I didn't think the answers would ever be found, not in this lifetime. I kept eyes peeled on our surroundings as I continued to wonder if the world was a better place before my existence.

Were vampires always here? Were stories about the genetic mutation all a myth?

That was a question for old Otis back at home base. Ashborne's crazy doctor more than likely knew something but no one was willing to ask. He gave me the creeps most days, but he was all we had.

The truck went over a bump and suddenly we were back on an actual road. Dirt kicked up behind us, sending dust into the air that clouded our rear view. It made me antsy, but I didn't show it. I didn't like being blinded from one side. Once it settled, so did my nerves.

I continued to replay what I witnessed in the previous town. Something broke through the side of the building, a fight of some sort—but what created that much power?

Gunner pulled into a field a few paces from what looked like an abandoned old-town style shopping center. Once we all parked, I whistled for everyone to get out and keep their eyes open. Everything appeared quiet beside the rustling of trees behind us. Cars looked to have already been looted and broken into. We would avoid them to save on time.

"Eliseo! There were three houses in this area the last time I scouted," Reed hollered at me.

Without looking at him, I tipped my head in acknowledgement and led my group, Team A, toward the shop in front of us.

"If you see any extra backpacks or bags, grab 'em," I instructed.

Samuel passed the message to the others,

followed by murmurs of agreement, as I lifted my shotgun and began to clear out the first store. A few of the guys looked through cabinets and drawers while Samuel and I continued toward the back.

"Clear." I lowered my gun and headed back to the front of the store.

"Anything?" Samuel asked.

"I found a container of seasoning," one of them piped up, lifting said item in the air.

"Grab it and let's go," I instructed as I headed out the front door. We needed to keep on a steady timetable.

Samuel cleared the next building but it was ransacked heavily so it wasn't worth our time. Crossing the street, the next store looked more promising. Once cleared, we all start combing through the shelves and walls.

"Got some pain killer," someone called out.

"Good. Keep looking," I told him.

"Shit, half a box of ammo," Samuel grinned.

Maybe luck *was* with us after all.

BOOM! A loud crash against the brick wall of the store shut us all up. Brick and broken pieces of cement came at us like shrapnel as we dove behind the counter, dust obscuring our vision and clogging our nostrils. Waving my hand in front of my face, I looked around the room to do a head count, when two extra bodies emerged from the gravel.

It looked like a sight from hell, skin boiling as they growled at each other while their flesh sizzled beneath the peaking sunlight. They instantly threw fists and grappled like two mad men, the only difference was the strength they showcased with each blow. It was incomprehensible—it was inhuman. *Bloodsuckers.* The fact that their skin sizzled in the daylight only reiterated what I already suspected.

As I low-crawled around the counter, I caught Samuel behind one of the shelves still standing. I flicked my fingers and wrist to catch his attention. He nodded when he saw me direct him toward me. We'd bust a hole out the back wall if we had to, but I thought I remembered catching sight of a handle to a back exit door.

BOOM! One of the vampires lunged at the other again, knocking them through another part of the wall. More dust and debris flew but I used it to my advantage as concealment, holding my breath for short bursts. Crouching low and covering my nose with my arm, I walked around and gathered my men, shoving them behind the counter. I could hear Samuel shuffling them to the back room when I realized we were missing one.

Where's the kid?

The sound of rustling beneath one of the fallen shelves caught my attention. A hand clawed at the ground and I quickly grabbed it and pulled.

We both coughed and sputtered as the two vampires outside continued to slam into each other, knocking more walls down. Some debris hit my left eye, but all I could do was shut it, wincing through the sting, while I held onto the kid.

The sound of a crunch made my heart skip a beat, followed by the groans of a man in throes of passion—or from feeding. I'd heard it once before and it was a sound I would never forget.

I shook my head and dislodged the past. *There's no time for this!* I pulled the kid out again with all my might and he finally broke free. I quickly bent down and tossed him over my shoulder. I was taken aback by how light he was.

The kid coughed against my back as I jumped over broken pieces of wood and concrete, careful not to slip my footing. As I ran toward the back, a growl broke my concentration. It sounded too close, and the hairs on the back of my neck stood on end.

Something slammed into me and took us both down, right into the back wall with a painful *thud*. The wind was knocked out of me, but the only thing I could think about was the damn kid.

"Seems I came at just the right time," one of the bloodsuckers growled. "I'm getting a little *hungry*."

Clenching my fist, I got to my feet and gave myself a few seconds to get my mind back on track. I *hated* vampires—they were the bane of my existence in a place where survival was hard enough.

"I think you've got the wrong fuckin' buffet," I spat as I turned around and glared at the creature before me. He still looked human, but everything about him was just *wrong*.

Despite being shaded by the roof of the store, it didn't hide his blistering skin that had begun to heal in front of my very eyes. He smelled like burnt hotdogs, and it made me want to gag. I'd never see the meat the same again, not after this. Half of his hair was singed off from contact with the sun. He had to be a *new* vampire, his actions were too erratic. They didn't usually come out in the light of day for a stroll. His nostrils flared, and my body tensed in anticipation. This crappy life kept me in survival mode 24/7, even at the age of fifty.

The creature in front of me bared his teeth and lunged, but I dodged in time to bring my elbow down on his back and roll away. I grabbed the pistol still strapped to my waist, aimed and let off a few rounds. He moved quickly, and landed right on top of me with his hands around my neck, knocking my gun to the side.

"On the contrary, *human*. That last vampire filled me up pretty well. You, on the other hand, can serve a different purpose," he taunted.

His sinister smile and lust-filled eyes made me realize I might not make it out alive. But I wasn't about to let him use my body for whatever nefarious reasons he had.

Slipping my forearms between his, I forcefully loosened his hold just enough for me to get a knee right to his crotch. I assumed it still functioned the same by his innuendo, so it should fucking hurt the same, as well. He growled as he fell to the side, giving me enough room to straddle him and grab the knife I kept in my boot. I pulled my arm up to slice his neck, but he didn't stop clawing at me.

Struggling to gain the upper hand, we grappled in place with dust kicking up around us until he landed a knee to my abs and tossed me off. Crashing into the broken concrete on my back, I groaned as a sharp pain shot up my spine.

"I'm too old for this shit," I grumbled after a few breaths.

Just as I was about to get up, something blurred in my vision. More dust kicked up making me cough up a storm. I got to my feet and looked around for the shotgun I dropped during the initial crash into the wall.

The sounds of grunts and growls kept me on edge until I finally saw what I was looking for. Grabbing it, I swung the barrel up and pointed at the primary location of the noise. The dust settled, and the sight before me made me cock my head in confusion.

The vampire's head was cut clean off, rolled into the sunlight, and had subsequently burned into ash. I watched in morbid fascination as the kid grabbed the carcass and shucked it into the sun as well, destroying what was left of him.

Before the ashes could float in the wind, Samuel drove our truck right over where his body would have been. He leaned half of his torso out the window and looked around.

"Did I get him?" he asked quizzically.

I shook my head and rolled my shoulders, then

looked at the kid whose head was still down. He was covered in dust, some of his clothes ripped in places as he silently walked toward the truck and got in. *What did I just witness?* I wasn't sure I could trust my eyesight when it still hurt from taking a piece of debris earlier.

Blinking a few times, I answered Samuel with a bark. "Where the hell were you? What took you so long?"

"I had to corral the guys and head back to get this damn truck. What does it look like? Jim over here was limping, and it slowed us down."

Whatever. They were here now.

"Come on, old man. It looks like you guys handled things just fine. Dust your rusty ass off and get in the car. We'll drive around a bit before we hit up the next spot."

Groaning as I lifted myself to the passenger seat, I put my head back and rested my mind. Samuel could lead from here. I needed a damn break. Fighting a bloodsucker in broad daylight wasn't part of my plan today.

We arrived on the other side of the old town streets after some careful reconnaissance. Exiting the car, we continued on our scavenge. The two vampires we came across earlier must have been an offshoot from Clan Sira. We'd heard rumors that some of them healed faster than they should. Images of the bloodsucker still fighting with half his neck sliced rebounded in my mind.

Could this be evolution? Were they changing on

us, gaining more advantage over humans as the years went on? I snarled at the thought. *What kind of survival of the fittest is this shit, if we're all meant to die, anyway?*

"Don't think too hard over there, you might bust a blood vessel," Samuel teased, his voice grating my nerves.

I punched his shoulder and he chuckled, pulling into a store farther down the old town. We all exited and dusted ourselves off, entering the largest store to clear it. The rest of the trip went smoothly. We were able to obtain some canned food and dried seed packets for a few vegetables.

"We need to head back to the meet spot," I threw out.

"Roger that." Samuel replied. "You want to drive, or me?"

"I'll drive." I probably shouldn't, but I couldn't let the others see any weakness. I needed to set an example of what we expected from each person who chose to go out and do this.

We ventured back to the original parking spot to find Reed and team B already there. As we pulled up beside him, he jumped off the driver's seat of the Humvee and walked toward us.

"You guys get anything good? Judging by the fact that you needed the truck, I'm assuming you found a good loot."

"Shit. I *wish*. We ran into some problems early on, but we handled it. You guys get anything?"

Samuel's demeanor smoothed this over easily without leaving anyone curious. *Good.*

"Yeah, we found some ammo and some canned meat," one of the other team members called out.

The crunch of gravel, pulled all our attention. We looked over to team C, who were just walking back to their vehicles, something trailing behind them on a leash.

"We ran into another group of people to the west," one of the guys I didn't recognize stated. "We traded a couple of guns for this guy." He pulled a single sheep forward, and I held back a laugh.

Gunner did chuckle then. "I had a few pistols I lent the guys. The group was only willing to trade for a couple of our rifles and a knife."

"You're lucky you didn't run into trouble on the way back," I told them, my back still aching from the fight earlier.

"Bloodsuckers aren't known to go that far into resistance territory," Gunner observed.

"We only *hope* that's how it works," I told him. "For all we know, they're just biding their time until they can make it a human blood farm."

With that morbid thought, we all headed back to our respective vehicles. Samuel jumped into the driver's side and mumbled under his breath for only me to hear. "We're going to have to prepare for that, you know."

Looking out the vehicle's front windshield, I

rubbed my fingers on my right temple with my elbow out the window. "Don't I know it."

The drive back left me with an uneasy feeling in my gut about what the future held for us as a species. Sneaking a glance at the rearview mirror, I stared at the kid who still hadn't said a word since everything happened.

First things first. I needed to find out what the hell happened back there.

2

THE MOMENT WE PULLED BACK INTO THE COMMUNITY and behind the gates was the moment my knees bounced with anxiety. My skin felt tight despite my clothes being loose and covering much of me. The tears in the fabric would have to be repaired, I didn't have too many other pairs to switch out. Forcing myself to calm down, I waited until Samuel pulled into our designated garage. When he put the vehicle in park, I immediately opened the door and jumped out.

I knew the big guy would have questions for me. It was stupid of me to lose sight of things, but my fight or flight instinct took over. My heart pounded with every step I took away from the group.

"Hey!" he yelled as if on cue.

I walked faster, kept my head down and my ball cap low.

"Hey, kid!" he called out again.

Biting my lip, I concentrated deeply on the path back to my residence. I picked a home closer to the back of the community, in the shadows, away from the main crowd. I swiftly zig-zagged around homes as I tried to get him off my trail.

Chancing a look back to see if I lost him, my body slammed into something hard, knocking me off my feet. Before I could fall, hard arms caught me, and my heart stopped.

Don't look up, don't look up. "S-Sorry."

I dodged around the body and continued on my way but only made it a few paces before a warm hand gripped my arm tightly.

"Where are you off to in such a rush?" came his deep tenor. "I just want to talk to you."

It was the big guy from the outing that pulled me from the wreckage. I shouldn't have jumped in. I shouldn't have done what I did.

It was too late now, I couldn't go back. *But I could still try to get away.*

I jerked my arm but he wouldn't let go. Panic set in and I kicked him in the gut, knocking him off me. I ran, jumping hedges that whipped and scratched me while I weaved in and out of different yards. I made it to the next house's backyard when his large frame slammed into my back. My face hit the ground with a hard *thud*, sending stars into my vision and the smell of grass into my nostrils.

Groaning, I turned and threw an elbow, only to have him block it with his forearm. I automatically moved my other arm, and we both struggled until he locked my wrists on either side of my head with his brute strength. He was a heavy son of a bitch, but my small body made it easy for me to pull my knees up and plant my feet on his stomach. He growled the same moment I kicked again, knocking him off just enough for me to twist and crawl.

"What the hell is wrong with you, kid? Are you *that* afraid of some questions?" he growled.

He landed on top of me, slamming my head into the ground again as pain radiated through my skull. I was going to have a concussion at this point. I growled and kicked back, but he held his forearm against the back of my neck, and his entire body weight pushed me down into the grass.

Breathing heavily, my mind ran with different escape scenarios... until I realized my baseball cap had flown off as I turned my head. My panic reached an all-time high as I struggled beneath him to get away.

"Fuck, I'm getting too old for this shit," was the last thing I heard before he manhandled me and forced me onto my back.

My eyes widened and so did his. We were both heaving as we stared at one another in alarm. Moments passed, and I could feel my face flame from how hard he stared at me—scrutinizing what he was seeing.

"Either my eyes are deceiving me and you're just a really feminine looking kid who hasn't hit puberty yet, or..." he trailed off and I scowled in annoyance.

He was such a rude asshole. *What if I was really a boy? Who says that kind of stuff out loud?*

His eyes roamed downward and landed on my chest, instantly making me feel insecure.

"Can you not?" I snapped in reaction. I'd been in hiding for so long, it was weird to have someone stare *right there.*

His eyes darted to mine as his face flushed, scrambling to get off me and onto his feet. I rolled the aches out of my body with a groan and stood up as well, dusting my clothes and giving him my back. I couldn't face him, especially now that he knew my truth.

"You've ruined my shirt even more, you jerk. You owe me a new one." *I was pissed. Why couldn't he just leave things be? Why couldn't he just let me go home in peace?*

"Look, if I knew you were a girl, I wouldn't have —" he started, and I gave him a sharp look over my shoulder.

"Wouldn't what?" I challenged. I wasn't normally this irate, but this man was doing something to me. I was always good at keeping calm, keeping quiet, just living my life.

He frowned and barked back, emphasizing each word from his mouth with a flailing arm. "What the *fuck* happened back there? That's the whole damn reason why I needed to talk to you. If you had just stood there instead of running off, we wouldn't be in this mess right now!"

Was he serious?

I turned to him fully and my fist moved before my mind could tell it to stop. The sound of the crunch came before the pain that shot up my arm. His face snapped and twisted to the side, but nothing was said.

Crap, I shouldn't have done that.

Backing up a few paces, my eyes darted again for escape routes. I chose a random direction and turned, only to have him grab me by the scruff of my neck. He dragged me and backed me up until I was cornered against the wall of the next house. His large hands slowly crawled up to my neck and began to squeeze. There was a fire in his eyes, and a red mark that began to bloom on his tanned face.

I needed to learn how to control my strength.

He licked his lips as he stared a hole into my head. "I would be more pissed if not for the fact that you definitely do *not* hit like a girl," he said with an eerie calm. "Now, tell me what happened back there."

Something flickered in his eyes and I didn't know how to interpret it. It made me nervous. I tried to choke out words, but his grip on my neck was so tight, I could barely get air out. My mouth gaped a few times before he noticed and loosened his grip, placing both of his large hands on my shoulders to hold me in place. His very presence was intimidating. He was so much bigger than me, towering in the shadows behind this house like Ashborne's sentinel. The short spurt of courage I had earlier dissipated in his proximity, now that my fight or flight was fading.

I physically shrank as I turned my head to break his gaze.

I took a deep, stuttering breath before answering. "I did what I was supposed to do. No man left behind. The perfect opportunity opened up and I took it."

I left out all the other details, like my fear of the bloodsucker exposing me to the people of this community. I was so tired of running. I just wanted a peaceful existence for once.

"I see." He slowly removed his hands from me but continued to stand there, blocking my path.

I took my chances anyway and swiftly twisted my body to escape, but he slammed a hand on the side of the house with a *thud*, stopping me with the barricade of his veiny arm. I shouldn't stare but I couldn't take my eyes away. He had a tattoo that wrapped around his forearm and trailed up into his sleeve.

"I don't think we're finished just yet. What's your name, kid?" he asked conversationally, as if we didn't just go a few rounds of fighting and grappling.

"What does it matter?" I shot back, unwilling to look him in the eyes.

He chuckled, and the sound elicited goose-bumps along my skin.

"I like your tenacity." He leaned in, and I could feel the warmth of his breath on my neck. "Just wanted to know whom I'll be keeping close to my groups. I don't like incompetent people, and you impressed me today."

The tension I didn't know I was holding relaxed a few fractions and a new emotion ran through me—*pride*. It wasn't something I was used to. I weighed his words around in my mind, replaying it again and again. It was a nice feeling.

Shoving his arm off the wall, I told him, "Fitri," and started to walk away.

"Eliseo," he said after a few moments. His voice was clear, confident.

Grabbing my hat off the grass, I placed it back on my head and looked over my shoulder. "What?"

"The name's Eliseo. Remember it, because you're stuck with my team." He smirked and turned, throwing a hand up in the air as a goodbye.

What was wrong with this guy? *Did he really mean what he said?*

I walked away from the spot, only a few houses down from my home. My mind whirled with thoughts of belonging to something. This outing was initially an attempt to get the frenetic energy out of my system. What would it be like to belong somewhere? Flashes of bodies burning on the stake made me gasp as I ran the rest of the way to my home.

With a relieved sigh, I grabbed the pin out of my hair as I walked up the front steps, and picked the lock. This place used to be a gated community in the past. I never lived during those times, so I couldn't be certain, but it had been whispered among the different flocks of humans I'd come across.

The sound of the *click* lifted my mood as I entered my home and made sure to relock the door behind me. Leaning my back against it, I slid down and put my head in my hands. How did today go from wanting to stretch my legs to running into a pair of newly-made vampires? No one really knew how they came to be; the world had always been the same in the years I had been alive.

I wondered if Eliseo would tell anyone my secret. Groaning, I slammed my head against the door with a *thud*, the smell of grass still in my nostrils.

"You're worrying over nothing, Fitri. It was bound to happen," I muttered aloud.

He still wanted me for future outings, though, despite knowing what he knew now. That had to mean he wouldn't let my secret out. Why would the community allow a woman to go scavenge for supplies? The ratio of men to women was severely unbalanced and everyone was aware of it. I grabbed the bill of my cap and tossed my hat to the side with more force than necessary. It slapped the other wall with a loud *smack* and fell unceremoniously.

This unnatural strength within me was going

to get me in trouble one of these days. Look at what almost happened today.

"Can't do anything about it now," I told myself as I got back to my feet.

I stripped as I walked toward the upstairs bathroom. How this place managed to have running water, I'll never understand, but I wouldn't question it, either. I was just glad I could make a home in this community. Besides the rumors about the crazy doctor, everyone had been pretty peaceful, friendly even.

A few steps up, and my oversized shirt was the first to go. This thing always felt like a blanket on me. Once I was at the top of the stairs, I kicked off my shoes and shucked my pants. I began to unwrap my breasts; the pain from ripping the tape off my skin made me groan in both relief and other feelings I didn't want to think about. Tossing it in the trash bin in the restroom, I rubbed my breasts to stimulate blood flow. My nipples pebbled the warmer it got, and my fingers pinched and pulled, trying to replace the ache with another type of stimulation.

The memory of Eliseo's eyes flashed in the reflection of the mirror on my restroom wall, and I shook my head to dislodge the image. *What was wrong with me?* That old bastard was a pain in the ass.

I stood there in panties and undid the tight bun I pinned under the cap. I had collected these bad boys over time and finally accumulated a good amount to keep my identity a secret, keeping me out of unwanted trouble.

As my arms performed the mundane task, pieces of my past floated through my mind.

"What do we have here, boys? Look at this fresh meat, all alone."

"Do you need a little help, sugar?" came the second male.

My eyes counted the men before me. Seven. All armed. Crap, how was I going to get out of this? I woke up in a field and couldn't remember what happened. The only thing I knew was that I needed to wash the blood and dirt off before someone else found me.

My nose led me to a river. The dead body nearby gave me enough clothes to replace the ones I had on.

"No, I don't need any help," I told them in a neutral tone. The hairs on the back of my neck stood on end as I tried to make my way around them, but they weren't having it.

One deliberately stepped in my way. "You think you're too good for us?"

"Your pussy is probably gaped open from how many people you let in. What's a few more, huh? For the good of humanity. We need to be fruitful, sugar," another one said from behind.

Gritting my teeth, I didn't see the first man move until he was on me, grabbing at my skin. Something within me grew to infernal heights. My body burned with a hatred I had never felt before. My mind found it difficult to catch up, when suddenly, the clothes I'd recently obtained became covered in blood once more, the copper tang of their life force drowning my senses.

The smell of their unwashed bodies singed my nostrils like I was back in the moment. The way their clammy skin touched me. The way their fingers roamed...

I removed my panties and jumped into the bathtub, turning on the shower head and letting the water chill my insides. I felt like killing them all over again, one at a time. My mind must have blanked out the memory for the sake of my sanity, but some days I swore I still tasted their blood on my lips. I just couldn't remember what came before or after the incident.

My mind sporadically supplied flashes of a heavy weight oppressing my chest, of the smell of fresh dirt as my hands clawed for air. *Nothing made sense.*

I wandered the lands, running into different flocks until I ended up here, broken and weary. They quickly took me in after interrogating me in the doctor's strange underground quarters.

The freezing water made me shiver while I scoured my skin with my nails, leaving welts behind. The sharp pain grounded me, forced me to concentrate on the moment and the sensation rather than the fragmented memories of the past —shards I couldn't quite put together.

Running my hand through my hair, I felt the ends tickling beneath my lower back. I might have to cut it soon before it becomes too difficult to hide. I massaged my scalp and tried to calm my senses as my skin began to itch and rapidly heal itself.

Once clean, I turned off the water and stepped out, walking toward the adjoining room. There was a lack of towels in the community so, to let myself air dry, I walked toward my weapon's stash in the bedroom closet. I didn't bring much today, assuming the daylight would have been enough to decrease the chances of running into hordes of bloodsuckers. *Boy, was I wrong.*

"Your lack of enthusiasm bores me, hybrid."

The last word the stranger spoke echoed in my mind as I grabbed the knives I hid in the pants I wore today, putting them back where they belonged.

Sometimes my nightmares gave me flashes of grey hair, of torture and of my *death*. And every time I woke up, I didn't know what was real and what was not. After all, I was here, bent down and counting my ammo. The death *couldn't* be real; that wouldn't make any sense. *So why did it keep playing in my mind like a vivid broken loop?*

I would gain no new answers here, so I continued with my task. Once everything was back in order, I rummaged through the dresser and looked for another pair of panties. I only had three. Grabbing the dark pair, I slipped them on. A *knock knock knock* reverberated through the front door downstairs at the exact same time, startling me.

Looking around for fabric or tape to bind my

breasts, my adrenaline skyrocketed when another knock came through impatiently. I still couldn't find my tape. Growling in frustration, I grabbed an oversized black shirt and quickly tried to braid my wet hair. Running down the stairs with light steps, I jumped the rail the last few steps and loudly skidded on the floor in an attempt to grab my baseball cap.

Shoving everything under it, I tightened it down and unlocked the front door, opening it an inch.

It was the tattoos I saw first. I didn't know whether to be apprehensive or relieved. *What was he doing here and how did he know where I live? Was he following me?*

"Fitri." His voice was calm, almost amused.

I didn't like the way his tenor made me feel when he was like this—not brooding or commanding someone.

"What do you want?" I blurted out with more attitude than necessary.

He lowered his arms slightly and leaned against the outer frame of my door, blocking anyone's view from behind him. I guess I should be thankful for that. I didn't want any unexpected visitors and I sure as hell didn't want him here.

He stared at me for a few moments and the air between us felt thick and awkward.

"I need to talk to you," he finally said.

"You already did."

He smirked, and I slammed the door in his face.

"Fitri, open this damn door."

There was the asshole from earlier. "What for?"

"Fitri."

I growled at his incessant use of my name out in the open and swung the door open a little further than the last time as I bared my teeth at him.

"Can you not?" I tried to look around him, but his torso was too broad; I couldn't.

He smiled, and my eyes widened. *What was he smiling about?* I quickly found out when he shoved his large body through the door and shut it behind us with a *bang. Damn these inward opening doors!*

"What is *wrong* with you?" I snapped, trying to keep my voice down. There weren't many who lived near me, but the ones who did didn't need to know anything about me. *I just wanted to be left in peace!*

Eliseo looked around my humble abode and then ripped the cap off my head. I gasped at the audacity and clenched my fists. *Calm down, Fitri. He's purposely pressing your buttons.*

"So why are you trying to hide the fact that you're a girl?" he asked over my head, still looking around, and then finally, down at my now loosely-braided hair.

Straight to the gut with this one. No manners at all. He wasn't even invited in.

Flashes of a different man's tanned face smiling at me while he gardened hit me with sadness. Why was this memory appearing now?

"It doesn't matter how much this desolate existence tries to suck the humanity out of us. There's still time for courtesy and manners. It helps us live in harmony. We are already at odds against one group; we need to keep our community together."

The memory of his voice was soothing to my soul and my eyes burned with unshed tears. This wasn't like back then. This was a whole other community, one full of different people.

A tear escaped and I ground my teeth together. Eliseo looked panicked and suddenly lifted both of his hands up in a supplicating manner. "Hey, hey now. It's just a question."

"I just want..." I gritted out but stopped. What did I want? What could this man before me, standing here like an intrusive no-mannered giant, understand about what it was like being a woman in this world?

He never will.

"What does it matter to you?" I angrily bit out. "I did what I had to do. We came back alive. I need you to take your large ass out of my house!"

His eyes flamed and his nostrils flared. I could physically see him grind down on his own molars, holding whatever he wanted to say back. His eyes scanned my face and I frowned. Here was a man who wanted people to follow his commands, yet he couldn't even follow a simple one.

"Listen," he started. My eyes narrowed at him in suspicion. *Yet, he didn't want to listen to me.* "I just wanted to be aware of any issues you might be having. Once you're part of my team, you're under my protection. We take care of our own, you feel?"

"No, I *don't* feel. I don't *need* your help. I've been doing fine all on my own. Now leave!"

"What are your skills with weaponry?" he continued, ignoring me.

"Did you not hear what I just said? Get out!"

"Let me know if you need training in anything. The guys will be up for it."

What. The. Hell?

I threw a fist at his face but his hand stopped me with a quick grip. Crap, he was fast.

He leaned in, and I leaned back to keep distance between us. He was overwhelming me again. "The thing you need to know about me—I can quickly adapt to something I've come to recognize."

My chest heaved, and I was unsure of what to say. Each inhale I took brought with it his unique masculine scent. I could feel his warm breath against my skin and it annoyed me that it wasn't entirely unpleasant. His grip on my fist tightened, sending spikes of pain through my knuckles, but I kept my face straight and my eyes on his.

Something crossed his features, but a strange silence descended between us. I was really getting tired of these staring contests.

As if he could read my thoughts, he finally shook his head and released his grip on me. "You got spunk. I like it. But false courage can also get you killed. Keep your temper in check, *Sili*."

Growling at his stupid nickname, I turned to look for my cap. What did *see-lee* even mean? I bent over to pick it up with more force than necessary. Eliseo cleared his throat loudly.

Turning with irritation, I spat out, "What now? I can't even wear my cap? What next?"

His face darkened with a blush as he grimaced. What kind of reactionary answer was that? What was wrong with him?

I tried again. "Look. I hear you. *Done.* Get. Out. Of. My. Damn. House!"

I walked past him, opened the door, and gave him a good shove. He stumbled over the threshold, and it was enough for me to slam the door in his face again. *Asshole.* Making sure I engaged the lock, I turned around and went back up the stairs.

The breeze passing through my legs reminded me that I hadn't put on any pants before I opened the door. Already halfway up the stairs, I stopped and groaned toward the ceiling. This was exactly why I hated being caught unawares. Trouble always seemed to find me.

Grabbing some loose cargo pants, I covered my bottom half up and looked for my second pair of boots. I found them on a dead woman a few months back and I was lucky they were only one size too big.

"Always make sure you have a good pair of shoes on your feet. It can be the difference between making it to your destination and dying."

The tanned man from my past always did have

the weirdest advice. A sense of longing hit me, and my eyes burned with unshed tears once again. I hated it when my memories plagued me back to back.

Going through my closet, I grabbed a couple of knives and a small pistol. Hiding them under my clothes, I finger-combed my hair to let it aerate enough to dry properly. I rummaged through my dresser drawers, looking high and low for some masking tape or anything at all to bind my breasts down. Without a bra, my nipples were much too obvious under my shirt. When I failed at finding what I needed, I decided to take one of my thread-bare shirts and rip them into strips, binding it on myself toward the back. It would have to do.

Once enough moisture left my hair, I plaited it and pinned it close to my scalp while I made my way downstairs. I needed to find another hat one of these days. Eliseo and his tendency to just grab it made me nervous. He might mess up my only one.

I looked in the small fridge and found nothing I could put together. I would have to go to the center of the town to the community store. *Damn it all.* I had hoped I could just hide away after today's events.

I made sure to lock the door from the inside as I left the house, closing it behind me. No one around me milled about, so it gave me a small sense of reprieve. I took in everything this community had created thus far as I meandered along. It amazed me how much could get done when everyone pitched in for the same cause—survival.

Some of these houses were well-kept, while others could use some fixing. One of the residents refused to put a door in, and it baffled my mind. How much privacy could that really offer? Maybe he didn't care. That wasn't my problem, I told myself, shrugging.

Old Mrs. Santos was on her knees to my left, planting her garden of vegetables along with a few of the other women. She claimed the biggest front yard on this side of the community and used it to her advantage. The smell of fresh earth wafted through the air, along with the acrid stench of whatever she used for manure. I refused to get to the bottom of that, afraid of what I would find.

They said the crazy old doctor who had a house with an underground bunker always figured out a problem. He plausibly mixed chemicals together to help fertilize the ground. Thinking of his bunker, I pondered why someone in the past would need it. What were they preparing for? Did they know life would be like this? Ashborne's doctor now used it for his experiments, working toward the cure to whatever happened that made our species split. If my memory served me correctly, rumors stated it all started with a virus of some sort.

Prior to it arriving, bloodsuckers apparently didn't exist—except for in books.

I couldn't even imagine a world like that. It sounded too good to be true.

Staring at the painted black door of the doctor's house now, a shiver ran down my spine. They said he healed people in his home while he did who knows what down underground. I had only seen him from afar a few times after my initiation here, the guy made me uneasy. Lucky for me, I had a tendency to heal faster than the average person so there wasn't a need for his assistance.

I was lost in my thoughts when someone called out, "Hello!"

It was one of the older ladies walking in the same direction. I tipped my cap and waved without giving a verbal greeting back. Everyone who came across me thus far knew I chose not to say much, and they all seemed okay with it. *Everyone except for what's-his-face.* Hopefully, I won't run into him again. I already had my dose for today.

When I came upon the larger homes located in the center of the community, my palms began to get clammy. I didn't like being around so many people at the same time. I didn't know who might have their eyes on me. Maybe I was simply paranoid, but some days I felt like my senses were on overdrive and I didn't understand why. Another part of myself I hadn't been able to pinpoint down.

A random resident walked by and my nose twitched. I could smell their unwashed body before they made it beside me. No one else was scrunching their nose or giving him looks. It further led me to believe that my sense of smell was more sensitive than everyone else's.

With my fragmented memories, I was still learning—or relearning—things about myself.

Ignoring that line of thought, I continued forth with the goal of buying what I needed. I had some homemade bread and mayonnaise at home. I needed to find something to put in the middle of the sandwich to complete it. The community had a small pen to the north for our farm animals, beside the main shop. With the addition of the sheep we accumulated from the recent outing, I wondered if we would get more wool for the colder months— or milk.

My stomach grumbled and I sighed.

Two houses down from the store, I observed a good handful of customers checking out the front crates before making their way inside. *Alright*, I told myself, *just get what you need and go home.* I walked through the double front doors and tried my best not to touch anyone as I dodged patrons milling about. The combination of multiple scents and body odor was enough to ward me off, I didn't need to add touch to the mix.

Grabbing a head of lettuce, I spied a cucumber and grabbed that, too. If they didn't have any meat available today, I could eat some sort of vegetable sandwich. It would be enough to hold me over.

"Hey! What will you be needing today?" the guy behind the counter asked. He had a friendly smile, and I found myself giving him a small one back.

"Meat?" I tried to lower the tenor of my voice so that it sounded more androgynous.

"Alright. Here, let me grab the clipboard. Choose one of the community services, and I'll be right back with what you need. We only have pork today, is that alright with you?"

I nodded as he handed me the sheet. Ashborne was run by service contribution instead of the use of money. Trade goods worked too. Since I didn't have a garden or anything good I found on the outing, I would have to sign up for community service to pay for my purchase today.

Looking through the list, I was at a loss of what I wanted to do. Everything seemed to have the possibility of too many people around me.

"Have you decided yet?"

I started. How did he make it back so fast? Or was I standing here that long?

A large arm went around me and grabbed the meat from the shop owner, meant for my order. I whipped my head around to say my peace when I saw a face I recognized. It was the other guy from the truck, the darker gentleman who hung around with Eliseo. Just as broad, he cocked his head like he was challenging me to say something.

My eyes narrowed as I calculated how far I would get if I kicked him in the balls, grabbed the pork, and ran.

He smirked and I began to wonder if, like Eliseo, he could read my thoughts somehow.

"Samuel!" the shop owner called out jovially. "What's up, man? This one's actually for the kid right here. You're going to have to get the next one."

Samuel stared at me, his smirk never leaving his face as he addressed the shop owner. "Nah, I got you. I'm just grabbing it for him. He's doing community service with me."

What?

"Oh, alright. I didn't realize you guys had an arrangement already. Let me know when he completes it, so I can clear out his tab."

"You got it," Samuel finished off.

He held onto my lunch, wrapped in paper, and I debated whether I should simply have that vegetable sandwich I was considering earlier. I didn't want to hang out with him or Eliseo any more than I had to.

Turning my heel without a word, I quickly walked out of the house, avoiding the bodies around me.

"Hey!" he called out.

He could shove that pork up his ass, for all I care.

"Hey!"

This was beginning to become deja vu. With my lettuce and cucumber in hand, I dodged the people milling about in the center of the community nimbly. Everyone looked at us strangely, while I ran into those that weren't looking at all. "Sorry!"

I avoided a poor old lady who pushed a wheel-barrow, but she tripped when Samuel ran into her, his momentum too much to stop. I was torn between using her as a diversion and stopping her fall because of my guilty conscience.

Dammit all! My feet moved before my brain made up its mind.

3

ELISEO

I watched in confusion as Samuel ran into one of the old ladies who helped with the gardening group. *What was that guy up to, and why was he running with packaged meat in his hand?* Only Oscar from the shop used that paper.

Something small flashed between the meandering bodies and my eyes sharpened. It was the tattered brown baseball cap that gave her away. She was dressed in all black, her dusty, sand-colored boots the only thing that popped out.

I watched as she gracefully leapt over the tilting barrel and grabbed the old lady before she could fall with it. Samuel ended up jumping backward like a buffoon, trying to dodge the metal full of what looked like manure from the back of the shop.

Shaking my head, I made my way toward them. Samuel hissed as Fitri turned and sprinted—

—right into my chest. I grabbed her arms to steady her, as she snapped her face to mine. There was a fire inside this little woman, and it intrigued me. *What made this girl burn so deeply from within?* This community was a human's dream in the world we lived in. What did she have to be angry about all the time?

With a robust water turbine and functioning solar panels to provide us with electricity, we were far better off than some of the other human settlements I had come across personally. Heck, our homes here actually had roofs.

"Can't you just leave me alone?" she hissed quietly, and my eyebrow quirked up in response. Was it not *her* that ran into *me*?

"Damn, you got some quick strides with that little body of yours," Samuel panted toward us. "Moves like a freaking ninja with the way you leaped into the air."

I watched as Samuel rolled his ankle, trying to stretch his strained muscles.

"I got your meat."

Fitri and I both snapped our gaze to him. He busted out laughing and wagged his eyebrows at her as I inwardly groaned, wondering why I kept him around. Fitri inadvertently leaned into me to create a larger distance from Samuel, and I was grateful for her discernment. Samuel was known for dipping his *meat* into anything that would let him.

It was partially why Hannah turned so irate when he left—she couldn't keep a good eye on him and his appendages.

"I'll hold on to the meat for ya," he continued with his perverted insinuations, "but you owe us some service."

I scowled. I needed to put a stop to this. I knew I shouldn't have let him weasel an answer out of me. He figured it out before I could give him a proper response as to where I ran off to right after our outing.

"Samuel, keep your dick in your pants," I commanded, my voice deeper than I would have liked. But something about his last statement grated on my nerves.

"I keep my dick in Hannah, thank you very much. She'd cut it off if it was anywhere else. Here." He shoved the meat at her chest, and my nostrils flared at their connection. "She signed up for weapon checks and cleaning," he said without moving his eyes away from her.

Fitri whipped her head around to face me and stared daggers into my eyes with accusation. The unease I felt from watching him touch her earlier morphed into something else entirely as my body began to respond.

"Well, now, we can always use some extra hands," I agreed. Samuel smirked, and I curled my lip. He laughed out loud and turned to limp away.

"Asshole," Fitri grumbled.

"He has his uses," I commented. "Follow me, and I'll take you to our weapon stores."

"No. I didn't agree to this."

"Judging by the meat in your hand, you surely did."

"What? I was still looking at the list when that asshole of yours showed up!" Her raised voice called attention to herself from the community and she tightened down the cap on her head.

Grabbing her by the arm, I dragged her toward the location of the weapon stores on the southwest corner of the community—near my residence. I didn't trust anyone near my cache but me and my men. And I knew for a fact that weapons cleaning was not on Oscar's list of services. Leave it to Samuel to wrangle this squirrelly girl.

She wriggled and jerked from me until she slipped from my grasp. Backing up with her vegetables against her chest, I tamped down the chuckle that wanted to escape at the sight before me. She looked like a rabid fox, fighting to protect her prize—a prize I was not here to fight for.

"Let's get your food home. How about that?" I offered. "Looks like you were fixing to make something to eat. Let me help you."

"No." She turned and jogged away.

This little cat-and-mouse game she was playing made my blood boil in more ways than one. My boots hit the pavement behind her, and suddenly she was sprinting.

I took a sharp right behind one of the empty homes and cut her off right before she reached her porch. She was moving so fast and knocked us both down with her velocity. *Holy hell.*

Wrapping my arms around her, I made sure to take the impact of the ground with her safely in my arms. The feminine growl and hiss at my face was just par for the course.

"What. Is. The. Matter. With. You?!"

"You're welcome," I snarkily replied. "Let's get a handle on your hunger, then we can talk calmly."

"I *am* calm!"

Her reddening face told me she would have punched me again if it wasn't for all the food she held. *Small blessings.* She hit like a freight train, but I wouldn't tell her that. Instead, I gave her a smirk and gently got her back on her feet.

She shouldered me and went up the steps with me right behind her.

"Go home, Eliseo. You're still not invited."

"Let me help you with that," I offered.

She turned with a blazing inferno behind her eyes. The veins on her neck popped out as her jaws flexed from grinding her teeth together. Every part of this woman intrigued me but I didn't let it show on my face.

When she closed her eyes and exhaled, I grabbed the food from her arms and caged her in. "Listen, *Sili*. Let's get this straight. I don't have to do shit for you, but I want to. There's a difference.

Let's get you inside and curb that hunger before you bite my head off, yeah?"

Her face flushed a different way as she turned toward her door, pulling pins out of her hair. I watched in fascination as her nimbly fingers worked the lock, listening to her grumble about not being hangry.

She completed the task with ease and I shuffled us both inside before she could kick me out again, slamming the door with my boot and walking toward her kitchen.

"What are you doing?" she screeched.

I poked around in her fridge, pulled out a single container, and spread the mayonnaise on her bread. I searched her cabinets for a plate and found none. There was a single dented pan, so I grabbed it and placed it over the hole on her stove. She shoved me away with an adorable little growl, and I finally lifted my hands in mock surrender.

"Alright, alright. Just trying to do something nice."

She grumbled a few more times as I leaned against her counter, watching her agile little hands start a flame in the leftover coals inside the empty burner.

She grabbed a knife from beneath her shirt and I glimpsed her smooth flesh before the glint of the blade stole my focus. The sizzle served as background noise, but the smell made my stomach grumble. I ignored it in favor of watching her hand-eye coordination. She was graceful, quick, and dexterous. The way she flipped her blade and wiped it against her cargo pants before tucking it away had me wondering what her past consisted of to make her this way. Not that it was a bad thing—*not for us*. Not with what we had to face out there, risking our lives when we scavenged for the town.

I was lost in thoughts of venturing further northwest to the midway point between Clan Sae and Lekim territory. Rumor had it, there was a community there that may benefit us with trade.

Fitri shoved a sandwich at my chest, and I frowned in confusion. "Where's yours?"

"I already ate it while you were staring off into space. Shove it in your mouth and leave."

She was precious, really.

I stuffed my mouth and contemplated how we would organize this outing. I wasn't sure I ordained the crew we had today as a success. We would have to take another walk around this community and observe the able-bodied again to take another mental census.

Wiping my mouth with the back of my hand, I swallowed the last bite and burped. Fitri wrinkled her nose, and I let out a laugh. "Meet me at the furthest house on the southwest corner of town tomorrow at sunrise. We train."

"What?" she sputtered, caught off guard.

Before she could say anything else, I left and slammed her front door shut. A stranger who was walking by jumped at the noise. I scowled at him and he scampered down the street. *This was the problem.* We brought in too much fresh meat—too young, too inexperienced. The men I fought with in the past while living in Ashborne had fallen one at a time with the rise of bloodsuckers around us, except for who was left with me.

The porch creaked with my weight as I made my way down. I didn't think she realized it was there and I took a mental note. I'd use it to my advantage to keep an eye on her and make sure none of the boys in this place caused trouble. Walking north toward Reed's house, my mind swirled with thoughts of trade, when someone called my name.

"Eliseo."

It was a voice I didn't hear often, but when I did, it made my hackles rise.

"Doc," I replied as I turned in his direction. "Did you need something?"

The crazy fool had a wild look in his eyes, his dark leather apron wet with something I didn't want to recognize. The goggles on top of his head left a crimson streak in one of his wrinkles. He smelled of chemicals I was both familiar with and not, making my nostrils tickle annoyingly.

"I need you to come to my quarters for a moment," he requested calmly with an undercurrent of authority.

My body tensed, but I nodded. Everyone knew the doc had been working on something down there, disappearing for days at a time. He was presumably trying to discover a cure to this hellscape we call life, to find the reason why bloodsuckers came to be, and to reverse it enough to take things back to the way they were naturally supposed to be.

Some days, I just thought he was out of his damn mind.

With heavy reluctance, I walked toward him, and he smiled wickedly in triumph. I didn't trust this fucker, but he was the only doctor Ashborne had. His task was to mainly treat the new residents upon arrival, and the groups that went out on runs if necessary—to make sure the infected weren't harbored back behind the wall.

"Good, good," he commented. "I'm going to need you to help me with something. I'm sure you can spare the time. You just came back from an outing, correct?"

"Yeah. Whatever you say, Doc," I replied carefully. His statement led me to believe that he emerged from his hole more than once today to know that fact. I filed the information away in my mind. Something was up.

He guided me toward his opened underground bunker, following behind me. The cold concrete stairs chilled me to the bone with each step. It felt like death every time I was here. Cold. Stagnant. A sterile scent, with a hint of something dark lurking in the corners.

When we reached the bottom, there were tables and chairs—some with straps, some without. No one realized it, but this bunker of his had tunnels that reached every corner of this damn place. He wasn't aware I knew, but I had gathered enough intel over the years to piece it together. Some of the residents whispered about hearing muffled noises in strange locations coming from underground during the daylight hours. Most chalked it up to the water turbine, but when things became too coincidental, one would be a fool not to start connecting the dots.

"Can you sit down in that chair, please?" He flapped his hand toward the one with the straps before he dropped his arms and raised his eyebrows with excitement. "Unless you prefer the table?"

Grinding my molars, I sat in the stiff chair. The last time I was on the table, I lost track of time. I wouldn't make that mistake again.

He threw his head back and cackled at my choice, the seal of his bunker door soundproofing anything that happened down here.

I stared at his face with unhidden disdain as he meticulously strapped my arm in. That blood streak from his forehead now ran down his temple like a bad omen. The left rim of his goggles was wet and shifting on his skin. My eyes scanned his face but saw no wound. Whose blood was it?

"Save that hate for the bloodsuckers. I've got a bigger purpose here, you know this." He hadn't wiped the smile off his face yet.

"What's about to happen?" *Dare I even ask?*

"Oh, you'll see," he taunted. "I'm going to need a sample of your blood, my friend. I'm so close to a breakthrough but I'll need to use you for my baseline. I ran out of Reed's donations the other day. Samuel was busy judging by the cries coming through his doors, and Gunner was nowhere to be seen."

The doc lifted his lip at the mention of Samuel and his choice of extracurricular activities, but all I could concentrate on was the fact that he just named off everyone on my team—minus Fitri. Every time I brought up the fact that he had my men and I on his radar, he assured me that he took blood samples from random residents here as well.

"This would be easier if I knock you out, you know." His words were laced with mirth. I bet he got off on that power.

My paranoia naturally grew. He had knocked us out a few times without us realizing. There was just something *off* about him. I refused to let him do it to me again. I had talked to my men, and made sure they were doing the same.

"No," I grounded out, annoyed at his delay tactic. "Let's get this over with."

He laughed before he turned toward his table and grabbed an empty syringe. "Alright, suit yourself."

A sharp pain accompanied the needle's entrance, and I flexed my jaw. I watched as he pulled a vial's worth of blood from me.

"Good, good." He pulled the syringe out and

smiled with satisfaction at the full vial. "Alright, if you see Samuel, tell him I need to talk to him about something."

The doc was already back at his table of metal wares before he grabbed something else and exited through one of his tunnel doors, slamming it shut.

"Didn't even unstrap me, fucker," I grumbled. Removing the leather belt from its loop, I released my wrist, rolling it to stimulate blood flow.

Walking up the concrete steps, I shouldered the bunker door open and climbed out. Not the way I saw today going. I wondered what he really did with the blood he collected. The door fell down with a hard slam, the sound bouncing between the houses, but no one came out to look. Seemed everyone on this side was used to the crazy doc's bunker.

Shaking my head, I turned the corner toward Samuel's, since I forgot what I needed to do earlier. The evening cooled the outside temperature, and the symphony of insects began to fill the air.

"Asshole!" a voice cried out.

I turned around, sure they were addressing me. *What did that say about my position in this community?* Not that I cared.

I saw a small figure in the distance walk toward me with their arms crossed until the familiarity of the face appeared clearly before me.

"*Sili.*" I knew she hated the nickname, but her firecracker attitude matched the small pepper my mother used to use in some of our meals—Siling

Labuyo. What I wouldn't do for another taste of my mother's pork Kaldereta. I could almost still taste the spice in my mouth. It was perfect for Fitri with a personality that matched.

"You never told me where the weapon store is," she groused. "How am I supposed to know where to go?"

Her little attitude made me feel things. Like the need to put this little girl in her place.

"So, you decided to seek out the *Asshole* and find out?" I scoffed. "How very assertive of you. Well, now that you're here, we might as well get to it, then."

I turned to walk toward my street and listened for her soft footsteps behind me. She moved like a graceful feline. It was no wonder she leapt like one too. She would do well with reconnaissance when we went on outside runs—her small frame gave her an advantage in tight spaces.

The walk was quiet until the voice of Mrs. Reyes cut in. "Eliseo!"

Groaning, I walked faster. Fitri chuckled behind me. *I was waiting for it.*

"Eliseo! I made some extra food! Do you want to come over?" she entreated.

Looking over my shoulder, I waved my hand politely. "That's okay, I already ate. Thank you."

With all the cooking she did, I was surprised she wasn't busier doing community service to pay off her ingredients. Why was she always out here waiting specifically for me to come home? I should throw Gunner on her trail, he had enough patience for it.

Mrs. Reyes continued to smile until she saw Fitri behind me, then her eyes turned curious. I was glad the kid wore oversized clothes and a cap. I didn't need any more problems on my side of the street. Lord knows, Mrs. Reyes had been trying to get into my house from the moment I made residence here. She's widowed, and lonely—a bad combination for me. A lot of these women had a worshiping complex for the men who went out on runs. They all craved a protector.

But the idea she had of me in her life was far from the truth. I was here to survive and make sure my men came back alive. That was it.

"Hello there! I haven't met you before, have I? You must be new. I've never seen you around with Eliseo." Mrs. Reyes wouldn't let up with her mingling of my personal affairs. I had to do something before it went too far.

Fitri choked, and I lifted a brow at her reaction, partially unsure if she was waiting for me to save her from the widow or if she was going to save herself. With a house between where we stood and our destination, I almost tripped when I heard Sili's voice come out loud and clear.

"Oh, yeah. Eliseo's been hiding me away. You know how he is, doesn't really like people in his business. And by the way, I've been feeding him just fine," she batted her lashes with a hand on her hip.

Her feminine voice was on full blast now, compared to the way she usually spoke when around strangers. I was caught off guard, curious to see what she was up to.

"Oh, I thought you were—I mean—I'm so sorry." Mrs. Reyes flushed deeply and put a hand over her chest. She looked like all her dreams had been shattered. Did it make me a bastard that I was trying hard not to laugh?

A hand touched me, and electricity rippled up my arm. Fitri's delicate fingers were slowly caressing my skin, and I didn't know if I should slap it away or see where this conversation was heading.

"Thought I was what? Or are you saying you thought Eliseo was bringing little boys to his house? I'm not sure whether to be offended for myself, or for the man," she said in mock offense, blinking up at me then casting an accusatory gaze back at the poor widow.

Could this get any worse... or more entertaining? My focus zoned in on the little hand touching me as my ears continued to listen to this crap shoot.

"I didn't mean—" Mrs. Reyes tried but was cut off.

"Of course, you didn't," Sili snapped in subtle female aggression. "You're just following Eliseo around, trying to get his attention. Sorry to inform you, Mrs..." She cocked her head, and a laugh slipped out of me. I tried to mask it with a cough, failing miserably as they both jerked their gazes at me.

"Reyes," she finished for her.

Fitri gave her a bright smile, and my eyes wanted to bug out of my head. The simple act transformed her face into something else entirely. *I never knew she had dimples and now I can't get it out of my mind.*

"Ah, Mrs. Reyes," Fitri continued politely. "I'll be accompanying him tonight. I'm sure your *husband* is missing you?"

Shit, I didn't get a chance to tell Fitri that—

"I'm a widow."

"I see," she answered easily as if prepared for it. "Sorry to hear. It's the world we live in. Goodnight Mrs. Reyes."

Fitri's fingers went from caressing to digging her little nails into my skin as she dragged me down the street toward our destination. We reached my porch, and I was both impressed and suspicious. *How did she discover which house belonged to me?* Pushing the thought back, I asked her the other question that was burning to come out. "What was that?"

"What was what?"

There was that little brat again. I ripped my arm out of her grasp, stomped up the steps, and took out my keys. "You know what. Why would you have Mrs. Reyes think that? She wasn't doing anything wrong."

I couldn't very well tell her I enjoyed watching the trainwreck.

"Pfft. She was sniffing you like she was in heat. I merely helped the conversation along, since it didn't seem like you knew what you were doing," she accused.

I turned to give her a piece of my mind when she shouldered me and went inside first. I slammed the door with my boot and stared at her, incredulous. "I knew exactly what I was doing. I was *handling* it."

She turned with fire in her eyes, and my hand itched to do things. It appeared, now that she came out of her shell, she was nothing but trouble.

"You weren't handling *shit*," she spat. "Now, tell me where the weapons are so I can clear my tab and get the hell out."

I laughed humorlessly at that. "Whatever. Fine. Let's get this shit done so you can get back and rest up before training tomorrow."

"What the hell?" she whinged. "Once I'm done here, I'm done. That was the deal."

I kept walking until I reached the back of the house where there was a dented cabinet full of weapons. "The deal, *Sili*," I started without looking at her just to annoy her, "was that you become part of my team while we keep pretending you're a boy. But with the way shit went down with Mrs. Reyes, I'm sure your cover will be blown by now. But who knows? She's a recluse. You might get lucky."

"Seems like *she's* the one who wanted to get

lucky. How did *I* end up with this asshole?" she grumbled under her breath, making me bark out a laugh.

I grabbed the first weapon closest to me and shoved it into her chest. She gave me a little snarl and yanked it out of my hand, walking toward the little table I had set up nearby. I watched as she sat down with more attitude than her little body should have and glared at me.

She shouldn't look so attractive with that gun in her hand.

"Well? Are you just going to stand there?" she complained. "I need some rags, or whatever you use to clean this stuff."

That little bite to her words had my insides boiling. *Rags first. Discipline later.* Narrowing my eyes, I ripped my shirt off and tossed it at her face. It fell into her lap and left her mouth hanging open.

"Use that. The old rags were too worn out. I expect half of that cabinet to be done by the end of today." Turning, I walked away toward the downstairs restroom and slammed the door.

The doctor's puncture wound on my arm still itched. The fucker probably didn't even sanitize his needles. Leaning my hands against the sink, I stared at my foggy reflection in the dirty cabinet mirror. I cracked my neck as the aches from today caught up with me. I really was getting too old for this crap. Opening the cabinet door, I grabbed the bottle of painkiller I had stashed away. There were only a few pills left. I popped one into my mouth and ground down with my teeth, letting the bitter chemical taste fill my mouth.

As I continued to torture myself, swallowing particles of the pill down dry, I stared at the old wounds I had on my chest—each one a memory from a time I couldn't seem to forget.

The smell of flames burned my lungs as I ran toward my home, hoping nothing had happened to her.

The crackle of the fire, the screams of women and children pierced my ears like razors while my heart threatened to beat out of my chest. I almost slid past the door as my hands grabbed the edge to stop my momentum. Waving my hand in front of my face to clear the smoke, the strong metallic smell overwhelmed my senses.

My heart stopped.

There, lying on the ground in a pool of her own blood, was my wife, with her stomach and legs mutilated beyond recognition. Her eyes were glazed over in an expression of fear, turned to the side.

My pulse throbbed against my ear, drowning out the screams and flames. Darting my eyes around the room, I took tentative steps, trying to see if our unborn child was alright... but there was nothing. Nothing but the blood of my wife christening the grounds of the place we once called home.

My fist landed on the mirror, coating it with red cracks. The pain in my knuckles dislodged the memory as I hung my head and buried my face in my hands.

4

FITRI

It had been strange around these men the past few months.

After clearing my tab and completing training with them to their satisfaction, I found a sense of camaraderie growing between us—one I didn't expect. When Gunner and Reed found out about my truth, they didn't skip a beat. Everything was business as usual. They had been good about keeping my secret around others, and that was something I appreciated greatly.

They were good to me. I still couldn't understand why. I was a nobody brought into their tight-knit team out of the blue. I thought back to our last training with a confused smile.

"Again!"

I threw my punch toward his face, but he dodged,

twisted, and shouldered me in the back then elbowed me into the ground swiftly.

I groaned and turned over, staring at the sky, trying to catch my breath. What the hell? How did he move so fast?

His hand stuck out in my direction and I grabbed it, letting him lift me up easily. Reed's smile took over his face as he released my grip and got back into position.

"Come on, kid," he called out. "You're getting better, but it's not good enough. What if you call for backup and we don't make it in time? You need to stay alive long enough for us to make it there."

He was right.

"Quit yacking, you two. Again!" Eliseo's voice boomed, and I flinched subtly. Asshole.

Reed's eyes sharpened on me but he didn't say a word, he simply lifted his hand and curled his fingers in the come hither motion.

Rolling my neck, I got back into a fighting stance and we circled each other. My eyes scanned for any possible openings or advantage points. Reed was almost as big as Eliseo, outweighing me by almost a whole other body. Most of the men on the team did. At five foot four, I stuck out like a sore thumb amongst these guys.

I lunged and twisted at the last minute, dodging his block, spinning until I could leap onto his back and wrap my arms around his neck and head with a firm grip.

He used his strength to throw me over his shoulder.

Landing on my feet, I lunged again toward his right leg, pulling him onto the ground where I straddled him with my hands around his neck.

He stared at me with his chest heaving, nostrils flaring while I stared back, waiting for his next move. But I couldn't anticipate what happened next. His eyes flamed with an emotion I couldn't name, and it scared me as his pulse rose beneath my palms. My grip loosened, but he grabbed my wrist before I could pull away, keeping me locked in position.

The tension in the air between us became thick and heady, my own chest rising and falling more than it should. Suddenly, I was pulled off him by the back of my shirt with a hard jerk, landing me on my ass.

"Alright, that's enough," came Eliseo's voice. "Get your ass up, Reed. You're embarrassing me. You just got your ass handed to you by a girl."

Reed brushed off his insult with a chuckle and continued to stare intensely at me beside him. "I'd gladly let the kid do it again. She's getting better, quicker."

"She's going to spar with one of the other guys," Eliseo barked out.

What was up his ass? Reed had been the easiest to work with so far. His instructions were the simplest for me to understand with how he broke things down.

"Whatever you say," Reed mumbled, dusting himself off.

"I don't—" I tried to pipe in.

"Gunner! Get your ass over here!" Eliseo instructed

after glaring at Reed with more attitude than normally called for.

Gunner ran up, his forehead already gleaming with sweat from sparring with Samuel. "Good. That asshole Samuel fights dirty and always smells like pussy. I'm tired of that shit."

A laugh burst out of me and I doubled over at his blatant comment. We all knew it. We all thought it, but to hear it out loud was something else.

Eliseo's scowl softened right before he chuckled along with me, his eyes scanning me from head to toe. He was such a hardass most of the time, it was rare to hear laughs slip out of him like this during training sessions. It made him more relatable.

"Alright, Gunner you're with Sili," he instructed. "Reed, with me."

"You got it." Gunner slapped me on the shoulder, and I almost fell over. He laughed it off before getting into position.

I couldn't take my eyes off the way Eliseo tackled Reed with full strength, taking him down to grapple. It reminded me of the first time he took me down, and my heart kicked up.

"Pay attention!" Gunner yelled before he swept my feet from under me, landing me on my back again.

I groaned and rolled to the side, rubbing the sight of impact. I didn't know how I felt about a group of men actually being kind to me. It had never happened before. The last man that was kind to me ended up in a pool of blood—

"Sili," Eliseo gritted out, pulling me from my

thoughts. "Quit standing around staring off into the distance. We got a trip to prepare for. Go get strapped up!"

Lifting my lip in a curl, I stared daggers into him. He merely chuckled at my reaction and waved me off. Eliseo and I had come to more neutral ground between one another, my initial paranoia about him dissipating the more I was with him, witnessing how he operated with his men. I could see why they were loyal to him. He had taken more of a protective, fatherly role with me since I joined his team, always making sure I stayed on my toes and kept others away from me when I started to get overwhelmed.

I didn't change the fact that he was still an asshole, and still got on my nerves from time to time. I honestly didn't think that would ever change.

The men were already strapped and headed to the front community gates. I jogged back toward my house and up the stairs to slip some blades into my boot, pistols into the waist of my pants, as well as grab the crossbow and bolts we found on the last trip. The weight felt good in my hands.

I ran downstairs with renewed energy and almost slammed into a large body. The familiar masculine musk hit me before the tanned, tattooed arm held me steady.

"You need to pay more attention to your surroundings." Eliseo's deep timber was so condescending. Or, maybe my pride was hurt by his assessment. I was trying to hurry because he was commanding me to.

Not only had I been forced to learn all forms of weaponry, the guys had been challenging me with hand-to-hand combat in case they didn't get to me in time during reconnaissance. My head was swimming with so much knowledge that I occasionally became distracted by what was expected of me. *Who was he to nitpick my weaknesses?*

I said nothing. Eliseo hated insubordination, and always had a gleam in his eye when my mouth got the better of me. It sent chills down my spine in more ways than one. Thinning my lips, I shouldered my way past him with emphasis. He chuckled behind me as he locked the door and slammed it shut. When we both reached the front of the community, there was already a decent group forming.

"What took you so long, kid? Was Eliseo holding you up?" Reed grinned, and his face softened. It made some of the tension brought on by Eliseo melt away. He was quite a handsome guy when he let his guard down. *I shouldn't be thinking about how handsome he is.*

Shrugging one of my shoulders, I broke his eye contact by pretending to pat myself down to make sure everything was where it was supposed to be.

It took me a while to understand how these men mentally operated. Samuel always had sexual innuendos, Gunner was the quietest, more patient of the bunch, Reed was the most level-headed, and Eliseo...

I turned to look at him with a sour expression. "You know how he is."

Reed and Gunner both laughed as Eliseo joined in with a chuckle while putting his hand on my head, digging his knuckles into my cap. I hated it when he did that, and he knew it. I scrunched my nose and slapped his hand away.

"Alright, where's Samuel?" Eliseo asked. "Is he rounding up the groups?"

"Yup, he should be done any minute," Reed answered.

"Alright, listen up!" Samuel commanded. Everyone around us stopped their conversations and turned to look at him with respect. "Team A is taking the Humvee, Team B the truck, and Team C the Jeep. We're heading out of Ashborne in the next fifteen minutes. This trip is going to be one of our longer ones, since we're heading farther up northwest than usual. It gets cooler up there guys, so make sure you're dressed appropriately. I don't need shivering fingers getting trigger-happy. Take note that we'll be close to Clan Sira and Lekim territory, so keep your eyes peeled for anything out of the ordinary. Stay together, safety in numbers."

When Samuel got down to business, he had a similar authoritative presence as Eliseo. Once his speech was done, everyone started to break up and murmur amongst themselves about what they might run across.

"Whose team am I on?" I asked the men.

Reed smiled and opened his mouth to reply, but was cut off by Eliseo. "Mine. Get your ass in the Humvee."

Frowning at the jerk, I gave Reed an apologetic look. He stared at Eliseo's back for a few moments before he waved me off and headed toward the Jeep. My eyes followed Reed, wondering what just occurred.

"*Sili!*" Eliseo snapped, and I stood at attention, running toward him.

"Geez, calm down. Samuel said we're leaving in fifteen," I retorted.

I grabbed the handle to the back passenger door, pulling it open, when Eliseo slammed it shut and caged me in with his body. I turned with wide eyes, staring at his chest. With his proximity, I could feel the heat come off his body. His scent enveloped me and I breathed harder through my mouth as I tilted my head up to look at him, curious as to what I did wrong now.

"*Sili.*" There was that tone again, the one he was always using when he wanted me to know I was testing him.

Was I? I mean, I was definitely annoyed he didn't let me go with Reed's group. At least he was fun to be around. Eliseo's eyes bordered with fire and mirth. I didn't know how to read him, always confusing the hell out of me with words and actions that didn't match.

"You're going to have to move if you want me in this Humvee," I told him.

"Is that right?" he hummed.

Wasn't that what he told me to do? He needed to make up his damn mind. I scrunched my nose in displeasure and he softly chuckled before opening the door for me. I hopped in and pulled it shut so I didn't have to see his face anymore.

When the rest of the group climbed in, I realized Eliseo seated himself next to me in the back. I turned to him with a frown. "Who's driving?"

"It doesn't matter. Strap yourself in." He then reached over and pulled the belt across my body, buckling it in.

The drive was longer this time around. Good thing we gassed up last week in preparation. I stared out the passenger window when a bump in the road made Eliseo's thigh hit mine. I knocked it right off me, and he laughed under his breath.

"What's so funny?" I snapped, annoyed at this weird game we were playing. I never agreed to play anything.

"You, *Sili*. You."

"Whatever."

Ignoring my retort, he continued to give me commands under his breath. "Stick with me when we make it to the destination, alright?"

My irritation dissipated. "Why? What are we expected to run into?"

"It doesn't matter. Just stick with me so I can keep an eye out on you."

I turned to look at him in disbelief. "You don't think I can handle myself?"

His eyes sharpened on mine as he leaned in, our noses almost brushing, making me flush with weird emotions. "I didn't say you can't. I need you to stick by my side for my peace of mind. I don't need to be distracted, wondering where you're at if we run into shit, you feel me?"

I bared my teeth and turned to stare out the window again. It seemed like the moment he found out I was a girl, he started treating me with protective gloves, and I was tired of it. What was all that training for if he was going to be this way when it was time to get down to business?

The air chilled the glass, and I knew we were close. Adjusting my long-sleeved shirt, my legs started shaking with anticipation. What would we run across? Would we find anything good on this trip? I really hoped we didn't run into any more bloodsuckers. I discreetly looked at the other people in this group and inwardly grimaced. I didn't need to bring liability to myself.

A warm hand held my left thigh down, and my head snapped to his face. Eliseo wasn't looking at me, instead, he stared straight out the front windshield intently while trying to calm my nerves at the same time.

With an audible swallow, I told myself to take a few deep breaths and calm myself and my running thoughts.

"We're going to pull off this road and hide the vehicle behind the cluster of trees," the driver said.

Eliseo inadvertently squeezed my leg as he responded to him. "Behind that one. Me and the kid will go do recon ahead of you guys. Wait for our signal."

"You got it."

The driver, an older gentleman—even older than Eliseo—pulled the vehicle smoothly to the side, crunching some of the fallen branches beneath our tires. I opened the back passenger door and jumped out with my partner right behind me.

He placed his large hand on my shoulder and directed me forward. There was a field clearing a few paces ahead. Crouching behind an abandoned, rusted-out truck, my eyes tracked everything in front of me. Eliseo's body heat was right beside me, keeping the chill at bay. There was an abandoned gas station and shop ahead about a mile out.

"We should head around the backside, use the trees as concealment," he whispered.

I nodded. Sounded good to me.

We moved quickly from tree to tree, trying our best to soften our footfalls, until we could see the back of the gas station. There was graffiti all over it, written messages that warned us away from the place.

"It smells like blood," I told him.

"I'm sure it does. It's probably old. This place

looks to have been abandoned for some time already."

How could I explain to him that my sense of smell was heightened? The blood didn't smell old at all.

"Elis—"

"Let's go." He moved quickly and placed his back against the wall, his pistol pointed up.

Dammit. I had a bad feeling about this. Something in my gut screamed at me to go back. "Eliseo!"

But he was already looking through the clouded windows and opening the backdoor with his gun pointed ahead of him. He lifted his hand and called me to his side. Growling under my breath, I did as he commanded.

We cleared the gas station and the convenience store next door. Heading back to the Humvee, we called the others in the group to come down. When we all made it back, half of us scavenged the gas station and the other half the store.

Eliseo let me choose which I wanted and followed me. The store was still pretty stocked up with useful things. Grabbing the backpacks we brought with us, I began stuffing it with cans of food and other useful necessities like toothbrushes and combs.

Guess that bad feeling from earlier was a spoof. Maybe it was some leftover bad taint in the air. Crouched down to the floor, I rummaged through the random items as far as my arms could reach.

My ears perked up when the sound of pills in a bottle rolled from behind the back counter. Turning to look, I saw Eliseo with a full-blown smile on his face right before he shoved it into his pack.

Maybe that was why he was such an ass. He was probably in pain all the time. No one looked at a pill bottle with that much longing unless they were suffering in silence.

He saw me looking at him and he gave me a genuine smile. Electricity shot through my body. It was weird when he wasn't being an asshole. I wasn't used to it.

Standing, I dusted off my cargo pants and threw the bag on my back. Eliseo took that as my signal that I was ready to go.

"Two minutes, and we head back to the Humvee!" he called out to everyone around us.

The other guys collectively murmured their agreement and zipped up their bags. We met up with the other half and it looked like all our packs were full. I was feeling good about this trip. We were going to come back with a lot more than the last trip we made.

"Alright, men." Eliseo checked his watch and looked at the sky. "We found a good loot early on. We still have another good hour before we need to head back to the meet spot. You guys want to keep moving forward or go back now?"

One of the random new guys piped in with eyes full of excitement. "I say we check out what else we can find. We'll just stash this stuff in the Humvee. There's plenty of room."

I looked around as Eliseo called for a vote. The majority wanted to try other locations. I really had no say since Eliseo would drag me wherever he went, anyway, like we were stuck at the hip.

When we made it back to the vehicle, Eliseo threw both of our bags in the back. Grabbing the back passenger door handle, Eliseo tapped my shoulder and jerked his head toward the front passenger side. I followed his direction and got in with him getting into the driver's side.

"Alright, let's head north for another few minutes and see what we find," he instructed as he started the Humvee.

The drive over the uneven terrain was quiet besides running over a few dead brushes. Soon, we came across a house in the middle of nowhere and pulled around the side about a mile away. There was a barn and shed to the side of the main home.

"Tools," I whispered under my breath, and Eliseo nodded.

"We might find something here. Let's check it out," he told everyone.

We all got out with our weapons in hand. Eliseo walked around the shed while the other men went toward the barn.

"What do you think happened here?" I asked him. My mind was whirling with different scenarios, none of them good.

"Who knows? But it looks dilapidated, like it's

been sitting alone for a while," he observed.

We bypassed the shed that had a door hanging on a single hinge. There was nothing inside. Walking up the porch of the main house, we both crept around and looked through the windows.

"I don't see any movement," I mumbled under my breath, mostly to myself.

"Me either. Stay behind me."

I quickly did as commanded right before he kicked in the front door. Dust fell in a cloud and we both covered our faces with our arms, coughing. Eliseo moved through the living room, his gun up. There were two levels to the house and the bottom was covered in the same dust that was on the door. Whatever was in here, never left judging by the lack of disturbance in the environment.

Walking up the creaking stairs, we found four closed doors. The pistol in my hand felt heavy with what we may encounter behind them.

Eliseo kicked the first door in, and the smell of mold and something else wafted out. Looking around his broad back, my heart constricted at the sight of two decayed bodies in an embrace on the bed, one smaller than the other.

The sheets were darkened with old blood-stains, and the shredded curtains moved with the breeze that filtered through the window.

Flashes of a woman holding me when I fell over my father's tools played in the back of my mind. She was my mother, wasn't she? It was the only thing that made logical sense...

"*Oh, poor baby. It's okay. What are you doing out here?*" *Her voice soothed me every time I heard it.*

"*I wanted to see what Papa was doing," I told her. "I wanted to help.*"

Her familiar smile wrapped around my heart like an embrace. "My dear, the best place for a child to help is to stay out of the way. Come on, you can help me cut up the vegetables we just harvested. How does that sound?"

"*I'm not good with a knife, the handle's too big, Mama.*"

Her smile softened her wrinkled face. She patted my shoulder and moved me away from the greenhouse. "Baby, every woman should know how to wield a knife. You'll learn. It's a skill you need to have to make it in this life."

"*Yes, Mama," I conceded.*

"*Sili?* Where did you go?" Eliseo stood before me with his warm hands on my shoulder, his face crouched right beside mine, staring into my eyes. I blinked a few times until he came back into focus.

"I-I'm sorry. It was a memory. Sorry." *Why couldn't I remember that she was my mother at first?* The memory that played back this time was so vivid—like it was yesterday.

Eliseo's concern was written all over his face, but he didn't address it. "Come on, let's clear out the rest of the rooms and get out of this house."

"Okay," I answered softly, still haunted by the memory that played back.

He kicked the next door in, and there was old

blood spatter all over the walls, sprinkling the ceiling. I frowned at the direction of it before my eyes cast toward a skeleton lying in a slump on the bed with a gun still in its hand.

Was this what our future looked like? So bleak that it became easier to just kill oneself? How long before we become like this family here? Withering away with hopelessness. Dust, stale air, and light decay tickled my nose as I continued to look around.

Eliseo walked in and grabbed the skeleton's gun. I followed suit, rummaging through the side table and dressers in case I found some ammo—and I did. Some of the clothes looked pristine, having been preserved away from the dust. I grabbed some shirts and shoved them into the small bag I brought along with me.

"Check the other room, too, in case you find some other useful stuff for yourself," Eliseo said as he walked toward the next room and kicked it in. More dust came down in a cloud and I held my breath as I left the room.

Reentering the first room, I tentatively looked through the dressers to find some feminine undergarments. *How did he know?* Looking at the embracing bodies again, the smaller one looked to have been a teenager. My heart ached, not only for the old residents here, but for the fact that my memories were still fragmented. *How could a person forget their parents?*

"*Sili.* Are you alright?"

"Yeah." Shoving the undergarments in some of my cargo pockets, I ran across a bra and stopped. I had been accustomed to hiding under my disguise that I no longer recalled what it felt like wearing one of these contraptions.

The bag I had with me wasn't big enough, so I made the decision to leave the bra behind and shoved the dresser door close.

We both walked down the stairs and turned into the kitchen to look around. As we opened and closed cabinets, the sound of a faraway gunshot rang in the air.

We both bolted out of the house toward the barn to witness blood spraying in front of us in a wide arc. Another ragtag group was fighting with our men. I pointed my pistol at the closest one, pulling the trigger and getting him in the chest. He screamed and fell to the side, rolling off one of our guys he had pinned under him.

I heard an animalistic growl before Eliseo tackled a guy who snuck up behind me. They grappled on the ground for a few seconds before Eliseo straddled him with his weight. The glint of the blade distracted me as he sliced the man's neck, spraying blood all over his front as he repeatedly plunged his knife into the man's chest cavity.

My adrenaline was running at full speed with this surprise attack. The smell of copper covered his normal musk, and it made my mouth water and tickled my nose at the same time. I couldn't comprehend what was happening and I stood there for a few moments, trying to collect myself.

My ears twitched when I heard leaves crunch behind me. Twisting with my gun, I fired off a couple of rounds before rolling on the ground and crawling behind a bush.

"Where the fuck did the kid go?" The stranger's voice made the hair on the back of my neck stand.

Memories bombarded me, flickering in and out with images of red, fires, smoke, and screams. A moan and cry of agony brought me back as I watched one of the strangers stab one of our own.

When the stranger turned to look at me, his face flickered, distorting his facial features, right before it flickered back. He jumped up and ran, and I leaped to my feet as well. I grabbed my crossbow and secured a bolt, but missed the target as he jumped over a fallen tree and dodged around a tipped-over wheelbarrow. Throwing my weapon down, I chased after him and decreased the distance between us enough for me to reach for my knife and throw it in his direction. It hit the target, but it didn't stop him. I watched as he took a few steps, turned, pulled the knife out of the back of his thigh, and threw it right back with an inhuman amount of force. In shock at what I witnessed, I didn't dodge in time, taking the blade right in my chest, knocking me to the ground with a crash.

My breath wooshed out of me upon impact.

"Sili!"

My vision blurred, my mind replaying the

strangers' flickering face and the memory of some-thing else from the past. I felt like the blade lodged in my chest broke a rib bone and pierced through to the other side. The excruciating pain coursing through my body brought back a familiarity and more faces, menacing grins, and roars. *How many times had they stabbed me?*

Hands roamed my body and I kicked and screamed, consumed by the mental cage of my memories. Smoke, fire, blades, and screams. Life flashing before my eyes. Darkness, unearth dirt. The smell of blood...

"You brought that among us!" they accused them.

"How could you bring that monstrosity here?" came another voice among the angry masses. "Do you not care about the safety of this community?"

My father stood tall like a sentinel with his arms crossed, blocking them from getting to me.

"Sili. Open your eyes. Look at me. Look at me!"

I cried out when he tried to move me, fighting a darkness that threatened to drown me in another moment in time.

"Stay away from me!" I threw my fist at the man before me, collapsing his face in. The crunch of bone was barely discernible in the moment. My strength was out of control, and it scared me.

"Caleb!" she cried before turning her glare on me. "You monster!"

"No!" I screamed as the community dragged me by my arms away from my family, away from all I had ever known.

The fires began to dance at my feet as my father attempted to get to me through the throng of angry faces that held him back. Tears streamed down my face while the heat exponentially increased as the flames came to life. It was my mother who broke through the crowd, jumping into the flames with her knife in hand, sawing at my ropes as her dress began to catch fire.

"Please!" I begged through my sobs.

"Get her off there!" one of the random community members screamed out, pointing at my mother while sneering at me.

"She's out of her damn mind!" came another voice.

"Faheemah. Just hold on, baby."

A mouth pushed against mine and I was pulled back to the present, my mind fading in and out of awareness. Eliseo blew air into my lungs and I was confused. Why did my limbs feel so heavy? He did it again and my fingers twitched and my eyelids fluttered. Another blow and I coughed, sputtering to the side, moaning as the skin on my chest started to itch in that familiar way.

"What the hell?" Eliseo growled above me.

He rolled me onto my back and stared at my chest as it began to knit itself back together at rapid speed. I tried to kick him off me, to no avail. *He would condemn me. They all did.* He leaned his head in with his eyes ablaze with something akin to fury as my body healed itself like nothing happened, leaving perfect skin behind.

When his eyes snapped to mine, his nostrils flared and his lip curled with a snarl.

5

ELISEO

I took too many knocks to my head. I couldn't be seeing what I was seeing. What the fuck kind of sorcery was this?

Fitri's skin healed completely before my eyes, leaving soft flesh and only bloodstains behind. I was so focused on bringing her back to life, doing whatever I needed to do, that it didn't register in my mind that she was probably already dead. I refused to believe it. The knife jammed deeply beside her heart, I had to dig my fucking fist in her wound to pull it out, still holding on to hope that maybe it missed the mark.

The suspect was already gone by the time I got to her. *I just needed her to open her damn eyes!*

"Get off me," she screeched, her energy returned.

"What the hell are you?" I snarled—seething

that I almost lost her, pissed at what I just witnessed.

She was *not* human. But what was she? She couldn't be a bloodsucker. I was covered in blood, and she hadn't tried to bite my head off. Nothing made sense, and she had better give me some answers before I dragged her to the doc's bunker myself.

"Get *off* me!" she cried out again.

Her arms covered her chest, and I remembered I had ripped off her shirt to see her injuries. I discovered during my panic that she taped down her breasts. It was no wonder she easily disguised herself as a boy. My fingers shakily lifted and trailed the blood left on her skin, trying to find the knife's entry point, but there was no evidence left behind. Her chest rose and fell with her rapid breathing, and my shoulders slumped in relief that she was breathing at all.

I almost lost her.

The little brat kept this fucking secret from me. I was affronted beyond reason over that fact. We were a fucking *team*. Didn't she know she could trust me?

You were just about to take her to crazy Otis, my mind supplied.

I stood up and paced back and forth, pulling my hair from my scalp. The pain clarified my tumultuous emotions as my mind attempted to reason and see logic in everything that happened.

We lost the group. Everyone's dead. The other

human group that ambushed us scattered the ground amongst our men, and I needed to decide what we were going to do from here.

"Who threw the knife at you?" I barked, unable to tamp down my anger.

"I don't know."

"Did you kill him?"

"I don't know. I..." She groaned as she stood, and my eyes zoomed in on her chest again.

Despite seeing what happened, I still couldn't fucking believe it. What kind of other shit was out there? What more do we *not* know?

"I don't think I did. I think he got away," she answered.

"Fuck." What if this was just a scouting group? What if he was bringing back other guys right now to follow us back to Ashborne? Shit, this was becoming a bigger problem than just a random ambush. "Get your ass in the car. We need to go. Now."

I watched as Fitri subtly rubbed at her breasts, moaning under her breath. She was fucking beautiful beneath her clothes. I had never seen skin as smooth as hers—without scars. Ripping my bloody shirt off, I threw it at her.

"Cover up and let's go." I was distracted. I needed to think. I needed to drive us around in circles just in case something tailed us.

"We should grab some of the guys' weapons and bring them back." She walked away before she even finished her sentence, and I growled.

She was stubborn. I loved and hated that about her. But she was right. Grabbing what we could, we shoved them into our pockets and made it back to the Humvee.

My foot slammed on the gas and we headed toward another cluster of trees. We needed to ride off-road so we were not easily seen. Glancing at my watch, we had about fifteen minutes before I needed to be back at the meet spot.

"Eliseo..."

I slammed on the steering wheel with pent-up frustration. *Do I report this to the doc, to the community? What if they exiled her?* The thought of losing her from my team made me boil with rage. I was *not* going to fail her like this. Not when I promised myself I would take care of her.

We drove in silence for a while, finally back on track. The other teams most likely already headed for the community, leaving us behind. Coming up familiar territory, I drove through a shortcut to see if I could catch up with them.

"Eliseo..." she called again.

My head snapped to the right, staring at her. "What?"

"Where are we going?"

Turning back to the main road, the Humvee bounced with the change in terrain, the springs of the seat creaking beneath our weight. "We're going to catch up with them another way."

A few moments went by before she said something again. "You're not going to tell them about me, are you?"

Her voice was so vulnerable, so broken, that it split my fucking heart in two.

"Of course, I'm not going to fucking tell them! But you *are* going to tell *me* everything I need to know before I lose my damn mind trying to figure this out. *What the hell are you?*" I growled, unable to control my emotional state of mind.

She turned her face toward the passenger window without answering me, and my rage transformed into full-blown fury. My mind replayed her dying in my arms and my mouth opened before I could filter anything that came out.

"*Sili!* You're going to do as I say or so help me..."

She turned to me with fire in her eyes, and I slammed on the brakes, skidding us to an abrupt stop, parking us right where we were. Dust floated around outside of the vehicle, concealing us for a moment. It was as if the world had disappeared, and nothing existed except for this brat next to me.

"*Sili*. Answer me!" I roared. "What the hell are you?"

"I don't know!" she screamed back.

"What the hell do you mean, you don't know?" What game was she trying to play? Had she been planning this all along? To infiltrate my men? Was she planted in this community? Was that why she was pretending to be a boy?

"I. Don't. Know!" she seethed. "My memories

are fragmented at best, coming at me randomly. Some things I *think* I know, only to be turned upside down with another memory that makes no fucking sense!"

My eyes narrowed in suspicion. It was a plausible alibi.

"Don't look at me like that, you asshole!"

"How the hell am I *supposed* to look at you?" The tension in this Humvee was ramping up hard and fast. The air was thick between us. What would Reed have done if this happened in front of him? Would he have tried to save her, too, or left her to rot the way I did with the men that came with us today?

Thoughts of Reed's mouth on hers made me growl.

She exploded in response and shoved my body, taking me by surprise with her extra strength, slamming me against the driver-side door with a hard crash, sending pain up my back.

"You're supposed to fucking look at me like you did yesterday and every other day. How does me healing fast change anything about me, huh? I'm tired of people trying to kill me for things that are out of my control!"

Kill her? Who the hell was trying to kill her? A new type of rancor seeped into my skin upon this revelation.

"Who tried to kill you?" I grabbed the front of her bloody shirt and straightened up. "Tell me who they are!"

Does it have anything to do with the guy that got away?

"What does it matter?" She tried to pull away, but I was too far gone. Images of my previous community flashed before my eyes. I couldn't save them. I came home too late. I was fucking too late to save her.

"Fitri. Tell. Me!" I roared.

When her eyes faltered from rage to unshed tears, my body automatically moved on its own volition, pulling her into my lap to wrap my arms around her.

Her breaths were harsh and hiccuped as she shook in my arms, against my shoulder. *Fuck. I'm an asshole.* Why did I push her when she was clearly already in distress over what happened earlier? I was torn between shaking her for answers and comforting her in this moment as she broke apart before me.

The more her scent infused into my nose, the more I calmed, rubbing my hand on her back. After a few moments, I broke the silence. "Dammit, *Sili*. Stop crying. I can't take that shit."

She laughed into my shoulder and my lips twitched.

"You're such an asshole," she mumbled against me, and I secretly liked the fact that she continued to seek me for comfort.

"I know. This is nothing new. Now, stop your fucking crying so we can figure this shit out."

Her hand slapped me in the chest as she pulled

her face away. It was splotchy from both tears and blood as she tried to wipe at her eyes. *She shouldn't be this fucking beautiful when she cried.*

"Stop that, you'll get nasty shit in your eyes," I chastised. "We have enough to deal with. I don't want to be the one dragging your infected ass back to the Ashborne."

"Ugh." She shoved me until I reluctantly released her and resituated herself back in the passenger seat. "I don't get infected. I heal, remember?"

Damn. What would it be like to not fear death when everything around you would shit for the opportunity? *Wait, she said people were trying to kill her.* My mind began to piece a few of her statements together. "Is that why people try to kill you? Because you heal?"

She sniffled and wiped her eyes one last time with the back of her hand. "No. Maybe. The memories break up, but...I don't know how to explain it. Can we just get back home? Please?"

Noting her avoidance tactic, I nodded and moved the Humvee back on the path. We made it to the front gates of the community half an hour later with weapons trained at us.

Coming out of the vehicle slowly, I hollered so they could hear my voice and know it was us. "We lost track of time. Shit happened! Open the damn gate!"

"Eliseo? Where the hell were you?" shouted the first guard.

"Open the damn gate!"

He did as I commanded and I got back in the Humvee, driving us into the garage. We both jumped out of the vehicle as other residents came forth to help grab the items and bags from the back.

Some of the male residents were malingering about and I scowled, looking around, wondering what the hell the hold-up was. Fitri subtly hid behind me and I went on high alert, trying to assess the threat. Some of the younger men kept their heads down, donning their backpacks and sneaking peeks behind my back.

What the fuck?

"Get your ass in gear and go! What the fuck are you all standing around for?" I barked.

The men scattered like roaches and I grabbed Fitri's hand to drag her toward the southwest corner of the Ashborne. I realized she lost her cap somewhere out there, but it was too late now. Her braid was pinned tight around her head but it didn't escape anyone's notice that she was all woman.

"Dude, what happened, and where the hell is your shirt?" Samuel ran up to us, looking us over with Gunner and Reed right behind him.

"Where's the kid?" *Of course, that was Reed's first question.* It pissed me off.

"The kid is fine," I gritted out. "Get out of my way, I need to check on something."

Gunner stared at Fitri in my blood-soaked

shirt. "Holy shit. What did you guys run into out there? Where are the other men?"

"Dead, apparently," Samuel answered. "Glad you two made it back alive. How many were there? Were you outnumbered?"

"Something like that," I mumbled as I continued to pull Fitri behind me. The men knew they weren't going to get another word out of me at the moment, so they left us and headed back to wherever they came from.

Except for Reed.

"How about you go wash yourself up and relax? I'll help the kid back home," he offered, keeping his eyes on Sili.

I swung around and snarled in his face. "*I'll* take care of the kid and *you* can go back home. You can talk tomorrow when we hit training again."

Dragging her faster toward my house, I ignored anyone else calling for me and pulled her up the porch steps and through my front door, slamming it shut. I let out a sigh at the resounding lock mechanism falling into place.

"Why can't I go back to my house?" She asked with her little attitude creeping up again.

"Go upstairs and wash up."

"Eliseo. What the hell is going on?"

My patience was wearing thin. "Go upstairs and wash the blood off. Then come back down and tell me everything."

She grimaced but hesitantly did as I said, stomping up the steps with her boots. I shouldn't have my eyes trained on the way her ass swayed, but here we were.

How fast would news of her being a girl fly through this community? What kind of other danger would she be in now? I needed to keep her out of the doc's radar. Didn't he check her in when she first arrived? He had to. It was protocol here. Why hadn't he found out anything about her?

Unless he was hiding shit about this, too, like he always did.

My back tinged with residual pain and I groaned. Fuck, I needed to shower, too, relax under the water. Rolling my neck, I jogged up the steps. The sound of water running grew louder the closer I got as my eyes scanned the dirty clothes scattered in front of the door. I divested myself of clothes, opening the curtain and stepping in to her screams.

"What the hell are you doing? I'm showering! Wait till I'm done, you asshole!"

Stepping the rest of the way into the tub, I shoved her forward so I could wash up, too. "We need to conserve water."

I ignored her curses. Grabbing the soap, I squeezed some into my hands and lathered it up. "Turn around."

"W-what?"

"Turn around, so I can wash the blood out of your hair."

Of course, she had no argument and turned around. It was the whole reason why she needed to shower after all. I chuckled to myself as my hands ran through her long, thick, dark locks. *How the hell did she hide all this under her cap?*

My fingers dug into her scalp and she moaned, making my dick jump. *Fuck.* Gritting my teeth, I quickly finished the task, squeezed more soap onto my hands, and washed myself while she rinsed her hair.

Once we were done, I shut off the water and walked toward my bedroom, looking for a fresh set of clothes.

"Can I borrow one of your shirts?" Her innocent voice behind me threw the image of her drowning in my shirt in my mind, and I groaned under my breath.

What the hell was up with me these days? Why couldn't I get her out of my mind? She was too fucking young for my fifty-year-old ass. She couldn't be passed mid-twenty by the looks of her. But life and lack of food did funny things to a person's development.

"Yeah." I grabbed the first shirt I saw and turned to toss it to her, only to glimpse at her tiny panties glued to her skin from her damp skin. Rubbing my hands down my face, I stared intently at her as she put her arms through the shirt, dropping the fabric to cover the knees.

My eyes drifted to her legs and she crossed her arms protectively. Her reaction communicated that something happened to her in the past to make her so skittish.

Leaning against the dresser, I asked my first question. "Where did you come from before Ashborne?"

"I'm not sure how to answer that. I flitted through a few human groups before running into some trouble." Her eyes were cast down and it made me suspicious, if not for the fact that she called them 'human' groups. Maybe I was over-thinking things.

"Look at me," I commanded.

She shook her head and rubbed her arms. Why was she timid all of a sudden? Where was the fire-cracker I knew?

"Fitri, when did you realize you were different?"

"When one of the guys at my home camp tried to molest me," she deadpanned.

My nostrils flared. Thoughts of another man's hands on her silky skin enraged me beyond reason. Judging by the way she looked now, she must have been pretty young when it happened. Did I really want to know?

"How old are you?" I blurted.

She lifted her head, blushed, and turned her face to the side. That was when I realized I still stood here buck fucking naked with my arms crossed and my dick at half-mast from the way her skin flushed down her neck. Turning, I pulled open the drawer, grabbed some boxer briefs, and put them on. I wasn't sure whether it was for her benefit or mine.

Rubbing my chin, I asked her again, cautiously. "How old are you, Fitri?"

Once she realized I was covered, her eyes flared. "What does it matter?"

"Relax. I'm just trying to fill all the holes."

Her eyes widened and she miserably failed at stifling her laugh. The crap that came out of my mouth sounded so much like Samuel, even I chuckled.

"Look. It's been a long day," I sighed. "We're back behind the walls of the community now, so stop being on edge. I'm trying to figure out what we need to do from here. You mentioned people trying to kill you. Were these people from your previous community?"

"Among other places," she admitted.

Was everyone out to get this girl? "Why?"

"What do you mean 'why'? You saw what you saw."

"Yeah, but why would that enrage so many different people? It doesn't make any sense. Make them cautious of you, yes. But I'm assuming you haven't gone around bloodsucking on anyone, correct?" She scrunched her nose, and I took that as a yes. "If that's the case, why so much hate?"

"I-I'm stronger than most," she stuttered as if afraid of letting the fact loose. I remembered the strength behind her first punch to my face. It was a pleasant memory. I would have to agree there.

"Is there more?" I prodded.

"Sometimes, I can't control my strength. Especially when I'm emotional."

She was slowly opening up. This was good. "Duly noted. You *are* a brat sometimes."

"I am not! What the hell is wrong with you?" *There she was. I loved that fire.* It filled a hole inside of me I didn't know existed. "Do you not think maybe it's *your* asshole attitude that causes it?"

"You *would* turn it around on me." She growled like an angry kitten, and my dick twitched in response. "I mean, it's the best way to take the attention off you, right? You have an avoidance tactic among other things."

I was pushing her buttons, I knew it. I needed to see what this emotional outburst brought. Maybe it would help us both understand.

"You are such an—"

"Asshole. I know. You've said this plenty of times. We're going to have to work on switching up your vocabulary," I teased.

She lunged at me and I caught her wrists in a tight grip, pulling her against my naked chest. Without the tape over hers, I could feel her little nipples pebble through the fabric.

"I wouldn't, if I were you," I warned, hoping it would push her to do the opposite.

Her eyes narrowed and my cock fully hardened. She didn't realize how fucking beautiful she was when she was like this. At that thought, more things began to click into place. Maybe this was why she was skittish around men. *Who the hell could keep their hands off this?* I would have to get more vigilant around her, especially now that the other residents of Ashborne knew she was all woman under her baggy clothes.

"Let. Me. Go," she snarled. "I want to go home."

"Not yet, *Sili*. Not yet. I got a few more questions," I breathed.

"I'm done with your stupid questions! This is getting nowhere!" She kneed me, and I twisted quickly enough for it to hit my thigh instead of my groin.

She struggled and continuously kicked until we were knocked off-balance and I ended up on top of her with her arms still firmly in my grip on the floor.

"Go ahead, *Sili*," I taunted. "Show me this strength you have. You're probably lying to me."

She kneed me in the gut, knocking me off her. Leaping on top of me like a crazed woman, her little hands scratched and clawed at me while my arms continued to block most of her hits. Her legs were straddled around me and I groaned when she ground down against my erection.

My hands slipped under the hem of the shirt and grabbed her ass, forcing her to grind down on me again. She panted on top of me, caught by surprise, her arms planted on the floor over my shoulders. She was so fucking innocent. I was in pain as I tried to hold myself back. Being the bastard I was, I ground against her panties, too, trying to add to the friction we were creating.

The adrenaline from the fight earlier to this fight at home, had my blood pumping. My previous anger morphed into lust as her eyes stared at me like a deer caught in headlights. *Was she untouched?* It was hard to believe, in this world where death was around every corner. Many lived like it was their last day, indulging in their carnal hungers.

Not wanting to frighten her any more than she already was, I kept her on top of me, giving her a sense of control over the situation. She could remove herself at any time.

"What are you doing?" Her voice was breathless, the attitude from earlier vanished.

If I knew this was all it took...

My hand slapped her ass with a loud smack for all the times she had been a brat toward me. She squealed and fell against my chest, breasts pressed up against my flesh in the worst kind of temptation.

"What is wrong with you?" she screeched, and I slapped her again, then rubbed the sting away with my calloused hands longer than I needed to.

"All that mouth on you needed to be taught a lesson. I wasn't done asking questions."

Our faces were so close, I could see the flecks of light reflected in her dark eyes, framed by the longest lashes known to man.

She was quietly scrutinizing me while her breaths came out in shallow pants. I massaged her ass a few more rounds before slipping my fingers under her panties, tugging at them then moving my hands up her waist. I watched her reactions carefully noting that she didn't move. I took that as a good sign.

A hard slap to my face came out of nowhere, stinging like a bitch, making me flex my jaw. She definitely did *not* hit like a girl, the full force of what she had been trying to tell me demonstrated in a single blow.

I guess she wasn't lying after all.

Unexpectedly, she grabbed my face and pressed her lips against mine, grinding her damp panties against my hard cock. This was a turn of events I welcomed. I groaned into her mouth, reveling in the way she took over. For once, I was grateful for a command—one that came from a tiny little spitfire that wanted to unravel me from the inside.

It had been years since I touched a woman— years since I even wanted to. What was it about this woman that made me fall so easily?

Her tongue tentatively touched the seam of my lips and I submitted for her exploration. She was new to kissing, this I could tell. I could teach her whatever she wanted to know. When her tongue touched mine, I took the lead and dueled with hers. She loved a challenge, especially when it came from me. It ignited her ire and I loved it. Just as I imagined, she came to life, fighting for dominance in the kiss. Her delicate hands caressed my scruff and scratched my face with unrestrained need igniting my own passions.

I flipped her over and she kept her legs wrapped around me. My lips traveled from her mouth to her jaw and down her neck as my hands ripped off the scrap of fabric between her legs in my way. She gasped and threw her head back, cradling my face as I kissed and sucked her skin. My body felt on fire, the shirt she had on irritated me with its barrier to her body. I ripped it off her and she yelped in surprise as I shoved down my boxers and rubbed my hard shaft between the apex of her legs.

"Fuck, *Sili*," I groaned against her waist. "You're so wet for me. Do you feel it? I want to drown in you."

"Oh, my god," she gasped.

My mouth latched onto her pert nipple and sucked hard. Rolling it around with my tongue, my other hand ran along her ribs. *She was too small. I needed to feed her more.* The scent of her arousal called to me and made my mouth water. Popping the nipple out of my mouth, I pushed the back of her legs against her shoulders and licked up the seam of her swollen pussy lips.

"Fuck, you taste so good." I groaned against her. Another lick up towards her clit, and she clamped her legs around me aggressively.

When I dove my tongue inside of her, she undulated, and her grip on me increased to an uncomfortable level. Using extra strength, I pried her legs apart and ate her like a man feasting on his last meal. I was starved—starved for a girl I had no business doing this with.

Why did this make me desire her more? I had self-anointed myself as her guardian, and now I was licking her cunt. How much more wrong could this get?

"Oh my god, don't stop."

Hell fucking no, I wouldn't stop. As if her words cracked a whip, I dropped one of her legs and sucked on her clit, rolling it in my mouth as my finger dove into her wet entrance. Her pussy squeezed my fingers, and my dick slapped my abs, thinking of how she'd squeeze my cock when I buried myself inside of her.

What the hell was wrong with me? I should be protecting her, not eating her alive. But the forbiddenness of what was happening only drove me harder.

"*Sili*." I whispered against her pussy. "Tell me you want me. Tell me you want this."

A rejection from her might snap me out of this lust-filled haze. *Hopefully*. Her hesitation had me diving my tongue inside of her in eager persuasion of her answer. I was such an asshole, but I knew she loved it. The way her fingers laced through my hair and pulled me against her told me she didn't want me going anywhere.

When her thighs quivered, I knew she was close. I increased my efforts, my hands firmly gripped on her ass until she cried out in pleasure, her hips wild against my face.

Before her pleasure could die down, I rubbed the head of my cock against her entrance, slipping the crown in and out of her teasingly, silently asking her to reject me before I lost my damn mind.

Much to my dismay and delight, the little minx widened her legs, grabbed my ass and pulled me in, plunging me inside, surrounding my cock with her inferno.

I was lost in carnality, lost in longing, lost in a sense of loneliness I never knew I was drowning in as my mouth covered hers and my hips began to pound her into the ground. Her arms wrapped around my shoulders and I shuddered in her warm embrace. Her hands roamed my back, feeling every scar I had accumulated over the years of my existence—a battle-worn body not worthy of the delicate beauty beneath me.

Fuck if I didn't want to keep her secrets all for myself.

She cried against my mouth when I twisted my hips on the next thrust and my tongue dove inside, stealing the sound for myself. I had been greedy for her attention, not fully comprehending why Reed's proximity and growing relationship with her pissed me the fuck off. Now, I knew. The buried truth I refused to face flooded through as I threw one of her legs over my shoulder and rammed into her wanting pussy, making sure she felt me in the depths of her womb long after we were done.

Her legs tightened and so did my abs. I repositioned her, reading her body, adjusting to everything she enjoyed. Turning her to her side, I pushed the back of her leg up, letting me finger her clit as I continued to bury myself inside of her.

Her pussy fluttered around me and my groin tightened with pain as I forced myself to hold off on my release until she found hers. When she cried out in pleasure, my fingers pinched and pulled at her nub, loving the way her pussy flooded my dick making squelching noises with every subsequent thrust.

I pulled out and she cried in distress, until I pushed her onto her back and fisted my cock over her chest. I needed to protect her. I couldn't run the risk of getting her pregnant in a time like this. As much as I wanted to fill her womb to the brim, there were more ways than one to find mutual pleasure.

Her eyes glazed over with lust as she watched me stroke my cock with a twist of my wrist. I took joy in the way she was mesmerized by me, the same way I was mesmerized by the way her breasts moved with each breath she took.

"I'm going to come on your tits. Would you like that? Fuck, your tits are beautiful. I want to mark them with my cum and rub it all over you," I groaned, lost in the smell of our coupling in this room.

"Oh, my god," she panted, her own hands slipping to the apex of her legs.

I chuckled. We really needed to work on increasing her vocabulary. An old, familiar tingle shot down my spine as my cock spent its release all over her skin and pulsed against my palm. Groaning, I tilted my head back and savored the feeling of our combined wetness coating my hand as I continued to pump it all out over her, marking her.

By the time I brought my gaze back down, her legs were still splayed open for my viewing pleasure, glistening like a siren's call. I rubbed the head of my cock against her inner thigh and slipped my dick back in, letting it take in her warmth as my left hand rubbed my release all over her breasts and stomach. Her nipples hardened, and I groaned against her shoulder, kissing her skin and taking in the smell of our mutual arousal in the room.

"I-I never knew it could feel like that," she whispered, running her fingers through my hair.

Nipping her shoulder, I pulled her chest against mine, keeping my cock nestled inside her pussy. Rubbing my scruff against her head, I let out an exhale—taking the tensions of the day with it.

"If you want to feel like that again, all you have to do is ask. I'm more than happy to be the one who gives it to you." I gripped her chin, tilted it up, and stared into her eyes. "Don't even *think* of asking anyone else, because if I find out, I'll kill 'em."

I slammed my lips on hers before she could give me any retort to my statement.

6

I WIPED MY CHEST OFF WITH A WET RAG AND SNUCK OUT of Eliseo's house when he began snoring. I probably shouldn't have, but I needed time to think about everything. It all happened so fast. Despite how good he made me feel in the moment, I didn't know how I felt afterward.

I was annoyed that he destroyed one of the three pairs of panties I was able to pack in my cargo pants. He knew how hard they were to come by, but did it anyway. But my annoyance made way for a different emotion. His sexual appetite for me was hot but I didn't have to admit to *him*.

I should be pissed. Right? I should be angry he took advantage of my vulnerable moment of discovery, despite the fact that I was willingly pulled into his carnal magnetism. Confusion muddled my every thought with each step I took away from his home. I could still feel the phantom sensation of his hard cock inside of me, and it made my pussy throb, weeping for him to come back and fill me up.

"What is wrong with you?" I chastised myself aloud under my breath.

I never had sex before, I didn't think, but I had seen it plenty of times. Flashes of another face flitted in my mind, and it made my heart hurt. I didn't recognize him, but I knew there were deep emotions tied to the memory. Who was this elusive person, and why was my mind bringing him up now?

Making it to my front door under the cover of darkness, my hands felt for my hair pin and used muscle memory to unlock it. Once inside, I turned on the light switch to the lamp on the side table. I quietly closed the door and turned the bolt, sliding down with my back against the door.

Eliseo was such a large presence. He over-whelmed me with how hot and quick his passion burned. How did we go from annoying each other to him taking a guardian position in my life force-fully... to this?

It felt wrong, but why? He easily was twice my age but that wasn't really the problem, not in this life. There were plenty of people in this world who had to take partners out of necessity and surviv-ability. But something told me, Eliseo wasn't one of those people. Something told me, Eliseo didn't take partners judging by the way he avoided Mrs.

Reyes' attempts. My hands slowly rubbed my breasts thinking about the way he did it to me, with such practiced ease. I bit my lip and replayed our tryst, stifling a whimper.

I missed him already, and I didn't want to. I didn't *want* to feel this way. I didn't *want* to become attached to something that wasn't mine to keep. Eliseo was an alpha with a tightly-knit pack. I didn't need any more complications in my life. What if I broke the team? I couldn't live with myself if it happened. I was the newbie in the group which also meant I could turn out to be the biggest liability.

Someone pounded on my door, vibrating it against my back. I jumped up and backed away, staring at it in silence, hoping the person would go away.

My heart hammered inside of my chest and I screeched when a large figure shouldered his way through my door, breaking it into pieces, sending splinters of wood every which way.

"*Sili*," he panted like an enraged beast with his arms against the door frame. "You left me," he accused. Was there a hint of pain beneath his voice? "Where the fuck do you think you're going in the middle of the damn night?"

I got to my feet and backed up on my until I hit the stairway post. Why did the wild look in his eyes make me feel this way—both afraid and intrigued? I was already too attached. I needed some time to think.

He was shirtless, muscles heaving. His cargo pants were undone and hanging on his hips deliciously. Even his boots hadn't been laced in his rush to find me. A pang of guilt ran through me at his worried expression.

You're a liability, Fitri. Look what you've done to him.

Breaking his intense eye contact, my gaze inadvertently roamed his body. The scars on his chest made my mouth dry, his dark tattoos a stark contrast against his sun-kissed skin. He slammed the remnants of the door shut and closed the distance between us until we were toe to toe, staring me down with his signature scowl.

His hands cautiously came up to cradle my face and I closed my eyes with a stuttered breath, letting his warmth seep into my skin. I shouldn't like this. I shouldn't want this...

"How am I supposed to protect you when I can't even keep you near me?" he gritted out painfully and I whimpered.

"I don't need protecting, Eliseo," I whispered. "I survived just fine without you."

He turned to punch a hole in the wall that connected to the stairs, making me jump in surprise. He released my face and pulled at his hair before turning back to face me with a storm behind his eyes. "You just told me people are out to kill you! You expect me to just ignore that?"

"Eliseo, *please.*" I couldn't understand why he cared so much. We barely knew each other.

His eyes dilated before he cradled my face with his busted hand and I felt my lips tremble. "Say that again," he breathed.

Shaking my head, I didn't even remember what I said. This was all so strange, so crazy. *What was going on with him? Why was he like this? Why me?*

Why didn't I want to run away?

He gently placed his lips on mine, and my heart melted. How could he go from a raging beast to someone I wanted to hold and rock at the drop of a hat?

"I need to know you're safe. I need to know where you are. Can you do that for me, *Sili*? Can you just give me that? I know I'm a hard man to be around. The world has brought out the ugly side of me, but I promise you I'll be everything you need. Just stay by my side," his voice cracked with a strange longing at the end and my heart constricted with yearning—yearning to be what he wanted me to be. But what if I wasn't enough?

I wondered what had happened in his past to bring us to this point. What good would two very damaged people do for one another? I could barely hold onto myself most days when my flashbacks got the better of me. And Eliseo? Eliseo seemed like a savage animal that had been forced to contain its rage in order to blend into society.

"I-I don't know," I admitted tentatively. "It's all just so much. I can barely remember my past, Eliseo. You don't want that burden on you."

He kissed me again until I was out of breath.

His lips teased mine until he licked the seam of my lips and asked for entry, to which I easily surrendered. His tongue enticed me, coercing me to believe in what he wanted me to believe. I wanted to, but what if the more I found out about myself...

"*Sili.* Stop thinking so much," he whispered against me. "Just be with me in the moment. Life is so fucking *short.*"

He ripped my borrowed shirt off an instant later, his hands all over my breasts, pulling my nipples deliciously before claiming my mouth again.

"The fuck?" Reed's voice came through the other side of the broken door. I yelped and quickly bent down to put my shirt back on right before he shouldered himself inside.

At this rate, I was going to end up like Samuel, with just a curtain to separate myself from the community.

"What is with you assholes and breaking my door?" I huffed, trying to distract them.

Reed stared at Eliseo, and Eliseo did the same. My skin prickled with how much the tension had ramped up in my house beyond the sexual one Eliseo brought with him. My nipples were hard as rocks as I stared at these two virile men locked in a silent battle.

What is wrong with you Fitri? Since when did you start thinking of them as virile?

Since Eliseo fucked the innocence out of me. I squeezed my legs together at the memory, and

Reed's attention zoned in on my movement, making me flush with embarrassment at getting caught.

Eliseo smirked and crossed his arms, a look of triumph stretched on his face. I punched him in the shoulder, knocking him off balance, and he gave me an incredulous look. I must have used too much strength in the hit, but he deserved it.

"What are you doing here, Eliseo?" Reed asked slowly. "Why is her door busted?"

"You just busted right through it yourself. I should ask you the same damn thing. I told you I was taking care of her," Eliseo responded in a clipped tone, making it obvious he was hiding something.

Reed's nostrils flared, and my pussy fluttered. This wasn't good. Could he tell I looked freshly fucked? My hands went to my cheeks with concern, trying to cool my blush. Would the whole community be able to see it on my face?

"Are you alright, Fitri? Did this bastard do anything to you?" Reed growled.

I was surprised by his question. Why would he assume Eliseo did something bad to me? Was there something I didn't know about? My face must have betrayed my thoughts, because he took a step toward the man in question.

Eliseo stood there with his arms crossed again, acting like he couldn't care less. "You got something you want to say to me, Reed? I did whatever she asked me to, have no doubt. I definitely didn't leave her wanting." He leaned in and gritted out, "But I don't remember her inviting *you.*"

"Is he lying, Fitri?" Reed snapped. "Tell me, and I'll kill him." He didn't take his eyes off Eliseo, and I wondered if they had some old beef between them. If so, why were they on the same team, spending so much time together?

And what was up with these guys always wanting to kill people at the drop of a hat?

Crap. Where's my hat? My fingers ran through my hair, and a pang of loss hit me. That hat had been my security blanket for as long as I could remember.

"Fitri!" I jerked back from Reed's tone, having forgotten he asked me a question.

Eliseo growled out, "Watch it."

"Fuck you, Eliseo! You knew exactly how I felt about her. You never once showed any interest and yet here you are, pissing around her like a fucking wolf marking his territory. What's really going on? You haven't had your sights set on a woman since I've met you. You've only cared about the mission."

"It's none of your damn business," Eliseo grounded back. "What the hell are you doing around her house in the middle of the night, anyway?"

What were both of these men doing around my house in the middle of the night?

"I wanted to make sure she made it home safely. After the way you dragged her around like a ragdoll, would you blame me? You'd fucking do the same."

This was becoming nuts. I needed to stop all this bickering and division. We were a team. "Guys!" They both snapped their faces to mine at the same time. "Both of you, get out."

"What?" Reed guffawed.

"*Sili*," Eliseo pleaded.

"Get out!" I was tired of this. I was just damn tired. I wanted some time alone to think, and I wanted to sleep. The testosterone in this room wasn't helping anything or anyone with clarity.

I pointed my finger at Eliseo first. "You, come back tomorrow and fix my damn door! I'm not living like Samuel!"

I turned to Reed with the same finger. "And you! Thank you for checking up on me. You guys need to take this shit out in training, not in my damn house!"

No one moved. They both stared at me with varying degrees of hunger, and my libido couldn't take it. "Get. Out!"

They both were reluctant to turn and leave. Eliseo made sure to gently close my door so it didn't completely fall off the hinge. Only when I was alone did I realize I wouldn't get any sleep tonight with the wood broken.

Growling under my breath, I waited a good amount of time after they left before I walked to the back of my house, opened my window, and climbed out. I needed sleep, but I needed it someplace safe. Making my way quietly through the neighborhood with the soft grass beneath my boots, I headed north until I reached a familiar porch.

Knocking gently, I looked left and right in case someone was following me. I had a weird feeling again in my gut like someone was watching me, and I didn't like it. No matter how diligently I scanned my surroundings when this feeling came around, I never saw anything out of place. That made the unease increase. The door opened an inch, and then all the way, pulling some of my hair with it.

"Fitri? What's wrong?" Gunner poked his head out and looked around before pulling me inside.

"C-can I stay here with you tonight?"

"What happened?" he prodded with concern. "Did someone break into your house? Do you need me to get the guys to go check it out?"

Good god, no.

"It's nothing. Just let me crash on your couch tonight. I'll be out before morning," I promised. I didn't want to have to explain myself yet again. My limbs were already feeling heavy from the events of today.

He looked at me quietly before nodding. "Alright. I'll grab you a blanket. If you get hungry, grab whatever you want. If you need me, I'll just be in the next room, alright?"

I watched as he walked away toward a hallway closet, his swagger one of a trained killer. Everyone on the team was alike. I wondered how they all came together and how they were able to work peacefully among each other when it was apparently this group was full of nothing but alpha men.

"Thanks Gunner. I owe you one," I mumbled sleepily.

He shoved the blanket into my chest and smiled. "Nah. From what I gather, you've done enough, coming back alive with that old bastard. Glad to have you on our team, kid."

I hoped he still felt that way once he found out my secrets.

Sleep came quickly as I situated myself on his couch. Before darkness could completely consume me, I found myself tossing and turning.

"What have we here?" came a dangerous voice.

I should have never gone east. The smell of burning flesh still clogged my nose as I leapt through the bushes and between the trees to try and escape. It wasn't good for women to be out here. Hasn't my father always warned me of that? But I couldn't stay. I couldn't watch...

"She's a bloodsucker. Look how fast she moves!" another male voice rang out.

"Get her!"

"Come here, little girl," the first one cajoled. "We wanted to invite you to a family barbeque."

The humans cackled, sending fear up my spine and my limbs moved quicker, determined to get them off my trail.

The sound of vampires shrieking echoed all around

us as the flames grew higher and higher around their crucifixes.

I jerked awake, groaning at the nightmare that threw me off Gunner's couch. Looking around, I scrambled out of habit until I realized the sun was peeking over the horizon, its rays peeking into Gunner's living room. I needed to get out of here.

"You dream like that every night?" Gunner's voice in a chair beside me made me jump, and I scrambled back onto the couch backwards, a hand on my chest to calm my racing heart.

"S-sometimes." Quickly gathering the blankets and folding it up, I told him, "I'll get out of your way. Thanks for letting me crash here."

He stood with me, and the silence became awkward. He didn't say a word as he watched me move around and then leave through his front door.

The morning air was crisp, I could feel the light humidity on my scalp reminding me that I lost my cap during the last outing. Irrational anxiety hit me as I quickly made my way through backyards until I was back at my own home. Climbing through the window, I looked around for a change of clothes so I didn't have to be reminded of Eliseo as I went about my day.

His scent clung to my skin, but not as much as the memory of the night before.

"It was just a slip-up. We were both riding high on strange emotions. That's all," I told myself aloud as I rummaged through my dresser for another shirt.

I ran out of tape for my breasts, so I decided instead to wear a long sleeve beneath my shirt. Switching out some weaponry, I sat myself on the floor and cleaned some of the ones I used yesterday. Not hearing much ruckus outside, I assumed the majority of the community probably hadn't risen yet. *Good.*

Replaiting my hair, my mind played back how Eliseo washed it and massaged my scalp. *Ugh. Stop thinking about it. You're going to make things weirder than they already are!*

Once I was done, I went downstairs and snuck out my back window again. Stealthily, I made it to the back of the community wall, looking around to find the best location for me to jump. Hoping for some overgrown branches to aid in climbing, I finally reached a corner that looked to be my best bet.

"We can't," a feminine voice whispered and my back went ramrod straight, stopping me in my tracks. Turning, I didn't see anyone but my curiosity got the better of me.

"I don't think you realize the position you're in, Hannah." I recognized that male's voice and it filled me with trepidation.

Crouching, I moved until I reached the back of the closest house. Peeking around the corner, my eyes widened as I slammed my hand over my mouth, preventing the gasp from escaping.

Her hands were on his chest with her head facing to the side. Doctor Otis kissed up her neck and grabbed her ass suggestively. His goggles were still on his head, but he didn't have his usual apron on. Instead, it looked like his pants were undone while he kissed down to the top of her breasts.

"We can't do this anymore," she whispered. "I'm with Samuel now."

Oh snap.

"What difference does it make? He's not going to find out. I can kill him in an instant." He grabbed her face and kissed her aggressively. "Would you like that? I can kill him while he sleeps and he wouldn't feel a thing."

She shoved him away and he cackled. Her chest heaved as she stared at him with what looked like a hint of fear. It was a look we all gave the mad doctor.

"No. This is it, Otis. This ends here. You need to stop looking for me. Stop calling for me. I'm with Samuel now."

The doctor licked his lips and pulled out his cock, stroking it for her to see. What kind of crazy response was that? There was something seriously wrong with that man.

Hannah stared at his movements, unmoving, biting her lip right before she snapped out of her trance, turned and ran off. The doctor watched her, still stroking his cock until he groaned, releasing himself all over the grass.

"Good for nothing woman. It ends when *I* say it

ends." He tucked himself away and walked off like nothing happened.

This place was full of secrets. Shaking my head, I waited a few moments after the doctor disappeared before I went back to the corner of the wall I was going to climb. With one foot planted on the wall, I grabbed the first brick that jutted out a little more than the rest about to leverage myself up. This was probably a bad idea, but a solo trip to look for another cap, and the chance to breathe away from the team sounded like a good plan when it ran through my head this morning.

Once up, I reached toward a low-hanging branch for my next step when suddenly, strong arms pulled me off the wall as if I weighed nothing. I threw an elbow back and a masculine grunt responded.

"*Sili*, what the fuck do you think you're doing?" Eliseo barked in my ear.

Turning in his arms, I stared at him incredulously. "Are you following me?"

"Are you trying to climb this fucking wall and leave the community alone?" he shot back.

I didn't miss how his hands lingered around my waist. I told myself that it was none of his damn business, but my face flushed when I remembered him spanking me for this mouth of mine.

He gave me a smirk, probably remembering the same thing, and I tried to elbow him again, only to have him throw me over his shoulder and walk back toward the heart of Ashborne.

"Put me down, you asshole!" I screeched.

"We got training today, I told you that." He slapped my ass and continued walking.

I was so mad! Lifting the top half of my body up, I wrapped my legs around his torso and threw the momentum back, taking us to the ground. He landed on top of me in a daze, not anticipating my move. Ignoring the pain in my back, I quickly twisted until my thighs were wrapped around his head and squeezed.

He sputtered but laughed. "If you wanted me between your legs, there are better ways to go about it, you know."

"You need to leave me the hell alone, Eliseo," irritated he took everything I did to him in stride. "I have things to do."

He slipped a hand through my legs and with his strength, one of his legs straightened and jutted out right before he twisted and broke my hold on him, turning us until he was on top of me from behind with my face down in the grass. *Why did I keep finding myself in this position with him?*

My body shuddered as he ran his nose behind my neck, inhaling me with a groan. This man was too much. I couldn't think straight when I was around him. That was precisely the reason why I needed a break.

"Did you have a good sleep at Gunner's last night?" he mumbled against my hair.

"Do you always stalk me?" I retaliated.

"I keep you safe when I can," he continued calmly, refusing to remove us from our position on the ground. "I need to make sure I know where all my team members are."

His hips ground into my ass, and my pussy clenched. *Fuck, get a hold of yourself!*

"Do you randomly take them down and grind against their ass too?" I huffed.

The low chuckle he let out against my hair made me close my eyes. The vibration against my skin teased me with other images I didn't need right now.

Without warning, the weight was gone, and my back was cool against the morning air. Turning around, I stared at him. His eyes were gleaming with something as he stuck his hand out for me to grab. I did, and electricity shot up my limb. Pulling it out of his grasp, I crossed my arms until I remembered I didn't have tape on.

Eliseo's eyes zoned in on my chest and I growled, walking away. My morning plans were already a crap shoot. He caught up with me in a few short strides, making it look like we walked out from between the houses after a naughty tryst. Thinking about what I witnessed this morning, I wondered how long the doctor had been rendezvousing with Hannah.

We made it to our usual spot for training, and most of the guys were already there. Samuel swaggered up a few seconds later with a huge, obvious smile on his face.

"I swear if you smell like pussy, you're going to have to spar with someone else, fucker," Gunner groaned.

"It's not my fault I can't keep her off me," Samuel laughed.

"You and Hannah need new hobbies."

I watched the men banter and mess around. My gut churned over what I discovered. It was not my business to say anything about anyone that I didn't really know. *After all, he wasn't fucking her, right? His dick was in his hand.*

I was torn at what I should do, guilt stabbing me again and again as I watched Samuel tell the guys about how wonderful it was to have a steady woman.

"Quit daydreaming, *Sili*! Get into position!" Eliseo called out.

Running a hand down my face, I turned and rolled my shoulders. *Just don't think about it. It's not your business. All you need to think about is sparring.*

"Samuel! You're up," Eliseo called again. "You and *Sili* are partnering today."

My heart quickened. *Shit.*

Samuel ran up with a cocky smile and blew a kiss my way. "Are you ready for this? I'll go easy on you, alright, now that it seems like you're coming out. I don't want people to think I beat up girls for fun."

I tried to smile at his tease, but it fell short. Maybe my guilt was misplaced. How did I know he was not fucking around on her while she was fucking around on him? I mean, this was a small community, after all.

"*Sili*! Get out of your head!" was all I heard, distracting me right before Samuel tackled me to the ground. We grappled, and I used my anger from Eliseo foiling my morning plans to gain the upper hand.

Samuel threw me over his shoulder and onto the ground, knocking the wind out of me before laughing like a lunatic.

"Shit, you're a slippery one, kid," he admitted happily. "I need to keep my eye on you. You got skills. Learn to counter the moves against you."

"Yeah, yeah." Getting up, I rolled my neck and got back into position, shaking my head to get the smell of grass and dirt out my nose.

I felt eyes on me, and my shoulders bunched up. Turning to look, I saw both Eliseo and Reed staring at me intensely.

"Seems you're distracting the men, kid," Samuel mumbled behind me. "Maybe it's *not* such a good idea to come out."

"Fuck you, Samuel. You know I didn't choose to. I lost my damn hat." I lunged at him and he dodged me easily. We circled each other, trying to find a window of opportunity to take our opponent down.

"Nah, I knew there was something up with you

the moment I saw you. Once the truth was revealed, it was easy to see through your tactics."

"What the hell am I supposed to do, then, hmm?" I asked, halfway serious. "Since everyone in this damn town probably knows it by now."

He threw a punch, and I leaned back, dodging his blow, pushing his arm down as I elbowed his face. His head snapped back and he shook it, rubbing his cheek. His eyes blazed as he came at me with full force.

We threw fists, elbows, dodged and tackled each other, but his weight got the better of me as he landed on top of my body, straddling me with triumph, my wrists pinned to the ground.

"You take the fucking bull by the horns and *deal with it, kid.* You're weren't going to be able to hide forever. Your moves are too unique, too noticeable for your size." He leaned in with seriousness. "You need to own that shit and shove whatever fear you have deep down inside. Weaknesses are exploited. You need to survive in this life."

I didn't see Reed move, but he shoved Samuel off me and pulled me up by the arm. Samuel stayed on the ground, laughing with his hands clasped behind his head.

"Fuck, you guys need pussy to loosen you up," he howled. "You're all pent-up with frustration."

We all ignored his comment as well as the elephant in the area.

"You alright, Fitri?" Reed asked as he looked me

over. His face lingered on mine when I didn't answer. "Fitri."

Blowing out a frustrated breath, I finally answered. "Yeah, I'm good. We're training. This is what we do. We take hits, we get better."

"At least someone has their head on straight today," Samuel grumbled before I heard an 'ow'.

Turning, I saw Samuel rubbing the back of his head and Eliseo glaring at him. Samuel laughed, and went to spar with Gunner while Eliseo walked toward us.

Now what do I do? The only person left to spar with was Reed, and that was not going to go over well with Eliseo, who was acting like a possessive prick.

Crossing my arms, I stared at them both. They looked at my stance and became tense. There was really only one thing I could do to keep these two from killing each other over something stupid that might happen during sparring.

"Well, what are you both standing around for?" I fumed. "Go fix my damn door."

7

ELISEO

THE DOOR WAS A QUICK FIX. IT WAS DONE IN SILENCE, and I couldn't care less. Reed and I were going to have to come to terms with what happened the other night sooner or later. He could stay bitter all he wanted, but there were plenty of other women here for him to choose from.

Sili was upstairs doing whatever she did while the two of us tested the door on its hinge to make sure it locked and stayed that way, securely.

"I'm going to the town store. I'll be back." Her voice floated down from the top of the stairs.

"We're just finishing up," I replied, looking her over. She was in an oversized t-shirt, cargo pants, boots, and her hair was wet. Thoughts of the other night made my dick press against the zipper of my pants.

"Reed, go find Samuel. The doc is looking for

him." Not taking my eyes off the woman in front of me, I gave Reed a task to complete so he could get out of my hair.

Her eyes flickered with an emotion before she schooled her features. Did she want Reed's company? Well, she was shit out of luck, because it was *not* happening.

She walked between us and tested the door, opening and closing it a few times. There was a slight gap between where the bolt met the door frame, but it did its job. She gave a resigned sigh and left the house with me following right after her and Reed breaking off to the right.

Fitri stopped, and I ran into her back. She turned and gave me a look I was used to seeing on her face at this point.

"Where do you think you're going?" she asked.

"To make sure you stay out of trouble."

"Me? *Me?*" She laughed humorlessly, and I leaned down toward her.

"I'm making sure no one touches you, you feel me? Because that's *my* job."

"The hell it is," she fired back, and I grinned.

"You weren't complaining the other day. In fact, you weren't complaining *at all* when I was grinding against you this morning. Your ass pushed right back into me, as if begging for me to take you again."

Her fist flew and I caught it, pulling her against my chest as I bit her earlobe playfully. "Don't test me, *Sili*. My restraint can only go so far."

She shivered and jerked away, pretending she didn't feel this thing between us growing.

Trying to placate her a bit, I told her, "I'll make sure to look for another cap when we go scavenging, alright? You don't need to go sneaking out into shit on your own when you have a fucking *team* backing you up. Don't be stupid, *Sili*."

Her eyes blazed as she turned away and continued toward the middle of the town. It was still early yet, the crowd small enough to make her feel comfortable. I had come to realize that about her. She got antsy when there were too many strangers around within touching distance. My mind wandered again to what happened in her past. If she was right about her fragmented memories, she wouldn't be able to supply me with information even if I tortured it out of her.

I quietly followed behind her a few paces, taking stock of the faces around us while constantly keeping her in my line of sight.

"Hey, guys! What can I get ya?" Oscar came from the back of the house with a towel in his hand and a smile on his face.

When he noticed Fitri, he stopped and stared, tilting his head. His eyes widened when he finally connected the dots. I stared at him, daring him to say anything right now. He was smart enough to stay quiet with his newfound knowledge.

"Any meat today?" she inquired.

Was it wrong of me to bristle at her choice of using her feminine voice with him instead of her false, deeper tone? He didn't deserve to hear her like that. I watched the way his face reddened and I made a mental note to keep an eye on this fool.

"Not today. The calf we have is still growing. It's going to be a while. We're hoping to get more piglets this summer," he conversed, leaning in on his elbows.

She nodded and looked around at the vegetables, grabbing a few.

Oscar continued to stare at her and I slammed my hand on his counter, startling him. "Mark her off for cleaning weapons. Her tab should be clear," I instructed.

He gave me a look before heading to the back.

Sili slapped me with the back of her hand, but I watched until Oscar completely disappeared out of my sight.

"Stop being such an asshole to people," she grumbled. It was adorable, and it further agitated me.

"They need to be kept on their toes and stop looking at what's mine," I warned. She might as well get used to it.

"I never said I was yours," she scoffed as she walked out the door with her little loot.

"Your body said enough."

"Asshole."

"I know."

We walked back toward the southwest corner of the community. My stomach grumbled, and she chuckled. I loved the sound. I needed to make her laugh more instead of being the ass she claimed me to be. Years of putting up with people's bullshit and surviving through sheer grit and determination made me this way. *Sili* was good for me, she reminded me of the man I once was. The man I thought lost.

"Eliseo! Who do we have here, hmm?" The sound of the doctor's voice soured my mood. What the hell was he doing out of his hole this early?

Fitri's body tensed in my periphery, and it put me more on edge. *Had he done something to her? Why would she react like that?*

"What do you need, Doc?" I cast my gaze at him with a blank face.

"I wanted to see if I could have a word with you, Eliseo. Samuel just left." His smile didn't reassure me one bit.

"I thought you got everything you needed last time?"

"Ah yes, well, there have been some new developments and I might need you guys to go out to find me something." His eyes drifted to the side of me to where Sili stood. "Who is she? I don't recognize her, though she looks familiar."

"She's none of your damn business. A resident. She's been here a while. What do you need us to look for?" I tried to redirect the conversation. I didn't like the way he was looking at her, like he was hungry for something more carnal.

"Why don't you two come inside, and I'll

explain further?" His smile was off-putting, to say the least. What was crazy Otis up to this time?

"Eliseo, I need to put the food away," she whispered.

Doctor or not, her desires trumped his. "Doc, we'll be back in about twenty, alright?"

His goggles were down, obscuring half his face but I could imagine how wild his eyes were to have more people in his bunker for who knows what. "I'm counting on it," he replied ominously.

We continued our way toward Fitri's home. She put the vegetables on the kitchen counter and began to wash them. Sitting down on her chair, I was surprised she hadn't tried to kick me out. She was getting used to me. Good, because I planned on being wherever she was. Clasping my hands in front of me, I watched as she put things together and brought it over in two bowls.

"I don't like him," she mumbled into her food.

"No one does."

"What does he do to you down there?"

I smiled. "You worried about me, *Sili?*"

"No." She refused to look at me and continued to eat whatever the hell kinda rabbit food she made for us.

"It's alright for you to care, you know. Don't be shy."

"Shut up, Eliseo."

"You can shut me up in other ways." Images of my face buried between her legs made my dick twitch under the table.

"I'm serious Eliseo. There's something about him."

"You keeping more secrets from me, *Sili?*" I challenged. "We never did finish our conversation the other night."

"No." Her retort came out too quickly, and I raised my eyebrows. She realized her mistake and shoved more food into her mouth. I let her off the hook for now. But I intended to find out everything about her if it was the last thing I did.

We finished up and unenthusiastically headed out toward the doctor's bunker. I was glad she wanted to be with me, but I was wary of what her presence would do down there. I hadn't heard or seen anything in regards to the doc and the opposite sex. I assumed his crazy experiments got him off plenty.

"You sure you want to come with me?" I asked *Sili* when we made it to his yard.

"Eliseo, I don't trust him. You need someone to watch your back."

And like that, my chest felt tight. This little woman had wormed her way into my life when I least expected it, one fist to the face at a time.

Jerking the ground door open, I let her go ahead of me so I could close it behind us. Walking right after her, I touched her shoulder to let her know I should go down the stairs first. She nodded and I cautiously looked around, straining my ears to listen for anything out of the ordinary.

It was the cackle that told me the good doc was in the middle of whatever he was doing.

"Doc!" I called out.

"Eliseo! Did you bring... ah, there she is." His smile was malicious when we reached the bottom of the steps, and I pushed Sili further behind me.

"What did you need?" I grounded out as he left the bottom of the steps.

"I remember her now. Yes, she came here a few years back. I thought she left, since I didn't see her again. Where were you hiding her, Eliseo?" He came around his table full of weird chemicals in different shaped vials and tools, trying to look behind me. His apron was on again, and stained with something fresh. His dark elbow-length leather gloves needed to stay away from *Sili*.

"You said you needed me to look for something? What was it?" Trying to redirect him again failed. He continued to stare at her with a dark hunger. "Doc!"

He threw his head back and laughed. "Like that, huh?" His eyes went from *Sili* to me and back again. "I got you. Alright."

He snapped his goggles down over his eyes and turned to head toward one of his tunnels.

I looked at Fitri and she shrugged. We both followed behind crazy Otis, who brought us to another, larger room. Bottles and jars of various sizes lined the wall on rickety wooden shelving that had seen better days. Otis read the labels, bent at the waist as he pushed things around. Most of the glass was dirty and clouded, concealing the contents.

The subtle sound of chains rattling floated to my ears, but I didn't see anything. Moans and other noises came through the walls, and my hand went behind me to bring Sili closer. There was a different chemical smell in the tunnel in comparison to his main room. I couldn't put my finger on it but it was something I came across before, outside of the community. I had never come this far in the doctor's lair. The hairs on the back of my neck stood on end with the darkness I felt lurking here.

Crazy Otis acted like he heard nothing at all, still rummaging around his collection. He tilted his head toward one of the labels and I noticed red welts on his neck that looked akin to claw marks.

"They say bloodsuckers from Clan Cirse can clone. Did you know that? Imagine an army of them growing exponentially, just from a mere thought," he rambled, his arms waving around to demonstrate.

That was horrifying news. Humans had created townships and groups among themselves in order to survive. No matter how big our community grew, we were still vastly outnumbered by what was out there. An army of clones would wipe out towns in an instant—or turn them into blood farms. The image of humans taken for slavery as mere cattle made me grind my teeth together.

The single bulb overhead flickered and I heard

metal on metal again. The walls down here were made from concrete, rough as stone.

"I happened to have some of their blood on hand," he giggled like a lunatic. "Trying to figure out what exactly makes them able to divide themselves as such. Is this nature, or is this nurture? Have they changed their own genetics, or have the years made them this way? This is why I need so many blood samples, you see."

He turned to look at Fitri, who grabbed the back of my pants like a safety net.

Crazy Otis pointed his gloved finger at her behind me. "I remember something about you. It's finally coming back to me. Yes... *that's right.*"

A loud crash echoed through the far end of the tunnel toward the darkness, but crazy Otis just continued to leer at Fitri.

"Why the hell are we here, Doc? You wanted to give us a history lesson? I thought you said you needed us to find something," I gritted out, agitated at how much attention he paid to her. *What the hell was going on down here? Were there others? Or could it be something as simple as a rat infestation?*

He cackled, his goggles glinting against the small uncovered lightbulb. "Yes, well. There are rumors that one of the human towns has something I need to further my research." He rubbed his hands together comically, but there was nothing funny about how serious he was right now. *This guy was out of his damn mind.* "Decayed wings from one of the bloodsuckers."

"They fucking have wings?" I was astonished at this news. I had never come across one in my years of living on the outside.

"Not all of them, no. Only a select few. I'm still not sure which clan they are from, but I intend to find out, you see." Otis crossed his arms and blood smeared on his exposed skin, stealing my focus for a minute.

"You want us to go in search of a dead body?" I snapped. "How the hell is this going to go over with everyone in the town? Sounds like a fucking wild goose chase to bring back something infected."

Little was known about how the whole world went to shit. Vampires appeared out of nowhere, breaking into four major clans. Their names were whispered in fear among humans as our kind began to dwindle more the more their numbers grew. Those who lived behind community gates like Ashborne lived in false safety unlike those who lived day to day outside of a gated wall, facing the reality of the unknown like my team and I, scavenging among the desolation and rubble of lives left behind by those who lived before us.

Thoughts of my previous community came to mind. Blood and destruction was what waited for me. Destroyed by a group from Clan Sira, nothing was left behind but a massacre of dead human bodies littering the ground—my late wife's among them.

Otis got toe to toe with me, his head level with my nose. He smelled of blood and other acidic chemicals that burned my nostrils. "That's the fascinating part. There is no body, only the remnants of decayed wings. So they say. The more I can gather, the more I can figure out how these creatures came to be and how to fight them. The cure is *so close*. Soon enough we'll be able to eradicate them from the whole world."

His smile turned sinister, his hunger for bloodshed easily written on his face.

"What the hell am I looking for? What is it supposed to look like?" I gritted out, pissed at his lack of personal space.

"Eliseo, I'm sure your men will figure it out when you get there. But I must warn you..." He walked off and rummaged through a dirty box that could fit three dead bodies in it. He pulled out something with a long tube and tossed it to me. Catching it, I turned it in my hands and investigated. It was an ancient gas mask.

"What the fuck do I need this for?"

"You and your men best take precaution. My research has brought me to the theory that the bloodsuckers were not born but made. Changed."

Fitri's grip on the hem of my pants tightened. This was some disturbing shit. "Explain it to me like a normal person, Doc."

He walked over with a few more masks and

smiled with yellow-tinted teeth. "There's something in the air, my friend. Something in the air. I'm not positive yet, but in the meantime, wear these. Who knows what kind of stuff comes off decayed wings? If my assumption is correct, vampires as we know it originated from an airborne virus."

"How is that possible? I've seen them bite and turn humans myself," I denounced.

Shoving the rest of the masks at my chest, I grabbed them before they fell. Fitri's little hand took a few and returned to hide behind me.

"Eliseo, in this world, who knows what else is out there? I don't make the rules, I only learn to play with what I got, discovering weaknesses where there are some, so that we as a human race still have a good leg in this game of war."

Crazy Otis went back to opening and closing bottles on his shelves, sniffing them one at a time and mumbling to himself, essentially dismissing our presence.

My mind was swirling with all this new intel as I dragged Fitri through the dark tunnel and back up the stairs to exit the bunker. Two houses down I saw Reed and Gunner standing on the street, talking to one another. I whistled to get their attention. Their heads snapped toward me and then to the items I had in my hand.

"Crazy Otis has got a mission for us," I told them.

"Fuck, what the hell does he want us to do to require *that*?" Gunner shot back.

"You wouldn't believe it even if I told you. Find Samuel," I ordered. "I don't trust anyone else on this but us."

Reed nodded, looking over Fitri before turning to do as I asked. My hackles rose. That was another problem I would have to take care of when we got back.

Fitri handed a gas mask over to Gunner who turned it over to inspect. "This shit looks like it's older than me. What the hell is this supposed to do? How do we know it still works as intended?"

"Let's head back to my place and I'll tell you what the good doc told me, yeah?" I patted his back. "I don't need anyone eavesdropping on us."

Gunner's eyes sharpened, understanding what I was not saying. It wasn't going to be good news and early, unsolicited rumors flying in the community might cause panic. There had been enough excitement going around with them finding Fitri's real identity.

By the time we made it to my front porch at the farthest southwest corner of Ashborne, the rest of the men were already there. This mission would only be between the five of us, and we would probably have to sneak out during the cover of darkness to reduce the likelihood of witnesses.

Unlocking the front door, I pushed Fitri in first, then followed after her. She headed to the living room and sat on the couch, deciding on a meeting spot for us.

"Alright, what's going on Eliseo? What the hell is up with these masks?" Samuel asked, turning one in his hands.

"Crazy Otis told me some shit I didn't want to believe myself. I don't know what the hell he does down there and how he even gets his intel, but the possibility of things going to shit by *not* believing him makes me take his word as the gospel until proven otherwise."

"Spit it out, already," Reed growled, sitting beside Fitri.

My temper flared not only from his attitude, but from the fact that he chose such close proximity to her, knowing what was going on between us. He stared right back, knowing full well what he riled up, challenging me.

First things first. I dropped the initial bomb. "Clan Cirse from the far north is rumored to be able to clone."

The guys' eyes bulged out before they all started firing their questions at the same time.

"That's not all," I lifted up a hand. "There's other rumors that say some of these bloodsuckers can fly—with *wings*."

"Fucking hell. Does the world want to eliminate the human race? How can they have all these advantages over us? What kind of evolutionary bullshit is this?" Samuel leaned back in the chair and ran his hand over his face, staring at the ceiling, lost in contemplation.

"I feel you, brother. The last thing crazy Otis told me is his theory that all this shit possibly started from an airborne virus instead of blood-sucking, like we thought," I added.

"Are you shitting me? How do we fight something we can't even see and probably already breathed in?" Gunner said with exasperation.

Tossing masks to the rest of them without one, I tilted my head to the item in hand. "Seems this is the only protection we're afforded, men. Crazy Otis wants us to get a sample of the decayed wings if they exist at all. Says he's close to a cure."

"I don't believe that old fool," Reed shot back quickly. "He's out of his damn mind on good days. Who's to say this isn't going to get us all killed? Fucking crazy doctor and his crazy ass requests. Why us?"

As much as I hated to agree with Reed right now, I felt the same. But what if the doctor *was* right? I leaned back with my arm behind the couch and stared at them all. "So what are you guys proposing? You want to skip this shit, or complete the mission handed to us?"

I might commonly take the role as head on most missions but at the end of the day, when it comes to life and death decisions, we were a team. I respected each and every one of these men as I patiently waited for their answer.

"Why us?" Samuel's question broke the pregnant silence. "Why not any other group that's been out scavenging? We're not the only guys capable of this job."

Samuel had his elbows on his knees, looking at me with eyes full of questions. Many days, I wondered the same thing. At the same time, I saw how *incapable* these groups could be. It was why we decided to start breaking into teams with each one of us leading. The death count decreased dramatically since we took over strategy and planning in Ashborne.

"I don't know, man. I'm just the messenger," I admitted easily. "He called me down to his bunker and told me all this shit. Handed me the masks, and that was that."

Sili fidgeted next to me. Yeah, I didn't forget the strange sounds coming from the tunnel either.

"Fucking fishy as heck," Samuel said, a thought that ran through all our minds. "His bunker has more secrets than everyone here combined. You know that shit goes under this entire place?"

"Yeah, I'm well aware, Samuel. As we all are. Look, I don't make the rules here."

"Pfft, the governor sits on his ass in his house all day," Gunner joined in. "He doesn't do shit either. Crazy Otis got more sway in this community than Sergio."

He wasn't wrong. Our makeshift governor only came out when he thought it was necessary to improve his position within the community. How? I had no clue, since there was really nothing higher than that here. We were all pretty self-sufficient in Ashborne, with competent men who maintained the turbines and solar panels to keep the place running.

"Hannah is going to sever my ball," Samuel groaned. "This trip is going to take more than a week at best." Samuel continued to stare at the ceiling, his thoughts elsewhere.

"What will it be, gentlemen?" I asked again.

"Fuck. If the world's going to shit, we might as well go down fighting. Let's find this decayed flesh and get home." Gunner had his arms crossed with a look of steely determination.

"Where is it located? Do we know? Or are we wandering until rumors get louder and things get warmer?" Reed inquired.

"It's in a human camp," I told them. "We just need to keep our eyes peeled around Clan territory and not disturb any hordes around us on the way."

"That's easier said than done," Gunner replied. "A few of them versus us might mean life or death with extra abilities like that."

My eyes burned when I noticed Reed leaning in toward *Sili*, the tips of his fingers dancing at the back of her neck. She looked uncomfortable. My hand shot out and knocked him away. We both threatened each other silently until *Sili* spoke up and broke our silent confrontation.

"People die every day," she asserted. "Let's just get this and go home. I ran across a few human flocks on my way to this community. We can start there and see where it leads us. Most of them were located toward the east and northeast."

Clan Lekim territory. Rumors had it, they were the worst and most ruthless of the bloodsuckers combined. How was it possible to have pockets of humans thriving on their territory?

"Where did you come from, Fitri?" Reed asked.

Her spine tensed, and I waited anxiously for her answer. Maybe this would help piece some of her scattered memories together.

"I-I have memories. Flashes. Fragmented at best."

"You got amnesia or something?" Gunner asked bluntly.

"I-I guess you can say that. The farthest back I can remember is my travel here. The rest comes to me in nightmares or during my waking hours and inopportune times."

"PTSD," Samuel interjected. "It happens to me too. Feels like you're living that shit again in a constant loop." He didn't talk about his past much, and I never asked. Most of us in the group had gone through some shit, surviving in this world.

"Fuck it. Fitri's right," Reed added. "Let's do this shit and come home. Might as well rest up before we head out tonight." My eyes burned as I watched Reed place his hand over *Sili's*.

She didn't push him away.

I jumped up, and so did Reed. We stood toe to toe until *Sili* squeezed in between us. "Can you assholes just go to a different room or something?

Damn. Cock fight another time, alright? We have shit to do."

I watched as she left us and headed to the kitchen. The other men were shaking their heads, but I ignored them.

"You're sleeping your ass on the floor," I snarled at Reed.

He didn't say anything, instead walked away to another room.

"This wouldn't have happened if you fools would have just dipped your dick like I suggest, to get rid of your built-up tension," Samuel laughed, and I kicked his crossed ankles before walking over it toward the kitchen after *Sili*.

I found her chewing on some vegetables, staring out the window over the sink.

"What kind of welcome did you get when you came across these human flocks you speak of?" I prodded.

She turned her head and gazed at me with a dreaded look on her face.

"I remember them burning me alive."

8

THE SMALL NAP WE TOOK AT ELISEO'S HOUSE ONLY DID so much. Some of the guys looked like they merely mimicked the motion of sleep instead of receiving any rest.

Hannah came by to scream at Samuel for leaving her again. It was heartbreaking to see. She really did seem like she loved him.

"Didn't you just come back, Sam?" she whined.

"What am I supposed to do, Hannah? I don't control this shit."

"You can say fucking no and stay home!" she cried out.

Samuel grabbed her by the upper arms, rubbing his hands up and down to try and calm her. She melted into his chest, and they embraced.

My face flushed from such an intimate scene, and I turned and walked away, unable to watch anymore without my own personal emotions boiling over. Reed followed after me, finding me in the back of the house running my finger along some of the cabinets in front of me.

"Hey. You alright?" he asked quietly.

"Yeah. Why wouldn't I be?" I turned to look at him with my arms crossed defensively.

His eyes softened as he walked up to me. I tilted my head back to look at his face trying to swallow whatever was happening inside of me. Reed was almost as tall as Eliseo—all the men in this group tower over me.

"If you need someone to talk to, you know you got me, right? I'm a good listener."

Reed touched my arm the way Samuel touched his girl and I flushed, warmth spreading through my blood. It was a strange comfort. I was surprised I didn't flinch like I normally would have reacted to the touch of another, but then again, the men of this team made me comfortable in their presence as they took me as I was.

The sun went down a few hours ago, and we waited for the community to settle into their homes before we took leave. The air had already become crisp once again, sending a slight shiver down my body, when a breeze filtered through the crack of an open window.

Reed came impossibly closer, and I could feel the warmth radiate off his skin. He was not as scarred up as Eliseo, and looked at least a decade younger. The crows feet around his eyes when he smiled made me want to smile back.

"I appreciate it. My memories are in pieces at best, most of them not happy ones. Maybe this trip will help me put the pieces back together?" I said hopefully. I wanted to know what caused my mind to be this way. Or if my mind was doing this on purpose to protect itself from something.

Both of his palms cupped my face, and my breath caught. My nipples pushed against the oversized shirt I was wearing, and I instinctually cast my gaze down to hide myself somehow.

"Don't. Don't do that. It's just me," he whispered.

We could hear Samuel's and Hannah's fight get louder until the door slammed and it became abruptly quiet. Was that what it was like to care for someone? I looked into Reed's eyes with all my mental questions, too timid to voice them aloud. When did I become this girl? My memories hazed in my mind every time I tried to inspect possible past relationships. The only ones that came to the forefront of my mind were my parents, and the bloodshed.

Lost in thought, I didn't realize Reed was slowly leaning down toward me. Not until I heard an angry growl cut into the moment, and my head snapped up.

"What the fuck do you think you're doing?" Eliseo stood a few feet from Reed, veins popping out of his neck.

My eyes took in his hostility and stepped away from Reed. I didn't need these guys to kill each other over me. I was the newest addition to the group. Guilt stabbed me in the chest.

Gunner walked by and saved the awkward moment by shoving Eliseo to the side to shake him out of his anger. The men's eyes never left each other, and suddenly I was feeling claustrophobic.

I left the room swiftly, not wanting to suffocate from the testosterone and found Samuel sitting on one of the chairs. "Hey."

Samuel looked up at me, his face tired. "Hey. Sorry about that. Hannah's kind of..."

"Worried," I supplied. *I get it.*

"Yeah, you can say that. She's also not happy with the fact that our mission includes another woman. But I told her she had no say in how we operate our team," he said with finality.

I sat down on the couch, checking the weapons I had in my boots, a different kind of guilt assaulting me. But Hannah had nothing to worry about. I was positive Samuel and I had no romantic feelings for one another—the idea never once on our radar. Again I began to wonder why Eliseo decided to integrate me into his team to begin with... before things went down between us. "I bet that didn't go over well."

"Such is life. We all gotta deal with something. We ready? Where are the other guys?" he asked, getting to his feet, looking around curiously.

Sighing, I stood up too. "Cooling down Eliseo."

Samuel chuckled and hollered, "Hey, old bastard! Let's get going!"

Multiple bootsteps got louder, approaching us. I turned to see all three men in the living room with scowls on their faces. There was a red mark on both Reed and Eliseo, but I didn't say a word. They needed to get this out of their system, because I didn't know what I could do to help—if I could help at all.

"Whiteridge," I blurted out. My mind supplied images of the human camp equipped with a small wall and a farm.

"Are your memories coming back, *Sili?*" Eliseo asked, coming closer to me.

I stared at him. The man who took me in and gave me a group to watch my back. Despite my guilt, gratitude spilled over. This fractured memory would give us a place to start looking at the very least. "I remember they had a place that housed criminals and such. We can start there. Maybe they'll have what we're looking for."

Flashes of chains rattling and tormented screams floated with the breeze brought me back to the moment where I escaped and ran.

"You're an abomination. You shouldn't exist, yet here you are, tainting the remaining human populace." His spittle sprayed out as he snarled in my face.

For such a small town, their hate for bloodsuckers was strong. The fact that I didn't require blood for sustenance wouldn't sway them, even if I mentioned it

—which I wasn't. There was no point. Not when they chained me the moment they saw my skin heal.

"Pity a womb like yours will go to waste." The man kneeled down, and all I could think about was how much I wanted to rip his face off when I got out of here. "I guess it wouldn't hurt to have a little fun before we kill you. After all, what difference does it make, in the long run?"

The chain beside me rattled, stealing his attention. The old man beside me has his sharp gaze fixed on the man before me. There was an aura hidden beneath the old man's frail body that screamed danger despite his appearance. I couldn't put my finger on it, but I could feel it.

"You getting excited, old man?" the leader of Whiteridge taunted. "Bet you wish you didn't try to steal that food right about now. You could have been partaking in the events."

I shivered in disgust. Whiteridge's leader smelled of fermented drink and a type of smoke I was familiar with back in my home village. The older ladies partook in the burning of the leaves, shoving it in their pipes during the day.

But this whole town hid their true faces. They welcomed you with open arms, only to see how they could exploit you and use you to their advantage. When one of them tried to blame me for touching their husbands, she stabbed me, only to witness my skin stitch back up...

"Be wary," I told the men as I checked all the

weapons on my body one more time. "It's a town of lies. Keep your guard up."

They nodded and we all began our last preparations for departure.

We moved under the cover of darkness, Gunner showing us an area of the wall that was easier to climb over than what I found when I tried. The second to climb, I jumped the edge of the wall and landed in Eliseo's arms. He smiled at me, refusing to put me down.

"*Sili*," he whispered.

"Put me down, Eliseo."

He slid me down his hard body until my feet hit the ground. My face heated up and I shoved him away only to have him chuckle quietly. The men quickly followed suit and we all started our trek outbound for the next few hours until the sun slowly crested the sky.

"Hey, guys. That car looks like it still runs," Samuel pointed in front of us.

We reached an abandoned town about a mile ago. This car sat off the road by itself at a strange angle. The top was rusted out, but the body was pretty much still intact. The sun had beaten down on us today, making us sweat profusely under our clothes. A vehicle would help us cover more ground quicker.

"You think it's fresh?" Reed asked.

"Only one way to find out," Samuel replied.

We cautiously walked around the vehicle and checked around the parameter. It was the loud crash against the nearby tree that stole all of our attention, then the splatter of blood spraying like rain in our direction. The tree creaked loudly as it fell over and hit the other ones nearby.

"What the hell?" Samuel murmured as he pulled his gun from his pants.

I readied a bolt and the rest of the guys all brought their weapons up, looking at the blood-splattered trunk.

A dark figure emerged from behind another tree, dragging a limp body behind him. His smile was menacing when he saw us, and he continued forward at a leisurely pace. His boots crunched the dead leaves on the ground and my hackles rose as he got closer.

His eyes, his eyes. They were hungry, and reminded me so much of—

Bang!

A shot rang out from Reed's gun, and then the rest of the guys followed suit. The vampire was quick. He threw the body on the ground and tackled Gunner in one leap.

I lifted my crossbow and aimed, but the bodies fumbling on the ground were moving too quickly for me to get a clear hit. Eliseo jumped into the fray, trying to pull the guy off, but got tossed against the side of the car with a loud crash, depressing the doors in.

"Nice day for a walk. Didn't think I'd find company. I *am* a bit hungry..." *A vampire? Out now?*

The guys got their blows in, but each of the

bloodsucker's hits were three times harder than theirs. In a last-minute decision, I ran up the back of the car's trunk and onto the roof, aiming my crossbow again.

"Hey! Bloodsucker!" I called out.

His fist threw Gunner against Reed, then all his attention focused on me. His nostrils flared after a step.

"Well, well, what do we have here? Didn't think I would ever run into one of *you* during my existence." His smile widened on his face, showcasing his extended fangs glistening with blood from a prior victim. He wiped his chin with the back of his hand and licked the remnants away, moaning suggestively. "Shouldn't you be bowing to a Lekim Clan member?" he chuckled. "Hunting does bring out *another* hunger in me..."

"Yeah, that so?" I snarked back.

My bolt hit him right in the chest, knocking him off his feet. As I got another bolt ready, the guys slowly got up and made their way toward us.

The stranger laughed maniacally and rolled to the side before getting back on his feet as if he didn't feel a damn thing. Were Lekim always this crazy?

"Oh, yes," the loon cooed. "We're going to have fun, you and I. I need someone who can keep up with my carnal cravings. I have a feeling you're going to taste delicious while you're under me, dying beneath my hands."

Eliseo tackled him from the side. He dodged,

only to get stabbed by Reed. The stranger snapped his jaws right against Reed's neck. Luckily, Reed leaned back just in time for Gunner to shoot a hole right through the back of his head, knocking him face down into the ground. Eliseo came up behind him and cut across the back of his neck deeply with one of his larger blades, separating his head from his body. The blood pooled beneath him, and I let out a breath of relief, climbing down the car.

"What the hell are these bloodsuckers doing out in broad daylight? This is the second time this happened." Reed rubbed a hand down his face as he stared at the dead body at our feet.

"I don't know, and I'm not hanging around to find out. Let's drag the bodies into the wooded area so they don't attract anything else." Samuel was already grabbing the vampire by the feet. Gunner threw the decapitated head onto the body's chest, grabbed under the shoulder, and they started moving.

"The other body is over there," I told the rest of the guys as I shouldered my crossbow.

"Yeah, we got it," Eliseo replied.

All three of us walked toward the dead human that was still intact. I looked over at the other one in pieces by the fallen tree, wondering how I should collect his remnants.

"I'll get...the other guy," I mumbled as I broke away from them and looked around for all the limbs, readjusting the crossbow behind me. I wasn't going to be able to get much of him, just the bigger chunks. His body basically exploded against the trunk.

Bending down, a breeze whipped my hair in my face. Footsteps from behind me crunched on leaves, and I called out, "I'm coming. I think I can only get this leg. I'll come back for the arm."

Grabbing the limb, I turned around and dropped it. There, standing a few feet away in the shadows, was another bloodsucker who looked like he just finished snacking—face still coated with crimson from his last meal.

"Would you do me a favor, sweetheart? I'm feeling kinda *horny* right now." His voice was gravelly, like it was raw from swallowing flesh and bone. It sparked a memory—*I had witnessed this before.* Some of these vampires didn't just drink blood, but consume so much more. Flashes of grey hair slammed into me and I frowned.

"Don't look at me like that," he cooed in complaint.

He walked forward and I took a step back, my hand going for one of my blades. *Where the hell are the other guys?* My mind ran through different tactics and my eyes searched for different exit strategies. This place was too open.

"I'll take it slow," he purred. "Would you like that? I'll fill you up until you beg for more. We could use more of us in this world."

He rubbed his crotch, and I could see the impression there, straining against the fabric.

Not wanting him to get the upper hand, I

lunged, only to have him twist and wrap his arm around my neck from behind. He licked up my neck and I flinched, expecting him to bite.

"You smell utterly delicious—a scent I haven't come across. But you've got something in you that calls to me. Be a good girl and get on your hands and knees. I'll make sure to make you like it," he mouthed against my neck while dragging me back into the shade of the trees. The light fragrance of burnt flesh wafted in the air.

I struggled and dug my nails into his flesh, drawing blood, but he didn't flinch. Trying to force him over my shoulder didn't work either, he outweighed me by too much. He continued to nip at my skin with an amused chuckle until I twisted my body behind his form and kicked his feet out from under him, taking us both down to the ground.

"*Sili!*" Eliseo cried out from a distance.

The guys came running, but the stranger was faster, jumping up and landing on Eliseo with a hand dug into his shoulder, ripping his flesh.

Reed fired his gun and hit the bloodsucker in the shoulder, throwing him off Eliseo, but he landed on his feet, snapping his head up with a grin like a predator.

"*Sili*, is it? Seems you're a greedy little cunt with all these men around you. Couldn't even let old Josh stick it in that hole of yours, hmm? What makes your pussy the golden goose?" he sneered right before he attacked Reed.

Gunner checked over Eliseo who was struggling to get up from the ground, his entire shirt stained with blood. Samuel had his gun aimed at Josh, still in hand-to-hand combat with Reed.

I secured my bolt and readied my crossbow, but the boys moved too fast. Samuel let out a shot, but it missed as both Reed and Josh fell to the ground. When the vampire got the upper hand and straddled Reed, Eliseo slammed into his side with a growl. A kick to the stomach threw Eliseo off, and Gunner let off a shot.

The vampire cackled as he leapt to his feet, ran with inhuman speed, and grabbed me by the waist, fleeing toward the thicker cluster of trees behind us. My crossbow went off on impact, hitting a tree with a *thud* as the men screamed my name.

Struggling in his arms, I elbowed his head, snapping it to the side. He skidded to a stop, growled, and broke my forearm with a loud crunch, making me cry out in agony before throwing me onto the ground and straddling on top of me. *Dammit, it was my dominant arm, too.*

"Now, why did you have to go and do that, sweetheart?" He groaned as he rubbed his crotch against mine.

I gritted my teeth, as my body began to heal. The bone restitching itself was excruciating, stealing my breath and distracting me from what I should be doing—*getting this piece of trash off me.*

I could feel his hands ripping the front of my shirt and down the front of my pants, sending sharp painful welts along the way. His hot breath hit my skin before his tongue lapped up the blood, making me grimace.

"Mmmm. What are you doing, hanging out with a bunch of human men? Do you keep them around for blood?" He grinded down again between my legs, disgusting me as he dragged his tongue downward. "I'd like to keep you alive for a while. Old Josh'll be good to you, if you're good to me."

The moment the pain in my arm became bearable was the moment I dug my nails into his head and ripped it off my chest.

"I do like it rough," he purred as he pinned my arms down and head-butted me, making me see stars.

His hands went around my neck and his knees kicked my legs wider apart. My head was still pounding from the blow as I feebly attempted to pry his wrist off to relieve the pressure. But he was too strong. His face was distorted, making his smile turn into one of nightmares. I began to panic, my skin flushed with fury as he rubbed the wet head of his cock along the inside of my thigh. I tried to scream, but only managed to open and close my mouth without a sound, my voice trapped in my throat.

He leaned in and whispered against my ear, "You'll stay warm long enough for me to finish. I don't need you breathing."

He nipped the side of my face and I broke. Deep

instincts took over my mind as I drove my nails into his eye sockets until it popped and splashed near the corner of my mouth. I wanted to gag, but the fury within me controlled my emotions. My internal temperature spiked, my body perspiring more than it should for not moving that much.

"Ahhh!" he screamed as his hands released my neck and went to his face.

I coughed and sputtered for breath only to have him throw a fist to my temple, jarring me. He ripped off his shirt to wipe his eyes, tossed it to the side, and landed back on top of me once more. His body slid against mine, and I could hear the men screaming my name, the sound coming closer and closer to our location.

"I'm going to fucking kill him!" Eliseo roared.

"Shit! Don't shoot, you might hit her!" Reed bit out.

His hands slipped as I continued to sweat profusely, struggling to get away. Suddenly, the body on top of me seized, and dropped to the side unceremoniously. Not stopping to figure out what happened, I scrambled onto my feet and stared in confusion as he lay motionless on the ground.

"What the hell just happened?" Reed asked as he skidded to a stop.

"Get away from him, *Sili*. Now," Eliseo commanded as if I wanted to be next to the creature.

I kicked him and a small groan escaped. The fucker was still alive. I was so furious at what almost happened that my hand moved on its own, pulling out one of the knives in my boot. With both hands on the hilt, my arm swung down again and again, his blood spraying all over me and inside my mouth as I screamed louder and louder for justice.

My mind was in a haze, the past melding with the present as my eyes coated the world in red.

He undid his buckle and brought down his metal belt in rapid successions to my front, making me hiss through gritted teeth at the sharp pain of each slice on top of the next.

I felt my skin fileted off the bone by the time Mistress Tyre came back with the intention of escorting me into the court before the Queen. Grabbing my arm, she broke both my wrists with a crack to slip them out of the shackles. I stifled my moan, pressing my lips together. My body was tossed onto the floor and kicked one last time for good measure.

Clan Cirse can burn in the depths of hell.

Darius. Darius was his name. *Darius can burn with the rest of them when I find him.*

My screams echoed between the trees, as birds scattered into the skies. My arms ached from the repetitive motion of bringing down my blade but I didn't stop. They couldn't just leave well enough alone. All I wanted was to leave and find a new life —to start over without their judgments and accusations, without their threats. I wasn't some stupid pawn in this game of war between the clans. I never was. I was nobody. The forsaken, after my truths came to light.

Strong arms came around me and I elbowed them. Their grip slipped from all the blood that saturated my skin and clothes. The guys argued around me, making me flash back to my previous community.

"She's an abomination!" my father hissed.

"She is my daughter!" My mother tried, but her cries went unheard.

"Patricia. I know you were desperate for a child, but this is not what we signed up for," he said with exasperation.

I knew they weren't my biological parents. It was never something they hid from me, but to hear my father speak in such a way hurt me to my very core.

"Would you have me leave a child so young with peddlers and thieves?" she asked, incredulous.

"That's not what I'm saying—" father tried to explain but was cut off by her furious words.

"That's exactly what you're saying! She needed us, John. She needed us to save her. She didn't ask to be brought into this world," she sobbed.

The sound of my mother's cries from the other room made my own tears fall. My father's rejection felt like a knife to the chest. I needed to leave. They didn't deserve the hate that was only going to grow in this community. There was something wrong with me. I was different. I couldn't hide anymore.

But I didn't understand it. I didn't ask to be born this way. What was wrong with me?

Sobs wracked my body as I dropped my knife and fell to my knees in front of the mutilated body.

Wrapping my arms around myself, I rocked and tried to stitch the internal wound that never seemed to heal.

Shaking my head, I was lost in grief and anger, the heaviness of it pushing me down like the weight of the world. Grief over my father's rejection. Anger over what clan Cirse did to me. My hands crawled to my neck, feeling for any scars, but found none. *Of course not.* My body was in cahoots with my mind, hiding away truths like a fucked up game.

"Fitri," one of the guys called, but I couldn't face them. *Not like this.* Not when I had been brought to my lowest point. I didn't know who I was. I didn't know my origins, or what my purpose was anymore.

I hung my head in my hands.

"*Sili*, please." Eliseo's broken voice made my tears burst forth exponentially. He should have never tangled himself with me. It only led to death.

"No," I whispered between gritted teeth. "Leave me here. You guys need to go and complete the mission. I'll be nothing but a hindrance." Turning to face him, his eyes were sharp, staring into mine. Did he see the truth of who I was? This bloodstained abomination before him. "I'll only attract more problems. Can't you see that?"

"What do you mean?" Samuel asked.

Shaking my head, I tried again. "I can't explain it. I'm not normal. I can't bring that kind of trouble your way. You guys don't deserve that, not after all you've done for me."

"You're talking crazy, kid. Get your ass up and let's go, before more of them show up," Gunner growled.

Eliseo grabbed my arm and pulled me up, but I shoved him to release me. He grabbed me again and I punched him. He let me. He let me continuously punch and claw at his chest until Reed grabbed me around my midsection and pulled me back, shushing me next to my ear. I was overflowing with a storm of emotions clashing and thundering within that I didn't recognize myself.

Reed's calm heart rate was a stark contrast against my rapidly beating one, and I let my body go limp with weariness. Why must I be doomed to always struggle in this life? Why couldn't I just have been born one way or another? *Why this?*

His grip loosened but he didn't let go, kissing my hair and confusing me ever the more.

"Let's get back to the car and find a damn lake for you to dunk yourself in. It wouldn't do good for us to walk into settlements looking like we just came from a massacre," Samuel decided for us.

Reed's hands moved to my front and closed the shredded shirt I didn't know was still gaping open for all to see.

Like deja vu, Eliseo took off his shirt and handed it to me cautiously. My eyes burned from the scratches I left on his skin. One of these days, the guilt that ate away from the inside will leave nothing behind, nothing of my fragmented life.

"Don't worry about it, *Sili*," he said calmly and my lip quivered. They were too good to me. I should be kicked out of their group. I couldn't even hold my emotions together. It was probably why they had been a group of just men for so long.

"Don't. Get that shit out of your head right now." Eliseo's eyes shot to Reed. "You can let her go. I think she's good."

Reed slowly pulled his arms away, his hands landed on my waist and finally, slowly, let me go to Eliseo. He took a step forward and pulled me into an embrace, coating himself with blood that was on me. He kissed the top of my hair and whispered, "I got you. We got you. Let's go."

Nodding my head, we followed Samuel and Gunner out of the cluster of trees and back to the road we left behind.

9

ELISEO

We found a lake and washed off the bloodstains. Not much could be done about the stained seats in the car, but we wouldn't be driving the car long, anyway. The gas gauge was already down to half.

Both Gunner and Reed were getting on my damn nerves with the way they stole glances at *Sili*. It didn't help that the bloodsucker ripped her shirt and pants right down the middle, exposing all her beautiful flesh for the guys to see. I couldn't stop myself from staring at how the globes of her breasts added definition to the blood that soaked her skin. Scratching at my own chest from the phantom sensation of our bloody embrace, my mind flashed to beauty in the lake.

The men air-dried themselves in the sun shirt-less, rubbing their heads with their dirty clothes. The sound of a splash made us all turn to look as

Sili broke through the surface, emerging like an inhuman siren as the water slid off her pristine skin. Not a scratch, not a scar. The globes of her ass peeked above the water, and Reed groaned. Gunner's eyes were unashamedly glued to the sight, and I couldn't blame him—*though, I did, anyway.*

My eyes snapped to them both and I curled my lip. Reed needed to keep his hands off her. He thought I didn't see the way he kissed her hair while he calmed her panic attack. He was just lucky I was willing to try anything to help relax *Sili* during her episode. As for Gunner, I would have to keep an eye on him, too. He was beginning to show favor the same way Reed did when we first started training together as a team of five.

Samuel was spread out on the ground with his hands clasped behind his head, and his eyes closed.

When I turned back around, *Sili* was bent over, wringing out her unbraided, wet hair. My cock twitched, and I tried to hide it. This mission would kill me. Trying to tamp down my erection, I thought about what happened with the last vampire that held her down.

One minute he was there, the next, he fell over without warning. What happened? Was there something else *Sili* was not telling me?

I was lost in my thoughts when Gunner and Reed jumped up. I turned to find *Sili* staring at me, covered in one of my shirts. Gunner was the smallest guy in the group at one hundred and sixty pounds. His extra pair of pants fit her better than any of ours.

She stood there looking like a drowned kitten as I rose and waited for her to say something. Her eyes roamed over my chest and shoulder, and my eyes burned with desire at her examination.

I watched in confusion as she leaned down and grabbed her ripped-up shirt, tearing it into strips.

"Sit down, Eliseo," she ordered.

We all obeyed as she tied the material together and wrapped my wounds. My chest felt tight, but not from her makeshift bandages. When she was satisfied, she addressed us all.

"You guys ready?"

"Yup. We got half a tank left, let's make it count. How far are we from the place you remember, Fitri?" Samuel dusted off his pants and grabbed his bag. We all followed suit, and began trekking back to the vehicle.

"It's about two miles off," she said with deep thought. "We'll make it with gas to spare."

"What do we need to know?" I asked her.

She scrunched her face and concentrated, a wrinkle between her brows. "It reminds me of a cult. Pleasant on the outside. Everything looks too good to be true. They had me in chains while I was there, so I can't tell you much more than that."

"How did you end up in chains?" Gunner asked.

She looked at him with a forlorn expression. "I healed."

Gunner's mind ran a mile a minute as he continued to stare intently at her. "Fitri, is there something I'm missing here?"

"Look. There's some stuff you guys are going to find out anyway. *Sili* is different from us, but she's not a bloodsucker," I supplied, placing my hand behind her neck for comfort, massaging her.

"And you're fucking. We got *that* part already," Samuel said with a smirk.

I slapped him upside the head, and he cackled. Gunner still hadn't stopped staring, and Reed had a scowl on his face.

We made it back to the car in silence and rode down the road for another two miles.

"Take a right here," *Sili* leaned forward between the front seats to point out.

Samuel twisted the wheel and took us all off-road, over uneven terrain. "You sure?"

"I'm sure. This site haunts my nightmares sometimes. It's hard to forget," she said matter-of-factly. I wondered what else happened here when she was put in chains.

"Alright," Samuel replied as we wove through the trees until we saw a clearing up ahead.

"Don't let them see you. We'll come in like we're traveling on foot," I told him. The guys nodded, and we hid the vehicle behind an over-grown bush.

Everyone checked their weapons and grabbed

their bags. *Who was to say the car wouldn't get jacked while we were gone?* I looked to Sili, who stood stock-still and stared at the town with a blank expression.

"Will they recognize you?" I asked to break the silence and pull her out of her trance.

She turned to me with worry in her eyes. "I don't know. They thought they got rid of me."

"Got rid of you *how?*" Knowing what I knew of her now, I didn't know what I was expecting to hear.

"They killed me. I don't remember much of anything after that." Her eyebrows bunched in confusion.

I took a few steps toward her, cradled her face in my hands, and tilted it up. I wanted to help ease her pain and frustration—to stand beside her on this journey of rediscovery. "Is that what happens? You forget when they kill you?"

I shouldn't be surprised with the rate of her healing, but when would it be too far? What would have to happen for her to never recover enough to come back to life? I feared the thought, but it was the only thing that made logical sense.

"I-I think so. Eliseo, what if one of these days, I can't remember anything anymore?" There was a vulnerability in her voice that pricked at my heart. I leaned down and pressed my lips against hers, and she sighed against me, surrendering herself. I could be this for her. I could be the one to take her fears away.

"Don't think about any of that," I mumbled against her. "Right now, we complete the mission. Once that's done, we can go home and I'll protect you."

She chuckled sadly. "But who's going to protect you from me?" She placed her forehead against my chest, and my heart cracked. "What if I discover things about myself that even I can't accept anymore?"

I rubbed her back slowly as the guys came to stand beside us as one. "We handle things as they come, *Sili*. No earlier. Come on, let's get this over with."

She lifted her head, wiped her eyes, and turned to face the town bravely.

"Do you remember who the leader was? What he looked like?" Reed asked.

"He was young. Has a scar on the back of his right hand. Dark hair and a beard, eyes as grey as ashes of the dead."

"How young is young?" Gunner piped in.

"I-I don't know. Possibly between thirties and forties, I'm not sure. The only person I remember clearly was the old man chained up beside me."

She must have been locked up earlier on in her life. It was my only guess. The guys and I looked at each other over her head and nodded. We were going in, regardless. If not for the mission, for *Sili*.

We automatically formed a barricade around *Sili* as we approached the town. There was a woman in a dress bending down to pull vegetables from her garden on the outside of the wall.

"Excuse me, miss," Samuel threw out with a smile and an extra dose of his charm.

She looked up and smiled until she noticed the rest of us. Her expression immediately fell, replaced with fear. She picked up her skirt and ran toward the heart of the town, causing others to come see what the fuss was all about. Samuel continued with his charm as he lifted his hand in greeting to the men who began to accumulate at the entrance.

Their wall was short, made from wood and random metal paneling. As we drew closer, the more we realized there was a scent in the air—meat cooking.

"What are you all here for?" One of the men approached us with his arms crossed in a defensive manner. He wore a leather apron that reminded me eerily of the doc.

"Well, you see," Samuel started, "my friends and I have been traveling for a while and were looking for a place to rest. We can provide service to pay off our debt, if you so choose. A mutual trade."

The guy's expression looked as if he was about to call his village for pitchforks when another voice joined in.

"Welcome! Welcome. Of course you guys are welcome to stay," came a jovial male. "We have a guest house available that you can share. My name is Devon, and our home is called Bellmore."

The newcomer's smile was exceptionally false and it crawled under my skin like a bad rash infection. Fitri's hand grabbed the waist of my pants and I knew this was the guy she spoke about. Seemed Whiteridge turned into Bellmore after her last visit.

"Thank you, Devon." Samuel replied courteously before turning to introduce us. "These are my friends, I'm Samuel. There are about five of us, and we would love it if we could stop and perhaps break bread?"

I lifted an eyebrow and stared into Samuel's back. *What was he, a damn disciple of the old ways? Break bread?* It must have been the perfect thing to say, because Devon's smile grew wider in response, if that were even possible. There was also a hint of something else there that was reminiscent of crazy Otis, and my eyes narrowed.

"Right, right. Come this way, gentleman." Devon turned to the people who looked at us the same way we were looking at them—with unbridled distrust. "Get back to work, everyone. We have guests. Let's make sure they feel welcomed. It's a harsh life out there, as you all know, and we've all been where they were."

The people looked to their leader and followed his command silently. Like creatures of a flock, nothing was said and everything went back to the way they were, as if we didn't arrive on their doorstep unannounced.

Samuel walked beside Devon as the rest of us followed close behind.

"Smells like a damn *barbeque* here. Where do you think they're getting all their meat?" Gunner whispered.

"They might have a farm, like we do," Reed answered.

"How do they keep large livestock in a place like this?" Gunner peered around, trying to find evidence of animals.

"I don't know. We'll find out."

I cleared my throat subtly to tell the guys to shut up. Devon stopped before a little cabin-style home that had seen better days.

"Claire! Would you come here, please?" he called out.

A young woman who looked *Sili's* age came running. She was in a modest dress very similar to the first woman we saw. Now that I thought about it, everyone here dressed alike.

"Can you please sweep through the home before our guests enter? I'll entertain them until you are done. You have ten minutes," he instructed with a smile.

"Yes, High Father Devon."

"That's a good girl."

Reed choked next to me, and my eyes sharpened on the way she interacted with him. A few religions cropped up over the centuries and scattered amongst different territories of the world. By the looks of this village, I didn't think it came this far, but with the interaction that occurred before us, I began to second-guess my assumption. Seemed we just hit the jackpot of cults.

Sili grabbed onto my pants even tighter, and my body tensed. I reached my arm back to comfort her—*a mistake.* The High Father's eyes went from eyeing the young woman's ass to snapping to *Sili's* location in a second.

"Oh, I did not notice we had another in your group."

"Yes, we all travel together often. Safety in numbers, you know," Samuel quickly interjected to throw him off course. "How can we help you in this community during our stay, Mr. Devon?"

"It's wonderful of you to offer, my friend, but we have plenty of workers here. Just enjoy your stay, and make sure you keep your doors closed at night."

Well, that was curious.

The young girl quickly exited the home, and 'High Father' Devon left us with his plastered smile. This place gave me the damn creeps. We all entered the home and shut the door, making sure to lock and secure it.

The men looked around, checked all the windows, and the first thing we realized was the fact that there was only one exit—the front door.

"Are all the homes around here like this?" Reed asked *Sili.*

"From what I remember, yes. There was a central area that served as a market for trade goods. The compound also has a blacksmith on hand and a forge."

What were we in, the olden days? A forge? One thing was for sure, they had metal weapons secured somewhere. None of the residents we had seen thus far carried any on their body, but I wouldn't put it past them just yet.

Gunner ran his hand across the walls as he asked, "Fitri. What else do you remember? Tell us everything you know. We're going to need all the information we can get."

Sili sat on the couch and rubbed at her temples. "The building I was imprisoned in was toward the far back. The rest of the houses here all look about the same, except for the one that houses the leader. I was only here for a very short time before...something happened...and they chained me up."

"What? What happened?" he prodded.

She snapped. "What do you want me to say, Gunner? My memories then were fragmented already. All I know is one of the women accused me of making her husband think impure thoughts, and she decided to kill me." Fitri stood up and stared at him intently. "When my skin stitched together, they tackled me to the ground and threw me in chains, locking me away from the world. The only person who didn't condemn me was the other prisoner."

Gunner walked forward, and I blocked him

with my hand. He stared at me in defiance, but I would kill him if he did anything to her. "All of us here have hunted bloodsuckers in the past, it's no secret. *Sili* is different," I placated.

He gave me an incredulous look. "You really think I'd do *anything* to her? She's part of the fucking *team,* man. I was trying to comfort her. No need to piss on your territory, I get it. We all do. You need to calm the fuck down."

My nostrils flared and my hands balled into fists. I was stopped before I could do anything stupid by gentle fingers on my arm sliding down to open my hands back up.

"Gunner, everyone," she sighed dejectedly. "I-I don't know what I am. I just know that once I passed a certain age, things started to become clearer. The fact that I'm not like others around me has condemned me everywhere I go. My senses are heightened and I heal faster than most. W-Whatever happened to that last vampire, I can't even tell you, because even I, myself have yet to comprehend it."

"We'll figure it out later, *Sili*." I placed my hand on her shoulder to comfort her and she exhaled. I loved the fact that I had that effect on her. "Right now, we need to recon this compound."

"We'll wait until nightfall. I'll stay here in case someone comes by. We can't all go out." Samuel kicked his feet up on the short table after sitting down on the couch next to *Sili.*

"Fitri is the smallest. She's the best for this," Reed supplied.

As much as that made sense, I didn't like the idea. She was put in chains once, what would stop them from doing it again? Did they recognize her? That was the main question still left in the air without an answer. "*Sili*, did you look different the last time you were here?"

"You mean, was I disguising as a boy?" she assumed. "No. But my hair was a lot shorter. I was dirtier, having just returned from something I shouldn't have survived."

Only to end up dying again. The world hadn't given her a break and probably never would.

"*Sili* and I will recon. If anyone asks, we're fucking in the other room."

Gunner choked, but we ignored him. A few seconds later, a knock came at the door. Walking over, I checked outside the windows and saw that it was one of the young girls from earlier. Opening the door, I stared at her in confusion.

"T-The High Father wanted me to let you know that the bathhouses are available for you if you so wish to use them. We keep the doors open until nightfall, to help keep everyone safe."

My anxiety rose. "Safe from what?"

Her eyes widened innocently before she leaned in and whispered, "From the vampires."

"They frequent this compound?" I could feel *Sili* stand behind me as I threw out my question.

"More like terrorize, sir. We have to make sure

we keep inside of our homes while The High Father makes a deal to keep them at bay. He's our hero, truly, with how he takes care of all of us. Without him, we'd all be dead," she said solemnly, with the uttermost faith.

I filed this information in the back of my mind as I nodded and took in everything she said at face value. "Alright. Thank you for the information."

"You're welcome." She hesitated to leave and I quirked an eyebrow. "W-would your female companion like to stay with one of the women's housing? We have some for the widows and unmarried girls."

"No," I deadpanned.

I shut the door on her and faced the men.

"Makes a deal? What the hell kinda deal do you make with a vampire?" Reed asked, crossing his arms.

"The only thing a bloodsucker wants is blood. There's no other explanation." I looked to *Sili*, who stared at me for direction. "It still doesn't make any sense, since they essentially killed you and casted you off. Why not keep you alive to offer up to a bloodsucker as live bait, if this is what they're doing here?"

"I don't know," she answered honestly.

"I know you don't. It's okay. We're going to find out." Staring out the window, I realized there was still an hour or so before the sun went down beyond the horizon.

"I'm going to head out to this bathhouse and

see what else is out there," I told everyone. "I'll report back in a few."

My eyes darted to both Reed and Gunner, telling them to take care of *Sili* mentally. They both nodded as I headed out the front door.

The smell of cooking food from earlier faded into the atmosphere, replaced by the increasing warmth of hot metal drifting in my direction. Following my nose, I was led to the center of the compound where Fitri indicated the main trade location. Weaving in and out of the stalls, my eyes located the sparks coming from the forge. With a welding mask covering his face, the blacksmith's perspiration permeated through the back of his shirt beneath his thick leather apron. Hiding behind one of the buildings, I diligently watched as he pulled out a long piece of bright red metal fresh from the fires of the forge.

He hammered it with expertise, tempering the steel as sparks emit with every blow. The roaring sizzle behind the plumes of smoke cloaked his presence as he quenched the metal, adding humidity into the air around him.

This place was more than what it seemed. The women here all dressed in similar dresses, and the men in similar trousers and a shirt of the same colors in varying greys. The blacksmith stood out amongst the crowd with his brown uniform as he continued to flatten the blade into something to be used for battle.

Why would a simple village compound need a

weaponry that large if the High Father made a pact with a bloodsucker? What exactly did they require the blade to kill?

If the number of residents in this community was a finite number, what purpose did it serve to continually craft weapons beyond their numbers? Surely they had since reached the requisite number for each person here. My mind logically supplied that the course that made the most sense would be Bellmore was crafting weapons for trade. My thoughts went back to the young woman and her cryptic statement.

Were *they trading with vampires?* Why did this solution sound too simple?

Forgetting the bathhouse, I made my way back to the men as the sun began to slowly set. I knocked twice, paused, and then twice more. Samuel jerked the door ajar and allowed me entrance. We developed our system among one another for the specific occasions when we found ourselves among unknown territory to ensure we knew it was our team that came calling beyond barricades and barriers.

"I located the forge," I began with the obvious. Pausing for effect, I looked at each and every one of them before revealing the next thing. "They might be trading with the bloodsuckers."

"Which clan? Who still uses swords?" Gunner threw out.

Good question.

"We're about to find out," I answered. "Fitri,

with me. The rest of you, keep your eyes peeled. I don't trust the young women here either. They're *too* innocent."

Sili got up from the couch and checked all her weapons. She set aside her crossbow in the bush hiding our vehicle for safe keeping. *Smart move.* We didn't need to draw more attention than we already did coming into this compound.

When she made it to my side, I threw my fingers up, letting the others know we would return in two hours' time.

"Keep your hair down, it'll obscure your face more. There's a chance they may still not recognize you since your last stay," I whispered to her as we rounded the back of the house and kept to the shadows, moving light on our feet.

"Things really haven't changed much at all. It's eerie," *Sili* admitted and I took her words as the gospel as we continued around the village, observing how the compound was laid out in relation to their protective wall. I no longer smelled the humidity of the forge as we trekked farther from the center trade area.

"You're telling me. I feel like we took a step back in time with the way things run around these parts. Did they mention any clan names while you were here?" I whispered back.

My hand shot out before she could step on a small fallen branch. She looked down and nodded, purposefully stepping over.

"No. Devon only talked about how he'd use me

before I died." She stated it so matter-of-factly, I was stunned. I wondered how many times she'd heard it to speak of it in such a way.

The sounds of grunts and moans broke the silence, stealing our attention. We both looked at each other curiously and followed it until we drew closer to its origins.

"The leader's house," *Sili* whispered.

It was bigger than the others around here, significantly so. What reason would he have to hide away in the farthest recesses of the compound when thus far, he had presented himself charismatically—and as one who basked in the attention of his people. It made more logical sense for a pompous man to flaunt his acquisitions in the forefront of the village for all to see.

We snuck behind the outer wall of the High Father's home as the moans transformed to cries. Straightening ourselves to peer over the closest window ledge, we witnessed a naked ass pounding between a woman's legs.

"God's called you today. He has a plan," Devon panted.

What the everloving hell?

"Yes, High Father. I want to be used," she whined. The girl's voice sounded young and the hairs on my back stood.

He grabbed her thigh and maneuvered her expertly on the bed, turning her face down and shoving his red-tinged cock inside of her once more.

So, the High Father was fucking virgins. What else was new? Couldn't say I was surprised.

I began to lose interest, casting my eyes to our surroundings, when *Sili* grabbed my hand. My sights snapped back to the inside of the house, and my brows furrowed. He didn't finish, his cock stood at attention outside of her body. We watched as he leaned in to kiss her and simultaneously reach to the side table for something, exposing the girl beneath him.

"Used you will be my child, have you no worry," he cooed and she bit her bottom lip innocently.

The girl looked like a fucking twelve-year-old, making me grimace, heartburn threatening to choke me in more ways than one. My hands balled into fists right as metal glinted against the light cast from within. *Sili's* fingers dug into my flesh as I watched slack-jawed as the High Father plunged the blade into the girl's chest.

Her gurgles floated through the air as he brought it down again, crimson blooming around her as if symbolically showcasing her innocence to the world—a flowerbud plucked before her time. The worst part was, she was smiling up at him.

The blood began to pool in a strange Rorschach pattern on the once pristine white sheets, morbidly mesmerizing me until he wetly pulled the blade out and shoved it into her cunt, and sliced upward an inch from her belly button.

A gasp escaped *Sili* before she slammed her

hand over her mouth. High Father Devon wiped the virgin's blood onto his cock with the flat of the blade and tossed it aside, stroking himself and groaning.

"You were so tight, so tight. It was right for you to come to me. You can't be left wandering around, bringing temptation to the men. There's a bigger purpose for you." He groaned again and climbed onto his knees over her motionless body. "There were too many men who came to ask for your hand, you see. You wouldn't be fit to take them all—but now, you can."

He threw her lifeless leg over his shoulder and started to fuck her limp body again with vigor, climaxing inside of her bleeding hole as a knock came at his door.

"High Father, the men are here," a raspy masculine voice filtered through.

What the hell was happening right now? What kind of sick, backward shit was this?

He removed himself and wiped his bloody cock on her slack lips before shuddering in ecstasy. We watched as he climbed off the bed, grabbed a robe to cover himself before he opened his bedroom door with another charismatic smile.

"Let them in," he instructed brightly. "They have ten minutes. When they're done, I'm going to need Mother Rachel to bury her in the garden."

The other man never took his eyes off the body on the bed, his own pants visibly tented. "Yes, High Father. The men will be sure to fill her up. She will help the vegetables flourish with our combined contributions. It was kind of her to volunteer herself."

Devon hummed and placed a hand on the other man's shoulder, pushing him to his knees. "Will you pray with me, brother Elijah? Before we start the harvest ceremony?"

"Y-yes, High Father," he stuttered as he licked his lips and opened Devon's robe.

I grabbed *Sili* to remove us from the house. He would be distracted for a good amount of time. Her feet were glued, but I muscled her away until we were back on track for the mission.

"*Sili*, show me where they kept you," I ordered.

She audibly gulped and nodded, moving quickly in the shadows like a ninja until we came upon one of the worst looking houses up against the back wall to the western of their compound. Pausing behind a thick tree trunk, I counted two men patrolling in the front. I signaled the number to *Sili* and we swiftly moved to opposite sides.

A blade across the neck with a hand clamped over their mouth was all it took for them to christen the ground with their life force. *Sili*, being short, had to leap on the man's back, twisting his head quickly with a soft crack.

Nodding to one another, we opened the doors with a creak and stood in place to allow our eyes to adjust to the darkness within. The village's curfew gave us the advantage of reduced likelihood of one of them catching us here. We looked around, but nothing moved. Cautiously entering, the only light filtering in was through the crooked slats of the dilapidated house.

"Old man," *Sili* whispered. "Are you still here?"

Chains rattled, and a leg pulled away from a stream of light with a scrap across the wooden floor.

"Old man, I need to ask you something," she continued confidently.

A dry chuckle came from behind a large, battered foundational pillar in the middle of the room. "And why do you think I'd know anything?"

My shoulders were tense, wanting to trust her yet not trusting a man I didn't know.

"You've probably heard enough of the leader's ramblings if you've been here this long," she answered.

"And you, my dear, should be dead," he replied with nonchalance. "*Quite fascinating.* Why come back here? Unless you seek death once more? He might have more answers for you than I."

This was getting us nowhere. Pushing *Sili* behind me, I leaned down to the man in chains. His white speckled beard reached his chest, covering a face which appeared weathered by the sun. "We're looking for specific information. Has there been any talk of something being brought into this compound?"

The chains rattled with his movements and his face crinkled with a grin. "The only thing to be found here will visit soon enough."

Scowling, I stood back up. What was the purpose of keeping this old guy prisoner? What could his frail body possibly serve to these people? Why wasn't he killed off with *Sili*? The intel compiled so far wasn't adding up.

Howls pierced the night air, ripping the silence of the compound away. I looked at *Sili* who continued to stare at the old man with a look of consternation. She knew something I didn't. The old man didn't move, maintaining his sitting position with his head against the pole behind him.

Instinct crept across my skin right as feminine screams cried out like a symphony. My frantic pulse quickened as snarls and growls accompanied them. I shot out my hand and grabbed Sili from behind, pulling her out of the building. We ran between the houses until we came to the northwest side where three women were tied to poles in white, flowing dresses. Wolves the size of small horses clawed and devoured their flesh, maws glistening with blood against the light of the moon, coating each sacrifice with an ethereal crimson glow. Innards spilled onto the ground in red cascades, eliciting snuffles and snorts of enthusiasm from the hungering beasts.

Backing away slowly, I kept *Sili* behind me, careful with each step as to not catch their attention during their feasting. Wet crunches continued, the wolves snapping their jaws at one another as they fought for shredded human flesh.

A howl retched from one of the bloodstained

nuzzles and I whispered under my breath to *Sili* behind me, "What the fuck? Did you know anything about this?" My statement came out more accusatory than I anticipated but nothing could be done about it now.

"The only wolves in my memory are—"

I grabbed her, silently communicating we needed to exit the area quickly before continuing our conversation. We turned to head back, with the sounds of beastial hunger behind us. When we came upon the prisoner's building, we witnessed another resident out in the open, kneeling in front of the dead bodies for inspection. Crap. Shift change.

As if sensing our presence, His head snapped to us. "Hey! Get back here! You killed brother James and brother Lucas!"

Perplexing wove through my mind as to why he would yell out when there were wolves nearby.

Menacing growls became louder as the beasts ran toward our direction, lured by the sound of the guard's cries. We bolted toward the shelter of the building. Throwing a fist at the newcomer's face, I knocked him off his feet. *Sili* pulled out her blade, jumped on top of him, and sliced his throat, spraying blood into the air, inadvertently sending out a calling card to the animals behind us.

She leaped through the doors of the dilapidated building and I followed right after her, slamming the doors behind us shut. Shifting around, I looked for a way to place a barricade against it as the old man cackled. The sound of wolves devouring bone and flesh drifted through the wood and we both backed away. The metallic scent of blood permeated the air as some of the blood seeped beneath the doorframe. A few minutes went by, and we heard the wolves pacing, but never attacking the door.

Peculiar and highly suspicious like everything else in this damn place.

"Seems you've met our nightly visitors," the old man chuckled. "Fun lot—when you keep them fed and happy."

My patience was at its last straw. "Let's cut the shit. There are rumors of a human group acquiring some petrified bloodsucker flesh. Do you guys have it here, or not?"

"Ah, well, if that's all you needed..." The old man struggled to his feet, rattling his chains loudly. The wolves growled and howled, but the door remained untouched. Narrowing my eyes, I watched as the old man rolled his neck, stretching his limbs as if he hadn't stood in a century. His posture was hunched over and his body was covered in splotches of dark bruises. He took a few steps toward us with his bare feet and smiled with dirty, broken teeth.

"You, my dear, have stayed on my mind for a long time," he purred, a wicked glint in his eye. "Seeing you here only confirmed my suspicions the first day you were thrown beside me."

"What are you talking about?" *Sili* asked, her

hand still on the blood-soaked blade from her last kill.

The old man crept forward until the chains on his legs were taut, preventing him from moving further. I lifted my lip in a curl as he glared at her from head to toe in examination.

I shot out my fist and grabbed him by the neck. His laugh turned maniacal as the wolves began to batter against the doors repeatedly, clawing and splintering the wood. *Sili* positioned her back to mine, her stance ready for whatever came.

I squeezed the old man's neck tightly, bringing his face toward mine. "Let me end your misery here, you old fool."

We didn't need him letting the rest of the compound find out about our mission. Something told me this old geezer knew more than he was letting on and we weren't getting any more infor-mation out of him than he had already given us—which was nothing.

A black wolf broke through and lunged at *Sili*, who swung her blade. Turning, I watched as the rest of the wolves entered slowly, circling us, none of them attacking.

The old man choked something, and I sneered. "What the fuck is going on here?"

He tried to talk, his eyes bulging as if they were about to pop out of their sockets. *I should kill him and get the rest of the men out of this damn place.* From the High Father to this joker, I was about to lose my mind.

"Drop him, Eliseo," *Sili* demanded.

"Why the fuck should I? He's good for nothing and knows we're here. I should kill him." I smiled as I watched the old man's eyes explode with broken blood vessels, coating his whites in reds.

"He's connected to the wolves. Don't ask how I know. I just feel it. Put him down!"

Fuck.

I dropped him like dead weight and gave him a good, swift kick to the ribs. He coughed and cackled as the wolves continued to circle us menacingly.

"Fucking bloodsuckers walking in the sun, crazy cults and sacrifices, what the hell is next?" I complained, throwing my hands up. "Why not an old man who controls wolves?"

Right as the words left my mouth, one of the wolves leapt toward the prisoner with a growl.

IO

MY EYES WIDENED AND MY BODY PREPARED TO SLAM MY knife into the wolf's back, but Eliseo grabbed me and pulled me toward him in the knick of time.

We both watched in horror as the old man moved faster than I could see and bit into the wolf's neck and drank his blood. *What the hell?* The beast whined as the old man shoved him aside and stood up, chin coated in crimson. His crazed eyes looked even wilder and inhuman with burst blood vessels.

Lekim, my mind supplied. But what did that clan have to do with anything? Unless it was part of their abilities...

But from the knowledge lodged in my mind, I knew none of the vampires could drink animal blood. So, how was he still alive? I frowned when I noticed his body began to change in front of us. His flesh slowly filled out despite logic telling me it wouldn't be possible.

The wolves all howled in unison at their fallen comrade, rattling the walls of the building, sending shivers down my spine.

"Do an old fool a favor and come closer. My eyes aren't what they used to be," he goaded, his finger calling me forth with glee.

Hell fucking no. I may not remember everything, but I wasn't stupid.

Eliseo pulled a gun out of the waist of his pants and pointed it directly at him. If he let off a shot, the entire compound would be alerted and he knew it. If this was a bluff, I hoped it worked.

The old man threw his head back and laughed then pulled the chain out of the wooden pillar with a swift jerk.

Was he a—

"I see it in your eye, girl." He walked around us, circling with his wolves, dragging the chain behind him loudly across the floor. His eyes flicked to Eliseo as he *tsks*. "Now, you know a gunshot will bring everyone out of their quiet little homes. Why disturb the peace? Who knows what these crazy humans are up to with how they so easily sacrifice their own people for their disillusioned belief of a good cause for the whole?"

The old man licked his bloodied lips and we both kept our eyes on him, ready to strike if necessary.

"They think I don't know, but *I know*," he leered with dark intentions. I took in his words and tried to piece what he was revealing in my mind. "A man leading a cult this easily? It was easy to figure out."

One of the wolves lunged at us and snapped their jaws a scant few inches away, taunting. I kicked its head with all of my weight behind it, making it whimper and skitter back. The other wolves snarled as I threw a knife, lodging it in its flank. But aside from it teetering a few times, it didn't stop it from circling.

What kind of inhuman ability did this old man carry to control their minds beyond pain and injuries? It was a frightening thought to know there were others out there with this same potential power roaming the world. Have the bloodsuckers truly evolved this much? Was there no hope for humanity?

"Now why would you harm one of mine?" the old man chastised. "You should be grateful I let them spare you. Three human bodies a month isn't enough to sustain them, you see." The old man's voice was no longer raspy, and his back was no longer hunched over.

"Fuck this shit," Eliseo gritted out, right as he shot the old man in the chest, the sound of the bullet firing resonating into the night. His body slammed onto the wolf he drank from earlier on the floor, making him yip in further suffering.

The rest of the wolves growled and snarled in reaction, thrown into a frenzy with no direction.

The old man groaned in both pain and what seemed to be pleasure as he rolled to the side and brought himself back to his feet. The bloody wound on his left pec dribbled down as he fingered the hole with a hiss before bringing his blood-coated finger to his mouth for a suck.

"You're making me excited, human. All this entertainment in one night," he smirked. With an unexpected leap, he landed on Eliseo's shoulder, claws digging into his flesh before he wildly ripped it away, and dropped Eliseo.

My heart hammered in my chest as Eliseo cried out in pain. My internal body heat rose from fury as I grabbed another blade and threw it, lodging it into the old man's back. He cried out for a split second before it morphed into a maniacal laugh as his feet landed on the ground. Without a hitch, he wrapped his arm around Eliseo's neck from behind.

Eliseo lifted his torso further and threw the man over his shoulder. The wolves barely made it out of the way in time and were now fighting amongst themselves as the stranger landed on his feet with feline grace and crawled on hands and feet toward us like a creature from nightmares with the hilt of my blade still sticking out his back. The smell of metallic scent of blood clogged my nares as my eyes burned with hatred. My chest tightened with growing antipathy toward my former prisoner comrade.

Eliseo got to his feet with a growl and pointed his pistol at the old man once again. The stranger's neck twisted to the side unnaturally right as his arm shot out to grab Eliseo's ankle, taking him down onto his back. A shot fired off through the ceiling of the building, sending dust down above us all. I turned to cover my face and cough, waving my hand in front of me to clear the air.

Eliseo roared, and my eyes saw red. I jerked my face toward them to find the stranger with his mouth latched onto Eliseo's calf while Eliseo continuously brought down the butt of his pistol on the back of his head to no avail. Heat suffused me from the inside like an internal storm as I tackled the old man to the side, ripping the flesh of Eliseo's calf in the process. It was unavoidable. The old man needed to be stopped. But as Eliseo's warm blood added to the atmosphere, my mind further went into a reddened haze.

I dug my fingers into the old man's mouth, his fangs piercing my skin as I pulled, screaming at his face with the tumultuous emotions running through my veins in deluge. He didn't fight back, surrendering.

My fingers threatened to slip with my clammy hands but I didn't let up on my grip—not until the crunch before his face tore in two. The surroundings disappearing in my vision, I slammed his head again and again against the floor despite his jaws flapping. Wet splashes cut through my haze and suddenly the growls around us grew to higher levels vibrating through my chest in a rumble.

The first wolf snapped his jaws into the old man's shoulder, shaking its head violently and knocking me onto my ass. I crab-walked backward, my eyes fixated on the macabre scene in front of me. Eliseo grabbed me from behind and hauled me to my feet, but I continued to watch the old man devoured by his own wolves, his life force coating the entire floor, making the beasts slip and slide as they fought over his carcass.

"Let's get back and get the fuck out of here," Eliseo panted as he limped back with me by his side.

We made it out the door, leaving beasts to their new meal only to run into another voice that sent a wave of fear through me.

"And where do you think you two are going?" Devon's voice was calm, like a simple inquiry during dinner. Eliseo and I stopped in our tracks, my arms under his shoulder as we warily watched Devon's soft smile staring at us.

What really happened after they killed me here?

Morbid scenarios ran through my head, and my simmering anger began to once again boil to infernal heights. Flashes of the young girl he mutilated on his bed were still fresh in my mind. With my body's regeneration rate, I would never know what became of my corpse.

Images of clawing threw dirt slammed into me and I choked on bile threatening to rise.

The community slowly gathered behind Devon one at a time, until they outnumbered us. Each individual stared at us lifelessly as if their bodies were devoid of souls. It was eerie, just like this place.

"Do your people know you're using desecrated flesh to fertilize your lands?" Eliseo barked out.

"Now, now. Let's not spread such blasphemy." Devon spread his arms out wide, palms facing out. "My people know all that happens in this place. I hide nothing. It is why they choose to follow my lead."

His smile morphed from calm to menacing as the people behind him began to march forward without any spoken order.

Ratatatat! Automatic gunshots rang out as the rest of our men came out from their hiding spots behind the villagers, spraying the people down with bullets. A row of humans fell to the ground like puppets with their strings cut, but it didn't stop the rest of them from continuously moving forward as if nothing had happened.

There was no fear. There was no hesitation.

Grabbing the pistol on me, Eliseo did the same as we let off shots to the ones closest to us. Moving back, we hid behind barrels lined up against one of the walls, adding to the gunfire when we could.

The people continued to mindlessly move toward

us as a can flew in the air, landing and rolling in a rattle toward Devon's feet. He swiftly kicked it and it hit one of his people in the head, knocking him against two others. No one got angry, no one said a word. The people climbed back to their feet and continued forth.

A memory pricked in the back of my mind and supplied me with what I needed to know. "Eliseo. We need to take down Devon. I think the people here are thralls—Devon is controlling them. He must be a vampire!"

"Fucking hell, can't missions be simple?" he said with exasperation.

Hsssss! The can finally released its smoke and the guys pulled down their gas masks. Ours were left back in the house, so we kept our distance and let the men mow down the rest of the people.

Was it wrong of me to feel no remorse for possibly eliminating an entire compound?

Like a phantom, Reed flew out of the smoke and was slammed against the side of one of the houses with a loud crash, groaning and falling to the ground. My eyes saw red again, my instincts heightening into a predatory mode, my nose searching out High Father Asshole.

Before Eliseo could hold me back, my body went into motion, cutting through the smoke at rapid speed. My consciousness was set aside as his strong scent drove me forth. Everything else around me disappeared in my vision, my instincts leading me right to the one I was searching for.

He stood there serenely with his back facing

me, hands coated in blood when I swept his feet from under him, taking him to the dirt ground in a crash.

The thralls around us began to moan in ghastly synchronization, and I was taken back to a different moment in time from the past.

"What is this? Someone Clan Lekim cannot control? How fascinating..." the first vampire purred as he gripped my neck tighter.

His many thralls stood by, staring into the distance with no expression on their faces.

"Hey, don't kill her yet. I haven't had my turn, you selfish prick." The second vampire licked his lips as his hand continued to stroke his cock in front of me, the crown of his head glistening with precum.

I gasped for breath as claws jabbed into my vagina. Struggling against the pain, a scream tore out of me despite the lack of air. He forced fucked me with his fist, spreading me open beyond my body's capability and scraping my insides right before he jerked his hand out and threw me onto the ground, face down. I coughed and sputtered for much-needed breath, each intake of air like shards of glass down my throat as tears blurred my vision. My body shook from the overstimulation and pain, pushing me toward shock as the second vampire shoved his disgusting cock against my lips on an exhale.

I bit down and the taste of warm copper overflowed in my mouth.

They would all pay for what they did to me! My mind screamed as the memory played in a loop, each time more vivid than the last, bringing forth details like puzzle pieces falling into place.

Leaping onto his back to stop his escape, my legs wrapped around his midsection as my nails clawed into his neck, pulling outwards. He struggled and gurgled on his own blood, trying to dislodge me, but I bit down and ripped the flesh of his neck with my teeth, spitting it to the side with glee.

He fell forward just as the smoke started to dissipate, the blood spurted in a wide arch from the severed artery like an elegant piece of art dancing in front of my eyes. Each spray of his life force on the skin of my face, did nothing to cool down the flames of my unearth subconscious, taking over me.

The old man. High Father Asshole. I growled and bit down again with savagery, but nothing could erase the memories of my defilement. *I will send Clan Lekim to the pits of hell!*

"*Sili!*" a familiar voice called out, but it was muffled by my rabid lunacy.

"Shit, someone grab her! They're still moving!"

Samuel's booming proclamation made me snap my head up and to see the thralls continuing their mindless walk toward me and my prey. My consciousness slipping back to the forefront, I patted my body and gripped my gun as I tried to aim at the closest one without letting it slip from my bloodied hands. A shot fired off but missed the closest thrall, until Gunner joined us, decapitating it in front of me. The head bounced and rolled until a black boot stopped it.

My eyes tracked up and saw the man from the High Father's room—*Brother Elijah.* He glowered at me in contempt, then to the dead body beneath me. His nostrils flared as he bore his fangs, his pupils dilating.

"You dare kill our High Father?" he sneered, moving with inhuman speed to grab me by the throat with both hands. His nails dug into my flesh and I kicked, my feet dangling above the ground.

Damn, another vampire?

My left fist landed on his face, snapping his head to the side as I proceeded to pistol whip him with my right to break his hold on me. A scarlet streak bloomed across his cheek as he slowly turned to me ominous. One of his eyes was blood-shot, and half of his face was caved in from my knuckles, but it didn't stop him from opening his mouth widely and trying to fit my head in it.

It was as if everything moved in slow motion, I watched his saliva string from his fangs as my nares picked up the oppressive scent of copper in the area. My breathing slowed as the heat of his mouth reached over my scalp. Blood dripped down my face along with sweat, tickling as it ran down my temples.

His teeth pierced my skull with a crunch and the agony stole my attention from the adrenaline running through me.

"Sili!"

"Fuck!"

Gunshots rang and the claws digging in my neck jerked, shaking me with him. He clamped his jaws tighter as his disgusting, wet tongue touched my face in mock reverence.

Suddenly, we both fell to the side but all I could feel was the throb rippling through the holes in my skull. How could blood smell both putrid and agreeably aromatic at the same time?

It was Eliseo who ripped the vampire's mouth open and pulled it off me. I sharply inhaled and sagged to the side right before he picked me up behind my knees and shoulders. My head flopped back as my body began to give in to my injuries.

I could hear the men's war cry as it faded in and out with my consciousness, the darkness in my periphery closing it faster than I would like.

"Faheema, you should have known it would be this way," my father's tone was laced with disappointment, adding to the guilt already weighing me down.

"I didn't mean it. I-it just happens." It was the truth. How else do I explain the unexplainable?

He stared at me in disscontempt and my heart cracked. When I looked at my mother, hers was full of pity. They didn't know what to do with me. I killed one of the cows when my emotions got the best of me. The entire town was enraged, and I did the only thing I could—I ran. I ran to my parents, who were now at a loss of what to do with me.

Each day, my father's disdain for me grew the more my abilities exposed themselves. His constant disap-

proval would be the death of me. I craved his approval like the air I breathed. How could I not? They took me in when they didn't have to and here I was... bringing the family down with my weaknesses.

"Nothing just happens, girl!" he roared, his veins popping out the side of his temples. "You understand the rules of this community as well as the rules of this house. You chose to do what you did, didn't you? You wanted to bring shame to this family!"

His hands balled into fists while I remained on my knees before him, begging for forgiveness—begging for a way to stop the madness inside of me from growing.

The sting across my face from the abrupt slap was nothing in comparison to what I felt on the inside. Was he right? Have I brought shame to the family? I was nothing but trouble. They didn't deserve this from me.

"*Sili*, open your eyes for me babe. Come on."

"She's fading again."

"I can see that, you prick!"

"Patricia, you can't save them all! She needs to go!" he growled.

"No!" My mother's screams morphed into the multiple cries of burning innocents nailed to crucifixes.

The scream was shrill in my ears, until I real-ized it was me. *My flesh singed and charred as the overwhelming fires stole my voice, drowning me in flames and losing myself to a darkness I never asked for.*

Images flicked back and forth, from dark to light, from dark to... *deep crimson.*

Everything was wet. I was drowning in the

blood of everyone around me until I sputtered and choked on my last breath.

I jerked awake, bolting to a sitting position... but a warm, calloused hand gently nudged me, returning me to a supine position on my back. I let him; my heart pounded erratically at the fresh nightmare behind my closed lids.

What happened? Where was—"Eliseo?" I whispered in desperation.

His arm wrapped around my midsection, pulling me closer to his warmth. Tears sprung forth uncontrollably when I turned to bury my face against his chest, hiding myself away from the world.

Just a nightmare, I reminded myself. Why were these crazy images running through my head? Wolves and old men. Robed masochists and a town massacre. What a bittersweet, beautiful macabre sight to behold.

My hands crawled up to cradle his face and pull him down. Opening my eyes, I stared at him, examining his skin meticulously to make sure I wasn't losing my sanity. I couldn't tell what was real and what wasn't anymore. The fabric of my existence, muddled between reality and some-where lost in the realm of nightmares.

He kissed my palm and let me stare to my heart's content, his eyes softening as he did the same.

"I had a bad dream," I croaked out timidly.

"Yeah?" His thumb brushed away my stray

tears but he didn't smile. No, his brow was wrinkled in concern, and my heart's tempo fluttered rapidly as my mouth went dry. How could I possibly explain the images flitting through my mind? How I, myself, struggled to put the fragmented pieces of my life together while tirelessly trying to survive in a world where everything and everyone was out to execute me.

"I-It wasn't a dream, was it?" Eliseo brought his nose down to rub against mine, sighing in defeat and my eyes burned.

"I wish it was." I couldn't form the right words, so I deflected. "What happened?"

I looked around, through the darkness of nightfall. Was this the same night or have I been out longer? The flames of a campfire behind us emitted a subtle glow and the relaxed air around me settled into my bones. I could hear the soft snores from some of the men scattered on the other side of the fire.

His hand pushed my hair back, and my own face scrunched up in concern. He was being extra gentle with me for some reason and I was afraid of the answer as to why. But how could I deny what I already knew, nightmares or not? It didn't make it any less true.

"D-Did I die?" I choked out.

The snores disappeared, notifying me the rest of the team was quietly listening to us, awaiting the rest of the conversation.

"You did," he said plainly.

The simplicity in his answer scared me. Why weren't his eyes condemning? A spike of irrational fear coursed through my veins—a fear of finally caring enough for someone... to want them to stay. Stubbornness finally aside after all we've been through, I didn't want them to leave me behind. But I also didn't want to face another rejection—It would break me at this point in my life.

Eliseo filled the silence with his voice as if he knew my mind was running a mile a minute, on the brink of fragmentalizing. The way his thumb played along the line of my jaw made me ache for what I didn't deserve.

"We made it back to the car and drove until it ran out of gas," he started softly. "It took us back to the lake where we all washed off. We were too coated in blood to not attract the attention of animals and enemies."

His eyes searched mine as he explained the events I couldn't remember. Still laying on our sides, I lifted my hand in front of my face to see my skin had been scrubbed clean, too—not even a trace of blood under my fingernails.

"You cleaned me," I stated, rather than questioning. *Of course, he did.* My throat clogged up as my sinuses added to the chest constriction. Eliseo always had a way of barging into my life and taking control of things. It annoyed me to no end, but this time... this time it submerged me in unfamiliar territory.

"Why wouldn't I? A random group of humans

who are concerned about the blood-coated goddess in my arms like a damn sacrifice couldn't stop me." His confident smile made me flush with embarrassment.

I shoved at his shoulders, unable to face the low simmering heat coiled in the depths of my gut from his words. He was so full of it. Turning away from him, I put my right arm under my head and mulled over the information. Why couldn't I remember him cleaning me?

I could feel his soft lips against my exposed shoulder, peppering slow kisses along my skin. Sighing in contentment, I closed my eyes and tried to force my mind to play back what happened earlier, but it only came back in bits and pieces, aggravating me to no end.

"*Sili,*" he whispered.

I bit my lip and tried again. *Why couldn't I remember?* I chastised myself, wallowing over my deficiencies as I ignored him.

He gripped my upper arm firmly, finally stealing my attention, making me snap my eyes open.

"*Sili*, if it wasn't for you we'd all be dead."

I looked over my shoulder, stupefied. "What are you talking about? It was probably *because* of me we were in that position in the first place. We should have taken a different route, chosen a different location to check out. We should have—"

His fingers trailed along the curve of my shoulder, eliciting goosebumps. "It was your skin this whole time," he mumbled as if to himself.

What was he talking about? What was wrong with my skin? I lifted my left arm in front of my face and examined it, trying to see what he was saying. It was smooth like it usually was, not a scar in sight. I frowned and stared harder.

"It was only when I washed you, the truth revealed itself," he continued. Lifting his own hands in front of me, we both looked at his palms. "My hands were numb, my fingers falling slack after a period of time. I had to call out to the guys to catch you before I dropped your body into the waters, drowning you in your unconscious state."

"What?" I got up on my elbow and I tried to see if he was messing with me.

He grabbed the back of my head unexpectedly and slammed his mouth against mine, his tongue invading between my lips like he belonged nowhere else but here. I whimpered in confusion but surrendered to his dominance nonetheless. I didn't want to think about all this craziness. I wanted this good feeling to wash away all the bad covering my life.

"I almost lost you—again," he growled against my lips and I gasped, my heart skipping a beat.

His other hand caressed my breast over my shirt, adding to the rollercoaster of confused emotions bubbling out of me. Scissoring my legs, I realized I didn't have any pants on, and the heat building between them was too fast for me to comprehend or control. How could I possibly feel this way after the horrors we apparently went through if my nightmares were correct? He nipped my bottom lip and then down my chin, pushing my face forward while he lifted my oversized shirt and pulled my hips back, grinding it against his covered erection.

The fire behind us crackled as a branch popped and the sound of the night began to increase—insects singing their tune, calling for mates and the flutter of disturbed wings from up above. The crisp air around us did nothing to cool the flames he continuously stoked inside of me.

Clothing scraped against the ground right before the heat of his hard cock slid between my thighs, rubbing against my core. Eliseo wrapped my hair in his fist, pulling my head up so he could pepper my neck with erotic kisses as his hips began a steady, slow rhythm.

"I've been dying to bury myself inside of you, knowing you'd come back to me. Your temperature cooled, and fuck if my dick didn't get the message, because it's been straining against my pants the whole time I've been lying next to you, *Sili.*"

Why did his debauched confession turn me on? But wasn't it the ultimate form of desire?—To crave you beyond death? Eliseo and his certifiable ways have shown me what it meant to be wanted for everything I was despite my shortcomings.

"I need you inside of me so badly," I whined, unashamed of who could hear us.

Knowing what his hard cock felt like inside of me made me whimper with unabashed need. I had never felt this hollow after coming back from the brink of existence before. I needed his brand of dominance desperately, I needed him to remind me what it felt like to be alive. Opening my legs, I forced him inside of me, my pussy wetter than the lake that erased the evidence of my guilt. I needed him to fill the void I felt inside of my heart. I needed him to make this life worth living.

He groaned as his arm tightened around my chest and shoulders, his hips pumped his hard length inside of me again and again with a delicious friction I grew to crave.

"You'd like that, wouldn't you? For me to fuck you while your body is coming back to life. My dick would warm you up faster, just like this," he arrogantly hummed.

His movements were voracious, my nipples scraped against the harsh fabric beneath us, and I could practically feel the head of his cock pushing my organs.

Pain mixed with a growing pleasure, drowning out all the worries previously swirling inside of my head. Sticking my ass out further, I met his thrusts with my own, both of us chasing what we could only bring to each other—a euphoria in the midst of this desolate existence that harbored nothing but death and destruction.

"Shit, look how good you're taking me in, clamping down on me," he praised making me preen beneath him. He pulled himself out torturously slow, before slamming himself back in deliciously.

My pussy fluttered around his girth and depth until he surprised me by changing the angle of his thrusts, hitting a point of pleasure I didn't know existed. His grip slipped to my hips, digging his fingers into my flesh as the sound of flesh slapping against flesh added to the sound of the night.

My inner thighs were slick with wetness, the smell of our combined arousal enveloping us here outside for all to witness. It was a primal claim and I fiended for more of everything he had to give me. His hand came forward to pinch and pull my clit, swirling it around in a torturous rhythm while he simultaneously never let up from his thrusts. I clenched down on my pussy, wanting him deeper, silently begging for him to ruin me.

He growled as his arm gripped me harder in response, sending a spike of delicious pain. It made me hot and wanton knowing how I affected him.

"Your pussy was made for me," he groaned, licking the lobe of my ear, sending a shiver through me.

Lost in a haze of lust, I swore I heard the other men moaning softly, stroking their own cocks behind us as Eliseo brought me to the pinnacle of no return. The sensation ran through me like lightning, making my entire body shudder when I fell off the metaphorical cliff with a cry of pleasure.

It was at that very moment... I knew he owned

me. I could never go back to the way things were. Not when he took care of me like this, stealing all my burdens onto his own shoulders while giving me nothing but peace in letting go.

As the high of my climax died down, a flicker of memory reminded me of Eliseo's ripped shoulder caused by our previous encounter with the old stranger. Opening my mouth to say something, his hand gripped the front of my neck seductively right as he buried himself inside of me so deeply it felt like it threatened to come out of my throat.

His cock pulsated against my walls, filling me up with warmth and I spasmed torturously again in response. I pressed my legs together for some sort of semblance of control, only succeeding in tightening around him.

"Fuck," he groaned, slowly thrusting inside of me, prolonging the sensation of his own release and mine.

Finally, his hand on my neck loosened, tracing his fingers along my jaw and sticking it between my lips. I sucked it in, swirling my tongue around the pad of his finger while I concentrated on another unexpected climax dying down to a whisper. He kept himself inside of me as he pulled me closer into his body in a possessive embrace from behind. My own hand slipped backward, threading my fingers in his hair, as I pulled him down for a kiss.

"Shit," was all I heard before one of the guys

groaned and finished in his own hands, the rest following suit.

When the sexual tension in the air dissipated, the sound of insects renewed around the flicker and snaps of the campfire between us.

II

ELISEO

THE MORNING TREK BROUGHT US TO ANOTHER abandoned vehicle, but this time, there wasn't any fuel in it. It did provide a nice pit stop for us as we tried to figure out the next direction. My right calf throbbed like a bitch, more than my shoulder did, but I ignored the pain. I wrapped it as best I could after cleaning it to prevent other debris getting inside the wound.

"Did you run across any other camps, Fitri?" Reed leaned his head back against the vehicle, sitting in its shadow from the sun.

"Perhaps, I just can't recall the direction," she answered dejectedly.

"It's okay, *Sili*," I reassured her, not wanting her to get lost in her thoughts. "We'll run across something."

As if serendipitously, another rag-tag group

walked down the road a visible distance away. I threw out a short, quick whistle for the men to pay attention. We all peered over the car. Their clothes were dirty but their bodies didn't look malnourished.

"Fitri, you're going to get them to lead you back to their location. We'll follow right behind you," Reed blurted out. I jerked my head in his direction with a scowl, reluctant to admit his spontaneous plan sounded good. I tipped my head up to the other guys to follow his lead and squeezed *Sili's* thigh.

She looked from me to Reed and nodded. I grabbed her chin and gave her a peck on the lips before we re-crouched behind the vehicle, out of visual line from the new group.

A few deep breaths and *Sili* stood up, dusting off her pants before she confidently walked out to get their attention.

"Hey! Please! I need some help." The vulnerability in her voice was convincing, even I was itching to leave my spot to answer her call.

"Walk farther out," I instructed.

She hunched her body, her arms wrapped around herself to play the part. *Good girl.*

She sniffed, and her voice shook as she informed them she had been wandering on her own for a while. The men easily fell for the act, surrounding her with pitying looks.

My men immediately changed locations, Gunner slapping me with the back of his hand to get my attention. I didn't like the way this scenario made me feel, but Reed was right, this was our way into wherever they came from. Following the men with a good distance between us, we hid ourselves behind the nearby cluster of trees off the side of the road.

"Hey, it's alright," one of the men placated. "Why don't you come back with us, and we'll get you situated. I'm sure the others won't mind a new addition."

My hackles rose. I *bet* they wouldn't mind another woman in their camp. Fuckers were going to lose their limbs if they touched her. Reed stared at me with the same intent shining through his eyes.

"Come on, sugar," the second one cajoled. "We're not that far. Just a few more miles."

Peeking around the tree's trunk, I noticed *Sili's* body tensed up. My own hackles rose in response. Did she know this fucker?

"O-okay," she answered meekly. "Thank you. I'm just so hungry. It's been hard out here alone."

"You won't be alone anymore. The guys will watch out for you." The line sounded practiced and overused. My hand gripped the butt of my pistol inside my waistband, itching to end his life where he stood.

Reed shook his head as he ground his teeth down, holding himself back from doing the same. Gunner had his gun aimed at the man closest to *Sili.* Samuel was crouched behind his tree, watching their every move with his gun pointed to the ground.

We followed them out of sight. About an hour into it, the other group stopped for a break on the side of an off-beaten path. We did the same, sitting and resting as we took a swig out of the water we collected earlier.

"Don't worry about Fitri. She can handle herself," Reed threw across to me in the silence.

The other group was far enough to not hear us as long as we kept our tones down. Wiping my mouth with the back of my hand, I gave him a side-eye. "Who said I was worried?"

"You say it in the way your body looks ready to kill everything in its path every time one of them gets too close to her. Trust me, I feel the same," he grits out. "She's one of us, and any scratch on her would make me explode. But we need her to make it back to the camp."

"Fucker, you think I'm going to mess up the mission over my feelings for her?" I bite back. "As a matter of fact, let's get it straight, right here, right now. She's fucking mine, you got it?"

Reed leaned forward and put his elbows over his knees. "I'm going to let her decide, yeah? She's not the kind of girl to be told what to do," he said much too confidently as if he knew a secret I didn't.

My hands balled into fists, itching to put him in his place—but he was right. At the end of the day, she could choose whoever the fuck she wanted in this group of dicks we had hanging around her.

Fuck, the thought made me feel like shit. She deserved better than a damaged man like me, one who could give less of a fuck about the world burning around them.

Reed was more mentally stable, more caring. My head twitched over the thought of him making her fall for him. It wouldn't be too hard, judging by how close they were growing already. I focused ahead of me, where Gunner chewed on a piece of dried meat. That fucker was more laid back than the rest of us. If anything, it should be him. He was closer to her age, as well.

What was I thinking, taking her for myself? What can my old ass offer her that she couldn't get from any of the other men?

I looked over to Samuel and my tension relaxed a fraction. Hannah would tan his balls. He wouldn't dare.

The selfish part of me said fuck it all. I wanted her. She was mine. I would burn the damn world down before I let her go to someone else. I scowled toward the distance. She would have to wait for my deathbed. Even then, I would haunt the rest of her fucking life.

Or finally kill her permanently and take her with me. Then I wouldn't have to think about this at all. We wouldn't have to struggle anymore. I ran an angry hand down my face.

"They're on the move," Samuel called out, catching all of our attention and pulling me from my morbid thoughts.

We migrated quickly, staying the same distance behind them until we came to what looked like a solid, concrete warehouse stronghold. Barbed wire ran across the top of a sturdy metal gate which rolled open upon their arrival. A short conversation was exchanged between the guards before they waved them in. The men and I hid behind some of the trees surrounding the compound, sitting on higher ground. Our location gave us a better view of the inside, beyond the metal gates rolling back to a close.

The windows were dark, revealing nothing. Cars and multiple motorcycles sat parked behind the wall in designated areas. Where were they getting all the fuel to power these things? Two small buildings sat on each end of the main one in the center, creating a strange row from our semi-aerial view from the hill.

Gunner tapped me on the shoulder and pointed. My eyes followed the direction of his finger to see another group come out to greet them. *All men.* I didn't like this, and it wasn't because of my irrational jealousy.

"We need to get in there," I told the guys.

They all mumbled in agreement as we slowly walked around the back parameter of the wall. We spotted another exit point manned with another set of armed soldiers. What the hell was inside this place needing such manpower?

"I'm going to look around the other side, see if there's a wall we can breach," Samuel threw out as he made his way behind the bushes on this hill.

The entire area was mostly covered in dirt and dust besides where we hid. Having higher ground within the same vicinity, put this stronghold at a disadvantage. Why would these guys choose this place as a home base?

"Well, hello there! My men tell me you've found yourself lost," came a voice much too friendly for my liking. The leader of the greeting party stepped forward. "Come, join us. We have plenty to go around. So, tell me where you came from..."

My men. This was going to be a shit show. *Sili* could only kill so many of them. Samuel made it back just in time before I decided to go rogue and got her out of there myself.

"We're shit out of luck, just two ways in," he reported.

"Alright, through the back it is then. Let's go," I commanded, unwilling to sit aside any longer.

We moved silently between the trees until the ground evened out with the back gates. The entry point from this end were double doors, compared to the sliding gate in the front. This was a good development—doors making less noise than rolling metal on a gate track.

"Reed," I called.

He nodded in understanding and threw a rock to the side, hitting the back wall to catch their attention. The guards spoke with one another briefly with their guns raised and one of them walked off to inspect the noise.

Reed and Gunner both went off in his direction while Samuel and I walked up to the remaining guard.

"Who are you and what the fuck are you doing here?" the guard hollered at us. *Welcoming, my ass.* These guys played the part when it came to women coming to their compound, but not the opposite sex.

Distracting him, I waved a hand dismissively and began spewing bullshit. "Shit, I kinda got lost. Do you know how you get to—"

Samuel quickly came behind him and sliced his throat deep enough to make his head flop back. Reed and Gunner came back at the same time with bloodstains on their hands and the enemies' weapons in tow.

Samuel grabbed the ammo off the guy we took out and tossed the rifle to me.

Opening the double doors, it creaked and I ground my teeth in annoyance. *Fuckers had a compound this big and couldn't find grease or some shit for the hinges?* We all slipped inside and moved between the parked vehicles for cover. Checking some of their condition, I appreciated the collection. We were going to have to hijack a few of these on the way out if we were too outnumbered.

Voices floated from the main middle building —particularly, the sound of men cheering and celebrating. When we reached the first small building, we slipped in and reconned. It was the size of a small home back in Ashborne, while the main building here was five times its size.

Crouching down, I leaned against the wall and checked my weapons before slowly rising to peer inside the dirty window. It was dark and looked to be housing supplies and crates. We should come back for this shit if we had time.

"Check the other small building and meet back here in ten," I signaled. Samuel and Reed both broke off.

Gunner beside me and looked into the same window. "Do you think they have food in here?"

"We'll find out soon enough. First thing is finding out where *Sili* is," I instructed. "Next, we see if they have what the doc needs. Then, we get our asses out *alive.*"

He nodded in response. "I know she can handle herself, but I got a real bad feeling about this."

"I know. Me too."

Time ticked by, and I started to get antsy when the other two didn't return. "Let's go," I told Gunner and we both stealthy made it to the other side of the compound. Reed and Samuel were nowhere to be seen from our new location. Might as well check out this building before we went looking for them.

"Ahhhh!" came a feminine scream and I jumped into action, led by instincts. Gunner was right behind me as I ran into the room, pulled the dagger I obtained from the last community, and stabbed it into the man's kidneys.

He fell to the ground and landed on top of a girl in chains secured around the neck, her arms, wrists and legs. *Why the hell would they need this much to hold a single woman?* The dead man's dick slipped out as he flopped to the side, a bloody saw clattering on the hard ground next to him. Her leg was freshly sawed right at the thigh, her blood spewing from her artery.

Was the world full of crazed people? Why do we keep running into bizarre shit? Gunner was standing next to me, staring at the sight before him. What the hell were we supposed to do? We needed to save *Sili* before she became...*this.*

The girl grimaced, her face wet from tears, before she kicked the body enough for her to bend forward and bite down on the dead man's neck. *So she was a bloodsucker.* We both watched as she moaned during her feeding right before her leg twitched, drawing our attention.

Gunner grabbed my arm in a tight hold right as we witnessed her severed leg stitch back together and regenerate. Images of *Sili's* healing came to the forefront of my mind and now I was more than infuriated. If these assholes find out she healed like this, she would become their next fuck toy—just like this bloodsucker right here.

Wait a minute...

"What clan are you from?" I blurted.

She smiled crimson-coated teeth before she

batted her eyelashes seductively. "Why? Don't you want a taste of me too, human? I can take you both if you want."

I threw my dagger right into her shoulder, watching her cry her crocodile tears. "I'm going to ask again. What clan are you from?"

I needed to know. I needed to tell *Sili*.

The bloodsucker panted with a grin, the injury making her pussy, still wide open on display, wetter.

"Clan Sira is going to burn this place down once they find me," she leered, licking her lips as her eyes tracked Gunner. "You might as well get your kicks in now before I kill you and your little friend."

"Right. That's why you let this limp dick over here fuck you and cut off your leg?" I spat back.

She bared her teeth menacingly and pulled at her chains, rattling them loudly like a musical tune.

"What the hell! We were looking for you guys. We got caught up in taking out some of the patrol and..." Samuel's voice tapered off as the rest of my men gathered around to stare at the prisoner.

"Smells like swamp dick in here," Reed mumbled.

"Clan Sira probably doesn't even know you're here," I reminded her. "What can you tell me about this place?"

"I don't need to tell you shit!" she cried out in defiance, pulling at her constraints until veins popped out. She was weak. Too weak to break free... unlike the crazed old man back in Bellmore. What was the difference? Why did his frail ass gain so much strength after a gulp of wolf's blood while this one here, continued to struggle after a feeding? There was so much about the bloodsuckers and their dividing clans we didn't know. If we wanted to gain the upper hand in this world, we were going to have to start paying more attention to the little details. It might be our ticket to better survival.

I signaled for the men to leave. We turned and headed out the door one by one while the sound of chains rattled louder and louder behind us.

"Wait! Please!" she called out in a much weaker tone.

I stopped. Looking over my shoulder, I gave her a suspicious glare.

"T-they eat flesh here. When the women can't bear any more children, they serve a different purpose."

My heart slammed into my chest thinking about what they were doing to *Sili*. Keeping my face stoic, I continued to stare in unbending silence to see if she would supply anything else under pressure.

"The assholes shot me from the sky," she added. "I was never supposed to cross this side. I was headed to meet my assigned commander."

Commander. The vampires had military forces? I didn't exactly know how these clans were organized, but it was not news they were at war with one another as evidenced by the bloodshed we occasionally came across. If she was headed toward her commander, war might already be here on our side.

Wait the fuck a minute...

"Did she say—" Reed frowned and came to the same conclusion I did. I nodded.

This was it. Our mission. The wings were hidden here somewhere on this compound. "You guys go ahead, get a sample for crazy Otis, and then look for Sili," I instructed without taking my eyes off the enemy before me. "We need to get out of here, now."

As my men left to do as commanded, I fully turned toward the bloodsucker. She smiled in triumph—until I leaned in and pulled out my dagger, wiping it on my pants, tucking it away and turning right back around.

"You asshole!" she roared.

"Yeah, so I've been told." I shut the door behind me so I didn't have to hear her annoying voice anymore.

I began moving toward and around the main center building to see if I could locate an unsecured entrance point. I did—through a single side door, and slipped inside.

"Eliseo!" Reed whispered my name from behind an open doorway. I stealthily moved until I met up with him. I assumed Samuel and Gunner were looking for the petrified wings.

"What did you find out?"

"They got *Sili* locked in a room with the welcome party," he informed me with a scowl.

"Fuck."

"Yeah, I scoped it out earlier with Sam. Their voices were floating through one of the windows. West side of the building, far end."

"Let's get her before she ends up in chains." The moment we made it out of here, I would tell her about my theory of her connection with Clan Sira.

Random men sat around metal tables eating, while some of them lined up with bowls like a soup kitchen. The walls to one side were lined with metal platform bed frames covered in weapons. *Shit; we weren't going to be able to take them all.*

I signaled to Reed to move behind the stack of barrels ahead of us. Gunshots and laughter went off outside, catching the attention of the men at the table. Reed and I both moved past them and made it to the room where they were holding *Sili*.

My ears strained to listen, but I didn't hear a sound. The door suddenly slammed open with a crash, bouncing against the wall next to us. Reed and I scooted further into the shadows and slowed our breathing. The sound of footsteps faded and we gave it another five minutes before peering around the wall. I signaled for Reed to move on the count of three. We both entered the room at the ready as we came up to a scene we didn't expect.

Well, after what the bloodsucker told us, I should have.

A woman lay on top of a table, her innards spilled over the side from a large open cavity sliced down the middle. All her limbs had been cut off, leaving only her head and torso. The skin on her face had been removed, exposing the muscle underneath. There was a drain beneath her to capture the blood. Looking around, there were axes, saws, and leather gloves hanging on the wall. The body hadn't started to smell yet, so she must be freshly mutilated.

This was a butcher's room.

"Travis, what you got going for dinner today?" came a voice from the other side of the wall.

"Slim pickings around here, Lawrence, so Slim got picked." The men cackled as the sound of flames roared, right before the sound of sizzling took over.

"Fucking hell," Reed whispered.

"Didn't you just fuck her last week, Travis?"

"Yeah, her used-up cunt wasn't even that good."

Reed and I both quickly exited the room and moved along the next line of shadows of the wall. *Sili, we're coming for you.* Soon enough, another room appeared before us, farther away from the main activity near the soup kitchen.

"Fuck, this is taking too long," Reed complained.

I agreed. Straightening, I let out an exhale and

opened the door. Lifting my rifle up, I cursed under my breath when all I saw were blood splatters covering the wall.

"What the..." Reed started.

"*Sili*. Are you in here?" There were dead bodies scattered about the room, some with their heads detached. A good number of them were half-naked with their pants undone. I was getting more furious by the minute, until a small body slowly climbed to her feet behind the wooden headboard of a bed frame in the middle of the room.

"Th-they should have listened," she said quietly.

"*Sili*? Shit." Lowering my gun, I ran to her. She was covered in blood from head to toe, but it didn't stop me from pulling her into a tight embrace.

"I didn't want to go out there. I knew you guys would find me soon enough. I waited. I was supposed to wait, right?"

"Yeah, Fitri. You did good." Reed's eyes were still assessing the damage she dealt.

At least she didn't die this time.

"Come on, let's grab a vehicle and get out of here!" I pulled *Sili* from her hiding spot and all three of us moved.

The smell of cooking flesh and charcoal began to fill the air, a lot of the men had made their way outside to get closer to the food.

One of the windows along the wall was open, metal crates sat right beside it. I signaled toward the location and pushed *Sili* forward first. She climbed the crates, slipping every so often but made it out the window. Reed went next as I watched their backs, in case anyone returned from the grill.

When it came to my turn, the window was almost too small for me. Wriggling, it scraped my skin, and my foot accidentally kicked something, landing it with a loud crash.

"What the hell was that?" came a voice from outside.

"It came from that side."

"Grab the guns."

Fuck! I landed outside and we all ran toward the parked vehicles. Gunner and Samuel whistled, masks in hand, and waved us over to one of the larger cars.

"This shit isn't going to fit us all. *Sili*, get in," I told her.

"What about you?"

"Just get in!" I commanded.

Shoving her, she fell into the back passenger side. I slammed the door and slapped the top of the hood to tell Samuel and Gunner to go. Tires squealed, throwing dust behind them.

"They're taking our shit!"

"Reed!" I yelled.

We both hopped on motorcycles and kick-started them. The one I chose took a few more kicks than it should, killing time I didn't have to spare and aggravating the wound in my calf. When the roar of the engine came on, we both rode and caught up to the other guys.

Bullets sprayed our direction, but we zig-zagged around the smaller buildings until we reached the front sliding gate.

The guards who stood there shot at us, but Samuel slammed on the gas and crashed right through, taking the damn gate with him as well as running over the guards.

Once the sound of gunshots faded in the distance, Samuel slammed on his brakes to let the gate fall off the grill of the vehicle. Reversing, he took a hard right and went up to higher ground with Reed and I following suit. Just when we thought we'd lost them, other motorcycles could be heard right behind us.

Keeping the throttle steady, I lifted my rifle and shot, hitting one of the riders, knocking his bike against the guy behind him.

Reed did the same but missed, letting two of the guys gain on us. One slammed into me, knocking me off my bike and against a tree. Reed slammed into him, taking him down right before he jumped off his bike and drove a blade into the enemy's chest again and again.

Two bikes followed Samuel, leaving one biker left with us. He skidded to a stop with his bike, letting it fall, coming up behind Reed. Gritting my teeth through the pain in my calf and back, I threw a knife into his side.

He screamed, but didn't fall. Instead, he turned

and threw a fist at my face, taking me to the ground. His body slammed into mine as Reed wrapped his arms around his neck to try and pull him off. An elbow to the face stunned Reed, knocking him to the side.

I threw a knee into his chest, dislodging him enough for me to reach into my right boot. *Shit, I already threw it.*

I didn't see the guy stand up, but I did see him pull a fucking blade the size of my damn lower leg out from a strap around his pants. With lightning speed, he brought it up and slammed it down across my right knee, shattering the bone, slicing halfway through.

I screamed in agony, rousing Reed, who pulled a pistol and let off a few shots, shooting the enemy right through his neck and head. His body fell on top of me, sending the pain all the way up my thigh.

While Reed pushed him off, our vehicle returned, and I could hear *Sili* screaming for me as my injuries throbbed with every pump of my blood.

"Was that the last one?" Gunner questioned.

"Yeah, I got him in the head," Reed answered. "How about you guys?"

"Ran those fuckers over, twice," Samuel answered.

"Eliseo, are you okay?" *Sili's* hands were all over me. The moment she touched my injury, I screamed bloody murder again. "Oh my god!"

"Shit, grab him and get in the car. Ditch the bikes," Gunner said it like it was a piece of cake. I fucking felt like I was dying here.

All the guys got their hands on me, and all I could think about was the pain amplifying, becoming too much for me to handle.

"On three," Samuel commanded. "One. Two."

"Ahhhh!"

They moved swiftly and expertly, throwing me into the back as Reed and *Sili* climbed in beside me on either side. The front doors slammed shut, and we started our trek back home, leaving the woods and hills behind. Each damn bump in the road made me groan, sending shooting pain through my limb. *Sili* situated my head onto her lap and pushed my hair back from my face gently, her hands still covered in blood.

"Dammit, Eliseo," she said accusingly, with a hint of tears.

"Fuck, it wasn't part of the plan, you feel me?"

"When does anything go to plan? Story of our damn life," Reed's statement made us all chuckle as Samuel pulled onto the paved road, saving me from some pain.

My right leg throbbed, but I could still feel my toes. That was a good sign.

"We need to get you cleaned up so you don't get infected," *Sili* said quietly.

"The only body of water we know about is the lake," Reed told the rest of the guys.

"Fitri, you need to wash off the blood yourself.

We'll do a quick pit stop, but we have to keep on moving, in case there's anyone else after us." Samuel drove faster as *Sili* opened the back window, cooling my skin down.

"I'll be okay. I'm just worried about Eliseo," she admitted quietly.

"I get it. Let's get the old fucker patched up and head back," Samuel replied with sympathy.

"Did you get what you guys came for?" she asked Samuel.

It was Gunner who said, "Yeah, was the ugliest shit I've ever seen. It was half mummified and almost disintegrated the moment we tried to pry a piece of it off. Smelled like shit, too."

When Samuel finally pulled the vehicle to a stop, one of the guys ripped the hem of their shirt, handing it to me. "Bite down on it, old man."

Fuck.

The moment they lifted me up, I thought my teeth were going to shatter from the intensity in which my jaws were clamped.

I was spread out over the grass as *Sili* stripped naked and jumped into the pool.

"We're running out of spare clothes. You think she's willing to go back naked?"Gunner whispered, looking after her form. Reed slapped Gunner upside the head. "Ow! Fuck you. You know you were thinking the same thing, Reed."

"I'm right fucking here, you perverted assholes," I gritted out.

"Us? Weren't you the one raw-dogging her on

the damn ground for all of us to hear? Rubbing it in our damn faces," Reed sneered.

If I wasn't in so much pain, I'd beat the shit out of this asshole.

Sili came back, dripping wet, looking like a damn goddess, and I was reminded of the fact that not only did I not deserve her, I might not have a leg left after this.

"Take mine." Samuel took off his shirt and threw it toward her. She caught it midair and put it on, making Reed and Gunner groan in disappointment.

"Bunch of assholes," I mumbled.

Sili still had a worried expression on her face as she stared at my leg. I didn't know what to tell her; I was worried, too.

"Give me a rag and some water. Who's got water left?" she asked as she pulled a blade from her pants and began to cut mine at thigh level. Every jostle made my eyes want to roll back from the pain.

"Here," Reed's voice came in muffled as my body began to heat up.

The moment the water dropped on my open wound, fatigue set in. My mind got dizzy as *Sili* tried to clean and dry my wound, pushing it, sending an insurmountable amount of pain through my body until everything started to go numb... right before everything went black.

12

FITRI

Eliseo passing out was a small blessing. I hated seeing him in immense pain. We wrapped his leg up as best as we could to try and prevent him from moving it so much.

I couldn't stop thinking about the last compound and the remaining five malnourished women there. I was introduced to the 'flock' as if I was to become one of them—a shell of their former selves.

The men were kind—too kind. From their touches, to the way their eyes tried to stare through my clothes as if surveying the quality of new merchandise.

When they brought me to the room with a single bed in the middle, I knew it was coming. It happened all too often. I was ready for them, but they weren't ready for me.

Was it wrong of me to feel elation after slaughtering them all? I was still riding the high The moment I saw the boys—my heart hammering from the adrenaline rush. The way their warm blood tasted on my lips felt like a new sensation despite having fragmented memories of it. New or not, it unlocked something I'd never felt before. I was too afraid to confront it, and was glad we had to move quickly to get out of the compound.

Putting my hand on Eliseo's clammy forehead, I could feel his body temperature rising and my concern for him grew alongside it.

We stopped for the night with a quarter tank of fuel left. The men found a good hiding spot for us to make camp, and now we were resting up. My body aches had all but disappeared, my mind tumultuous with what other mishap we might run into tomorrow. Expect the worst and hope for the best.

Kissing his forehead, I stared at the blood seeping through the makeshift bandage. He was losing too much. Lying beside him, my hand caressed his chest while I silently prayed for a solution. Eliseo was a vital part of this team and seeing him like this...

"We're running out of fabric," Reed stated.

"I know," I answered quietly, unsettled.

"He needs to change his bandages."

"How much longer until we make it back?" I tried to digress, wanting to hear good news to ease my soul.

"If nothing goes wrong, maybe another few days. We have to take the roundabout way in case we have a tail. The last group didn't grow to their size without good reason. To have a large collection of vehicles? They've been traveling far to collect the numbers they had. Who knows if we'll run into one of their groups on a supply run," Samuel explained.

"What if—" I started as bad-case scenarios ran through my mind. Flashes of biting into Elijah's neck and the way the blood tasted back at the last compound flitted behind my eyes. I was changing. Something was changing inside of me.

"What if what?" Gunner asked.

Turning and sitting up, I ran my fingers through my hair. The fear of them condemning me still debilitated me at times. I had to remind myself we had been through so much together already, and they would never leave me behind.

"What if... I'm a vampire?" I said weakly, hoping they didn't hear me, and at the same time, hoping they did.

"Impossible," Reed retorted immediately without thought. "I've run across too many of them to know that much. Could you have vampire blood in you? Possible. But I haven't seen you go off on any killing sprees when you've gotten hungry. You're still eating normal food like the rest of us."

"Reed's right. After the shit we've been through? Hell no. You're still Fitri," Gunner said with a finality.

My eyes watered over their acceptance. *What if I was still changing, though?* None of us knew the actual process, because none of us had been privy to this kind of information, living behind community walls. And the crazy doctor wasn't forthcoming with any of his intel, not unless it benefited him.

"What if I slowly become like them?" I asked, wanting to hint to the team at the direction of my thoughts.

Samuel stood up and added another piece of wood to the fire. Embers danced around the flames. "Even if you did, you think Eliseo is going to let anything happen to you? He'd massacre everything in his path. So would we. You're part of the team. If we have to leave shit behind, we will. It's not like we haven't done it before. Hell, you were surviving out there on your own before you arrived."

Letting out a sigh, I placed my head in my hands. *What if Eliseo wasn't there to protect me anymore? What if this infection got the best of him and poisoned his body slowly, killing him in silence?*

My heart constricted at the thought, the pain almost palpable. With a stuttering breath, I was taken back to a moment in the past.

"It's only been you, Faheema. You know that," he whispered. *"Come on, just a kiss."*

Maverick's hands rubbed my arms as I rested my face against his chest. Father would never approve of this. I was too young.

"Father would kill me," I told him.

"Would he? Nah. You're his only daughter. Not going to happen. Come on," he coaxed as he tilted my head up to place a chaste kiss on my lips. "He's not going to find out."

I had never felt about a boy the way I did him. He had always been there around my family with his dimpled smiles and his chivalry. Maybe Mother would approve. Maybe it would be okay.

The smell of burnt flesh and blood imprinted in my nostrils, reminding me of exactly what happened at my once-home community. The bloodshed and hate pushed me to the brink of drastic fear that Maverick ultimately became a part of the casualties around me. I didn't know if he was alive. If he was, he would have never forgiven me.

It was my fault for getting hopes up for a future never meant to be mine. Am I setting myself up for disappointment again with Eliseo? My heart ached fiercely, I wanted to tear it out. I didn't realize I was shuddering until Reed sat down beside me and wrapped his arm around my shoulder, pulling me into his strong embrace.

"He'll be alright," he comforted. "The old fucker is too stubborn to die."

I laughed a little. He was probably right.

Reed's hand went to the back of my neck, massaging it, and I found myself feeling exhausted. How long had we been awake? With all we had gone through, I was surprised we were all still sitting upright.

I could hear the other men's snores across the fire and it influenced my own mood. My eyes wanted to flutter closed the more Reed made me melt into him with his special hands.

"Fitri..." he whispered against my hair, and my body molded against his further, seeking his heat. Memories of the way Eliseo woke me the last time we made rest beneath the canopy of trees floated behind my lids. I spasmed between my legs, wishing there was something to fill the void, to take my mind off things.

Reed kissed my neck slowly, traveling down to my shoulder, and my heart skipped a beat. His hands moved from the back of my neck, down to the underside of my breast over my shirt, making me pant. My nipples were hardened against the fabric, the cold of the night not helping.

We shouldn't be doing this, I mentally chastised myself. *But why does it feel so good? Why does it feel like it was supposed to be this way?* Ever since Eliseo had his way with me, my libido had a mind of its own. I licked my lips, reminiscing the metallic taste on my tongue. I was never one to freely offer myself to men, so what was happening to me?

Has Eliseo's dominant ways conditioned me? If so, I didn't hate it. But it couldn't be right. How often had women been forced into positions for years, still fighting against it to the very end? No, there was more at play beyond my comprehension at the moment. My mind was currently clouded by the warmth enveloping me and the heated trail left behind Reed's lips on my skin.

He kissed across my jaw lightly until he fisted my hair and slammed his lips against mine. Despite his dominance, his kisses differed from Eliseo's. There was a rhythm to the way his tongue danced inside my mouth calling me to sweetly submit, but not too quickly. I found myself leaning in, wanting more.

Eliseo groaned, and the spell was broken. I pulled away, disoriented and flummoxed. My lips were swollen from Reed's kiss as my tongue poked out for another forbidden taste of him. The air around us was thick as we both sat there, breathing heavily.

"If you don't stop looking at me like that, I'm going to fuck you right here next to him," Reed threatened with a gravely voice. I didn't mean to affect him like this... like the way he affected me with his solid presence. How could it feel criminal and marvelous at the same time? I bit my lip, my mind warring within itself as Reed's pupils dilated, staring at my lips.

"*Sili*, no. *Sili*..." I jumped away from Reed, bumping into Eliseo's arm. Turning, I found him in a fever dream, his eyes flitting back and forth behind his closed lids.

Cradling his face, I leaned in. Reed reluctantly

left us as I continued to give Eliseo my full attention, trying hard to tamp down the emotions Reed pulled out from me.

"Come back to me," I pleaded. "Open your eyes, Eliseo."

His eyelids fluttered at my request, and hope bloomed in my chest. "Eliseo, please."

"*Sili*," he whispered. He wasn't waking up, but it seemed he could hear me according to his responses. "I need to tell her..."

Tell her? Tell me? Tell me what?

"Eliseo!" I kissed him all over his face and massaged his shoulders, trying to stimulate him into awareness. What I really wanted to do was shake him until he opened his damn eyes.

He groaned and my trepidation morphed into anger—anger over the shitty hand life dealt me. Lost in my emotions over the injustices in my life, I straddled Eliseo and brought us skin to skin. I needed him. I needed him desperately to keep me sane when all my mind wanted to do was break. He was the strength I didn't know I had—the only one who saw me for who I was and what I had to offer besides my body. He trained me, built my confidence. *He couldn't leave me now.*

I grabbed his face and firmly kissed him, invading his mouth with my tongue, needing him to fulfill the longing Reed left in me earlier.

He groaned, still under the influence of sleep. Without warning, his hands crawled up my leg and grabbed my hips, grinding me against him.

"You're going to have to wake me up like this every time, *Sili*," he mumbled groggily. I laugh-cried against his lips.

"As much as I love your little body taking advantage of me, can you get off for a minute? My leg hurts like a motherfucking bitch."

Still laughing, I gave him one last kiss before climbing off. We both stared at his right leg and noticed the blood pooling out of the bandage had multiplied.

Eliseo cursed beneath his breath.

Worry threatened to overtake me until an idea popped in and stopped it. Crawling down, I bit my wrist, groaning in both pain and a hint of pleasure against my pierced skin. Pulling my blade out of my boot, I cut away Eliseo's bandages before placing my wrist above the wound, I squeezed it with my other hand to release more blood. I watched with rapt fascination as my blood dripped inside.

"What the hell are you doing?" Eliseo bit out. "Are you out of your damn mind, *Sili*?"

He tried to kick me away, but I slammed my hand down on his left leg, holding it in place. *Come on, come on. If my blood heals, it should heal him too, right?* My eyes prick with tears of hope.

"Do you feel anything? Is anything happening?" I asked Eliseo frantically.

"Woman, if you don't get your ass up here right now, I'mma feel more than pissed off you did that," he grimaced.

My skin itched as it stitched itself back together, sealing my life source back where it belonged. I covered my face as I sobbed while my hope shattered. *I couldn't even do something as simple as heal the person I cared about. What good were these stupid abilities?*

"*Sili*, get your ass up here," he commanded.

Climbing up, I nestled myself against him, crying silent tears as he rubbed my back in comfort. A small laugh escaped over the messed up situation. I should be comforting him right now, not the other way around.

He kissed the top of my head, pulled me across his body so I could use him as a mattress. We laid there until we both succumbed to much-needed sleep.

The next day, we ran out of gas a few miles away. Of course, this would happen. Eliseo had been fully awake thus far, limping along as we trekked the rest of the way back home on foot.

"*Sili*, I need to tell you something," he threw out of the blue.

"Yeah?" I took the initiative and threw his arm over my shoulder to help relieve some of the weight on his right leg. He kissed my forehead in appreciation as we continued to follow the other guys ahead of us.

"There was a prisoner at the last compound. A bloodsucker. Female. She's the one the wings belonged to," he continued conversationally.

"Okay… why are you telling me this?" I asked curiously, unsure of where this was going.

"One of the men was raping her. I killed him, thinking it was you. When he fell to the side, I saw her leg was getting cut off."

I was not surprised. They were fucking cannibals.

"What happened after, filled in some of the missing pieces to the puzzle."

I still wasn't getting what he was putting down. "What puzzle? What the hell are you talking about, Eliseo? You're not making any sense."

"Her leg healed right in front of my eyes, *Sili,*" he emphasized.

I stopped walking and so did he. We stared at one another intently before I found my voice. "S-she healed? Like me?"

"Yeah, like you," he said much softer. "She said she was from Clan Sira—they fly among other things. Do you know anything about them?"

Scrunching my nose, I tried hard to remember. "I remember being a prisoner with Clan Cirse. I was promptly marked for execution." Flashes of the memory played in my mind clearer. "They called me a hybrid."

"I figured as much. Your blood has to hail from the same clan. But I haven't seen you in a feeding frenzy so it reiterates half of you being human. The only thing I've seen you eat are vegetable sand-wiches back in Ashborne. It would explain why you don't show the same characteristics as the vampires we've come across—just similarities. How did you stumble across Clan Cirse if their territory is far to the north?"

I shrugged before we started walking again. Eliseo's hand rubbed my shoulder to ease my mind. It was full of so many questions and not enough answers. But this was closer to anything I could piece myself—one of my biological parents was a vampire from Clan Sira. Where was my human parent from? Were they still alive? Should I be out looking for them?

Do they even want to be found? They got rid of me, didn't they?

"*Sili*, let's get home first," Eliseo directed. "Whatever is going on in your head needs to be planned out, okay? Let's not rush into things before we can get enough information."

He was right. I was too high on emotions again.

"Alright guys! We're about a mile out," Samuel hollered back.

"Thank fuck, I'm tired of walking," Gunner groaned.

"Quit being a pussy. It's just a mile," Reed countered and they shoved each other playfully.

Their spirits were up. We were so close to home. I was filled with renewed energy. We ran out of food a day ago with just water left. We had been sharing and sipping along the way.

The last mile went by quickly. I could tell Eliseo

had been trying to tough it out with the way he leaned more of his weight on me toward the end.

The guards at the top of Ashborne's towers on either side of the gate pointed their guns at us, but the familiar sight still brought me comfort.

"Hey! It's Samuel!" he called out with a wave. "I got Reed, Gunner, Eliseo, and the kid with us. Open up!"

"Fuck, where the hell have you been? We didn't see you leave. We assumed you were all dead a week after your disappearance." The guy at the front rolled his hand in the air and the gates creaked open slowly.

"Fuck, home sweet home," Gunner grumbled as we all walked through the gates together as a unit.

We crossed the threshold with relieved sighs but my shoulders were still tense.

"Call the doctor!" I hollered before Eliseo could stop me. He gave me a glare, and I glared right back. He was not coming back home simply to die from some stupid infection. I refused to let it happen.

"Welcome back, gentleman! Glad to see you've decided to return." The governor, Sergio, greeted us with a smile more false than this farce of an existence. But I had to admit, the familiar smells of grass and manure made me homesick. A few of the other residents began to come out of their homes to see what the ruckus was all about.

"You've brought me something to play with, I see," the crazy doctor laughed as he parted through the growing crowd.

"Samuel!" Hannah launched herself into Samuel's arms, kissing him and doing more than she should in the middle of the town. Samuel laughed and pulled her away from the crowd without removing his lips from her. They wouldn't come back up for air for a while.

"Eliseo, Eliseo. Seems you've run into some trouble out there, hmm?" Crazy Otis spoke again. "Hopefully the other guy looks worse."

"The other guys are fucking dead," Eliseo stated flatly.

"Even better." Crazy Otis rubbed his hands together, staring at the infected wound on Eliseo's leg. He looked too excited for his own good. "Well, come on, I'll fix you right up—"

"In the house," I cut in. I was not trusting him in his secret bunker, not with this. I needed him where I, and everyone else, could see him.

He stared at me for a few moments and threw his head back in a maniacal cackle. "Alright. Alright. Take him to my home and put him on the table. I'll be right there. I need to grab some of my... equipment from the bunker."

His eyes sparkled as he spoke of his tools, right before he turned and walked away.

"*Sili*. What the hell? I don't want crazy Otis near me," Eliseo hissed as we walked past the crowd, who continued to stare from me to Eliseo and our close proximity.

"You're a crazy old fool to not want to get your leg checked out," I countered. "You know he's the only doctor we have here!"

Was he really going to put his life at risk for stubbornness and paranoia? So what if Otis was a lunatic on good days? It was better than nothing. He definitely wouldn't last another trip out there in search of another person with medical experience. Ashborne's crazy doc was it.

I dragged Eliseo until we made it to the doctor's house above ground. There was a small coating of dust in his living room from disuse, and doubt began to crawl into me. *Eliseo might die from the dirtiness of this damn house.* Maybe this was a bad idea after all.

Before I could change my mind and leave with Eliseo, the doc came in with his apron and gloves donned. Reed and Gunner followed behind him distrustfully—they were watching him, too.

Their presence put me a little more at ease... until I saw someone else come in with his tools. Scalpels, knives, hacksaws, bandages, and a whole lot more.

"Fuck this shit," Eliseo blurted out, trying to pull me out of the house.

Reed placed a hand on his chest to stop him with a scowl. "Your leg is fucking infected. I can smell that shit from here."

"It's fucking fine!" Eliseo snapped.

"Suck up your pride and get this over with," Gunner retorted before shifting his gaze toward crazy Otis. "We'll make sure the doc don't try nothing else but what he needs to do."

"Now why would you say that?" the doctor grinned as his makeshift assistant left the house without looking back.

Gunner turned around with his arms crossed in a defensive stance. "Because if you fuck this up, you're not getting the shit you sent us out to find," he gritted out.

The doctor snarled and slammed his hand down on the counter of his kitchen. His face went from pissed, murderous, to a maniacal smile in mere minutes. "Have it your way."

He turned to Eliseo and his eyes went wild. I took a step back with Eliseo, unsure of what to expect.

"Put him on the table," the doctor instructed, confident I was going to do what he said.

Looking at each other for confirmation, the boys and I lifted him through all his curses and kicks. Gunner and Reed physically held him down when he started throwing fists, dodging his attempts at stopping them.

I grabbed his face and kissed him firmly, forcing him to concentrate on me and me alone. The tension ever so slowly left his body as his hands threaded through my hair, kissing me back just as passionately.

I ended our liplock, panting, placing my forehead against his. "Please, Eliseo. *I need you.*"

"Fucking hell, *Sili*. Dammit!" He slammed the back of his head onto the table and ran a frustrated hand down his face.

The doc shoved me aside rudely and leaned into Eliseo's ear, whispering something I couldn't hear. Eliseo glared at him.

"Reed give me something to bite on," he barked. "Gunner, get me some fucking whiskey."

The boys did as he ordered, moving around the doctor's home while I continued to stare at crazy Otis, watching his every move. If he tried anything other than what needed to be done, I would bleed him out alive.

The doctor looked at me with a demented smile before going to his tools gleefully.

I didn't catch Reed leaving the house, but he reentered through the front door with two belts in hand. He folded one and shoved it in Eliseo's mouth while creating a tourniquet around Eliseo's right thigh near his groin, making him groan in pain.

Gunner came back with two bottles of whiskey, one in each hand. When Eliseo spotted him, he spit out the belt and said, "Give me some of that shit."

"You got it, old man." Gunner poured a few gulps down Eliseo's throat before shoving the belt back where it belonged.

Crazy Otis sneered as he grabbed one of the bottles from Gunner's hand, opened it, and poured it all over the wound. Eliseo screamed bloody murder behind the leather belt, the veins on his temples and neck popping out.

The doc cackled, shoved the bottle back into Gunner's chest, and grabbed his scalpel to cut around the skin above his knee. My hands grabbed Eliseo's fist when he tried to throw a punch at the doctor's head. I kissed his knuckles to calm him down as he threw his other arm over his face to cut off visual from what Otis was doing to him.

The sound of metal clattering on metal made us all jerk our heads as Crazy Otis grabbed a bigger knife to cut through the muscle and tendons still intact around the bone.

"Whiskey," the doc called out. Gunner handed it to him.

More was poured over the wound, washing away the fresh gush of blood. Eliseo turned his upper torso to hide his face against my belly. I caressed his back, praying it would be over soon... But it was only the beginning as the doc climbed onto the table with a hacksaw, placing the serrated edge against the exposed bone.

"Hold him well, dearie," he said to me with a psychotic smile right before he began sawing.

Eliseo spit out the leather and screamed in agony. The townspeople who had accumulated around the open doorway of the doctor's home all screamed with him, some covering their eyes and briskly removing themselves. Why were they here to begin with if they couldn't handle the sight?

The sound of someone hurling outside made me lift my lip in disgust. I was infuriated by the community wanting to use Eliseo as part of their entertainment. My eyes burned with retribution as I stared at the doctor's glistening forehead, his arms and entire body putting forth full effort to cut Eliseo's leg off.

"Get out of here folks, there's nothing more to see." Reed tried to corral the remaining crowd away, and I was grateful.

Gunner took a swig of the whiskey, his skin getting pallid as he stared at the doctor's brutal handiwork.

Snap!

Eliseo groaned against my stomach and I pulled him in tighter against me.

"Ah, there we are," the doctor exclaimed before hopping off the table with his bloodied saw, tossing it onto his other table full of tools haphazardly. He wiped his hands over his apron and looked over his shoulder at me with a smirk. "My dear, are you good with a needle? I do hope so, because Eliseo wouldn't want my hands on him after this."

I audibly swallowed as I caressed the back of Eliseo's head before casting my gaze down at him. His body was starting to go slack against me from exhaustion. I was conflicted. I didn't want to cause him further pain than he had already gone through... but if he passes out, he wouldn't feel it, right?

The sound of glass hitting the counter made my head snap up to see Gunner. "Fitri, do it. I got him."

I bit my bottom lip and nodded, shakily walking toward the doctor's table of instruments. Otis came up behind me, making the hairs on the back of my neck stand as he leaned in to whisper, "I have full faith you'll make it through this. Pain probably arouses you—you seem like the type. If it gets too much, old Otis can take care of non-medical needs, too."

I frowned and elbowed him away from me, but he dodged, snickering as he walked away with one of the bottles of whiskey.

"What the fuck did he say to you?" Reed growled.

"Nothing."

Grabbing the needle and spool of thread, I made my way back to Eliseo on the table. Reed walked over to the counter, grabbed the other bottle, and handed it to me to sanitize the needle.

Taking a deep breath, I pulled one of my knives out and cut the thread. Looking to the guys for courage, they both stood on either side of Eliseo's upper torso, ready to hold him down.

Leaning over him, the first stitch went smoothly, Eliseo fading into unconsciousness. The smell of his blood close to my nares made my mouth water and I shook my head, endeavoring to stay focused. In and out the needle went, pulling his flesh together to suture the wound around the bone. The doc left enough flesh behind to create a meaty cushion around the bottom of the amputated bone. Toward the end of my sewing, I was drunk on his scent and needed to sit down to regain my bearings. Breathing through my mouth, I tied off the thread and sliced it. Leaning my hands against the table, I tried to catch my breath and slow my heart.

"You alright, Fitri?" Reed asked with worry.

"Hey, we got it, go get some rest," Gunner added.

Maybe they were right. Maybe I was just tired from our trip. "I-I'll see you guys later. Let me know if anything changes, or if he wakes up, okay?"

"Yeah, we got it," Reed answered softly. "Get some rest."

I nodded and walked toward the small crowd still milling about the front of the doctor's house.

"Don't you guys have anything better to do?" I barked out, maddened they were still here. Some of the crowd dispersed with fear in their eyes as I approached them, some stayed with stubborn curiosity.

Shouldering my way past the remnants, I went home. Standing in front of my door, I reached in my hair for a pin, only to realize, I hadn't worn my hair up since we were gone. Slamming my head against the door, I slowed my breathing, trying to calm myself.

"Fitri!" Gunner's voice came from behind me.

When his hand touched my shoulder, I turned around and buried my face into his chest, frustrated over everything life threw at us during this journey.

"Hey, it's alright. Shhh." He rubbed my back and led me to his house, gently placing me on his couch beside him.

"Wash up. Then rest. I'll be back to check on you," he assured me.

"What about you?" He wasn't looking too good during the surgery, swigging whiskey every twenty minutes. At least his color was coming back.

He smiled gently before standing up and kissing me on the forehead. "I like that you worry about me, but I'm alright."

I watched as he left the house without looking back or saying another word. I was too tired to attempt to decipher what he meant. Standing up from the couch, I walked to his kitchen and turned the sink on. It sputtered aggressively before finally giving me a steady flow.

My hands were still coated in Eliseo's blood. My heart pounded as I brought it to the front of my lips, slowly turning it around.

Still drunk on his scent, I stuck a blood-coated finger into my mouth and savored his taste, humming in appreciation. I throbbed between my legs, missing his cock, and I choked back a cry at how messed up this was. I shoved my hands under the running water, scrubbing until the welts on my skin began to bleed, going down the drain with everything else.

Wiping them on my pants to dry, I went back to the couch, kicking off my boots and pants, falling to the side. I buried my hands under my head, letting the exhaustion of the day finally take me over.

I3

ELISEO

"Here, let me help you."

"Fuck this! I don't need your fucking help. I got it!" I yelled, right before I fell on my ass out of bed.

"You're such a cranky asshole!" *Sili* screamed back, rushing toward me to help me back onto the edge of the bed.

I flopped backward and ran a hand down my face, then covered it with my arms. This was exactly why I didn't want her to do this shit. Why did she have to go and get crazy Otis? He had been dying to cause me misery from the moment I met him.

It was probably why he sent us out on the stupid mission to begin with. He wanted us all to die and never come back for whatever nefarious plans he had. In the end, it was a win-win for him because we did come back—*with the shit he requested.*

"What am I here for?" *Sili* sighed. "I'm here for *you*, you cranky bastard."

She climbed on top of me and pushed my arms away from my face, rubbing her cute little nose against mine. She melted my damn heart, even when I was being an *extra*, irate asshole these days.

"You're just a little frustrated," she whispered. "I can help with that, too."

She slowly kissed me and my anger dissipated with every swipe of her lips against mine. Her sexual appetites have elevated lately, and I perceptively questioned why. But the moment it crossed my mind to ask, she had a way of distracting me. Like now. Her hand ran down my chest seductively and into the waist of my pants, stroking me to life.

I groaned at her tease and flipped her over, losing balance a bit since I couldn't seem to remember I only had one knee.

She chuckled and pushed my pants the rest of the way down, letting my dick spring forth and slap her naked inner thigh. Grinding against her, another groan slipped out over how wet she was. She never did accumulate panties again after our trip, and I was glad for it.

Well, not when we were around the other guys. The hunger in their eyes was a growing irritation, but then I remembered I was just an old bastard with one leg, and she continued to *choose* to be with *me*.

Damn this line of thinking. *One fucking leg.* It was making my dick go soft until she dug her claws into my shoulders, pulled me in, and bit me on the neck. My erection grew at such a high rate, I became lightheaded as the blood rushed through my body into her hungry mouth.

She confessed the smell of my blood got her drunk with need and lust after the guys dropped me off back home post-surgery. Both she and I knew she was evolving again, but it didn't stop me from protecting her and providing her what she needed. In fact, I swelled with pride.

No one had to know. As long as we kept it to ourselves, everything should go on the way it always did.

"Eliseo," she moaned against my neck lustfully. "Your blood is like a drug to me. It tastes so damn good and makes me so horny." My cock strained toward her, wetting her inner thigh with precum.

When her tongue lapped up the puncture wound, she caressed my face, turned it, and shared the taste of blood in my mouth. It was erotic, and I was a sucker for everything that was Fitri. Her other hand grabbed my shaft firmly and shoved it between her legs with ease.

Thrusting slowly inside of her, she gasped in my mouth. "Look at how well you stretch around me, taking my cock."

I cursed under my breath with the next thrust. I gave her all my passion through our kiss, broadcasting how much she meant to me. But *Sili* had other plans as she flipped us over with her inhuman strength and rode my cock like we were both going to get executed tomorrow.

"I need to feel you deeper," she whined, throwing her head back. "I need you so badly."

"Shit, *Sili*. You can have whatever the fuck you want, especially if it's my dick inside of you."

I grabbed her hips to slow her down, but she was too strong when she was lost like this. Beautiful in her rage and her passion, she ground her clit against me until she cried out in pleasure, clutching my cock with a vice grip and forcing me over the edge with her.

She fell limp on top of me, panting, exhausted, and stretching like a damn feline as her hands continued to roam my body, secretly begging for more.

"*Sili*, we should get up." As much as I wanted to lounge around with her, I needed to train with my damn makeshift prosthetic the guys got me.

"Why? I like where I am," she complained, heavily breathing against my chest.

It appeared during our absence, Ashborne acquired a welder who was able to utilize the extra metal we had lying around to fabricate a false leg with a hinged knee and spring-hinged ankle. A supply run was made on my behalf by the guys to find a mannequin leg they could use to help the project along.

And who would have thought a damn tree lover and gardener would be the one to inform us of a way to acquire natural rubber to coat the inside of fabric to protect my stump?

Sili's tongue traced the wound on my neck and my dick twitched inside of her. I was conflicted with what needed to be done and what I wanted to do. "*Sili*, baby, we gotta get up. I want to be buried inside of you everyday, but I need to get used to this leg of mine."

She made an adorable sad sound and I chuckled, sitting up with her still on my lap with her arms around my neck. Kissing her chastely, I detached us and moved her to the side before reaching over for my prosthetic.

She placed her delicate hand on my chest as she bent over and grabbed it for me, teasing me with the sight of her glistening, swollen pussy lips. Slapping her on the ass, she yelped and handed it over with a mischievous smile.

"Get your ass ready for training. Stop trying to tempt me to stay here," I snapped with pseudo agitation.

"That's what I'm doing!" She laughed and walked to the other side of the room to find her pants and boots, bending at the waist seductively in front of me.

"Dammit woman," I growled in frustration, debating whether I should stay here and fuck the bratiness out of her.

We miraculously made it out of the house after another quick fuck over the arm of the couch, emerging in time for the community to start their day. With the additional residents we accumulated during our mission away, the mornings were louder than what they used to be with people hustling and bustling in the center of Ashborne.

Fitri walked a step ahead of me, bracing for any accidents as I descended the steps of my front porch. I had fallen a few times, but not lately. I appreciated her caution nonetheless. She was good for my cranky old soul. Honestly, I was surprised she put up with me on bad days.

"Eliseo! You down to train today?" Gunner called out, walking beside Samuel and Hannah.

Fitri waved shyly at Hannah, who enthusiastically squealed and ran toward her. My lips twitched in a suppressed smile. Hannah had taken to *Sili* since our return, glad her man made it back home alive and intact—unlike myself.

"Hey..." *Sili* said weakly and I nudged her. "Hey."

"Hey, girl!" Hannah yelled over, causing some of the residents nearby to turn and look.

Sili was wary about the friendship at first, but was slowly getting used to the idea. Hannah still didn't know all the details about her extra abilities, and we let *Sili* decide when it was the right time to expose her secrets. Margaret, the old lady *Sili* saved while she was running from Samuel, had also become one of her friends, gracing us with extra vegetables on our doorstep on random mornings.

"Fitri! I heard the last run was a trade and they got some new livestock. Did you see the baby lamb born the other week? It's so cute! Come on, let's go." Hannah pulled her away as *Sili* gave me a 'save me' look I ignored.

"Hey, man, how are you feeling?" Samuel asked as we hugged and slapped each other's backs in a masculine greeting.

"Fell off the damn bed today, but *Sili* fixed my mood," I chuckled. "Didn't fall on my face coming down the porch steps so I say that's progress."

"That's fucking great, man. You down to do some hand-to-hand this morning?"

"Maybe."

"Yo!" Reed ran up beside us with a wave. "I just saw the girls. Well, I mean I just saw Hannah pull Fitri away like there's free food offered somewhere."

"Baby lambs," I told him.

"Ah, okay. That makes sense. We training today?"

"Yeah, I gotta get used to this prosthetic and bearing the right amount of weight," I admitted.

"We got you, Eliseo," Reed replied. "We'll make sure to kick your ass."

I threw a punch and Reed dodged it. Gunner and Samuel cackled with mirth, not helping my sour mood one bit. Sparring used to invigorate me, knowing I could beat 'em all and teach them a thing or two. Seems like these days, they were teaching more times than not.

"You boys are still at it, huh? I haven't seen any of you take a break since you got back," Margaret smiled at us, pushing another wheelbarrow of manure down the street.

"No rest for the weary, Marge. You know this," I told her with a smile.

Her face crinkled up as she chuckled, lowering the wheelbarrow. "I was hoping to run by Fitri to let her know the new harvest was taken down to the shop in the town center. I know how much she loves those vegetable sandwiches of hers."

"Hannah took her that way about a few minutes ago," Gunner supplied.

"Ah, okay. Well, don't overdo it today, Eliseo. I wouldn't want poor Fitri to be sad over something as stupid as not controlling yourself."

I sheepishly hung my head as the men snickered behind me. I promised her I would do my best. Walking to our usual location, we got into position and started with moves requiring weight shifting and changing center of gravity. I sweated profusely as it tried to reacclimatize to putting pressure on the stump and compensatory strategies in order to perform moves I would have done with my eyes closed in the past. Time flew by. Gunner's stomach rumbled as he leaned to dodge one of my hits, and we laughed. Looking around, I realized the sun had started to set, and *Sili* hadn't come by to check up on me.

I patted the guys on the back and told them I would see them tomorrow as I made my way toward the center of the town. Entering the shop, I called out Oscar's name.

"Hey, Eliseo! What's happening? Looking good on that new leg. What can I do for ya?"

"Oscar, have you seen Fitri or Hannah?"

He leaned his forearm on the counter and frowned. "I don't think so. Were they supposed to come by for something? There isn't much left."

My heart rate spiked and I turned to leave, on a mission to find her. I almost ran into a man standing around looking at some of the fresh vegetables in the crates when someone called my name.

"Eliseo!"

"Not now Margaret, I'm busy," I mumbled, bent on finding *Sili*. With quick strides, my stump started to throb with the impact of my steps hitting the hard pavement. Margaret left her wheelbarrow, lifted her skirt in a jog, and caught up with me, wrapping her frail hand around my arm.

"I saw her," she blurted out, out of breath. My panic increased.

"Saw who?" I growled.

"Hannah," she panted. "The girl who hangs around Samuel. She was pulling Fitri toward the back of the west side of town. I saw her go down a doorway, but I didn't see them come out. I'm worried about her."

My anger rose. I still hated the old fucker for sending us out on the mission and then chopping my damn leg off. "Go find Samuel and tell him exactly what you told me. Go!"

She nodded frantically and jogged away.

I made a detour to my house and grabbed extra weapons before heading toward the one location I disliked about this place.

FITRI

"Can you come with me? I have something I need to do real quick," Hannah pleaded.

"Okay."

I should have made an effort to hang out more. I didn't think I would make a good friend. I wasn't used to connecting with other women, spending most of my previous life out on the run. Old Margaret never needed me for anything, but Hannah was the complete opposite.

"Thank you!" she squealed. "It will be quick, I promise."

I nodded, and she led me toward the far west side of Ashborne, near the back wall. When she reached for a rusted steel handle on the ground, I frowned in confusion. I thought the doc was the only one with a bunker. Maybe I was wrong. Curiosity got the better of me, as well as worry for Hannah being alone down here. I followed her down a metal ladder.

When we reached the bottom, the smell of moldy wetness hit my nostrils, tickling it with its pungency. Hannah didn't react, instead following the tunnel until it forked. Taking a right, she grabbed a torch off the wall and pulled out a lighter.

The flame glowed, casting dancing shadows behind us as she led me further until the wet smell started to dissipate.

"Where are we going?" I whispered.

"We're almost there."

The darkness of the tunnel began to disappear until we entered what looked like a concrete room from floor to ceiling. A few wooden crates lined the ground, but there was nothing else special about the place.

"I need to talk to someone really quick, and then we can be out of here," Hannah continued.

Following Hannah, she led me to another room which broke off into three tunnels. The sound of moans floated to my ear, making it twitch. The frequency was too low for Hannah's human ears to pick up. She chose the path straight ahead and continued forth with her torch, lighting the way. We passed at least three to four more segments of the tunnel until we came across another one that split into four.

Footsteps echoed from a distance, and I pushed Hannah behind me, going on high alert. The extent of the tunnel's vacancy made for bouncing sounds, I couldn't tell where it was originating. A glow entered from the left and my body tensed, preparing for whoever was about to join us. Hannah didn't say a word as we both held our breaths, until a dark cloaked figure came forth.

"Well, I didn't expect to see anyone else down here. Are you guys lost?" The masculine voice was deep and raspy at the end.

"No. We're heading toward the bunker to meet up with Otis," Hannah answered. *Otis? Why didn't she just say that in the first place?*

"Ah, you're in luck. I'm heading to see the doc myself. May I accompany you girls?" He took a few steps forward and lifted his head up, the flame of his own torch glowing against his marred skin beneath his hood.

His face had been burned on the left, one of his eyes clouded over. The other side of his lip hadn't been scarred, but there was a severe cut at the corner all the way to the side of his ear. Embarrassed from being caught staring, I turned away and let Hannah lead us again.

There was something entirely too familiar about this person, yet not. I couldn't put my finger on it. He was as tall as Reed, but not as broad, his skin deeply kissed by the sun, like Samuel. Maybe I had run into him in the past, but his face was not sparking any of my memories.

We all walked with some distance between us, the tunnel turning dark once more before it lit up again.

It was the crazed cackle letting us know we

were close, but the moan accompanying it was not what I expected at all.

"You're doing so well, don't fail me now, dearie," Otis cooed.

I froze in place when we entered the next tunnel chamber that doubled as a room and I saw what was happening in front of my eyes. Crazy Otis had his booted leg up against a metal spring frame leaning against the concrete wall. A woman was chained to it. Well, one of her arms since the other three limbs were scattered nearby on random carts and boxes. The smell of blood was overtaken by the smell of cauterized flesh as smoke billowed from her left thigh.

She moaned in pain again, her skin pallid as she shook against the metal bed frame. The most disturbing part? The doc was naked beneath his apron and boots, his dick at half-mast. A welder's mask sat on his head as he smiled down at what was left of the woman who looked dirty and malnourished. What was probably once blond hair now appeared brown at the singed ends.

Hannah retched beside me, and the stranger remained quietly stoic.

Otis looked over at his new company. "Ah, Hannah, my dear. You made it."

His eyes became wild as they looked over in my direction. I took a step back as the doctor came toward me.

"I-I'm so sorry Fitri," Hannah stuttered as betrayal lanced through me.

The doctor grabbed my arm and I saw red, reacting instinctively with a punch to his face. He dodged, and the stranger grabbed me from behind. *He was in on it, too? He acted like he didn't know Hannah earlier.*

"He threatened Samuel, Fitri. You have to understand! I never wanted to do this!" she cried, her sobs echoing around us.

Growling, I shut out her voice and kicked the doctor in the head, knocking his mask off, while twisting in the arms of the stranger and elbowing him right in the eye.

"Ahh!" His grip loosened around me enough for me to slip down and sweep his feet from under him, taking him to the ground. He grunted but jumped back up quickly, tackling me.

Hannah's light footsteps faded into the distance as she removed herself from the situation —too guilty to be a witness. *I trusted her and she backstabbed me. Samuel trusted her.* But she mentioned the doc was threatening him. I was so conflicted over how I should take this.

The doctor grabbed a blowtorch and rolled his neck before grinning down at us both.

"Get your ass up, Rick. You're embarrassing me." The doctor kicked the stranger, forcing him to roll away from me.

He leaned down and I grabbed his neck with both my legs, twisting and taking him down in a chokehold. The tunnel air cooled me as I held on tight. But the stranger pulled me off right as the sound of other bootsteps entered the tunnel.

Schwink. An arrow landed on the doctor's left thigh, making him roar in pain. I let go, but the stranger didn't, forcing me to my feet.

"Get your fucking hands off her," Gunner growled, pointing a crossbow right at his face, the one he picked up from his last supply run.

"Chill, my man. I was just helping her up," he placated calmly. "The doctor was going nuts, and I had to intervene. I accidentally walked in on all this."

He let me go, backed up, and put his hands in the air. *What the hell? Am I going crazy? Wasn't he with crazy Otis on this?*

"What the fuck, you bastards!" the doctor yelled out, but no one paid him any attention. All of them stared at the woman chained to the metal bed frame with disconcertion.

"What exactly do you do down here, Doctor?" Eliseo growled, his prosthetic tapping heavier on the concrete than his other foot. I ran into the safety of his arms while he never took his eyes off the stranger and the doctor on the ground with a bolt sticking out of his thigh. "Ah. Seems karma made an appearance," he chuckled.

"Does the community know she's down here? Where the hell did she come from?" Reed snarled.

The girl in question moaned, her eyes fluttering open and closed.

"That's my business," Otis snarled. "She's a

bloodsucker. I'll do what I see fit to keep the community safe. If I decide to have fun along the way, what's the problem?"

The doctor pulled the bolt out of his naked thigh, groaning. His erection was on full display as he got to his feet, a grin plastered on his face. Reed and Samuel both had their hands wrapped around a pistol, standing behind Eliseo.

"Who the fuck are you?" Gunner barked.

The stranger, Rick, crossed his arms and didn't reply.

"Rick is my assistant. He doesn't go out much," the doc said as he booted the prisoner's cauterized stump to rouse her. She moaned in pain but didn't open her eyes as her head hung.

So he *was* with the doc?

"Is that right?" Eliseo narrowed his eyes and held me tighter. "I'm only going to warn you once, Doc. Stay the fuck away from us. We completed your stupid mission and owe you nothing."

"Indeed, you did," his grin grew impossibly wider.

We turned to leave, Gunner being the last to follow, bringing in the rear. Four more chambers in, we reached the doc's normal bunker entrance and climbed up the concrete steps. Thank good-ness there wasn't a ladder here because Eliseo wouldn't make it up, but I didn't voice this out loud. Once we were all back on the surface, Reed slammed the door shut with a loud bang. It was already dark outside, and I felt a loss of time. *How long was I down there? Shit, where's Hannah?*

"Eliseo!" I grabbed the front of his shirt to pull his attention. "Hannah, she—"

"She's back with Samuel," he finished for me. "Reed saw her run toward his home without you in tow. I was beyond furious, I could have strangled her. But I wanted to make sure I got to you first."

"She..." *What should I say?* It would break Samuel's heart to know she was blackmailed into doing something because he was threatened. Dammit! I needed to think this through. I needed to figure this out before making a rash move. "Nevermind," I mumbled.

The guys checked me over, and when they were finally satisfied I was alright, let me leave with Eliseo back home. Once we entered the house, Eliseo broke the silence with his pent-up rage.

"I'm following your ass wherever you go now. That's final. Can't deal with that shit again," he growled, falling onto the couch, pulling me with him.

I wrapped my arms around his neck, burying my face against his skin, trying not to feel guilty over the fact I couldn't tell them the whole truth. It might break our team apart. Our mission together would have me think we were stronger than the situation, but I had never run into something like this before. I was at a loss at what to do.

Eliseo rubbed my back, and I could hear the rhythm of his heart slowing down. Training with his new leg took a lot of energy out of him, I felt bad for forcing him to work through so many steps below ground. Pulling my head back, I kissed him until he fell to the side of the couch, getting comfortable. I hadn't gone back to my home since we returned, Eliseo needing help during his recovery. Ending the kiss, I quietly laid on top of him, my mind in chaos.

Exhaustion pulled him into sleep quickly, his quiet snores filling the room with a soft buzz. I closed my eyes, trying to lull myself to sleep, but the sound of Hannah's stricken voice informing me she had no choice burned under my skin.

Gently climbing off Eliseo, I grabbed a few weapons and headed out the back door to release some energy. If the doctor knew my secret, why hadn't he said anything to Sergio or the community? Everyone continued to stare at me the same, with curiosity about the girl who hid herself as a boy until she was forced to come out in the open.

The cool breeze outside chilled my skin. My forehead perspired thinking about the prisoner Crazy Otis had underground. Who was she? He mentioned she was a bloodsucker. Was he using her to find the cure he was always rambling about? Recollections of his cock half mast with a blow torch came back, and I cringed. The doctor had eclectic carnal tastes.

Pulling a blade, I cut through the air with some training moves.

Wasn't Hannah with the doctor before we left, behind a house?

My left arm came up as I twisted to drive the blade down onto the grass.

It sounded like they had a previous relationship. Or were they still in a relationship while she was with Samuel? How long has she been with Samuel to begin with?

Throwing the blade up, I caught the hilt and jabbed it sideways.

Does Samuel know anything about this? Why hasn't he come to check up on us?

"Fitri…"

I startled, turned and threw my blade in the air, lodging it into a tree trunk. Hannah gasped behind said tree, peering around at me. "I'm so sorry!"

Fury overtook my senses, the sweat coating my skin increased. "Get the fuck out of here!" I growled. "I don't want to see you right now."

"You have to understand! I love him!"

"Love who?" At this point, I wasn't even sure anymore, especially after all I witnessed.

"Samuel! God, I'm so stupid. You have to believe me. Please! I-I had an affair with Otis a long time ago, but I swear it's been over for years! He would tell Samuel. I couldn't let him! He threatened he'd get Samuel killed if I didn't come back to him in his bunker. I didn't know what to do!" She sobbed.

This was too much information bombarding me at once. "Just get out. I-I need to think."

She nodded her head frantically as tears shone in her eyes. When she didn't move, my untempered rage came full force. I could have died. Where would that leave Eliseo? He needed me. He was the air I fucking breathed these days, and she threatened to take it away all because of something *she* selfishly did in the past. Baring my teeth at her, she whimpered and ran back to wherever she came from.

Grumbling under my breath about the stupidity of friendships, I pulled the blade from the tree trunk.

Damn her. Damn her for making me care, and damn her for her betrayal of not only me, but one of the guys on the team. Samuel and I had grown so close, if I were to have an actual brother, he would be it. *I couldn't believe her! And she dared to say she loved him? What the fuck kind of love was that?*

My father's face came to my mind. Images of his hugs and kisses, to images of his disdain and rejection, while acting like we were a happy family in front of our community. Screaming inside my mind, I fell to my knees and repeatedly hit my temples. It shouldn't be this complicated! Why couldn't we all just live peacefully without the cloak of so many lies?

You're one to talk. You hid everything about yourself for most of your life.

...until Eliseo. He freed me from that guilt—he took the burden I carried and distributed it among the men.

Dammit! Maybe it would have been better if none of this happened. But then I would have never felt Eliseo's embrace—the love he poured out of himself to fill the hole in my chest left behind by my parents.

Needing to feel something other than the hurt from her betrayal, I took the knife and sliced it across my chest. The pain grounded me, clarifying my mind as I concentrated on feeling my wound stitch back together.

The smell of blood tickled my nose, and my mouth watered. What if I kept changing? Was it possible for me to become a full bloodsucker like the rest of them? The community would exile me, if not kill me. The guys didn't deserve that kind of trauma.

Standing up, I walked back into the house and stared at the weapon's cabinet. Grabbing my bolts, I made a spontaneous decision. The doctor and the stranger weren't going to stop and leave us alone. Not now. We were fools to even consider it.

Taking the bolts out one by one, I cut my chest with their pointed tip, making sure to coat the metal with my perspiration. My pussy throbbed by the fourth one, but I needed to prepare for what may come. Once it was done, I fingered my wound and brought the blood to my mouth as I walked up the stairs to take a shower.

Shedding my clothes, I grabbed them and threw the pile into the tub while I showered over it. I didn't need Eliseo feeling the effects of my paralyzing ability by accidentally touching it. I cataloged everything he discovered about me over the course of our time out there. My skin stitched itself back together, and my pussy ached. Running my hand down between my legs, I swirled my clit and sighed. Dipping my fingers inside the slick heat, I tried to satisfy myself under the spray but only ended up frustrated.

Eliseo had ruined me in the best possible way. I could still feel the phantom sensation of him inside of me from this morning.

Quickly washing my hair and body, I stepped out of the shower and wrung my clothes, hanging it on the curtain bar. Rummaging through his dresser, I grabbed a shirt and put it on as I descended the stairs to the first level. Eliseo was still there, peaceful in his slumber. It didn't escape my notice that the nights following his surgery brought on many nightmares.

What a pair we made when we would both set each other off. But I had come to find the more I spoke to the men about it, the more my nightmares faded away. Of course, some nights remained worse than others.

It was why I appreciated and cared for them as deeply as I did. They had done more for me than anyone else—besides my mother. My sour mood returned with thoughts of my adoptive father's disappointment in me as a daughter.

Climbing on top of Eliseo, I undid his pants and pulled him out. Swirling my tongue around his crown, I swallowed him whole with a soft hum. He shifted and grew harder inside of my mouth, making me squirm in response. Popping him out, I licked up the underside of his shaft, savoring his taste. His hand went to the back of my head and I moaned, taking him deep inside of my mouth again. The curse slipping through his lips told me I woke him up. His hips slowly undulated into my face while his hand kept my head still. I crept my touch under my shirt, continuing what I started in the shower while Eliseo tried to push his cock down my throat.

Humming and swirling my tongue around the crown on my way out, I nipped at him and then climbed up, forcing his hand out of my hair, pulling my scalp deliciously. He grabbed my hips harshly, dragging me the rest of the way until the head of his cock lined up against my entrance, and slammed me down.

I moaned, digging my nails into his shirt as I rode him torturously. He squeezed my breasts and pulled firmly at my nipples, sending exquisite lightning through my body. Since my enhanced strength had further exacerbated, Eliseo's been rougher with me—and I loved every bit of it.

He sat up and wrapped his arms around my lower back, and began pounding into me from below. Pushing his chest, I grabbed the hem of my shirt and pulled it over my head, throwing it to the back of the couch. I bit my bottom lip, squeezing my muscles around his cock on every downward grind.

He groaned into my chest and I pulled his face up for a kiss. I had worked myself up in the shower, the hunger inside of me a wicked inferno. What would it be like to carry Eliseo's child inside of me? The world was so fucked up, and I shouldn't want to bring another innocent life into this, but damned if this man didn't give me a taste of hope. I needed to bury everything about him inside of me, to desperately become one with him. Life was so short.

Licking his jaw, I clawed at my chest, creating a wound. Grabbing his face, I lowered him down to the top of my breasts where he lapped up the blood, tonguing the cut before it closed. It was so hot, so dirty. I could feel my pussy fluttering around him inside of me.

"I need you to fill me up, Eliseo. I want it so bad. Don't stop." Wrapping my legs tighter around him, I clamped my pussy down, trying to keep him inside.

I forced him to chase away everything I felt today and he didn't disappoint. He cursed under his breath as his hips slapped against me, the sting of our impact taking me over the edge.

He exclaimed against my chest right before he pulsated and finished inside of me, some of it leaking out, wetting the couch beneath us.

14

ELISEO

Sili KEPT ME UP ALL DAMN NIGHT AND MORNING WITH her irresistible appetite. I should be exhausted but I was currently stroking my cock to the sight of her sleeping soundly beside me on the bed, blood-stains on the sheet beside her chest.

Last night was the first time she wanted me to taste her directly instead of the other way around. We stumbled into the bedroom toward the end as her hand clawed at her neck and chest for me to lap at her again. I never knew it could be titillating, and I found myself wondering if I could sneak another taste of her now. She had alluringly come into her confidence and constantly hungered for me. The knowledge made me tense up and come all over myself.

She was the beauty the world kept trying to

take from me. What did crazy Otis want with her, and where the fuck was Hannah? I would have to gather further intel about who this Rick guy was.

Wiping my hand on a nearby makeshift towel, I leaned over her and ran my nose along her cheek, taking in her unique scent. She sighed happily and I crawled down her naked body. I felt energized today and extra aroused. My dick was already at half-mast again as I pushed her legs apart and licked between her legs.

She tried to close her thighs around my head but I forced her further apart, opening her up for my tongue's invasion. My eyes wanted to roll to the back of my head, she was delectable.

"Eliseo..." she began to rouse.

"Shh. Be a good girl and just take it."

Sucking in her clit, I nipped and swirled it around my tongue before diving back inside her heat. She squeezed me and I hardened to the point of pain.

"Oh, god," she whined prettily.

My thumb played with her as my mouth continued to devour her center. When her legs shook and her pussy fluttered around my tongue, I knew she was close. I was lost in the scent of her arousal, the heat of her body when she grabbed my head and whimpered, pulling me tightly against her. I spread her wetness along her inner thigh and bit down, breaking her skin. The blood rushing forth from her frantic pulse made me release on the sheets. My hips continued to thrust on their own in aftershocks. She cried out in pleasure as my fingers entered her, filling her up, and my thumb grinded against her sensitive spot.

"You're such a dirty little slut for me," I whispered, pulling in her blood into my mouth and returning to the apex of her legs. "Always ready, always so damn wet."

I groaned again when her skin healed while I cleaned up the remnants of her blood on her inner thigh. It was the most erotic and intimate thing I had ever experienced.

Sili pulled me up with her inhuman strength and wrapped both her arms and legs around me as we shared a lewd kiss.

"That was so hot," she sighed against my lips, licking up the bloodstain on my chin.

"You shouldn't taste so good," I told her. "A man like me is weak, unable to say no."

"A man like you is known to just take what he wants, from what I remember." She laughed melodically, and it made my heart light.

"I needed to make sure you knew you were mine the moment you punched me in the face," I teased.

"Oh, really?"

"You didn't hit like a girl. It left a good impression."

Grabbing her ass, she squealed as I rolled off her, reaching for my prosthetic leg. She embraced me from behind and licked along the column of my neck. Looking over my shoulder, I smiled at her display of affection.

"What are we doing today?" she whispered against my skin, running her teeth along a secret trail.

"Not a fucking thing. I need you next to me. Can't trust anyone in this damn place."

With her cheek pressed against me, she sighed in contentment. *She gets it.* She shouldn't trust anyone, either, besides old Margaret.

"Where the fuck was Hannah?" I asked.

She pulled away from me, and I *knew* there was a fucking problem. There was something she wasn't telling me. Turning on the edge of the bed, I glared at her to give me an answer.

"*Sili*," I tried again. "Where. The. Fuck. Was. Hannah?"

"Let's get out of the house today," she said with a smile. "We can just stick by the guys and nowhere else."

Evasion tactic? *That was what she's going with?* Grabbing the stump covering, I rolled it on tightly and tied it before sticking my thigh into the prosthetic and securing the leather belt straps. I watched her naked ass parading around the room, pretending to look for something to wear. Standing up, I stalked over to her and pulled her into my arms, forcing her to look at me—which she couldn't. She looked everywhere but at me.

"*Sili*, quit with this shit and tell me what happened," I gritted out, annoyed.

Her chin quivered and I cursed. I needed to know for *her* own damn good!

"Don't tell Samuel!" she whimpered.

What the fuck?

"Hannah got blackmailed by crazy Otis. He wanted me down there for something. I haven't figured that part out yet. Th-the stranger ran into us and ended up there, too. I'm still not sure if he was in on it or not. I'm conflicted about it all. I don't want Samuel to be pissed at her," she rambled.

"He doesn't need to be pissed at her, I'm fucking pissed! You could have died!" I roared.

She cradled my face in her palms, cooling my temper a fraction. "I always come back."

"What if you don't? It's not a chance I'm willing to take. What the hell does the doc have over Hannah for her to be so easily blackmailed?"

Sili turned away, then buried her face into my chest. *Was this girl code?* Was she not going to tell me? What good was girl code if the fucking girl in question put her in dangerous situations? After seeing the prisoner down there, who knew what crazy Otis had in store for her? I highly doubted he wanted her down there for a fucking talk.

I let *Sili* go and exited the room. Since the amputation, I had moved most of my stuff downstairs. I was glad for it now. Walking to the kitchen,

I washed my hands in the sink, wet a cloth, and wiped my dick down, tossing the dirty rag back into the sink with force. Grabbing the shirt on the back of the couch, I put it on. I snatched the cargo pants off the floor and got dressed with jerky movements.

"Eliseo?"

"Get your ass dressed, *Sili*," I ordered. "I'm going to have a talk with Samuel."

"What? No! You can't!"

Turning slowly with my eyes ablaze with fury, I asked, "Why can't I? *His* fucking woman almost got *mine* killed."

She choked but didn't talk back, because she knew it was true. "*Sili*. Don't make me tell you again. Get your ass covered with something and let's go."

Her eyes burned, and my dick twitched. I didn't have time for this attitude of hers. Once she was dressed, I grabbed her hand, and we headed out the door and across to the south side. When we reached Samuel's street, we could already hear them fighting through his curtained door.

"What the hell were you doing, Hannah?" Samuel snarled.

"I didn't mean to!"

My head snapped to *Sili*, who flushed sheepishly. Climbing the steps, I pushed the curtain to the side to find Hannah with her arms wrapped around herself and Samuel putting holes in the wall.

"You could have gotten her fucking *killed!*" he roared.

"He was going to kill you!"

"I don't give a shit! I can die any day out there going on stupid runs for this damn place," he pointed angrily at the door. "We shouldn't have to prepare for war on the inside of our own damn community!"

"What did you just say?" I cut into their conversation, making them both turn their attention in our direction.

"Fitri! I swear I'm sorry," Hannah sobbed.

Sili's eyes burned hot, and now I was about to kill Hannah. Whatever the reason became irrelevant if she was going to put us all in danger.

"Hannah, I can't be with someone I don't fucking trust anymore. Get the hell out of my house!" Samuel roared.

"Samuel! I love you!" she cried out pathetically.

"What the fuck?" he scoffed. "You love me enough to get one of my own killed? That doesn't make any damn sense. Listen to yourself!"

"I didn't know what to do!" she cried again.

"You should have fucking told me!" he snapped. *"Me!* The threat was against me! I would have handled it!"

"Please..."

"Get. Out! I don't want to fucking see your face right now!" Samuel flipped a side table, taking a plugged-in lamp with it, crashing to the wall.

Hannah screamed as she flew out the front door, skirting beside us.

"Dammit!" Samuel yelled.

"What the hell was the doc threatening her with?" I asked.

"Some bullshit about killing me, I'm sure. You know that crazy old fucker has always been out to get us. He probably has all our blood down in his bunker for some nefarious reason or another. Killing wouldn't be a surprising next step. He wants control of this damn camp, I just know it. For what purpose, that's the real question."

Samuel's chest was heaving as he spit out all this information. *Sili* walked up to him and wrapped her arm around his midsection. He stared at the ceiling, covering his face with his hands as he growled in frustration.

"I'm sorry, Samuel," she whispered under her breath.

Sam laughed humorlessly. "Sorry? You're fucking sorry that worthless sack of shit I called mine was trying to get you killed? Fuck sorry!" I watched as he hugged her back, rubbing his head on top of her hair.

We had all come to love her in our own way. She was a part of us, weaseled her way into all of our hearts, and saved our asses on the side.

"We need to find out who the other guy down there is. I don't recognize him." My mind ran through all the faces I had seen so far since we returned from the mission. His didn't come up. *How long had he been down there?*

"I wouldn't be surprised if Otis has a damn team down there," Samuel grumbled.

The thought made my skin prickle. *Sili* released Samuel once she realized he had his emotions under control.

"Fucker is always talking about the war between clans. Maybe he's been preparing for war inside these damn walls," I muttered.

"Why us? If he's so damn power-hungry, why not just take out Sergio? Hell, take out half the people here who go to him for medical needs." Samuel crossed his arms and stared at the doorway behind me as if he expected Hannah to run back inside.

"Because he knows we'd never go with it," I told him. "We'd be the one to take him down."

"So he sends us out on a wild goose chase, hoping we'd die or fall off the face of the planet, only there was actual evidence to collect and bring back," he continued, trying to piece it together.

"Maybe he wanted *me* to die," *Sili* piped in.

We both turned to look at her and considered her statement.

"Why? You're only one person." Samuel spoke for the both of us, knowing I was thinking the same thing.

"He said he remembers me, but never said anything else afterward."

"You saying he knows about your abilities?"

Samuel inquired. "How? You can't tell through blood samples, can you? You'd have to witness it, like us."

I mulled over Samuel's logical line of thinking. I was not a scientist, or anything close. I didn't know what you could decipher through blood.

"I don't know, Samuel," she replied dejectedly.

"Maybe he's just keeping a close eye on you because you've become one of us," Samuel added.

"It means we're all in danger. Get Reed and Gunner here ASAP. Seems our stay has been shortened," I instructed.

Samuel nodded and went into the other room to grab his weapons. If it was too good to be true, it probably was, and this place has been too damn peaceful. Memories of the town we massacred came to my mind. Bellmore was too friendly, too. Creepy as shit. I didn't want to be a part of it if this place was transforming into something similar.

"Suit up, *Sili*. Grab a bag and get whatever shit you want to keep with you," I told her, coming to a decision. "We're going to leave this place by nightfall."

I grabbed her hand and pulled her out of Samuel's house. His boot steps pounded down his porch behind us, splitting off to the west to gather the other men.

"Do you have anything back at your place you need to get?" I asked.

"No. I brought most of the important stuff to your place," she admitted.

"Good."

We reached our front porch to find old Margaret setting down a tray of fresh vegetables. "There's the lovely couple! I hope you guys are hungry. Some of the women were able to fertilize the ground really well this season."

"Thank you, Margaret. You are too kind." *Sili* walked up to her and gave her a hug that lasted too long to not be suspicious. My hackles rose as I did a double take of the old lady. Margaret looked over her shoulder at me while she rubbed *Sili's* back. Her lips moved silently against *Sili's* ear and *Sili* nodded as she pulled away.

I bit out a thanks, unsure of what else I should say to get her off my damn porch so we could get things moving.

Margaret walked down the steps slowly and placed a hand on my arm. "I don't blame you. Take care of her. Her mother would have been proud of the woman she's grown into." Her eyes sparkled and she left quickly. Caught by surprise, I didn't get a chance to ask her further questions about *Sili's* past.

"Come on, Eliseo!" Sili hissed.

"I'm coming." *How did old Margaret know Sili's mother? Was she in the same community? What were the odds of two residents from the same community, migrating and ending in the same place at the same time?*

Walking up the steps, I laced my fingers in *Sili's* as we unlocked the door. "Grab your shit and some extra, in case we run into trouble. Even the holey clothes, in case we need to make makeshift bandages."

Sili stood on her toes and kissed me on the cheek before doing exactly as I instructed. Heading to the back of the house, I checked my weapons store and contemplated what to leave behind. We needed to leave unencumbered for a successful exit. Staring a bit longer, I ran a hand down my face. *We might have to steal the Humvee.* It was the better vehicle, but a truck would help more with supply runs, I debated.

"Eliseo! You here?" Reed's voice came through the front of the house.

"Yeah, he's in the back," *Sili* answered.

"Samuel told us what he learned." The door slammed shut and the sound of the lock engaged. "Shit's gonna go to hell in a handbasket. We might as well take our chances out there."

"I never trusted these people. The doc was already here when I arrived." Gunner's voice came toward my location. Looking over my shoulder, I nodded in agreement.

"Yeah, crazy Otis has always been here," I concurred.

"Why now? If he wanted to plan some crazy shit like a coup, why not do it already?" Gunner pondered. "Why wait this long?"

"Who the fuck knows?" I said. "At this point, who the fuck cares? We need to get out of this place before it happens. It's about time Sergio steps up and takes command of this place. Besides the guards he posts by the front gate, we've never really had any changes or improvements." Turning to the group, I stared at each and every one of them.

We all arrived at Ashborne at different times, coming from different journeys in life. The moment we clicked, we knew nothing else but sticking with the team to increase our chances of survival. Now, life had thrown us another wrench threatening to tear us from what we considered home.

There was a pregnant silence until Reed spat out, "I was getting bored of this place, anyway."

"Bored? This isn't the kinda entertainment I was thinking about," Gunner replied.

"Eliseo's leg was enough entertainment for a lifetime," Reed chuckled, and I smirked at the bastard.

"Collect your shit before I stick this fake leg up your ass," I commanded. "We leave at nightfall. The Humvee is what we're going to take. It's stronger than the truck. We might need the coverage we can get on the way out, in case we run into trouble."

Gunner prepared to leave as Reed continued to stare at me. "You think they're gonna shoot us down before we exit the gates?"

"It's possible," I told him truthfully. "For all we know, crazy Otis has been the one who organized all the runs from the background, using Sergio as a front."

"Alright, we're going to lay low and keep our ears open in case anyone gets wind of our exodus before we make a break for it." Reed tipped his head up at me and exited the front door.

"I brought your veggies in," Samuel said, leaning against the wall.

"We should eat before we go, get our energy up." *Sili* looked to me for direction. My chest swelled with pride and apprehension. I didn't know if I was making the right decision, but I knew it felt like a smart one.

"You're right, *Sili*. See if we have enough to make some sandwiches to go."

She nodded and left for the kitchen. Samuel walked up to me once she was gone.

"You know Hannah might go back and tell crazy Otis about all this. Even if she doesn't know the details of the plan," he whispered.

"Possibly." We had no other choice. *What's done is done.*

Samuel walked past me and began grabbing some weapons. I did the same. We worked efficiently in silence until the guys came back with their packs one at a time and *Sili* came out with food.

Gathering in the living room, both Reed and Gunner posted themselves next to the front windows of the house as we discussed strategy and which direction we should head first.

"Largest bodies of water to the southwest. There's a larger inlet to the northeast but it sits smack dab in the middle of clan Lekim territory and those bloodsuckers are worse than the rest," Samuel stated as he placed random items on the coffee table in front of us. "We're closer to Clan Sira if we choose west but as we know, there's a multitude of human camps scattered about."

"Northwest has the highest concentration, along the clan boundary lines," Gunner stated, still staring out the window.

"Margaret told me about a town at the middle intersection between Clan Sira and Clan Lekim lines. Silverforge. We might be safe there," *Sili* added quietly.

"Are you sure? Is this what she whispered into your ear?" I prodded. *How do we know it wasn't a setup? Why was the old lady the only one who saw Hannah?*

Sili nodded, and we all contemplated the possibility.

"Bellmore was friendly, too, look how that turned out," Reed supplied with a scowl.

We all mumbled in agreement, except for *Sili*, who continued to stare at the items on the table. "I-I think I've been there before."

"You sure?" I asked genuinely.

"No, but something in my gut tells me I have. I haven't had too many nightmares recently, thanks to you guys and Eliseo. Maybe it will come back when we're closer," she said hopefully.

"Alright, so we'll head northwest first."

The sun began to fall over the horizon and we double-checked our bags, weapons and food stores. The men divided the bags up evenly between each other, giving *Sili* the lightest one.

"Really?" she said with exasperation.

"Really," I deadpanned. "Suck it up, buttercup. You're going to be carrying the bolts for your cross-bow, too. Don't worry. Make sure you double down on knives on your body, just in case."

She nodded and went to the back to grab extra weapons.

Turning to the guys, I reiterated our plan. "Reed, Gunner, and Samuel, you guys go along the southside wall. Make sure no one sees you when you take out the guards on the south tower over the gate. *Sili* and I will weave in through the houses and go along the north side to take out the other tower. Do you remember which garage has the Humvee?"

"South garage, last I saw this morning," Gunner answered.

"Good, grab it and get it ready."

Darkness covered the town, and the hustle and bustle of the outside died down. I signaled to the men to exit the back. *Sili* caught up with me just as the team broke in two.

"*Sili,* north side wall," I instructed.

Weaving behind yards and trees, we subtly made our way across the grass to soften the sound of our footfalls. The slam of a bunker door made us freeze one house away from the doctor's. Crazy Otis was mumbling to himself, his apron and forehead splattered in blood. He had his goggles over his eyes as he stomped into his house and slammed the front door.

A few minutes went by before we continued our path. Just past Gunner's house, something pulled my prosthetic foot, taking me down. Fists landed on the back of my head until *Sili* tackled the culprit and grappled him a few feet away from me. The back of my skull throbbed as I turned over and checked the straps on my thigh. They were still tight, but pulled the stump out from its cradle.

"You little bitch!" The masculine hiss snapped my head up, making me search the darkness. The stranger from the bunker had a choke hold on *Sili's* neck while his legs wrapped around hers from behind, both of them lying on the ground. His ugly face was in a sneer as he stared directly at me. Slipping my leg back in the cradle, I got on one knee. "She's a pretty one, isn't she? I don't blame you for wanting to sink your dick in her. I did as well, for a time, back in the day."

Back in the day? I gritted my teeth, feeling my temperature rise from this fucker's audacity. I'd cut off his dick before he could stick it in anything. My hand crept down my leg toward the knife I had in my boot.

"Tsk. I wouldn't do that if I were you. I've studied with the doc enough to know if I sever her head and take it with me, she won't come back.

You're more than welcome to her body though, what's another hole, right?" He licked her face and she elbowed him. He grunted and laughed darkly against her.

Rolling my neck, I tried to control the fury rising within me to keep a clear head about what needed to be done. But quicker than I could manage, my vision was red with rage. My shoulder bunched up in preparation for me to aim.

"You never did want to play with me, Faheema," he purred. "Always scared what your father would think about you—until you took the whole damn community down during one of your tantrums."

She gripped the arm wrapped around her neck, trying to pry it loose while my mind went through different possibilities of how to throw this knife in his good eye.

"Who the hell are you?" she gritted out.

"I'm offended you don't remember. How could you? We were too young. My face wasn't fucked up yet. Thanks to you, I was able to slip by without even stirring a memory. To think, John's only daughter showing up here with not one man, but four. What would your father say about that, hmm?"

I watched as *Sili's* face morphed from concentration to hate, my own mood mirroring hers. Quick as lightning, she twisted enough to force his knee into the ground, slipping her hand down to grab her knife. I threw mine with more strength than I anticipated, missing him as he turned to try and mount *Sili*. The blade lodged into the grass beside him, the hilt barely visible. Unlucky for him, he met her blade in his inner thigh, blood spraying on her cargo pants from the artery she severed.

He opened his mouth to scream, but I quickly threw my fist in his face, shoving my knuckles in his mouth, shattering his teeth and jaw, lodging it in his throat. *Sili* pulled her knife out and he fell to the ground, unmoving except for his eyes, filled with evil intent.

"*Sili*, is your skin..." I trailed off, not wanting him to hear it.

"No. It's on my knife." *Fucking hell*. My erection grew so quickly from her brilliance, I got lightheaded.

Jerking my fist back, his head snapped with a crunch. Bringing my knuckles to the front of my face, I watched in awe as the broken skin turned into light scratches.

"I do remember you, Maverick. I never meant to hurt you then, but I mean to now, after what you've done. Fuck you." *Sili* slammed her knife into his neck, then his chest, and finally buried it in his good eye, leaving it there.

She leisurely grabbed the backpack that fell and stretched her hand out to me. "Let's go. They're waiting for us."

Shoving these new developments to the back of my mind, I grabbed her hand and we continued our way along the north wall until we reached the guard tower.

Sili watched from the bottom as I quickly climbed up and leapt into the tower, taking out the guard with a twist of his neck. He dropped like a ragdoll and I took his rifle, looking down the other side to see where the rest of the men were. Samuel came out the side door of the garage and waved at us. Sliding down the ladder, *Sili* and I quietly made it across the other side toward him, slipping inside.

"We're going to have to break through the garage door and gate. You think this vehicle is going to handle it?" Samuel asked.

"Why do we have to break through the garage door?" Sili questioned.

"It's automated. If we open it up, the neighbors can hear the electric mechanism."

"So we need a distraction." This girl would have me tossing her down in this car to fuck her with all this quick thinking.

"Reed, you got anything we can use?" I asked.

"Let me look."

We all waited as he rummaged through his bag and pulled out a grenade.

"Where the hell did you get that?" Gunner exclaimed.

"Dude, I've been saving it for a rainy day. Found it a while back. You never know when you need one."

"You got that fucking right. Who's going to

throw it?" Gunner looked at all of us. We all looked at each other.

"Let's get this garage open and just toss it in the direction of the town center. That should cover the sound of us driving through the metal gate," Reed suggested.

"Sounds like a damn plan. Let's do this," I told them as we rearranged ourselves so that Reed could sit by the back passenger side window.

"Let's go!" Samuel barked.

The garage hummed loudly as it moved up. The moment it gave us enough room to exit, Samuel stepped on the gas. Shifting to reverse, he went back far enough to give us enough momentum to slam into the gate.

"Now, Reed!" I called out.

Reed leaned out the window, pulled the pin and tossed it. I grabbed the hem of his pants and pulled his ass back in right before we slammed into the gate with a loud crash that could wake the dead. The bomb exploded, sending debris and shrapnel every which way, ringing our ears.

Samuel drove into the night without looking back. None of us did. The good thing about Ashborne was that they always kept their vehicles full of gas. It was the main reason why they never collected any more vehicles to store.

"You guys run into anything? You took kinda long," Reed asked on our second mile out.

"Yeah, but we took care of it." Like that, *Sili* buried that part of her life with Ashborne. I didn't say a word, respecting her decision. But I also buried the name John in the back of my head.

We drove until daybreak, and Samuel switched out with Gunner. A few miles later, a man appeared on the road and we swerved, almost hitting a tree.

Reed leaned out the window and aimed his rifle, letting off a few rounds. He hit the man, but the body dissipated into thin air, making us all take a second look.

"Did he just..." Reed trailed off, squinting.

"Fucker just disappeared," Samuel grumbled.

"Maybe I'm sleep-deprived," Gunner added.

"I know him," *Sili* stated flatly. *Of course she did.* This girl had died everywhere. I shouldn't be surprised. "At least, I *think* I do. He's tortured me in the past. We need to go, now," her voice turned to seriousness.

We all tense up, grabbed our weapons and readied ourselves as Gunner slammed on the gas and got back on the road. Looking out the rear window, I saw nothing but dust kick up.

Boom! Something large crashed landed on the roof of the Humvee and clawed through, the sound of metal screeching piercing my ears.

"Fucking hell!" I roared.

We shot up the roof only to have the thing jump onto the hood, staring at us with an evil grin. His body was covered in some sort of camouflaged ghillie suit. His face sizzled in the sun, and the smell of burnt flesh wafted into the car. His flesh began to boil and pustule in front of us while his hands turned into monstrous claws. He slammed his fist into the front windshield and Gunner swerved, throwing the guy off the hood of the vehicle.

"What the hell kinda mutant shit is this?" Gunner yelled as he backed up and ran over the body again. The bump tousled us about in the back as Gunner slammed on the gas and tried to get away from the dead body—if he was dead at all. How could he continue to fight while his skin burned in the sun?

"First winged bloodsuckers, now this shit?" Reed growled. "When the hell does the human race get one leg up?"

His statement brought back a memory of the conversation I had with crazy Otis back in Ashborne.

"They say bloodsuckers from Clan Cirse can clone. Did you know that? Imagine an army of them, growing exponentially, just from mere cloning," he rambled *with his arms waving around in demonstration.*

"It's Clan Cirse," I blurted out.

"Of course it is," the men grumbled in unison.

"We can never catch a fucking break in this place," Samuel complained as he leaned out the window to make sure the body remained lifeless. "Fucker's not moving."

"Good. How much gas do we have?" I asked.

"Enough to get away from that shit if he decides to start reanimating."

The sun passed the highest point in the sky, and we finally decided to stop for a rest.

"Hey, what is that over there?" Reed leaned toward the front and pointed to the right of us. We all peered out and tried to see what he was seeing.

"It's a recreational vehicle, an RV. Smells like dirty humans in there," *Sili* stated. I could smell the pungent scent too. In fact, since running into *Sili's* ex, my body had been feeling a little different. I wasn't able to investigate it during our break out, but now, sitting in this Humvee, my mind flitted through reasons why things were happening the way they were.

"I don't smell anything," Samuel said.

"Because you probably fucking stink to high heaven, too," Gunner replied.

The guys chuckled as we pulled off the road and half a mile into a cluster of trees. Their statements proved that their sense of smell hadn't enhanced like mine. *Was I just going out of my mind?* We jumped out and threw some of the shrubbery around it to further camouflage the vehicle.

"If anything, we can steal their gas," Reed mentioned.

"If anything, we could just steal their damn RV," Gunner threw out. "The Humvee is busted to shit from that last bloodsucker. I can barely see through the front windshield."

The guys bickered amongst themselves about what we should do. I pulled *Sili* closer to me as we walked toward our destination. "*Sili*, what else do you smell?"

She gave me a confused look but replied, "Wet moss to the left."

"Me, too."

She stared at me in confusion before her brows raised and her eyes widened. "What does this mean?"

"I don't fucking know yet, but the crazy doc's been doing shit to us we don't know about, knocking us unconscious," I supplied. "Once we found out, we never let him do it again, but who knows what kind of shit he put into us while we were out cold?"

"How come the other guys aren't showing any changes?"

"I've been thinking about that," I told her. "When I slammed my fist into that fucker's face back at Ashborne, my body closed the biggest wound on my knuckles and healed it into scratches."

She stopped and grabbed my hand, turning it to investigate. Her little fingers fluttered over the semi-healed flesh.

"I-Is it—"

"Your blood, *Sili*. You've been changing. Getting hornier. After I got a taste of you... I started feeling the same. It probably caused a chain reaction of some sort, or became a catalyst for—" I motioned my hands to my body. "—This."

She took a deep breath. "Does that mean you're...?"

"What are you lovebirds whispering about over there?" came Gunner's voice. "We got shit to do, keep it in your pants, Eliseo!"

The men already walked ahead of us. Shaking my head subtly to let *Sili* know to drop it for now, we caught up and made it back to the main road.

15

FITRI

Was Eliseo like me now? That wouldn't make any sense, because I was made through conception with one parent being a bloodsucker. So why would that make him change on his own? Unless...

A memory of Otis' last ramblings popped into my head as we continued to walk side by side.

"There's something in the air, my friend. Something in the air. I'm not positive yet but in the meantime, wear these. Who knows what kind of stuff comes off decayed wings? If my assumption is correct, vampires as we know it originated from an airborne virus."

I turned to look at Eliseo, wondering what the hell crazy Otis injected him with, and if our mission was the catalyst to his change, rather than me. He wasn't looking at me, but staring straight ahead with the men at the RV, their weapons raised.

Reed knocked on the door and plastered himself to the side of the vehicle with his head out of the line of sight of the window. Gunner hid around the bottom corner near the front half of the RV while Samuel, Eliseo and I stood in front of the door in plain sight.

The barrel of a rifle came out of the door first, pointing directly at Eliseo, before a half-naked old man with his pants undone. "What do you want? Who the fuck are you?" he barked.

Reed knocked the gun from his hand and elbowed him in the face, knocking him down to the ground where Gunner quickly put his knee on his back and tied his arms behind him.

Samuel jumped over the old man's body and went to clear the inside of the RV. Feminine screams made my legs automatically move as I ran in after him. Jumping through the door, I was met with a small kitchen area. To my left, all the way in the back, was a woman huddled around a teenager in the farthest corner. Their eyes were full of fear, staring at Samuel, who continued to look around the RV, investigating the rest of the inside. His gun was pointed down, but his large presence could be intim-idating.

I tried to step around him to ease the women's fright by letting them know I was female, too, but their attention was stolen when Reed and Gunner dragged the old man inside with us, slamming the side door shut.

Eliseo reopened it and stepped inside. The women shuddered and tried to make themselves smaller than they already were. The team was full of large men. I didn't blame them.

"So, where are you all headed this fine evening?" Gunner asked nonchalantly, making me side-eye him.

The old man spat a mouthful of blood onto the floor and glared in the direction of the women, making Reed sneer in distaste. *How uncouth.*

The old man bared his crimson-coated teeth as he mentally sent some sort of message to the girls huddled in the back. I could feel the hateful tension radiating off him in waves, clogging my nostrils. I narrowed my eyes in suspicion. *What exactly was going on here?*

"We have nothing to do with him! We were sold. Please don't hurt us!" The woman whimpered, and my back went ramrod straight.

I saw red. *Sold. Sold? What. The. Fuck?* Staring at the youngest girl, who looked to be about eleven, then back to the old man on the ground, I could see a resemblance. The mother was sold, but the kid was *his.* He was easily in his eighties or more, while the older woman looked to be in her late twenties. *When the hell did he buy her?*

"Where did you get her?" I snarled in his face before punching his temple, stunning him for a second. I was wrathful, I could feel my body vibrating from the need to kill something—some-one. *This man.*

He shook his head and gave me a sardonic smile that boiled my blood to unnatural heights. "Wouldn't you guys like to know? But you already have yourself a whore on the go. One pussy is really all you need these days, I'm just lucky enough to have two."

I straightened and smashed my boot into his skull with a loud crack, caving it in and splattering blood all over the leg of my pants. The woman and her child screamed at the top of their lungs, but it sounded muffled to my ears as my eyes burned with rage from what he dared to reveal in front of us. Bringing my boot down again and again, the jagged edge of his skull scratched me and caught on the fabric of my pants as I yelled profanities at this pathetic excuse for a human. My foot slid on the last kick from the amount of blood that was pooling under me if it weren't for Gunner catching me.

The smell of his life source was thick in this small space, taking over my mind, clogging my nares, seeping into my pores. My hands wanted to claw at the rest of his body, my mouth watering for retribution for these two innocent women in this RV. My arm shot out and I attempted to rip his spine out, but Gunner pulled me back. I kicked and struggled like a feral animal as the women behind me sobbed in fear at my display of temper.

"Fitri. Breathe. He's dead, babe. You got him,"

Gunner whispered against my ear. His hot breath sent a different kind of passion and hunger inside of me, one that I had come to find went hand in hand with the current emotion that was crashing inside of me like a tidal wave.

"I got her," Eliseo blurted out aggressively as he grabbed me from Gunner's arms, secured me in his, and took me out of the RV side door.

We both breathed a sigh of relief when the air thinned out the scent of fresh, warm blood. My pussy throbbed and I groaned as he continued to drag me to an unknown location. Eliseo didn't stop walking until we were behind a tight cluster of trees, out of the line of sight of the RV. Suddenly, he slammed my back against the trunk and kissed me with lustful fire. His hands frantically undid my pants while mine undid his and pulled out his hard cock, wet with precum.

Stroking it roughly, he groaned and bit my lip hard, piercing the skin and making it bleed deliciously. The pain only increased the sexual high I was drowning in as Eliseo continued to invade my mouth with his drugging kisses. I pulled at his hair with force, wanting him to feel the same sensations I was, and he growled, turning me around and bending me over with my ass exposed to the open and my legs still trapped in my pants.

"Naughty girls get punished," he said in a guttural voice.

"He deserved to die," I snapped, still angry about what that shitbag revealed. "What are you going to do about it? I'd kill him again if I had the chance."

Eliseo wasted no time and slammed his dick into me fiercely, pulling at my wet pussy lips just enough to cause a little bit of added pain for my supposed punishment. I was panting, clawing at the bark as Eliseo pounded away and I scraped my hands. His own nails dug into the flesh of my ass, pulling me against him with every slap of his hips. The squelching sounds of our combined arousal made me spasm from how dirty and sinful this all was.

He leaned over me, his hot breath against the crook of my neck, his balls slapping my clit with every thrust. "You're such a dirty little slut for me, *Sili*. I love it. I love the way your pussy wants to swallow me whole and keep me there. I should also punish you for letting Gunner whisper in your ear."

"He wasn't fucking doing anything," I gasped.

Eliseo leaned back and slapped my ass. "He was too damn close to what's mine," he growled.

"Who the hell says I'm *yours,* Eliseo?" I taunted, looking over my shoulder.

He forced me back down and bit the crook of my shoulder, making me scream with pleasure. The feeling of him pulling a mouthful of blood made me clench around his cock so desperately, my stomach muscles ached.

He licked my neck and groaned, expanding inside of me and spilling his release until it leaked out the side onto the ground between us. I could feel his fingers pushing it back inside of me and it made me whimper.

"I do," he scratched my asscheeks until I felt wet welts. The moment my skin stitched together was the moment I groaned again, my pussy fluttering one last time around his cock still buried deep inside of me. When he pulled out, his release splashed against my inner thigh, making me bite my bottom lip.

"You're such a dirty old man," I whined.

"You love it that way. Now pull your pants up so we can get back in the RV," he ordered.

Sighing with satisfaction, I did as he commanded and we walked back to the location. Reed and Gunner both stared at us with heat-filled eyes while Samuel held a rope tied to the woman and her child.

"What the hell did you guys decide?" Eliseo asked calmly.

"You mean, while you two were fucking like maniacs out there?" Reed snapped, nostrils flaring.

My face flushed, turning away from the woman who stood slack-jawed, staring at us in astonishment.

ELISEO

"She told us where he bought her." Samuel looked at the woman who shrank a little, her daughter hiding her face in her mother's chest. Samuel's eyes softened at the sight. "It's a human settlement a little northeast from here." He turned to me and continued, "Eliseo, I think you've mentioned this place before. What was the name of the community you were originally from?"

I frowned and answered, "Marnmouth. But we don't have flesh peddlers there."

"Perhaps flesh peddlers came through the town?" Reed offered. The probability of this was high.

Flashes of a pool of blood, smoke, and the smell of charred flesh slammed into me. The memories turn into visions, like I was there again.

Her body laid on the ground; I couldn't take my eyes off her. The scream of women and children pierce my ears like physical razors. My wife's stomach and legs were mutilated beyond recognition, her eyes glazed over in an expression of fear, turned to the side.

Darting my eyes around the room, I took tentative steps, trying to see if our unborn child was alright...but there was nothing. Nothing but the blood of my wife christening the grounds of this place.

Fucking flesh peddlers. Of course. That explained—

My heart beat erratically, my hands closing and opening into fists, digging my nails into my palm until stings of pain shot up my arm. My head felt tight, my jaw popping from my teeth grinding down. What the hell was wrong with humanity? At this point, I was starting to think it wasn't worth saving. Crazy Otis' efforts in all this were mute.

Sili touched my arm and I automatically knocked it off me in reaction, still lost in the haze of my wife's murder. Immediately feeling guilty, I pulled her into a tight embrace, buried my face into her neck, and breathed in her scent to ground me back to the present.

"You alright, man?" Reed asked cautiously.

"Yeah. Yeah, man. Just shit from the past," I mumbled. "I haven't gone back since they pillaged us while I was out on a run with some of the men. I came home to straight genocide."

"I'm sorry man."

"Not as sorry as I am." I lifted my head up and kissed *Sili's* forehead. "They killed my fucking wife when I should have been there to protect her."

It went deathly silent, the air thick and cloying on my skin like grime that refused to wash off. I didn't need their fucking pity. That was another lifetime ago. Looking down at *Sili*, I pushed her dark hair back behind her ear and stared into her hazel eyes. She filled every hole I had inside of me.

"We don't need to go there. We'll keep heading north," *Sili* said. Her eyes were clear, her stare intense as she tried to comfort me between the lines. "I was sold by traders, too. I know how they feel. I can't stand hearing about it. It boils my blood."

"We see that," Gunner said solemnly. "I'm glad we found you, though. You're stuck with us."

His statement lightened the mood, but my mind mulled over the little piece of information she just shared with me.

We grabbed the rest of our stuff from the parked Humvee, packing us down with everything we took with us from Ashborne. Gunner brought a tube he found in the RV on our walk and we were able to siphon the gas from the tank of the Humvee into the RV. When I asked about the dead body, the men told me they dragged his carcass out in the opposite direction of where we parked and threw him behind a bush.

The decision to utilize the RV was a good one as the vehicle held all of us with room to spare. We had gone from a party of five to a party of seven in a split second. Reed volunteered as the next driver as we got back on the road and continued our journey northwest.

A few miles in, and my mind was restless. Sitting near the exit door across from the kitchen, I pulled *Sili* onto my lap and wrapped my hand around her waist, forcing her closer to my body.

"How old are you, *Sili?*" I whispered, the meaty flesh of my lips grazing against her delicate neck.

"What does an old man like you care about age? You've already fucked me twelve ways to next week by now," she answered breathlessly.

I squeezed her ass and she wriggled on top of me, making my cock ache to be inside of her again. "Just answer the damn question."

"I'm not sure, but the people who took me said I was just a newborn. They made my adoptive day my birthday. That was around twenty-seven years ago, if the fragments of my memories are telling me the truth."

Twenty-seven years. I filed that away in my mind as I continued to listen to her talk about her past.

"My mother, Patricia, couldn't have kids of her own. She was desperate, and her husband was willing to go to whatever lengths necessary to make her happy. She told me that I was still covered in blood, wrapped in a dirty sheet with my umbilical cord still attached when they sold me to her. She tried her best to raise me as her own."

Her voice had turned sad. I didn't like it when she was sad. "What do you mean 'tried her best'? What exactly happened?"

"M-my abilities started to manifest, and it brought trouble to our doorstep. The details are hazy, but I think I had an outburst, and many died, many more becoming casualties... like Maverick."

Rubbing her back, I stopped asking her questions. I didn't need to know anymore. The guys were all quiet, probably listening to her story as well. We all had a past, a journey we had been through to get where we were now. It didn't matter what happened, or where we came from. We were given the opportunity to make a new life away from Ashborne.

"How long do we have to go?" I asked Reed. We had been driving for a while, and night had already fallen again.

"Not sure, but if my estimates are correct, we're probably over halfway to Silverforge," he informed us. "I'm directionally running the camper along the border of Clan Sira territory."

"We should keep driving through the night and only stop during the day, in case we run into bloodsuckers," Gunner said.

"Roger that," I replied.

The two women were silent as they sat beside Samuel. The mother looked malnourished, but the daughter did not. I watched as Samuel handed her the sandwich he brought with him, breaking it in two. She smiled softly, cautiously taking it from him and handing half of it to her daughter, who devoured it like she'd been starved for days.

In this shitty existence, we had to not only be wary of bloodsuckers, but of human monsters, as well. Crazy Otis talked about having a leg up in this war. I say, let the vampires kill each other off, and let the rest of us survive and thrive with what we could gather. Half the human population needed to be eradicated, anyway—the stains of humanity.

Tapping *Sili*, she stood up, and I grabbed her hand to walk to the back where the seating could be pulled out into a bed. Doing just that, I lied down, pulling *Sili* on top of me, running my hands through her hair.

I was changing. Crazy Otis talked about airborne viruses making the first wave of vampires, but I had a gut feeling that he injected something in all of us. Maybe it started as a vaccine, but even those were just weaker versions of an actual virus.

Sili's scent of arousal grew as she crossed her leg over me, using her knee to tease my crotch.

My mind ran through what I knew about newborn vampires. Their strength, speed, hunger and need for sex. Was that why my libido was quickly matching hers? My dick pulsed behind my zipper as I ground her knee down against me further, humming against the exposed skin of her neck.

"I love the way you bite me. It makes my pussy wet," she whispered.

My cock twitched in response as I ran my tongue along her skin. I liked it as well, a little too much. I would have to tell the guys to keep an eye out on themselves in case they felt any changes.

"This is when I should tell you to not tempt an old man like me with your young, supple body."

She giggled and it made me smile.

Twenty-seven years.

The number kept looping through my head as I nipped at her collarbone while she slipped her delicate fingers under the waistband of my pants, running her fingers along my slit.

"Is everything okay?" I asked my wife, Myra.

"I-I think I'm pregnant," she whispered.

My heart jumped in my chest. I was elated. She was carrying my child. But as quickly as it came, my elation turned into a spike of fear as I wondered how I could protect something so precious in this life.

Myra grabbed my hand and kissed it. "I'm about a month and a half along, I think. I didn't get my last period."

Pulling her into an embrace, I rocked us both, kissing the top of her head. "I'm going to need to go on a supply run to find stuff we need."

"Eliseo, why can't they get someone else?"

"Because no one is competent enough. You know this. The last time I tried to stay behind, they barely came back with anything."

She sighed, and I promised her I would stay home this run.

Sili's hand grabbed the head of my cock, stroking and twisting it. When she dug the tip of her finger inside my slit, my hips thrusted uncontrollably toward her, wanting more.

"You've been on a lot of runs, man. You sure the baby is yours?"

"The fuck you just say to me, asshole?" My fist landed on Wyatt's face, and blood spurted out of his nose.

Sili's nimble hands undid my pants, giving my cock room to breathe as she pulled me out and quickened her strokes, running all the way down my shaft and teasing my balls. The pleasure mounted up, knowing that the guys were just a few feet away.

My wife's stomach and legs were mutilated beyond recognition, her eyes glazed over in an expression of fear, turned to the side. The smell of blood was strong, cloaking the air.

The phantom smell of blood made my dick throb as I released in *Sili's* hand, groaning against her neck. This was so fucked up. I shouldn't get turned on by my dead wife's blood, but here I was. I watched as *Sili* brought up her hand and licked it in front of me, plunging her cum-coated fingers inside of her mouth like it was a delicacy. Groaning, I reached into her pants to find it soaked and ready for my fingers to penetrate.

Twenty-seven years.

I was an old bastard. I shouldn't be doing this with her.

Twenty-seven years, my mind chanted as my fingers brought her wetness up to swirl against her swollen clit and pussy lips. The facts lined up and I couldn't stop myself from inserting another finger inside of her, then a third, listening to her sharp inhales as she continued to lick up my cum from her hand, her eyes glazed over with lust and desire.

Fucking hell, twenty-seven years. My fingers pinched her clit hard and I pulled her face against the makeshift mattress to stifle her cries of ecstasy as she fluttered and spasmed, coming all over my fingers. I slipped one of my fingers inside her tight ass and bit down on her skin, sucking in her warm blood and making us one.

Licking her healing skin, I nipped at it teasingly. The world could burn down tomorrow, and I still wouldn't regret a damn fucking thing between us. She was mine and she always would be, now and forever.

"We're going to have to get a bigger fucking vehicle. First Samuel, now Eliseo. I can't take this fucking shit," Gunner grumbled.

The men laughed at Gunner who scowled, staring right at us without shame. His own hand was down between his legs, his dick sticking out of his undone pants. The head of his cock was angry and purple. I smirked as I continued to play with *Sili's* pussy for my own enjoyment, torturing him. She mewled against me, trying to hide her reaction, but it was much too late for that.

"That's a good girl. You don't have to hide. I love the noises you make," I cooed, staring directly at Gunner as he spilled all over himself with a growl of frustration.

The vehicle jolted back as Reed slammed on the gas, speeding up. Samuel stared daggers into me, tilting his head toward the young teenage girl inside the RV. *Shit, I forgot about her.*

Pulling my hand out of her pants, I got up, fixed my fly, and grabbed a random piece of fabric to wipe off. Walking past Gunner, I tell him, "That's *my* pussy."

"Fuck. We all know, you selfish old bastard."

Sili threw her head back and laughed, rolling in the back as I continued forth until I reached the passenger seat beside Reed.

His face was still scowling as he stared at the road. I looked at him, but he didn't give notice.

"I fucking heard you. She's yours," he grumbled.

I snickered, putting my hands behind my head and stared out the front windshield, kicking my feet up on the dashboard with only a small amount of difficulty.

"You're such an ass."

"I know, so I've heard," I told him without a care. "She likes my ass, though, that's all that matters."

"She puts up with you, you mean. I don't know why," he grumbled under his breath.

I threw my head back and belly laughed, startling everyone in the RV. We drove into the night and decided that since sunrise was not too far away, we would stop and make camp off the main road.

"Gunner and I are going to see if we can catch some meat," Reed announced as they broke off into the woods.

"I'm going to take these ladies to see if they need to relieve themselves, and gather some wood. We could use the extra hands," Samuel announced as he took our guests with him.

"Guess it's you and me, jailbait. Let's set up the

fire pit and find something to roast the meat when it gets here," I purred.

"Who are you calling jailbait, old man?" *Sili* sassed as she exited the RV with her crossbow and bolts. "Maybe I should be calling you cradle robber."

I choked on the term as I strapped up. *If only she knew.* The fact didn't change anything about us, not here, not now. Slapping her on the ass, I closed the RV door and exited with her.

We walked around the area, gathering large stones, when Samuel called out her name. "Fitri! You got a sec?"

"Yeah? What's up?" She handed me the stones in her hand and went off to meet Samuel.

"The ladies don't feel comfortable with me standing watch as they piss. Can you stand guard?" he requested.

"Of course, yeah. I can do that. Watch Eliseo for me," she said with a wink.

What the hell do I need watching for?

"I'll make sure he keeps his dick in his pants. Yes ma'am." *Is this fucker kidding me right now?*

She laughed as she gathered the two guests and headed toward an area surrounded by high bushes for concealment.

Dropping the rocks down, I began to make a circle and dug the middle in preparation for the wood. The sound of footsteps over the crunch of leaves snapped my head up. Reed and Gunner returned with a small creature they secured. It would be enough to keep us going for now. Beggars couldn't be choosers.

"What the hell is that?" Samuel asked.

"Dinner. It doesn't matter what it is," Reed deadpanned.

He got that right.

"The RV has a pot we can use. We can skin and skewer the meat over a roast, let the drippings fall into the pot and save the fat for something later," I threw out. With the amount of food we had on hand, there wasn't enough to make any sort of stew to increase the portions. We would have to make due.

"Yeah, that sounds good. I'll go grab it. Reed can start skinning," Gunner said as he walked past me.

"Why do I end up doing the dirty shit?"

"Because you're a fucking dirty bastard. Suck it up. Everyone's hungry."

We all chuckled as Reed groaned and sat his ass down with the kill, pulling out his knife, grumbling about assholes as he ripped the skin off.

16

Once we were a good distance away from the men's sight, the mother told her daughter to relieve herself first.

"What's your name?" I asked her, trying to ease her feelings about us. I didn't know what the future held, but I didn't think the men were going to kill them ruthlessly. Samuel already seemed protective.

"Emma. And my daughter is Remi."

"I'm Fitri," I answered.

She nodded, staring where her daughter disappeared behind the bush until she came back, rubbing her hands down her pants.

"I'm done," Remi said sheepishly.

"That's good. I'll be right behind you. This is Fitri; she's going to stand next to you, okay?"

Watching their interaction, my heart panged

with a longing for my own mother. Though, she wasn't really my mother, was she? She loved me enough to make up for my father's disappointments. If Maverick survived everything that happened, I wondered if there was a chance my parents did.

Emma came around the bush, fixing her pants, when my ears twitched with the sound of a light rustle of leaves.

"Ahhh!" Emma cried out in horror.

"Momma!"

Emma was pulled into the bush, her screams echoing between the trees.

"Go to Samuel. Now!" I yelled at Remi. She sobbed, and I was stuck between finding Emma and pushing her toward someone who could guard her.

"Fitri! What the fuck happened?" Samuel's voice didn't sound far. Good. My adrenaline was rushing through me as I grabbed the girl and threw her in the air toward Sam. He caught her with a grunt, and I ran in the direction I last saw Emma. A trail of her blood was left on some of the leaves and the bush. Using my heightened sense of smell, I followed her trail, the bolts on my back making a racket as they jostled.

Something slammed into the tree trunk next to me, making me stop. Rolling toward my foot was Emma's decapitated head, her eye sockets dark and empty with streaks of crimson running down like tears. Her mouth was gaped open, her jaw broken off its hinge.

Growling, I yelled out, "Show your fucking self!"

The sun had already gone down by this point, just a hint of it left over the horizon. The bushes shook beside me and I pulled my crossbow from my back, securing a bolt. My hair bristled when a dark figure walked out, dragging the rest of Emma behind him. Her neck was still spurting blood as he dropped her like a rag doll and sucked his stained finger into his mouth.

He was covered in something that camouflaged him, his presence large and domineering. *He couldn't be the guy we ran over, right?* Crazy Otis talked about clones and Clan Cirse—

The stranger threw off his cloak when the rest of the sun went down, his face scraping the inside of my mind with images of torture in a military compound as his belt came down repetitively.

"You!" I growled with hate as my bolt went off.

He twisted and moved with super speed, dodging it and landing on top of me, disarming my crossbow. His hands circled around my neck and tightened as he leaned in and sniffed. "Just as sweet as I remember, hybrid. I see Sira blood runs strong in you. How did you survive?"

Eliseo leaped over me in an attempt to tackle him but missed as the vampire practically disappeared in thin air from his inhuman speed, landing beside me.

"Fucking bloodsucker!" Gunner screamed out a distance away from us and I gasped, fearing for Remi. Jumping up, I grabbed my crossbow and scrambled to get back to the camp.

Gunner and Samuel were in hand-to-hand combat with him while Remi crouched beside the RV with her hand over her ears, crying and rocking.

The smell of blood elevated the moment Samuel growled and landed on the ground. Darius, my torturer from Clan Cirse so long ago, smiled menacingly as he circled around Gunner, who had a blade out in front of him.

Eliseo caught up to me right as I locked in another bolt and aimed. Darius lunged, but Gunner dodged, slamming his knife down only to miss the killing blow when Darius twisted, slicing his arm in the process, and threw Gunner against the camper with a loud crash, almost tipping it onto its side, leaving a dent behind. Remi screamed in terror, which made Samuel growl and pull his gun from his waistband, letting off a few shots that missed and hit the trees.

My ears rang as Eliseo fired from behind me, hitting Darius in the leg, but it didn't stop him from continuing forward with the intent to kill and feed. His eyes were wild; his fangs glistened with saliva. Gunner was missing from the last spot and Samuel grabbed the vampire from behind. Eliseo was still aiming his gun, but with so much movement, we both couldn't get a good shot.

Darius threw Samuel over his shoulder and

slammed him onto the ground. Eliseo let off a shot but missed again when Darius twisted, stood up, and brought his booted foot down on Samuel's left thigh, breaking it with a loud snap. Gunner came in from behind a tree with one of the blades we acquired from Bellmore. It looked almost like a shortsword as he brought it down across Darius' back, taking him to his knees.

Reed crept up behind Gunner who ducked and pulled the blade sideways, cutting Darius' hamstring as Reed jumped over him and slammed his own knife into Darius' neck from behind.

I finally let off a bolt the same time Eliseo let off a shot. It hit the target, twisting his body and taking him to the ground on his back. I didn't see Samuel move as he grabbed the pot with his shirt and poured animal fat onto Darius' face, making him cry out in agony as his flesh began to melt and peel away from the bone.

The combined smell of burnt flesh and animal fat actually made my mouth water as I watched him unable to roll around in his pain since my bolt was lodged in his shoulder.

Flashes of his torture ran through the back of my mind as Samuel limped over to the fire, grabbed a piece of wood, and stabbed it into Darius' throat. The animal fat that stuck to his skin caught fire, sending tendrils of smoke into the air. Samuel fell onto his ass as Remi ran into his arms and wrapped her arms around his neck. Gunner used the shortsword to push himself up to standing, leaning against it while he watched the paralyzed vampire continue to burn and sizzle alive.

Eliseo placed a hand on my shoulder and I covered it with my own, dropping the crossbow on the dead leaves beneath me.

"You coated the arrowheads. Good girl," he whispered.

"Didn't we run over this guy?" Reed asked, perplexed, knife still in his crimson-coated hands. *Where was he this whole time, and why was he covered in what smelled like animal blood?*

"Clones," I answered.

The fire crackled as we all stood there, watching the vampire cook in front of us. His hand twitched, and I pulled out a gun, shooting him twice just for good measure.

"Babe, you're going to have to get off poor Samuel. My leg hurts like a motherfucker." Samuel tried to pry Remi's arms off but failed. The girl was shaking with fear, her mother having died only a few moments ago. *What a damn shit show.*

"Remi, come here. I got you. How about you and I go relax in the RV, huh?" I coaxed her.

She shook her head vehemently as Eliseo stood beside Gunner and Reed, talking about where to chuck the vampire's corpse. *What was Clan Cirse doing so far out here?* The last thing I remembered was them wanting to use me as a treaty gift to Clan Sira. Cirse was way up north, toward the snowy regions, much too far to be here. Unless, they had been searching for me, since the 'gift' obviously didn't make it. Like that, another mark was on my head for execution. We were going to have to find a solution to all this, or else risk being on the run for the rest of our lives.

Samuel rubbed Remi on the back, murmuring things until she finally nodded and let go. We could see him physically exhale when she took her weight off and ran into my arms.

"It will be okay. We'll protect you, alright?" Crouching down, I rubbed her shoulders. "You know, I lost my mom, too, when I was young. But I'm okay now. I found this great group of people who took me in when I thought I had nothing left, nothing to live for."

The men groaned as they carried Samuel under their shoulder and helped him sit down on a fallen log a few feet away. Darius broke his leg, but it wasn't a compound fracture, thank goodness.

"*Sili*, grab me some bandages when you guys get in the RV, yeah?" Eliseo called out.

I straightened and patted Remi on the back, taking her into the vehicle for safekeeping. "You stay in the back and just relax. Get some sleep. I'll bring the food to you when it's done."

"Are you guys going to leave me? Please don't leave me!" she begged through new tears.

Corralling her to the back, I laid her down on the fold-out bed. "Of course not. Where would we go? We need the RV to travel. We'll be right outside. How about I open up some of the windows so you can hear us talk? Then you'll know we're still here."

She wiped her face with the back of her hand and nodded, snuggling in a blanket. I grabbed a smaller one beside her.

Leaving her, I looked for one of our backpacks we brought with us and took out an old piece of cotton fabric. Using my knife, I ripped this particular one into strips, walking out of the RV toward the guys. The men were shaving off a branch to use as a splint as I handed Eliseo the makeshift bandages. Gunner carefully cut off Samuel's left pant leg without jostling him.

"Here," I called out. Eliseo began wrapping Samuel's naked leg. Reed placed the branches on either side of Samuel's thigh, and I started wrapping it together.

"Just my fucking luck," Samuel grumbled. "What happened to the older woman? Did the bloodsucker get her?"

I nodded, tying off some of the bandages.

"Fucking hell," he exclaimed, running his hand down his face.

Eliseo stood up and went to turn the meat that miraculously remained on the skewer over the fire. Reed, no longer needed to help, went to one of the bags we had outside the RV, grabbed water, and tried to wash his bloodstained hands.

"What are we going to do with the girl?" Gunner asked.

I looked over my shoulder at him. "What do

you mean 'what are we going to do?' She stays with us. I'm not going to drop her off in the middle of nowhere to fend for herself."

"That's not what I meant," he rebutted.

Straightening, I crossed my arms. "What *did* you mean, Gunner?"

"I'm fucking this up." He scratched the back of his head with a sheepish look. "I'm just pretty much asking where we're going from here, guys. We can't stay here in case there are more from Clan Cirse following the fucker we just killed."

"Let's eat real quick and go," Eliseo piped in.

"Yeah, that sounds like a good plan." Reed wiped his hand on his pants and took a swig of water.

Grabbing the meat off the roast, I divided the food between all six of us. The men shoved the meat in their mouths quickly, chewing as they grabbed their things to be brought back into the RV. Climbing back into the vehicle, I let the guys help Samuel in.

"Remi, are you still awake?" I asked. "Here's a little bit of food. We're going to head out again soon."

She uncovered her head and sat on the edge of the bed, her eyes puffy from her tears. "Where are we going?"

I handed her the meat and she took small bites.

"A nice old woman told me about a place that might give us a home. I don't know if it's true. We have to get there first."

"We'll get there." Samuel barged in. "The boys and I will make sure of it. How are you feeling?"

"Remi," I said.

Samuel smiled through his pain, limping and landing on the bed next to her with his left leg sticking out. "Remi. That's a beautiful name. How are you feeling?"

The girl in question crawled into his lap and wrapped her arm around him again, laying her head on his chest. My heart made a little somersault at the sight. She was good for him. She would help take his mind off Hannah's betrayal. Leaving the back of the RV to give them a moment of privacy, I walked toward the center where Eliseo sat.

"They good?" he asked.

"Yeah, they're good."

"Sit next to me," he requested before pulling me into his lap. I started to unstrap his prosthetic. He leaned back, groaning in relief as I pulled off the fabric covering his stump. His skin was red and angry-looking. I was surprised he hadn't mentioned anything.

"You need to give your leg a rest," I chastised him as my hands began to massage and soothe his skin.

"Fuck, that feels good," he moaned.

"Keep your dick in your pants, Eliseo. I'm tired of that shit near me," Gunner yelled from the driver's side. Reed groaned and ran his hand down his face before looking out the passenger side window.

"I'll rest when I'm dead," he told me before turning to the guys and saying, "It's not my fault it slips in."

Reed choked and Gunner grumbled under his breath as he opened the window to lean out, slamming on the gas pedal to drive us northwest toward what could possibly be a new life ahead of us.

17

ELISEO

"So you've been changing?" Gunner interrogated.

"Yeah, you can say that."

"It makes sense. It all makes sense now. That's why they can't fucking stay off each other," Reed ran his hand down his face and rubbed his temples.

"We've seen it among the newly made vampires. This is similar." Samuel stared at me like he could see through my mind to the other side. "Does this mean we're all teetering on the edge of something similar? Walking time bombs?"

"Well, not as dramatic as that," *Sili* said. "My abilities came out so slowly at first, I didn't notice until my first temper outburst."

"And she's half," Reed explained. "Eliseo, you would be whole, right? Full-blown bloodsucker? I mean, that's what crazy Otis was concluding. If it started as an airborne virus and entered the human body, transforming them, that means whatever is currently in our body could morph into the exact same transformation."

"We're all carriers," Gunner flatly stated without emotion.

"Yeah, we are," I concurred. "Can't go back now."

"You said blood could have been the catalyst?" Samuel questioned further.

Sitting back, I pulled *Sili* between my legs and wrapped my arms around her lower back, rubbing my hand inside her shirt. "That's the theory. I don't know if it's true or not, but it's the closest thing my mind could connect from what I know."

"But you will be good vampires, right?" Remi asked weakly, clinging to Samuel's side.

"Yeah, babe," he reassured. "We'll still protect you, don't you worry about that." She smiled up at him and he returned it with one of his own.

We all sat in silence, digesting everything I divulged. They took it better than I anticipated. Then again, we all knew Crazy Otis was up to no good when he brought us into his bunker constantly. My assumption was that he wanted to create some sort of super soldier under his thumb, fighting for the human race or for his coup—*now, I wasn't sure.* Whatever his purpose was, he could suck a dick, because we were *not* going back.

The temperature continuously dropped the closer we got to this elusive town Margaret mentioned, sitting over a thousand miles north-west from our last home: Silverforge. If my conclusion was correct and this was her prior residence, what was her reason for leaving? I kept my guard up, not wanting to give into hope that we would finally find a place to settle.

The young girl, Remi, had been stuck to Samuel's side like glue—a shadow that refused to leave his protection despite his broken leg. I was just glad he was able to occupy himself with something. She responded well to *Sili*, but not always to the rest of us. I didn't blame her. She would get used to the team soon enough, because she was part of our crew now. Change could be good.

"Guys, there's something ahead," Gunner called out from the driver's side.

All of us gathered toward the front of the RV and looked through the windshield. My eyes had sharpened these past few days as well. I was able to clearly see the top of what looked like an outer gate to a community similar in size to Ashborne.

"What do you think? You trust old Margaret with her intel? Are they friendly?" Gunner asked, slowing the vehicle down. The arrow of the fuel gauge was right above the letter E. Even if this wasn't the exact town, we were going to have to stop soon anyway and try our hand.

"I have no damn clue. We're about to find out," Reed answered.

"Keep your weapons close and concealed as a security measure." I turned to look over my shoulder at *Sili*. "Keep your crossbow in the RV. We don't want to look too aggressive."

"You got it," she answered easily.

"Samuel, let us do the talking this time, alright? Just keep Remi close," I told him.

He scoffed, "Hell no, you're not doing the talking, Eliseo. You'll get us all killed with your asshole attitude."

"What the hell do you mean? I know how to be civil," I shot back.

Sili patted me on the shoulder and kissed me on the cheek. "You don't. I can do the talking. They might respond better to a woman."

"She's right," Reed agreed.

"You guys all against me now? How far have I carried us through shit?" I was a little offended, but deep down, I knew they were telling the truth.

"When shit hits the fan, you're good. When we need to come in with peace, however..." Reed chuckled as he clasped his hands behind his head, watching the community get closer and closer.

"*Sili*, tell them I can be civil," I told her. "I can speak without causing trouble."

Her eyes sparkled as she wrapped her arms around me from behind. "I remember distinctly how you made my acquaintance, you asshole."

"But you still love me. Tell me I'm wrong," I said endearingly, pushing her hair behind her ear. She smiled, and my whole mood lightened. I could hear the sound of her heart picking up as she looked back at me with adoration. *How the hell did I get so lucky?*

"Yeah, I do. You guys have become the family I never knew I desperately needed," she confessed adoringly.

"Nah, you're the one good for us, Fitri. We were just a bunch of ragtag guys with no purpose," Gunner said as he pulled the vehicle to a slow stop.

"You guys ready?" Reed questioned, sat up and looked around to the back. Everyone's heart rate picked up with anticipation.

Sili tightened her embrace. "As ready as we'll ever be. Let's go."

Taking a deep breath, I opened the side door and let *Sili* go out first. The guys brought Samuel and Remi up the rear of the group.

"Hello! We're looking for sanctuary," *Sili* said with a light, feminine voice. The patrol in front of the gate walked toward us slowly with a friendly smile, looking us all over. There wasn't any evidence of others in our view. Where were they hidden? I scanned beyond his shoulder and didn't catch any other movements. Guards without anything to guard. My shoulders tensed up.

"Where are you guys hailing from?" he asked.

Sili put her hands in her pockets while shrugging her shoulders adorably. "A compound not far from here called Ashborne. Life put us on a path toward something new and this is where we ended up. Do you have any room for new residents? We'd be so grateful. I swear we'll be a good addition to your camp if you let us. We're not troublemakers. We just want to find a new home, if you have room. No hard feelings," she rambled.

Who was this woman in front of me? Sili had grown much from the shy girl I knew when I discovered her secret. I looked at the backs of my men scattered around her. We all have grown. Taking serious note of what the men stated earlier about how I presented myself, I rolled my shoulders and forced myself to relax.

The guard's smile didn't falter as he took a quick head count with his gaze. "So you got six or do you have a few more in the RV?"

Sili lifted her arm toward the vehicle. "Just the six you see. One of ours is also in need of some medical attention if you guys can spare some?"

"Yeah." He flicked his head in the direction of the wall, calling us to follow. "We'll get you guys checked out and see what our Chieftain thinks. I'm sure our Healer Pata can spare a few moments to give you all a good once over."

I watched curiously as the guard easily turned his back to us and led us toward the gates. Was he not worried about us turning on him? We were strangers and he was gravely outnumbered. But judging by the relaxed way he proceeded, I knew we were being watched. So did the team. Keeping Samuel and Remi in the back, I indicated for Reed and Gunner to flank *Sili.*

Beyond the wall stood a few dilapidated buildings reminiscent of ancient religious houses. The sun's rays cast long shadows over their sharp peaked roofs as the grass began to become higher with each step we took. The only thing in front of us was a thick forest and I began to wonder if they lived in the trees as concealment. But how could the place possibly have a healer if they lived in the trees?

"There's nothing out here," whispered Remi as she continued to help stabilize Samuel.

"Things usually are never what they seem," Samuel answered her under his breath and I had to agree.

Out the corner of my eye, a few bald men appeared, jovially conversing. Their strange attire matched and the longer I stared at them the more I remembered running across some of the religious groups in my past life while out on runs.

"Ah! Good morning Father. I hope your day has been going well," waved the guard.

The other two men waved back, the long fabrics of their robes fluttering in the breeze. "Yes! It is a good day to be alive as usual. Nature continues to confound us as we pray to our ancestors to give us clarity. A few of them have blessed us in dreams, giving us tidbits about how we can continue to thrive in the world," the first man called out. His voice was light and devoid of worry. What would it be like to be disillusioned as such in this day in time? An ancient saying flitted through my mind: ignorance was bliss.

The second man waved, then cupped the side

of his mouth. "We hope to meet with the Chieftain soon with what we discover."

"Good. Good. We'll see you at dinner. Stay safe out there!" the guard concluded and we all remained silent, taking in the interaction.

Sili looked over her shoulder at me for a brief second, curiosity sparkling in her eyes before she faced forward and continued to stare ahead.

"I don't think we caught your name, I'm Reed—"

The guard looked at him with a genuine smile. "Right. Sorry about that. You guys were a surprise for my day. I'm Daniel, one of the post guards for the morning shift."

We all mumbled greetings as we continued to walk toward the cusp of trees up ahead. I had never experienced tree houses but I guess there was a first time for everything. Beggars couldn't be choosers and our RV had no more gas in the tank. A few more feet and I squinted.

The closer we came, the more it dawned on me that these weren't normal trees. No, shrubbery, vines and roots encapsulated a second wall with such density that it camouflaged it to the naked eye. It was clever and I began to look at the guard and think of his community in a different light.

Sili tilted her head back with her mouth in a little 'o' before shaking her head and pretending she didn't come to the same conclusion I did. The rest of the men were more subtle in their observations. Remi was too busy concentrating on Samuel.

Daniel looked over his shoulder when we were a few yards away from the second entrance, manned by a couple of other guards. "Impressive, right? I thought so myself. It took our resident botanist a while to find out how to accelerate the growth of the plants to our advantage. Science is such a wondrous thing and what we need out here if we want to gain any sort of advantage over the enemy."

He turned to wave at his men and they waved back before eyeing us all curiously.

"Hey guys! I got a few stragglers here and one that needs to see Healer Pata. His leg looks pretty bad," he informed them.

They both opened a gate behind a canopy of thickly roped vines. Roots wove itself along the metal, hiding the element from plain view. As we passed the guards, we came upon what felt like a bustling little town, one twice the size of Ashborne.

People of varying ages walked by us across cobbled roads, some manually pulling carts with full bags. A few waved at Daniel while others remained too busy to give us a second glance. When the laughter of children came toward us, we all stopped as they skipped and ran, chasing each other with a red ball.

A younger child struggled behind the group. "Wait up guys! I got short legs!"

The little boy stopped to pull up pants two sizes too big for him and looked over at us, then at Sili. He gave her a goofy smile with missing teeth.

"Gee, you're real pretty," he blushed before he shyly cast his gaze away and continued to run after his friends.

We stifled our laughter as Daniel continued to lead us past homes with thatched roofs until we came upon a sturdy mid-sized building on the west side of their community. A sign hung over the door, stating exactly what the building was used for. A few residents came out with bandages and tipped their heads in greeting at Daniel, casting a short glance at us and moving along.

There was something to be said about people who minded their own business. It was refreshing.

We followed Daniel in a single file as we crossed what looked like an infirmary, with metal beds on either side of the wall. An office was located in the back where a woman with greying hair sat, staring at a folder.

"Healer Pata, I got another one for ya!" Daniel happily chirped.

The healer's shoulders slumped as she pinched the bridge of her nose, her back to us. "What did you boys get up to now?" she grumbled before turning around with a surprised look. "Oh, hello. I don't think I've seen your faces around here before."

Daniel rubbed the back of his neck sheepishly. "Yeah, I just picked them up. The guy in the back looks like he broke his leg or something."

"Leg. You mean the whole thing? Where exactly?" she prodded as she got to her feet, putting her file down on the desk.

"Ah, I dunno Pata. You know I'm not good at this stuff. The high part."

She slapped him upside the head and shoved him toward the exit. "Daniel Shoemaker, you need to get your ass back in those anatomy classes before I whoop you. Make sure you do so right after your shift. This is unacceptable," she scolded and I even wanted to shrink from her glare.

"It's not like that, Pata. They were needing more men to cover different shifts and Roger fell sick the other day—"

"If I don't see you in classes tonight, I'm going to—"

"I'm going! I'm going! Geez!" Daniel complained as he quickly exited the infirmary.

"Well, not that he's gone, let me have a good look at you." She adjusted her glasses higher up on the bridge of her nose and looked between us, her gaze landing on Samuel. "Oh dear, you're bleeding out hun. Here, take this bed right over here and let's get something to clean the wound so I can take a better look at it. The rest of you... well, find a wall to stand by but stay out of my way."

We all nodded as we assisted Samuel onto one of the neatly made metal beds. He grimaced and locked his jaw as we straightened him out, Remi refusing to leave his side, holding his right hand as she knelt on the floor beside him, her eyes full of worry.

"Now, how on earth did you manage to break your femur like that?" the healer asked as her gloved hands began to cut through his bandages around our makeshift splint with scissors and tipped a jar full of clear liquid onto cotton fabric.

"It's a long story," Samuel gritted out.

The healer nodded. "Hold him please." We immediately did as ordered while she cleaned his wound with what smelled like strong alcohol.

Samuel growled and Remi began to cry, caressing his arm as she looked away. Despite him fighting us, he never once gripped Remi enough for her to hurt.

"Yes, vampires are quite a problem, aren't they," the healer mumbled as she pushed his flesh to get a better look at the wound. "But it seems you're among a smart group here. The splint saved you from further injury. This looks really fresh. You'll heal but you'll take some time rehabilitating back to the way things were."

"We got that covered. We'll make sure he does what he's told," I answered.

She chuckled as she got up and went back to her little office, returning with more medical supplies—ones that looked much more state-of-the-art than what Otis could acquire. I wonder where they found them, or if it was always a part of the community and they just managed to maintain it.

"Why, no one said anything about you guys having to do the hard work," she smiled at us. "That's what my assistants are for. They're currently helping in the communal kitchen but once mealtime is over, they come to the infirmary to check up on all the patients."

We all looked at her curiously, unsure of what to voice despite a million questions running through all our minds. We watched in silence as she rubbed another chemical around the wound before suturing his wound shut. Samuel's brows slowly relaxed as the minutes ticked by, far from the reaction I had when Otis amputated me. I wonder how they came to find such an agent to help with pain.

Once she completed her task, wrapped his leg and created another splint. She gave Remi a towel and bowl of water, watching proudly as the girl took on the caretaker role for Samuel while his eyes began to flit in and out of consciousness.

She nodded after a few minutes, put her hands on her hips and turned to the rest of us. "Well, what are you all waiting for? Go grab a bite to eat and get that energy up. I'm sure the chieftain has plenty of places for you to stay and roles for you to fill. Welcome to Silverforge."

18

FITRI

THE SCATTERED MEMORIES I RECOLLECTED WAS NOTHING compared to what we experienced upon our arrival. My mind told me this was where I grew up but my eyes told me differently. How many years had it been since my departure? I couldn't recall exactly when I escaped but I knew my time between then and now was full of things I was glad to forget.

"I think I've died and gone to heaven," Reed mumbled over a mouthful of beef stew.

Gunner was trying his best to get the last of the soup into his mouth by tipping the bowl up. Eliseo ate in silence, savoring each bite while keeping a doubtful eye on everyone around us.

I stared at my bowl of vegetable stew and brought another spoon to my lips. Flavors burst on my tongue and I had to hold back a moan of satisfaction.

"Do you think they'll let us get seconds?" Gunner mumbled as he licked his lips, his eyes on the food line.

"Don't push your luck just yet, Gunner. Wait and see how the community operates before we stand out too much," Eliseo told him and Gunner sighed.

Another hour passed and the conversation in the room began to rise. I wondered what was happening.

"Chieftain Bradshaw!"

"Chieftain!"

A few of the residents called out with pride. Some of the kids got to their feet to get a better look at their leader as if his very presence was a gift not often graced.

The tall, middle-aged man raised his hand and signaled for the others to continue on as they were as he scanned the crowd and found us sitting on one of the tables closest to the farthest wall from the entrance.

I watched with rapt fascination, finishing my last bite as he made his way toward us. "You must be the newcomers. Greetings," he announced in what sounded like practiced speech.

How often did new people come to join a place that was hidden in sight? Unless they heard about it through word of mouth like I did. My mind went back to the old lady in Ashborne and our last conversation.

"Things have changed, Faheema. I don't know what life has brought you but I know you never deserved what happened. But time can be a wondrous thing. Perhaps this was the ancestor's way of showing you the right path. One that will lead you to what you need to discover in order to finally find peace."

Was she right? Was this what she meant? I didn't recognize this chieftain despite his age and the more I tried to think back... the more I recalled, we never had a leader at all during my childhood. Perhaps, everyone from my past had since moved on from the small community I remember. Maybe Silverforge had somehow found a way to give birth to a new community altogether.

"I'm Eliseo, and this here is my team," Eliseo began before proceeding to introduce us all casually.

"What kind of residence are you all looking for? By team, do you mean you all live together or..." the chieftain questioned, looking between us.

"We have two more in the infirmary. But yes, a single residence is fine for my team here. We would like to request a second right beside us for when our other two are well enough to leave the healer." Two residences? What did Eliseo have up his sleeve, what was I not seeing? And what were the odds they would have two right beside—

"Easily done. We've had a couple of residents choose to move on from us from the southeast corner by the potato farms, so a vacancy just opened up. I can move the resident beside it, as he's single and spends most of his time outside of his home anyhow," the chieftain informed us. "Now, in regards to what you can offer our community, we do not want to press you on your first day here. You all deserve a few days to settle and take the time to see how we operate in Silver-forge. New residents usually discover how they want to contribute quickly as they integrate. So, enjoy your meal, and I'll come by to check up on you all in... let's say, a week's time."

We all nodded and watched as he exited the communal kitchen, taking some of his fans with him.

"That was... strange," Reed commented, his eyes still glued to where the man left, observing how the people around him reacted to his presence.

"I'm with you guys. Can't trust anything but at the same time, we've been fed, Samuel's been rebandaged and smooth sailing so far. I say we settle in and see how this goes," Gunner added.

Eliseo nodded but didn't say a word, lost in thought.

I placed a hand on his shoulder and massaged it, hoping to ease his worries. We had been through hell together. Whatever happened here, we would be able to handle, I was confident of it. But like Gunner stated, why not soak in what good we were given by whatever higher power there was out there. Leaning my head against him, I sighed. "Let's enjoy it while we can. Whatever happens. We got each other."

Reed and Gunner nodded before they collected our bowls and returned it to the end of the food line, on a rolling cart.

"Once we rest up, we'll think clearer," Eliseo told me, wrapping his arms around my waist.

"Yeah," I placed my chin on his shoulder and looked at him. "Why two residences? Wouldn't it be better to have us all together?"

Eliseo turned to look at me with a smirk. "Remi is still young, and skittish. She's hard to pry away from Samuel and Samuel is going to need some much-needed rest. You saw how she was in there. I think it will be good for them to have some peace and quiet, for her to not only acclimate to us as a team but to also give her time away from her new surroundings until she's ready to explore. What better way than to give her a job she's doing anyway? Taking care of Samuel."

I stared at Eliseo, taking in his wisdom. I didn't think that far but here he was always thinking ahead. This was part of the reason why the men followed him so easily despite their clashing personalities at times.

"You guys ready?" Reed asked upon return. "That Daniel guy is waiting for us outside. Guess he's been given the role of tour guide."

Gunner snickered. "I'm amazed they let the younger guys guard the outside perimeter. They must really have a low rate of running into blood-suckers out here."

His statement left a lot to think about as we all got to our feet and made our way outside to meet up with Daniel who was flirting with one of the kitchen girls who was carrying a basket of fresh vegetables.

"Stop it, you know I need to get back to work," she giggled and I rolled my eyes.

"How about I come see you later? Maybe at the infirmary?"

She playfully slapped him. "You know Pata will have your head!"

Daniel stood straighter. "I'm not afraid of that old woman."

The girl threw her head back and laughed before walking around him back to the kitchen.

"Oh! I didn't see you all standing there. Well, where would you like to go first? The greenhouse? The schools? Or maybe the well. The flowers are lovely this time of the year," he offered.

"The house," Eliseo deadpanned and the poor boy's happy face morphed into a pout.

"Alright, follow me," he said, throwing a hand up in the air as if he was directing traffic. There was no one around us. Judging by the way the community ignored his antics, it told me this was part of his charm. Despite Eliseo's command, it didn't stop the poor fool from giving us a tour anyhow, telling us everything he knew about the areas we passed on our way to our designated residence.

"And here we have good 'ol Wren, one of our teachers. Don't judge a book by its cover, despite her looking about a century old, she still has a sharp wit about her. She oversees the feminine studies after the teens graduate from their secondary studies."

"This guy never shuts up," Reed grumbled behind me and I stifled a laugh, patting him on the thigh behind me to hush him up. I was actually fascinated with everything he revealed, appreciating how much this place has changed...for the better.

"Here we are. Ignore grumpy Maxwell, his joints are beginning to bother him as the years go by. He really doesn't mean to bite your head off, it's just part of his charm. All the kids are used to him and are instructed to leave him alone. On the rare occasions he comes out for fresh air, we have one of the girls from the kitchen bring him whatever he needs so he doesn't have to travel far for a good meal."

As if on cue, the sound of something breaking floated through the window... right before a basket was thrown at Daniel's head, knocking him off his feet.

"You stay out of my business, boy! I'm tired of your chattering. Let an old fool sleep, why don't you? This is why you youngins are stationed on the other side of this damn community!" the old man growled, hobbling to his front door with a cane.

Daniel rubbed his head and scrunched his face. "I didn't mean to wake you. Was just trying to show these guys to their house."

"You don't need an hour just to walk someone to their damn house!" The old man yelled, raising his cane threateningly.

"Well, guys. It was nice seeing you," Daniel squealed as he immediately turned on his heel and ran in the other direction.

The old man pointed his cane at us. "I expect you all to respect your elders while you're here. Keep your trap shut after hours and your dirty business down to a minimum. You're lucky I'm hard of hearing but don't use that to your advantage. This old man has been through more than you can imagine and I'm not afraid to handle you all if necessary."

"Respect goes both ways, old man," Eliseo rumbled and both Reed and Gunner groaned. I kept a soft smile on my face, wondering what exactly this old fool meant when he spoke of going through things. Was it before coming to live here?

"You the leader, eh? Well, that means you'll be the one to catch all the crap if I catch any of you getting on my damn nerves." He waved his cane a few more times before jabbing it into the ground for stability.

"And you'll catch crap if you start shit. We're not here to live in misery. You stay on your side and we'll stay on ours, you feel?" Eliseo crossed his arms and glared, never once backing down despite the old man being half his size, hunched over.

An awkward pregnant pause passed between us before the old man mumbled something under his breath, turned and slammed his door shut.

"Well that was interesting," I whispered, my lips twitching with mirth. "He reminds me a lot of someone."

"Don't you start with me, *Sili*," Eliseo snapped, storming toward one of the empty homes beside us. I looked at the other guys and rolled my eyes before following right behind him.

The interior was sparse but nothing we couldn't work with. In fact, it was already proving to be much cozier than the cabin High Father tried to corral us into back in Bellmore. There was a couch and a table in the first room, a decent-sized bed in the back bedroom. One restroom equipped with a single towel folded and ready to use. They even had toilet paper.

"Wow. We're moving on up, aren't we?" Gunner whistled and we could hear our neighbor throw something against his wall.

Ignoring old Maxwell, the guys began to explore the home, running their hands along the non-crumbling walls while Eliseo went into the bed and sat down with a sigh, taking his weight off his prosthetic. I quietly sat beside him and began to unstrap it, gently placing it against the wall and massaging his stump.

"Thanks, *Sili*," he groaned as he let his body fall back and clasped his hands behind his head. We all quietly accepted the piece we were given as we took in the silence around us with the occasional muffled curses coming from the next house over.

Soon, Eliseo's snores buzzed and I carefully left the bed without jostling him, letting him catch up on rest to sit between the other guys on the couch.

"What do you think?" I asked them.

Reed had his hands on his knees in quiet contemplation as Gunner stared at the wall ahead of him. There was a large mural hanging without a frame, tacked on each corner to keep it up. It depicted a life of serenity with soft clouds and a bright morning sun shining down on children playing in a field. We all stared at it until the sun went down, darkening the inside of our new home.

"It feels weird, you know?" Reed whispered behind his hands.

"Yeah," Gunner replied.

I placed my hands on both their knees in agreement before getting to my feet and opening the front door to look out. Leaning against the frame, I watched as the residents on the streets dwindled, ushering their children back into their homes while those without, lingered around each other in laughter.

Was this what the world looked like before everything? How was it possible for something to destroy all humanity ever knew? Was Otis right? Was it an airborne virus?

Reed came up behind me, leaning his forearm above me while Gunner stood beside me, leaning against the other side.

"Hard to believe, right?" Reed whispered.

"What?" I asked, unsure if we were both on the same line of thinking.

"You ever wonder why some of these religious men," he pointed in front of me over my shoulder to the ones we saw beyond the inner wall, "believe what they do? What makes their faith so strong that they entrust everything they know to prayer and supplication through... their interpretation of dreams?"

"Sometimes I wonder if they're high on something in order to reach a different level in their mind. Who even dreams anymore in this shitty life," Gunner mumbled. "I've run across a few, some of them led by different belief systems but all of them having certain foundations that are the same. A single basis of what they pray to, an entity, a higher power and their belief that through going to this being, they are able to get answers if they pray hard enough."

I turned to look at Gunner as Reed dropped his hand and placed it on the crook of my neck softly, playing with my hair. "You sound like you were sucked into something like that without your consent in the past... to know so much," I gently prodded. He didn't have to tell me if he wasn't comfortable. But there was something in the way his gaze went past the men in robes that told me there was more to his story.

He blinked a few times as if chasing old shadows before turning to me with a soft smile. "I'm glad Eliseo's catching some sleep. Can you imagine his cranky ass in here and that old fucker out there? I'm glad we're separated by a couple walls and a few yards. It's no wonder they threw them together," he snickered.

Deflection. It was a coping mechanism of mine too, per Eliseo. I smiled back and laced my fingers with Reeds to try and bite back my tongue. I cared about him and wanted to know how I could help... the same way they all helped me heal. But I also didn't want to create division by forcing him to speak of any past horrors he may have lived through. After all, I knew exactly how that felt.

I turned away from the doorway, leaving the guys there to check up on Eliseo. He had turned to his side but was still peacefully lost in slumber. I felt along the walls until I hit a switch, hoping for the best. A dim light flickered on before gradually getting brighter. Another hum started up in the far distance and I tilted my head to listen.

"What's wrong?" came Reed's voice from the living room. He was always watching me, wasn't he? It felt good to have someone at my back. I knew I couldn't always rely on Eliseo. He was only human.

"I think I hear a faint humming. Can you guys hear it?"

Their footsteps got closer as Gunner moved past me to lean out the open bedroom window. A light breeze billowed the lace curtains, bringing in the light scent of manure and wet dirt, as he looked left and right one more time before bringing his head back inside.

"What is it?" Reed asked, standing beside me while I continued to peacefully watch Eliseo's chest rise and fall with his relaxed breaths.

Gunner frowned for a few moments before answering. "I think it's a generator."

19

"You getting a little comfortable here, Samuel?" I teased, looking at his frustrated face when all his attempts at escaping got thwarted by Healer Pata who had taken to carrying a switch around with her.

"You little shit, I can't stand being cooped up in here," he gritted out and I laughed before he sheepishly looked at Remi whose lips were quivering as she held onto his hand. He let out a sigh and smoothed his features. "I'm just frustrated, Remi. Not with you. You have been an amazing nurse to me and I thank you for it. But you have to admit it feels like the walls are closing in as the minutes tick by, especially with the amount of traffic that comes in. I can't even take a piss alone in this place."

"That's because they don't want you to fall on

your ass and patch you up again," I supplied the obvious.

Samuel cut a glare before ignoring me. I let him. Looking over at the other occupied beds, everyone came in with varying degrees of injuries. From simple splinters to someone's detached sole lodging a rock inside of a man's heel during his plowing. But nobody complained as the healer mended them followed by some of the young nurses informing them of how they should take care of their wounds in order for them to have a speedy recovery.

This place was a well-oiled machine. There was a system in place that all depended on one another, all pieces of a larger whole. Was this what Ashborne was missing? Watching how smoothly things moved and the smiling faces of the residents as they went about their day, I had to admit invigorated me in ways I had almost forgotten was possible.

The same girl from the soup kitchen came toward us in what I mentally labeled as a nurse's apron. I wondered if Daniel kept his promise in meeting her that day. She was a hard worker and didn't deserve a flake. My thoughts floated to *Sili* back home with the other guys. The plan today was to see where we fit in as we force ourselves to integrate and settle down. We were all tired of running.

"How are we doing?" the nurse asked softly,

looking over a file folder full of handwritten notes and images.

"Claustrophobic. Tell the doc I'm ready to leave the infirmary. Walking around will be good for my muscles," Samuel snapped. Remi gave him a little frown and shake of his hand and he let out a frustrated sigh.

His attitude didn't perturb the nurse as she thoroughly read through the papers. "Lucky for you, Healer Pata recently just assigned you to our rehabilitation team on the south side of Silverforge. Would you like me to show you where it is or send someone to take you? Your first sessions start in the next three hours," she said with a smile, efficiently closing the file and clasping her hands in front of her.

"What do you mean? Can't I get a chance to rest in my own place for a day at least?" complained Samuel as he sat on the edge of the bed carefully.

"You'll have to take that up with Healer Pata. See you around Samuel!" The nurse turned on her heel and left us without another word as she checked the file for the next patient.

"Geez, if she smiles any wider, I'm going to have nightmares. This place is too happy. Get my ass out of here," Samuel grumbled, getting to his feet. I stood beside him as he took his first few steps. A few wobbles but he regained his footing, limping along beside Remi, occasionally stopping to lean on my shoulders. "I might need some of those homemade painkillers they have," he gritted out as we continued forward.

"Is that what they've been shooting you up with to keep you in their infirmary?" I inquired but was genuinely curious. What other kinds of medicines did they have here? My own joints ached when the temperature drops.

When we reached the cluster of homes in the southeast corner where the rest of the team were waiting for us, eager for our reunion.

Sili ran up first and greeted Remi before eyeing Samuel from head to toe. "You back?" she teased.

"You can't force me into one of Pata's beds. I'll fight you, even with one leg down. Those mattresses feel like I'm sleeping on metal. I'd rather sleep on the ground," he growled.

"We're glad you're back. The team wasn't the same without you," *Sili* told him before turning to Remi. "I see you took really good care of him. Thanks, Remi. You did a great job. Far as I know, I didn't hear anyone screaming or yelling from the infirmary so it must mean he was being good."

"He wasn't," she deadpanned and Samuel gave her a look of betrayal. "What? It's true."

Gunner and Reed joined in on some banter as we all shook our heads and helped him into the vacant home beside ours. Maxwell must have been asleep. There wasn't anything being thrown against the wall during our conversation.

"How were you guys able to secure this place in such short notice? And right beside each other,"

Samuel asked as he struggled to sit down on the couch, stretching his leg out. The springs groaned under his weight as some dust visibly fell beneath.

Remi curiously went to go check out the bedroom that was an exact replica of ours.

"Have you guys discussed where you wanted to contribute," I blurted out, now that our reunion had settled.

"I'm thinking the kitchen," Gunner replied quickly and we all looked at him knowingly. "What?"

"I might check out what they have going in regards to their hunting strategies. With the meat we were provided on our first day, they must have hunting or trapping groups established. If not, I could always suggest a trapping group to work smarter and not harder," Reed piped in.

I nodded and looked at Samuel, knowing he would be occupied with his rehabilitation for the most part. I was sure they wouldn't push him to contribute in his state, especially because he also needed to take care of Remi and vice versa.

"*Sili*, how about you?" I was preemptively cautious of letting out of my sight. We still didn't know anyone here enough to fully trust them but they hadn't proven guilty of anything... yet.

She hummed and I turned to look at her, catching her braid Remi's dark locks into a thick plait.

"What's going on in that pretty little head of yours?"

She bit her lip in concentration before turning her brown eyes in my direction. "Despite getting comfortable with you guys, I'm still not partial to crowds. I'm going to have to think on this a little further, check things out before I make a decision. Maybe they'll have something where I can work on my own and still contribute. It would also let me hang around here, in case Samuel or Remi needs me," she thoughtfully replied.

"I don't need anything—" Samuel started but flinched when Remi hit him in the arm with a glower. "Geez. Relax. I got it."

"Since everyone keeps cutting up pants, maybe I can... help sew and repair things for Silverforge?" *Sili* thought out loud.

Looking at my team, my own mind ran with the possibilities of what I could do here. Though my gut told me to stay by *Sili*, she was fully capable of handling herself. I needed to keep in mind that she survived before us, out in the open among the bloodsuckers as well.

The aromatic smell of garlic and herbs drifted through the open door and Gunner's stomach rumbled.

"Well, that's my cue. Might as well go meet everyone's acquaintance and see where I sign up," he said with a grin, rubbing his stomach.

"You are too much. How can they trust you if you're eating the food before you can pass it on to the residents?" *Sili* teased, stepping away from Remi toward him. I enjoyed watching our team grow comfortable and relaxed. When was the last time we were given a chance to just be ourselves?

"Hey, I take offense to that. Look at me. Do I look like a person who steals food from others? Come on, *Sili*, give me more credit. I'll have you know, I am highly skilled in cooking when I have the right ingredients and tools. I just never had a chance to fully utilize it... until now," he pouted before leaning in to whisper conspiratorially. "But I will try to bring the leftovers home," he chuckled before leaving Samuel's new home.

Shaking our heads, I gave Samuel a once-over before nodding to Remi. "You got it from here, kid?"

Remi straightened and nodded her head.

"Some of the residents came by earlier today to bring you some extra clothes," I explained. "For both of you. Samuel, don't be late for your rehabilitation. The team needs you in top shape."

"Yeah, yeah. Got it," he grumbled, throwing his arm over his face and resting comfortably against the back of the couch.

"Remi, I'll bring you something from the kitchen, okay? Tell me what else you need while I'm out. I'll see what I can get or find out," *Sili* offered in a motherly manner. It came to her naturally and I admired her beauty while she was in her element from where I stood. That wasn't to say she didn't have other amazing qualities, but that this was the first time I was given witness to this part of her. I watched as she interacted with Remi, making sure all worry dissipated from the girl's face before turning to face me.

"We good?" I asked, taking heed of her pace.

"Yeah, let's go grab a bite and see if we can find something that interests you, Eliseo. You still haven't told us what you wanted to do for your contribution here."

Letting her grab my hand we left the house and I mulled over her words. Most of my life, all I could remember was being a soldier or positions lateral to it. No matter how much I tried to get away, the calling never left me alone. Each community or compound I resided in constantly ended with me on the team that performed the essential runs.

I blamed it on my father, a hard man who lived the same. It was the only example I had growing up besides my mother and sisters who stayed behind, keeping the home and making sure we were stocked with food supplies. Without the pressure of survival stress, I pondered over where some of my sisters ended up once they found partners. Two of them decided to stay in the same community with us but the eldest left with her husband who was part of a nomadic trade group that graced our home every fall.

"What are you thinking about?" Fitri asked as we found ourselves standing in the breakfast line with a tray in our hands.

"Life. Family. Where people are now and if they're still alive," I answered her and her expression softened before she lifted her tray for the kitchen girl to fill her bowl with something vegetarian.

We quietly made it to the end of the line where we found Gunner covered in an apron and a hair net on his head. "Laugh it up guys while I enjoy sneaking in a bite of food throughout the day."

Sili stifled a laugh and I shook my head as we found an empty seat at one of the tables in the communal kitchen building.

"Did you have a big family?" *Sili* asked cautiously. I knew she was thinking of her own and I kicked myself for answering her earlier. Here I was, reminiscing all the good memories I had while she was still trying to piece hers and understand if they were good at all.

"Somewhat. It doesn't really matter. How do you survive off all these vegetables, *Sili*? You can't possibly gain weight this way," I told her.

She puffed out her chest and my eyes dropped before she cleared her throat, pulling my attention back to her face. "I gain weight just fine, Eliseo. Unless, you want to feed me another way..." she trailed off seductively and I sat up straighter, only to have her chuckle, pull out a pickle and shove it in my mouth.

I scowled but she continued to laugh musically, relaxing my expression to join in on her contentment. This was what she deserved. A life without looking over her shoulder. A life where she could laugh—as a woman—with her found family without a care.

I promised myself I would strive to keep providing her with safety, to keep her at peace if it was the last thing I did in this life.

The day went on uneventfully and for the first time, I began to wonder if all my suspicions were for naught. *Sili* relieved Remi of her duties, telling her to go explore a few houses down and see if she could meet new acquaintances. I didn't overlook the fact that she didn't tell her to go look for new friends. Hannah's betrayal cut *Sili* deep and I wasn't sure if she would ever recover from it.

Sure, she had the team, but didn't women need other women?

After putting up with Samuel's complaints and whines after his first rehabilitation session with some of the nurses, I made sure to find Remi and bring her back home, keeping an eye on everyone she said she spoke to. She reminded me of *Sili* in many ways, her timidness and the way she kept her head down. But after a good bowl of spaghetti and meatballs for lunch, her face brightened as she skipped into the living room to bring Samuel his share.

"Where do they keep all their supplies?" Samuel asked through a mouthful of pasta.

"I think I saw a small mill beyond their vegetable farms," *Sili* answered, rubbing my back as we sat on the edge of the table, watching Samuel eat contently.

"What don't they have?"

"Are you interested in something, Sammy? Can

I come too?" Remi asked, looking up at him adoringly.

"What do you think we should do here?" he humored her. Like *Sili,* I had never seen this part of him and wondered how life would have turned out if Hannah wasn't compromised by crazy Otis. I guess, we'd never find out.

Remi tapped her chin thoughtfully as she scooted closer to his side, staring at him bringing another fork to his mouth. "Maybe we can do some sewing like *Sili.*"

Samuel choked on his food and looked at her. "You can't trust me with needles, look how large my hands are!"

"What do you mean? You'll have me! I'll do the needles. I watched the healer and it didn't look that hard. If you're worried about your large hands, just cut the fabric," she said her logical conclusion aloud.

"She does have a p—" *Sili* started but was cut off with Samuel's hand. Samuel never took his eyes off Remi.

"Babe, I'm a man. I'm not cut out for that stuff. Look at me. We fight. We might cook. We protect, we provide. I mean, I might join Reed in hunting to bring back skins if that's what you're talking about," he tried to reason but Remi placed her hands on her hip and mirrored his scowl with the same intensity.

"That doesn't make any sense. Do you see anyone around here walking around with skins?

Everyone here has clothes. Just like when Healer Pata cut off yours. What if that happens again? You going to walk around naked?" she shot back.

It was my turn to choke as *Sili* held back a laugh, rubbing my back. If only Remi knew... but better it, it was good she didn't.

"What happened to that quiet little girl we picked up, huh?" Samuel teased, nudging her with his elbow, but she refused to back down.

"You were hurt because of me," she began to tear up. "I can never repay you for saving me f-from that man. And I couldn't do anything to help the healer while you were in the sick room. I want to do this for you. I want to be helpful. I want you to know that I can be useful. I don't—" she rambled uncontrollably until Samuel placed his hand on her shaky ones to stop her.

"Remi. Stop. Don't ever think that you're disposable. Nothing is going to happen to you. You're part of the team, you got that?" he reassured her and her lips quivered before tears fell onto their joined hands.

"I-I can be useful," she whispered and my heart cracked. What did that bastard do to her? We came to discover that Remi was about thirteen. Flashes of the bastard's mention of having two viable women for his sexual gratification made me grind my teeth. Was that what he convinced her of? Her only purpose in life to serve others in disgusting ways?

I was about to say something in rage when

Samuel beat me to it, pulling her into a tight embrace.

"Your only purpose in life right now is to live it. Be happy. Let me take care of you and the rest will come. Don't worry about worth or any of that shit because none of us are perfect and none of us are without our shortcomings." He pulled back and tipped her chin up. "But you, you were made for something special. I knew it the moment I saw you. Don't ever doubt that. I might have a bad leg right now, but know that I would fight for you to the death if it came to it. You're the future in this shithole existence, babe. Let me live vicariously through you so I can forget all the crap that's been thrown my way, alright?"

I knew his mind went back to Hannah and Otis. He needed a new beginning, and Remi was it. Remi would be the one to heal him.

Sili sniffed beside me and I pulled her into an embrace as well.

"You gave me a second chance and I want to show you how much I appreciate that, Sammy. That's all. Y-You've been the only one in my life t-to—"

He kissed the top of her head and handed her the empty bowl. "Well, if you want to be useful, you can start by taking this back for me because as much as my ego hates to admit it, I can't."

Samuel awkwardly looked anywhere but at Remi as she obediently rose and did as he told her to. *Sili* and I both watched as his eyes followed her retreating form, leaving the front door.

"Stop all that damn racket over there!" Maxwell shouted.

"Shut your pie hole before I shut it for you!" Samuel growled before staggering to his feet and heading to the bedroom without giving any of us a glance.

20

"Why do you have to go?"

My irritation grew and I didn't know why. Three weeks in this settlement, trying to occupy my time with helping Reed and the trapping group but there was a different itch beneath my skin, one I couldn't put my finger on.

My rage was getting the better of me and I chalked it up to pent-up testosterone from being too complacent here. I needed to release my energy and none of the jobs at Silverforge fit the bill. The only thing I could think about was working with wood to build a new home but the chieftain told us we were running out of room for any additional homes.

I ran a hand down my face as *Sili* continued to pester me with her questions. "But why do you need to go if you're already working with the men who are going on the outing? Hunting and trapping are by the community, why not go with them?"

My blood boiled and I shot to my feet, pointing my finger into her chest. "Because, as a woman, you won't understand. I just gotta do it. Why are you holding me back? It's not like I haven't done it before. Hell, I met you while we both went on an outside run," I growled in her face.

Her own pupils dilated as she leaned in to snarl back at me. "Because, Eliseo, you're not the same. It's not the same!"

"Would you all shut up!" came Maxwell's voice through the open window right before something crashed against his wall.

"I'm going whether you like it or not," I snarled before turning away from her and grabbing a coat on the way out.

"Don't you walk away from me!"

I threw my hand up in the air without looking back. I already was. There was no point in her arguments. She couldn't hold me down. Not when there was a growing fever inside of me that made my skin feel like it was coated in grease. I needed fresh air, I needed to get away. I needed to fight something to get this energy within me out.

I growled out loud and kicked a wayward can, startling some of the residents around me. Stomping forward I made my way to the team preparing to leave on a supply run.

"Hey, Eliseo," came Cameron's greeting. He

was one of the team leaders. Reed looked over his shoulder at me and frowned. "You joining us?"

"Yeah," I threw out simply, putting on my coat and rolling my shoulders. Reed didn't say a word as he broke away from the group. I kept my eyes on Cameron, orange hair and freckles as I crossed my arms, waiting for orders.

The light throb on my stump only further irritated me as well as the fight with *Sili*. But I forced myself to focus and grabbed one of the guns they passed to me, tossing it over my shoulder.

"Alright guys, today we're going to trek toward the northwest, along the border while keeping a good distance away from The Steel Fang," Cameron began, looking at his map on one of the boulders.

"The Steel Fang?" I questioned, coming closer to get a better look at where he was pointing to.

"Yeah? Have you heard of it? Supposedly it's neutral ground for both humans and bloodsuckers but I wouldn't hold my breath. A bunch of bloodsuckers in one place? Fuck that. But if they're all distracted, it gives us a good chance of having less probability of running into one that's just hanging out waiting for food."

"That makes sense," I mumbled, wondering if *Sili* had any past experiences or runs with the place. But I kept in mind she was only half vampire, adopted at that. She wouldn't have had anyone give her any information about how the bloodsuckers and their operations worked.

As we all began to follow one another toward the first outer wall, I looked back once to see if *Sili* followed me. The fact she didn't pissed me off and I didn't understand why. Why was I so agitated? And why was she? Were we just building off each other's energy? Sex had become explosive, gaining us some complaints from Maxwell to the chieftain.

The chieftain promised to keep an eye out for vacancies but that was over a week ago.

We gathered in a total of four armored vehicles with all-terrain tires and skidded onto a dirt road that led to a field. One of the men threw a compass on the dash as Cameron navigated the lead vehicle toward our destination.

"There should be a few abandoned towns on the way, we'll see what we can ransack. Not too many humans come out this far, their fear of being caught between clan wars high," Cameron admitted.

"You're not afraid?" I asked.

"Nah. I've navigated these roads too much, and know too many exit points. Plus, it's easy to spot a bloodsucker from Clan Lekim. They have similar colored hair, so it takes them a minute to figure out I'm not one of them," he chuckled. "And they're too cocky to assume any human would be brave enough to go up against them. It works to my advantage when necessary."

The chill crept in despite the sun being high and I was reminded of some of the vampires we caught in broad daylight. "Hey, do some of them walk in the sun? I thought all vampires burned in its rays."

One of the guys in the back seat leaned forward to answer as the outside noise threatened to drown out his voice. All the vehicles had their windows down. "That's the thing. We've only seen it among Clan Lekim. They're a different breed of demon. A few of them can stand the daylight for short periods of time while others call on the power of wolves like a fucking animal whisperer or some shit."

Flashes of the old man back at Bellmore sent a shiver down my spine. "Do they drink wolf's blood?"

The others around me scoffed. "How could they? No way. Animal blood kills them. It's why they try to gather as many human stragglers as they possibly can for their farms. Wherever you got that intel man, I wouldn't trust that person again."

The only problem was... I saw with my own eyes. Could it be possible to build up tolerance to animal blood? The same way some people built up tolerance to different kinds of venom? Well, the old fool was dead now, but I filed the information in the back of my mind to tell the team upon my return.

The first town was pretty sparse, but I was able to gather a few herbal plants according to some hand-drawn paperwork the botanist gave us for the mission.

It was the second town that made my skin

prickle with awareness. A sense of foreboding clouded my mind as we set on foot, searching through the abandoned stores and gas stations.

"Make sure you check any abandoned vehicles as well. As much as our moonshine distillery continuously works, it's nice not to have to use the alcohol for fuel," Cameron whispered before we nodded and dispersed into smaller teams of three.

"Hey, check this out. I can't read the label," Dean, one of my teammates called out. We both stepped over debris and crumbling drywall to see what he was talking about. Colt clicked his flashlight and pointed it at the label but half of the words were faded.

As we leaned in closer to try and read some of the letters, a body crashed into the wall and I was taken back to the first time *Sili* and I went on an outing together. Before the growl could emerge from the plume of smoke and dust, my eyes quickly adjusted and spotted a large looming figure, then a hint of red hair. On instinct, my body leapt forward, tackling the intruder to the ground with my hands around his neck.

"I see we got a live one," he hissed beneath me before he kicked me off and launched me against the farthest wall.

Gunfire peppered the air as shouts rang out from every direction. I shook off the dust and snarled with elation before running back into the fray. Colt flew beside me but it felt like he moved in slow motion as my arm shot out and grabbed the bloodsucker by the scruff of his shirt. His grin turned wicked as he opened his fangs and came at me. Dodging, I wrapped one of my arms around his neck and pulled until I heard a small crack.

"Oh, I like to play dirty too, human. You're quicker than the other one, and I was just getting bored," he taunted as he flipped us back, smacking my skull into the broken concrete inches away from a steel bar.

"Where the hell are you? Eliseo! Dean!" came Cameron's coughing voice. The other men's boots thrummed around me like a war drum as I rolled right before the bloodsucker slammed his boot into my chest. He stomped again and I grabbed it, pulling his foot from under him and getting into the dominant position above.

He laughed maniacally as he twisted and took me with him right as a shot hit his shoulder. He leaned in and grinned. "You lied to me. Tsk, tsk tsk. If you didn't want to play fair, I would have put more effort into it," he cooed as he leaned in and sniffed my neck.

A primal urge forced my movements as I bit into his neck, making him moan and then scream in agony with every pull. As he jerked his head away, my fangs pulled some of his flesh with it. Spitting it out, I watched him carefully as he covered his wound with his hand.

"What are you?" he sneered.

"Your worst fucking nightmare," I responded,

right before I leapt onto him again and twisted his neck with a loud crack.

As the dust settled around me, I licked my lips and slowly stood, taking stock of my other team and their positions. But what I found was myself surrounded by the other men as they stared at me slack-jawed, some with disgust.

"Take him," was the last thing I heard out of Cameron's mouth as he lifted his gun at me while the rest of the men tackled me to the ground right over the bloodsucker's dead body. Every touch and every breath oversensitized me as I gasped for air under a new cloud of dust kicked up from their struggle to keep me down. My eyes watered as the sun's rays seemed to amplify the longer I fought.

"Fuck, he's too strong!"

"Grab his other arm!"

"Watch out for his fangs!"

I snapped in the air, trying to gain any sort of semblance of control as limbs tangled themselves around me. My body felt like it was on fire from within and from without. Everything was too much and not enough, my throat throbbing from a hunger I couldn't contain. Each pulse near my face only served to torture me as they all kept their distance from my mouth, forcing my throat to become dry.

"Get your fucking hands off me or I'll kill you all," slipped through my lips as my mind tried to placate me with images of *Sili* letting me drink from her and the way her body writhed against mine this morning, taking me over the edge of ecstasy. I groaned as my cock strained against my pants, wondering if I should keep one of them alive until I can get this frantic energy out of my system before I made it back home to *Sili,* to beg for her forgiveness—for her to take me back into her.

When someone's sleeve pulled up his forearm, a new burst of energy emerged. Knocking two of the men off me, I shot my arm out and grabbed his, bringing it toward my face for a bite. Warm blood spurted deliciously down my throat and my eyelids fluttered to the sound of agonizing screams.

Another pull and I thought of how wet and pliable *Sili* was beneath me as I claimed her again and again to the sound of her pleas, Maxwell's complaints be damned. Too quickly, I was pulled away, tearing his flesh as I made sure to chew on what I could gather in my mouth as Cameron threw me over another pile of broken concrete.

With a new surge of energy from my feeding, my mind was drunk in a red haze, hungry to fill the void that gnawed at my insides. Whether it was to feed or fuck, or both, my eyes zoned in on all the different heart rhythms sporadically thrumming around me.

"Eliseo!" Cameron barked but it was drowned out by the sound of the closest heartbeat. I licked my lips and took in a deep inhale, testing the air for the best delicacy among the crew. Surprisingly, it was Cameron's. All his talk of Clan Lekim and red hair, little did he know he was a carrier as well, his scent slightly different from the other men.

"Cameron, you sneaky bastard. I knew you were playing for both teams," I taunted.

"What the hell are you talking about?" he barked, never letting his gun down. The warmth of the barrel told me he already let out a shot. How many more bullets did he truly have with his bluff?

"You sure you getting by Clan Lekim because of simply your hair or is there something you want to tell the other men?" When the guys turned to look at him with suspicion, I took my opportunity, taking Cameron down and knocking the gun out of his hands. As the men around me roared and shot into my back, I laughed aloud right before I sank my fangs into his neck, giving in to the craving for liquid sustenance.

Vitality grew with each pull of my mouth. A few more gulps and Cameron's struggle began to die right as one of the guys slammed the butt of their rifle into the back of my skull for the last time, plunging me into darkness.

21

FITRI

I DIDN'T FEEL WELL. MAYBE IT WAS BECAUSE OF MY fight with Eliseo but my stomach was rolling as I sat in the communal kitchen with Reed.

"Why did you stay back again? I thought you were going out with the other guys. You were excited for it all week," I reminded him.

He scowled at me and lifted a spoonful of soup to my mouth, forcing me to take a bite. I did so reluctantly, knowing I was being stubborn and that an empty stomach would do nothing but make me angrier.

"Eliseo looked like he had something up his ass," Reed grumbled. "I couldn't leave you here by yourself."

I tilted my head in confusion. "Gunner and Samuel are here."

A few of the other residents walked by and

looked at us curiously but I ignored them, my mind occupied with more important things.

He scoffed. "Samuel gets tired from walking a mile and Gunner always has his face in a bowl of food by the time he comes home from the kitchen. Even Maxwell is losing things to throw because of his sawing logs when he gets back home."

I hung my head in shame. Reed always strived to watch out for me and take care of me when Eliseo wasn't around—which was rare. Why was Eliseo so hellbent on leaving anyway? We had been doing fine the whole time since we settled here, learning how to live life like regular people.

"I see it in your face, Fitri," he slowly shook his head before bringing another spoonful into my mouth. "You know Eliseo's got the hardest head in the group. How do you cage a wild beast and force him to live a life he was never meant to live? Just because he's usually calm around you doesn't mean he's tamed."

I knew he was right but my mind kept refusing to believe it. Yes, he was an irrational man who was hellbent on getting his way when we first met, but we had been through so much together as a group, he was different now. What in the world could have happened for him to... regress back to the way he was, with extra attitude on top? It didn't make any sense and it frustrated me to no end. Out of the blue, the smell of frying garlic in the pan over a roaring flame made me scrunch my face in disgust.

"What? Is there something wrong with the soup?" Reed asked curiously, examining the bowl.

My heart hammered in my chest as if I was injected with some sort of chemical to kick-start it out of the norm. "No—I don't know. I need some air."

Reed whistled for Gunner's attention to collect my unfinished bowl as he followed me out of the building. The moment fresh air hit my face, I realized that my entire body was exponentially perspiring. Pulling the fabric of my shirt away from me to fan myself, I darted toward home with Reed's boots chasing behind me.

"Fitri, what's wrong?" he called out.

"I'm hot. I-I need to wash off," I mumbled as I barged through our front door, straight for the restroom to turn on the overhead shower. My heart wouldn't let up, my body itching.

"Fitri—"

With my mind solely on my task, I stripped, threw the clothes to the bottom of the shower and stepped in. The moment the cascade hit me, I sighed in relief. I yelped in surprise when Reed stepped in too, fully clothed minus his boots.

"What the hell is going on?" he asked again, forcing my eyes on him as droplets ran down his face, distracting me for a second.

"My skin," I gasped, not wanting any of my weird abilities to affect him. I leaned back as far as I could, plastering myself against the tile wall, while scrubbing the sweat away furiously with my bare hands, raking my nails across my flesh in the process. I remained unsure whether it was *all* of my sweat that produced the toxin, or if it was the reaction my body took when it thought it needed to defend itself.

All the times Eliseo and I passionately came together naked—that particular light sheen of sweat never did any harm. I never heard him complain about going numb like he did out at the lake.

But with my stomach violently convulsing and my internal body temperature rising, I made sure to push the handle of the shower to cold. The rumble of the generator in the distance hummed softly in the distance as Reed pulled me into his chest, replacing my hands with his to wash me, running over my healing welts.

"W-what are you doing?" I asked him through chattering teeth, the chill of the water finally seeping through.

"Taking care of you because that asshole left you here. Stand still," he commanded as his hands continued to roam clinically until he was satisfied I was clean and unharmed. I watched him turn the water off and grab the towel from the rack, wrapping me in fluff before lifting me out of the shower. I stood there like a drowned waterbeast as he began to undress in front of me, slapping his wet clothes onto the floor beside us, while trying to dry me at the same time.

Was it unfounded of me to crave his particular

brand of attention right now? Despite being fully capable of doing this on my own, something felt off inside of me and my mind was discombobulated. As he stood there naked, I stared into his intense eyes as he concentrated on what he was doing.

When he nudged me to lift my arms, I did, letting him pat my underarms and travel up to my hair. He took a step closer and I could feel the warmth radiating off his skin toward my cold, shivering one.

I stuttered when he leaned in beside my cheek to make sure he gathered all the wet strands into the towel, squeezing it dry instead of rubbing it. He had been watching me, studying how I did things.

"Reed..." I breathed. I shouldn't like the fact that he watches me, even when I was with Eliseo. I shouldn't like that his voyeuristic tendencies made me hot when it shouldn't. To know he was always within reach but forbidden, made me bite my lip and sometimes fuck Eliseo harder.

What was wrong with me? It wasn't normal to feel this way, was it? Was this another part of my quirks that further separated me from being human? Guilt washed over me like a maelstrom.

"Let me take care of you, Fitri. You don't need to say anything. I want to, okay? Just give me this," he whispered against my ear as he brought the towel forward and rubbed the hair at my temples gently away from my face.

"What are we doing, Reed?" I stammered.

"Drying off. What does it look like we're doing?" he answered easily.

"I don't feel so good," I admitted as the internal windstorm made my legs weak.

He immediately let the towel fall to the floor and picked me up, taking me to the bedroom. I leaned into his familiar scent, letting my hands crawl along up to wind around his shoulder... letting it calm my nerves as my back hit the cool cotton sheets. Reed leaned over to wrap me with the other side of the fabric. Before he could leave, I pulled him, making him stumble beside me on the mattress.

"Stay with me? I don't want to be alone right now," I pleaded, refusing to break contact, yet hating myself for craving him so. Reed growled and nodded, mumbling something about Eliseo being a dick before he pulled me against him, cocooning me.

"Do you want to tell me what happened back there?" he whispered against my shoulder, his breath dancing across my skin.

I shifted in the sheets, the light rustle sounding loud in my ears, grating my flesh for some odd reason as I placed the tip of my nose against his lightly furred chest. Everything right now was at odds with logic. Why was my skin overly sensitive? My nipples pebbled while my mind told me I needed to pry everything off, it was too constricting.

"I'm not sure. Someone was frying something

and I felt like I was going to be sick. But I think I wasn't feeling well before that, so I don't really know," I rambled before my eyes began to burn with unshed tears. "Maybe I'm just upset he left me even though I expressed that I wanted him to stay."

Could it really be as simple as not having him with me? All logic flew out the window. I felt raw. The past few days confounded me. From explosive spontaneous sex that threatened to break our furniture to fights of the same intensity the next minute. Our highs and lows scared me and I began to wonder if it had anything to do with our bodies having gotten used to fight or flight for so long, it didn't know what to do with itself in a time of peace. When Reed placed his lips on my forehead, scalding tears fell into the sheets and I began to sob.

"It's alright," he whispered, holding me tighter, rubbing my back.

"But what if it's not?" I hiccuped, irrational thoughts and emotions swirling inside of me like a tempest.

"Why wouldn't it be?" he asked as the temperature in the room rose. *Or was it just me?*

I shook my head, unable to explain what my gut was telling me. The foreboding that weaved its way into my pores like a living thing. Each breath it metaphorically took shook me to the core. What was it trying to tell me?

"I don't know, Reed. I don't know. I feel like I'm

drowning but there's no water," I broke down as my emotional rollercoaster dipped and peaked, dipped and peaked. I shook, despite the sheet covering me, despite Reed surrounding me in everything. I shook and wiped my tears with the back of my hand until Reed grabbed my chin and forced me to look at him, making me sharply inhale in surprise.

The pools of his eyes reminded me of a hot summer day where the dry earth began to lighten under the sun. Talks of the western wastelands flitted through my head as I tried to remember who exactly said—

Reed covered his mouth with mine and I let out a sigh. His kiss pulled away my worries, my fragmented memories, forcing me to concentrate in the moment as he tentatively licked the seam of my lips without forcing his way in. Opening my mouth with each pass in invitation, he purposefully teased the tip of his tongue with mine and then retreated, making me chase him. His own body shivered as he pulled away and groaned against the top of my head.

"You torture me, Fitri," he gritted out. "Every time you walk by, you take a piece of me with you. Every time I see you with him, envy becomes my demon—the harbinger of my downfall. You cannot comprehend the depths in which you've buried yourself into me since the day you knocked me on my ass during training so long ago." His voice broke as his arms tightened and I felt myself choking with him.

In a perfect world, I wouldn't have to choose. I wouldn't have to feel this guilt as my stomach continued to churn angrily into a knot. But this world was anything but perfect. This world was everything that continuously goes wrong.

Reluctance in every movement, Reed pulled himself away from me completely and grabbed one of Eliseo's boxers in his drawers before heading to the living room without another word passed between us. I despised myself then for doing this to him, for torturing him the way he described. I was undeserving. I shouldn't pull him along, but I also couldn't imagine life without him in it.

"Hey, is everything alright? Reed, where's Fitri? She ran out of there like something was on her tail, man."

"She's resting in the bedroom. She needed to cool down quickly," Reed replied and I could hear the couch springs creaking under his weight. My supplied an image of him raking his hands through his hair the way he always did as he rested his elbows on his knees, deep in thought.

"Why are you half naked?" Gunner asked slowly.

"She needed to wash," he said with nonchalance and the couch creaked again.

"Okay..." Gunner crossed the threshold of the bedroom and looked at me with seriousness. "Fitri?"

Another sob escaped and he quickly came to my side, pulling me into his arms. Gunner's scent makes me think of freedom in an open field, where this wicked world never existed. If there was truly a utopia like the rumors say to the west, it would smell like Gunner—peace, calm and serenity in the face of adversity.

"Take a deep breath, *mi reina.*"

I did as he bid and closed my eyes. Where was Reed? I was falling apart without Eliseo. I needed my found-family around me. "R-Reed?" I sniffed.

Immediately the bed dipped and both men had their arms around me, trying to hold my sanity together as I continued to take in their scent. I didn't know how much time passed but my mouth went dry at their proximity, listening to the thrum of their heartbeats—this was the same reaction I had when Eliseo's pheromones invaded my senses, driving me into carnal madness.

I was famished, my abdomen constricting with hunger. But wasn't I sick a few hours ago? What was going on with me? The void was growing into a chasm as I began to ache fiercely. Groaning in pain, I shoved their arms away as my internal temperature spiked once more. Kicking the sheets, I tangled and fell onto the ground, trying to crawl away from their delectable scent but failing after a couple of feet, spasming in place.

"Fitri!"

"What the hell is happening?" Gunner asked.

"I don't fucking know!"

My eyelids were heavy, I felt like my face was sticking to the floor as I forced my body to turn to my back so I could take in the breeze. But there was no breeze, just the guys rushing around me, trying to lift me back into the bed. Their hands were scalding and I screamed, another echo coming from Maxwell's house.

"You all can go to hell!" he roared from his side, followed by a crash. How many things did he have in there to throw daily?

I laughed and cried, then deliriously moaned as vertigo set in.

"Stay with me, *little iris*," Reed's desperate voice cut in.

"Fitri, come on, *mi reina*. Open your eyes for me," Gunner pleaded.

They tried to wrap me in the sheet but I whimpered and Reed cursed under his breath.

"Fucking nuisances!" came Maxwell's next scream. "The ground needs to open up and swallow you all whole!"

What he didn't realize was... it felt like I was already there.

22

ELECTRICITY RAN THROUGH ME, INCAPACITATING ME FOR the next few minutes as my veins felt like they were being melted from the inside. The gawking eyes of spectators made my skin prickle as they murmured between each other in my haze. I snapped my head up when one of them mentioned my name, pointing in my direction. Grinning, I took in his scent and my mouth watered. With inhuman speed, I slammed into the metal bars of my cell only to be electrified again, sending me spasming on the ground of their stone prison.

Built beneath Silverforge was an intricate dungeon that housed not only myself, but what looked like other bloodsucking prisoners kept for experimentation. It wasn't Healer Pata down here, but the Chieftain as he spoke in hushed whispers with the rest of the men from the outing... minus Cameron.

I let out a raw laugh as I could still taste his life force on my tongue. I was delirious from the taste, wanting the rest of these fools to step a bit closer so I could have my fill.

"He's rabid," one of the men stated with repulsion.

"All the better to keep him for observation. We've never been able to witness a newly made—"

"That's just the thing!" the next man hissed. "He wasn't bitten!"

"How is that even possible? All evidence points to newly made vampires needing to be given the venom by the selected host," came the Chieftain's calm voice.

Oh, if only crazy Otis could see me now. He'd have the time of his life here, especially with their sophisticated tools and shit.

They pulled my blood and I broke the guy's arm, stabbing him instead and injecting him with it. He foamed at the mouth and smelled rancid as I tackled the next guard who tried to take me down. It took five men to throw me behind these bars and the ache in my muscles gave me life. I was beyond invigorated. This was the high I was searching for. It was as if everything fell into place and a new calm overtook me.

But fuck was I desperate to sink my cock into *Sili*. I twisted onto my hands and knees, staring at them all, watching their every move as if they were prey. They thought to keep me away from what was *mine*? I snarled with vehemence, leaping toward the bars but stopping an inch away, making the closest man stumble against the next.

I felt my eyes flick at inhuman speeds, cataloging everything in the room, every tool, every sound, and every rattle of chains from the other cells. Oh, this place had an arsenal of weaponry, all hidden beneath the ground. They portrayed themselves as a happy village for all to see, but the truth was in front of us the entire time.

I wonder how many of the residents knew and how many of them were brainwashed into thinking their lives were nothing but pleasantville. Simply knowing that Healer Pata, a woman who carried a lot of authority above ground wasn't here... told me everything.

"We can't trust him. He's lost all humanity after his first bite. I saw it with my own eyes!" one of the soldiers spat.

I slowly stood and never took my eyes off him. "Yet you dare stand here and say you were unaware you had a bloodsucker among you, leading you," I argued, before letting out a humorless chuckle. "Pathetic."

"What is he talking about?" the Chieftain questioned. "Who was the bloodsucker?"

"It's all lies, sir. It's not like Cameron is here to answer. If Cameron was a bloodsucker, wouldn't he have survived the fight with this guy? What he's saying doesn't make any sense. He's just trying to divide us from the inside!"

Dennis, my mind supplied. That was the idiot's name. Older brother to Daniel, the young guard we met the very first day. Guess it hurt their parents to think too hard over names.

"And what do you propose we do then?" came the Chieftain's voice as he rested his chin in his fist, staring in my direction. I blew him a kiss and mentally noted how his pulse raised in fear despite his stoic expression. He was an idol here, the one who held the power of persuading the people that this was a utopia under his thumb. It was no wonder the younger generation admired him like a higher being, willing to swallow down anything he fed them.

The politics in this place was so deeply interwoven with all the supplies they produced. I began to understand exactly why none of the clans have invaded Silverforge. If anything was to be learned from the experience we went through with the High Father, there was trade happening somewhere, somehow underneath everyone's noses in order to keep the false pretense of peace.

"We bring some of the old ways back," Dennis blurted.

"What do you mean?"

"I'm sure you heard the tales, seen the history drawings of the crucifixes, Chieftain."

"Those were the days of barbarism, Dennis. We're much beyond that. There's no point in going backward when we're already ahead of every-thing." There was so much to unpack between those lines as I listened intently, flitting my eyes between the two conversing.

"There's a power in making examples, chief-tain. It will reiterate what you've established here," he compelled with his choice of words before turning to glare at me over his shoulder. "A life for a life. Eliseo must be marked for execution."

REED

I watched her fitfully sleep, calling out his fucking name again and again.

I wanted to kill him, if not for her, for myself. Both contrition and apathy warred within me. I followed Eliseo's leadership for well over half a decade and despite our differences and occasional clashes, this was the first time I was willing to put my loyalties aside. It was his fault. I saw his remorseless face... and I saw hers—the shell of herself after he left.

He was unhealthy for her. I probably was unhealthy for her. But consequences be damned, I wanted her like my last breath.

Gunner was back in the kitchen, keeping the

residents away from what was happening here by pretending it was just another day. He was reluctant to leave her side just as much as I was but logic won during our plan of action, and I wasn't ashamed to admit I manipulated the solution in my favor.

My fingers trailed across her naked arm, watching as goosebumps rose in reaction. She knew I was here. I was always here, savoring the way she never pushed me away despite knowing how Eliseo feels about me around her. As much as we both fought it, it was futile.

Leaning in, I ran the tip of my nose across her shoulder, taking in her unique scent and judging her temperature by my touch. She was hot again and my mouth watered over the image of her soaked from head to toe.

You're a bastard. Let the woman sleep in peace, my mind scolded me. I gritted my teeth and slowly pulled back, crossing my arms to prevent me from wrapping them around her again.

Yet, the way she called my name... *begged* for my return to her side to keep her from falling apart. My cock rose as I ran my hands through my hair, jerking it from my scalp as punishment, letting the pain ground me in rational thinking. My demons locked horns inside of my mind as I locked my jaws in frustration, irritation, and resentment toward her for choosing Eliseo... toward Eliseo for forcing her to choose him.

My eyes burned as I leaned forward on my

knees, sitting here in his damn boxers, watching her body rise and fall from her breaths. Did I make her pulse as frantic as she made mine? Some days I swore my eyes sharpened back and forth when my gaze was upon her, noticing little details I never saw before—like the light dusting of soft freckles that gathered on her tanned shoulders.

The way her eyes would dart to my flesh in hunger. Thoughts of her teeth grazing across my skin as the heat of her breath hits my neck, makes me shiver in a blazing desire that robs me of air. Taking a shuddering breath, my knuckles cracked from the tightening of my fists.

Where the fuck was Eliseo and why wasn't he back yet?

Samuel came by with Remi earlier, making sure our girl was alright. He planned on keeping an ear out around town to see if there was any buzz on the return of the outing crew. It gave him a good excuse to exercise and keep his muscles and recovery going while still getting something done.

I leaned back in the chair and pulled my eyes away from her form, staring at the ceiling then casting my gaze out the open window. In a different world, Fitri wouldn't have to choose between a bunch of assholes.

Unlike Eliseo, I was willing to compromise to a certain extent if it meant I could have more of her to myself beyond the relationship we had established in regard to us as a whole team.

"Please."

I leaped from my chair and was at her side the second it left her lips. "What do you need, *little iris*," I whispered against her, scooping her into my arms.

She sobbed and wrapped her scorching arms around me, threatening to burn us both with her internal fire. What was going on? This couldn't possibly be from her distance with Eliseo. This had to be something beyond what we could physically see.

When she moaned and licked along the crook of my neck, the action forced all the blood between my legs as I shifted her into an awkward seated position on the bed with one of my legs hanging off the edge, trying to combat my dizziness.

"Tell me what you need," I encouraged with a choke, rubbing my hand down the slope of her back, feeling her curves and mentally dying from her nakedness pressed against me.

"You smell so good. I'm so hungry, Reed," she cried, fighting her natural instincts. I wasn't a fool who allowed denial to cloud my reality. She was changing, always had been. Was this another part of it? I had seen it in the way Eliseo grew possessive, the way he gravitated around her. She was pulling us all into her orbit and the way my mouth watered in response to her taking blood from me told me all I needed to know.

Grabbing the back of her neck, I shoved her face against me and gave her access to me. She fought against my hold, trying to pull away and I growled, nipping the lobe of her ear to put her in her place.

"If you don't drink from me, *little iris*, you're going to be punished," I panted, desperately wanting both despite her decision.

She moaned in pleasure, molding against me as if becoming one before her lips moved and fangs sank into my flesh, throwing us both to our sides from my lightheadedness. Every pull of her mouth made my cock weep as my body convulsed against her aggressive ministration. She straddled me to keep me laid out like prey, her the elegant predator in her element. I savored her dominance, willing to submit as long as it made her crave me. My hands roamed across the globes of her ass, forcing her hips down to either give me reprieve, or torture me for my purposeful transgressions. Each prick of pain from her forceful feeding made me want to release right against her inner thigh.

When her tongue swirled around the wound, it throbbed as if wanting to answer the call of its mistress.

"R-Reed? Oh my god, I'm so sorry," she stuttered, coming back to herself from whatever delirium that influenced her decisions. My chest constricted as she leapt off me, and scooted back as if wounded against the pillows.

"It's fine," I assured her. "Don't worry about it. I didn—"

"What's wrong with me, Reed? What if I can't control myself? I didn't mean to take so much from you. What if I can't stop myself next time?" she rambled beneath hiccups of tears and an irrational rage began to boil beneath the surface of my skin.

I shot to my feet and began to aggressively pace in the bedroom, pulling at my hair in exasperation.

"I said, don't worry about it, Fitri! Fuck!" I roared, my vision shrinking, my focus entirely on her as if she hung the fucking moon and stars. "I bet you never say any of this shit to Eliseo when you drink from him. But me? Why me? What's wrong with me, Firti? Am I not good enough for you?"

I was something that crept into my nightmares from time to time. The doubt. It started with my family, to the people around me... to this. I could still smell the damn iris', heavily cloaking my coffin before the dirt hit the top. But those were just bad memories trying to pollute the truth of what was real. I knew it couldn't be it. My logical mind told me I was being stupid and irrational, spouting venom that would only cause more confusion in a muddy situation.

But damn if her rejection didn't feel like a stab to the heart.

"What? Don't say that, Reed. I never—I wouldn't—that's not—" she stammered and the coiled beast inside of me exploded.

I didn't feel myself move until I was face to face with her, caging her in. "Not what, Fitri? Not see how you've doomed me to worship your shadow?

To beg for scraps whenever you decide to give it to me?"

Grabbing her face, I slammed my mouth onto hers and tasted myself. But it wasn't enough. Why was I pushed away when all I had ever done for her was love her as much as she would let me? Growling against her lips, she gasped beautifully when I bit her tongue and forced our blood to become one between us, to give in to the intimacy we both owed ourselves after all we had been through.

As much as my inner alpha told me I was doing what I was supposed to, it didn't escape my notice that her dainty little fingers crept upwards to cup my face gently and passionately return my kiss.

She told me she was drowning, but she couldn't see the man that was drowning with her, willing to give up his life to save her—from herself.

23

ELISEO

MY DEATH SENTENCE WAS GIVEN. YET I WAS STILL HERE.

Over the course of the next day, I was able to hear the light footsteps of Silverforge's residents above me. The more I concentrated, the more I could pinpoint exactly where this dungeon was in comparison to the upper layout of the community. My cell was located at the heart but leaning toward the southwest corner, toward the outskirts of the farms. The far end of this underground chamber, beyond the five cells was another room, rarely utilized for anything but storage. I couldn't explain it but the echoes of their boots did. It was in the way the sound bounced back that let me see what I couldn't with my own two eyes.

But it wasn't the room that intrigued me. It was the small window.

A tray was dropped on the ground as I stood in

the shadows of my cell, leaning against the wall with my hands in my pants and my boots crossed.

"I don't know why they even want to feed you if they're just going to kill you. But the chieftain is a pussy with this talk of humanity." The guard kicked the tray, holding a filled bowl, beneath my bars and leaned in, sneering. "Humanity is reserved for humans, not bloodsucking scum."

He spit in the soup before turning to leave, the ringing of his keys hitting one another fading into the distance with him. With their talk of how far they had come, they continuously showed their hand and idiocy time and time again.

I could smell the blood in the soup. I highly doubt it was edible. If anything, I would bet it was animal blood so they wouldn't have to put on a show for public viewing. The Chieftain knew his position was precarious here and that standing can be crumbled in mere seconds as a result of a bad decision.

I had lived among the likes of Sergio too long to not pick up on how politics and makeshift politicians made their decisions based on self-interest.

An hour after his departure, I took a few steps toward the bowl and picked it up... slowly pouring it out onto the bars to test it. It hit cold bars. With a smile, I stepped closer, keening my ears into the distance as I tapped the metal rhythmically, feeling how the sound carried and bounced back.

When my ears picked up on something nearby, I closed my eyes and concentrated on it. My breathing was loud, but my pulse was louder beside the shell of my ear as my mind formed an image of the creature beside the window.

It was a bat.

I hadn't seen one since my youth.

Letting myself escape my environment, I lost track of time, counting all the creatures around the trees that lined the edge of the community farm when the jingling of metal stole my attention.

My hand immediately sizzled and I jerked it away from the bar, spilling the rest of the bowls contents on the floor and all over my boot.

"What? Our food ain't good enough for you now? We don't serve human if that's what you're waiting for. Too bad our graciousness was lost to you because that was supposed to be your final meal," the guard said with disgust as he paced in front of my cell with pure hatred in his eyes.

I was content to wait until his next departure when he slammed something against the bars, rattling my eardrums.

"I can't wait to watch you burn back to the depths of hell where you belong, bloodsucker," he smiled menacingly.

I kept my eyes on the wall ahead of me, thinking back on some of Fitri's memories of bodies in the pyre. Her screams for her mother had all but faded but now haunted my own dreams. When the constant stories of her pieced torture would invade me, I fucked it out of my system by burying my demons in her.

Was I giving it back? It was selfish of me but it never crossed my mind in the heat of the moment until now.

"Fucking look at me when I'm talking to you, prick!" Spittle flew in my direction and I snapped my head to his, making him stumble backward.

"Be careful what you ask for... human," I purred.

His eyes widened as if a shadow demon rose from my back. Screams erupted when an explosion of bats shot through the little window of the room and circled him, each little black shadow diving like bombs with fangs, hungry for what their master ordered.

I watched as he was devoured alive through my mind's eye, then observed with glee as it came to pass before me.

As the colony of bats feasted, a few of them detached his key and dragged it toward the bars. I clicked my tongue in thanks as I bent down and casually released myself from my holding cell.

The colony scattered back to whence they came as I circled what was left of the guard's corpse. Bits and pieces of flesh over bone beneath his clothes, his hair strung out away from him. The smell of his fresh blood made me hungry, but I was sure I could find a snack on the way home.

Dropping the keys on his carcass, I whistled as I ascended the cold, stone steps as if in deja vu. Seemed these crazy scientists all had the same taste for torture chambers.

REED

I groaned against the sink of the restroom, her blood swishing in my gut as I kept the contents down.

Everything was in a haze, my mind unsure of how we ended up feeding on each other without actually fucking. And as full as I felt, there was still a void that wasn't filled with our... tryst.

My little iris was crying into her pillow and I wanted to choke her, force her to see what was right in front of her face. If that asshole left and hasn't returned yet... What did that say about his feelings about her?

I punched the glass cabinet in front of me and shattered it into the bowl of the sink before leaning my head back and running my fingers through my hair. He didn't deserve her. He never did.

She gasped and ran over to me, pulling me away from the sink. Growling, I turned and slammed her against the wall, stealing another kiss as my knuckles throbbed from the warm blood dripping onto the floor between us. Lifting my hand to her face, I wiped it against her cheek and watched as it beautifully bloomed across her skin like an artist's canvas. My nostrils flared as I leaned in, invaded her mouth with mine, and swiped my tongue across the blood.

I felt drunk and it reduced my inhibitions the way I wanted it to be. I groaned as her hands drifted tentatively downward and was lost in all the sensations around me when someone called out my name.

"Reed! The fuck are you? I think I found Eliseo!" Samuel was frantic and sounded far away but the name was enough to pull me from Fitri like a serrated knife across my skin.

Fitri gasped and slipped through beneath the cage of my arms, leaving me bereft with the breeze she left behind upon her exodus. Dropping my forehead against the wall, I listened with agony as she ran away from me—from us.

Growling, I punched the wall and fell to my knees, crying out to a god I couldn't see, asking why I was being punished when all I ever wanted was to give her the heart she keeps eviscerating in an infinite loop—a hellish nightmare that refused to release me from its clutches.

My pulse pounded behind my ears and I let my demons loose, too tired from fighting, struggling to keep them at bay all the time.

My surroundings sped past me, I couldn't see my periphery and yet I saw everything as Samuel scowled in my direction, pulling Remi back as if in slow motion. Gunner ran out the kitchen as people in the community center screamed when a bloody

Eliseo emerged like the devil himself from the depths of wherever he came from.

His eyes were glued on Fitri as she slowed her run, watching in horror as he grabbed the closest resident and bit into her neck, spewing blood down his chin and chest like a crimson fountain. His visible gulps could be seen as his pupils dilated. Bats shot down like black rain, attacking those close to him, including Gunner, while he took another step forward, tossing the limp body against someone.

He didn't see me. He couldn't. His sights were set on Fitri who stood there at a loss, both yearning and confusion across her features. She reached out and I knocked her hand down, before throwing a punch to his face, snapping his head back inhumanly.

The hood he had on dropped and the smell of cooking flesh grew. Sizzles and smoke emerged from his face as he turned to look at us with skin boiling and peeling from his muscles, the fat melting down the front of his shirt.

Screams of terror rose as some of the guards pushed their way through the thick crowd, stabbing him with cattle prods, the electric pulse snapping as it was delivered into his body, taking him to his knees.

"Eliseo!" Fitri cried and ran toward him, finally finding herself again. But I was quicker. I grabbed her in her midsection and ran back toward home, ignoring the way she continued to cry out his name with a broken voice, struggling in my grip to get back and save him.

But there was no saving him. Not with him that far gone. I didn't know how he affected the bats but I knew enough. Otis was right. We were all changing and Eliseo was the first to fully manifest himself.

It was the wrong place and the wrong time as the guards cried out for pitchforks and wooden beams to be erected.

"No! Eliseo! I need to save him! We need to go back!" she cried as she beat my back while I crossed the threshold of our home, slamming the door shut and locking it.

Gunner and Samuel were going to have to figure shit out from here because my sole job is to keep these people from finding out about her.

"Shh," I cooed, pushing her hair back, trying to push my calm energy into her.

"Shut the fuck up out there, ya dirty bastards!" And then came the crash which only amplified Fitri's anger.

She punched and clawed me as we both struggled to fight for dominance, dropping hard enough to crash into the living room table, breaking in two.

"Get off me, Reed! We need to get him!"

"Stop! What the fuck do you think you can do against a whole damn town, woman?" I snarled as she kneed me in the groin, knocking me over to the side with a curse.

She twisted and turned haphazardly over the

broken pieces of the table, bleeding in the process from the splinters as I shot my foot out and tripped her. She landed on her face and I pounced, grabbing her arms as she bucked and bit my arm, trying to loosen my hold. I aggressively transferred both her wrists to one hand while using my knees to knock hers together from above before I bit down on her shoulder.

Her warmth filled my mouth as she moaned and writhed, before she used her inhuman strength against me, knocking me against the couch as she lunged for the door.

"You little fiery bitch, get back here!" I roared as I shot my hand out and grabbed her ankle, dragging her back toward me with an aroused grin. The adrenaline coursing through my veins had my other hand clamping on her thigh possessively as she turned onto her back to try and kick me with her other foot.

I dodged the first attempt but didn't account for her agility as the next one landed against my temple. But this time, I kept my grip on her, taking her with me against the back cushions of the couch from the impact. I bounced and landed on top of her as she shoved me in the chest, clawing at my skin before scrambling toward the bedroom to increase the distance between us.

Wiping the back of my hand, I licked the smeared blood and felt my body contort, sniffing her scent as if I was out tracking a kill. Every one of her movements slowed in my mind as I calculated all her possible outcomes and what training move she was most likely going to utilize next to escape me.

"Come on, baby. I'm dying to see what you do. Try me," I taunted as I prowled toward her.

Her nipples peaked behind her shirt and my skin along my chest began to itch. I watched with wicked satisfaction as her chest heaved the closer I got. She stood there for a good minute, mocking my ability to hunt her before she darted to the right. The chase was on—my muscles moving on instinct as I dove for her. Oh, but the little fox had a few tricks up her sleeve as she used her forward momentum to jump against the wall, leaping over me and landing on the bed with a bounce.

My senses heightened; I quickly pivoted with a growl as she chaotically moved over the sheets, tangling herself in the process. Snapping my jaws in her direction, I taunted her, letting her get out of my grasp. My cock was heavy as I crawled on hands and knees toward her, watching with heinous amusement as her pupils dilated in response.

"Run, little fox. I'm getting aroused just watching you try."

"R-Reed, we need to get Eliseo. Please," she begged prettily and I groaned.

"For fucking what? So we can all die with him? He knew what he did! The same he left you," I pointed out, my pulse throbbing with fury that she still chose that bastard over me! I didn't need to see her broken face to see what my punctuated words did. My demon knew exactly what he was doing when he threw it out there like daggers, wanting to hurt her the same way she had hurt me time and time again.

"Please—"

A male scream rented the air and Gunner came barreling into the house. "Reed! Reed!"

I curled my lip in a snarl, never taking my eyes off her as he ran into the room, oblivious to what was happening.

"They're going to fucking burn him! They erected a pole in the middle of the damn town, man!"

"Where's Samuel?" I barked.

"Taking Remi somewhere safe, somewhere beyond the farms so she doesn't have to see—"

My demons warred inside of me again, one beginning to gain the upper hand over the other. Guilt assaulted me like a machine gun as I slapped the side of my head, wanting to pull my hair out over this shit.

My nostrils flared as I took in her scent to calm me, right before I turned, grabbed a fucking shirt, and stomped passed Gunner who was awaiting his next order.

"Stay with her!" I growled before forcing myself away from the reason for my existence and slamming the door behind me.

The crowd was wild, some of them with actual pitchforks while a noticeable number of them kept to the farthest sidelines. The town was divided. Some were hungry for retribution while others were unsure if they were back in a period before our time.

I shoved my way through the crowd, until Eliseo's melting face snapped his head toward me. The fire hadn't been started but he was already burning beneath the sun.

"I smell her on you!" he roared, jerking against his metal chains, rousing the crowd into fear.

"What if the chains don't hold him?"

"Hurry! Throw the fire!"

Before the next resident could add their suggestion, the guard in front tossed his torch into the piles of tinder and wood beneath Eliseo's feet.

He roared like the beast he always was, calling for *Sili* as he cursed me under the same breath. Apathy overtook me as I watched the flames come alive from beneath, twitching my nose from the mixed smell of wood and flesh.

The people around me cheered, raising their weapons as Eliseo gritted his teeth—visible through the lack of flesh that already pulled itself away.

He choked and coughed before he let out a breath, opening his eyes one last time in my direction.

"Take care of her," he croaked before he let out a final cry of anguish.

24

REED

I GRABBED HER ANKLE AS SHE DOVE TO CLIMB THROUGH the open window, sobbing, scoring her stomach as I pulled her back, perfuming the air with her wounds. Her cries tore at my heart but she would heal. She always did, even the scars on the inside.

"No! Let me go!"

I was the bastard Eliseo claimed me to be but the darkness inside of me couldn't care less as I grabbed her by the back of her neck, jerked her around, and slammed my mouth against hers while I shut the damn window and locked it, smearing her blood on the window pane.

She fought beautifully—she always did. When she sighed against my mouth, I was lost in yearning until she slapped me across the face with inhuman strength, taking me to the ground. She tripped over my ankle and climbed over me, desperate to get beyond the threshold of the bedroom but couldn't as I grabbed her leg with mine and twisted her down to the ground with me, relishing the physical pain she caused me.

Samuel hadn't returned with Remi yet and I didn't blame him. I would wait until the smell of death left Silverforge too before bringing her back. She had enough trauma.

Gunner could be heard pacing the living room beyond the closed door but that was the least of my worries.

"Little fox, let's not do this today," I cajoled but she let out an angry kitten growl before she twisted and sent a love punch right into my face.

I saw stars, my head pounding, and then all I saw was red as I grabbed her by the back of her hair and dragged her to the bed, tossing her onto the mattress. My own strength was changing, and I virulently let it take over. She didn't think I noticed the way she responded to my dominance when it got the better of me, but I did.

She loved it. I knew she did. It didn't matter what she said in the heat of the moment. Her words were passionate despite her choices.

Her every scratch, every blood draw, every spit in the face—was an expression of what she was afraid to accept... because she invariably molded into me during her weakness, pulling me in for the chase. I let her play with me. Hadn't I always? Except now, the playing field was level and I wasn't letting her go.

"Do what, Reed? You're delusional!" she cried out, throwing a pillow at me. "You let him die, you asshole! How could you? How could you do this to me? How could you do this to us?"

Was she really trying that manipulation shit on me, thinking her tear-streaked face would add to her flare? I straightened and glared at her, daring her to keep going with a curl of my lip. Her lips quivered and my cock twitched. Fuck, she was beautiful. "How dare I? How dare I try to keep you safe while the entire damn community was out on a hunt? Listen to yourself. Just fucking listen to yourself!"

She threw another pillow and I caught it in my hand, lowering it with a fury that defied human nature. I wanted to kill her. I wanted her to scream in my face beneath me, clawing my flesh off as I finally made her see reality for what it was. We lived. We died. We fought to survive. It hadn't changed.

She had.

"I hate you!" she hurled.

I blinked, and blinked again. Then let out a howling laugh as my mind broke in two. "You... hate...me. You...hate...ME?"

I didn't see him until the door crashed in right as I dove for her neck, but missed by a scant few inches as Gunner pulled me back with all his might. I snarled and fought like a wild animal, ready to finally get a taste of the prey that kept eluding me—she had starved me of her to the point of insanity. Her scent of arousal coated the room thickly as my body responded in kind.

She hated me. She fucking hated me. I fucking hated myself! Did she not understand this? Did she derive pleasure from torturing me with her words and her actions as they contradicted themselves again and again?

"Reed! Calm yourself! She didn't mean it! She's mourning, man!" Gunner tried but I wasn't hearing it. I wasn't seeing it. My body necessitated I be near her as she rejected her gravitational pull on me. The room was closing in on all sides the same way it did when they buried me so long ago, nailing the coffin against my screams. My lungs refused to cooperate as I gasped for breaths, clawing at Gunner's hold, trying to touch her just once more.

I saw it in her eyes, the way they yearned for me—her soul baying like a female wolf calling for her mate. I specifically perceived the way her lips parted before she shifted her legs as she scooted back in the bed.

It was as if she was in heat and I, the poor, sorry creature caught in her web of lies.

"What the fuck is wrong with you?" Gunner growled, almost losing his footing with my next lunge.

"Can't you smell her? Can't you feel her calling to you?!" I bellowed.

A crash came from the other house as Gunner tensed. He didn't respond but I knew, I just knew he was fighting it too. The only difference was... he was winning and I wanted to desperately lose. The urgency to claim what was mine trumped all rational thought as I elbowed Gunner in the face with a crunch and slipped through his grasp, leaping at Fitri who didn't run.

No, she sat there, watching me with awe as I tackled her onto her back and licked the column of her neck, groaning at her taste. Gunner grabbed my neck and I twisted, biting down on his. He roared and punched my face but I was lost in the taste of sustenance going down my throat, my body taking over every next move. Fitri sobbed beneath me, but I continued to cage her in, unwilling to let my pretty prey go now that I finally had her.

Soon, Gunner's body fell limp and I let him fall beside us as turned and slammed my mouth on hers, mixing her tears with the taste of *us*.

She weakly fought, crying, passionately kissing me back as I caressed her face and coaxed her to let go.

But she kept whispering his fucking name.

Even beyond death, the asshole pushed me from my rightful position. I snarled and bit her lip, distracting her depression enough for me to pull the elastic waistband of her pants down to her ankles, locking them together. Releasing my straining cock, I rubbed it against her skin as I grabbed her hair with both hands and held her still for the assault of my lips.

She whimpered through her sobs and hiccups but didn't push me away. Slipping my tongue out of her, savoring her taste, I trailed it down until I hit the neck of her shirt.

"Fucking piece of—" It didn't stand a chance as it tore right down the middle with a jerk of my hands.

"Reed, please!" She pushed but instinct led me as I nipped her skin, closing my mouth on her right nipple and piercing her skin with my fangs.

My hips undulated as I pulled in a gulp of blood. The hands that pushed, now grabbed my head and brought me closer to her bosom, begging for me to rid her of her internal pain. When her nails dug into my scalp, I trailed my mouth down her abdomen and toward the apex of her legs. She pretended the pants kept her shackled but I knew she wanted another struggle. She was the strongest of us all.

Chuckling, I gave it to her—slapping her mound before wrenching one of her legs out of the pants and pushing the back of her leg up toward her shoulder.

Gunner laid unconscious beside us, his depression on the bed a reminder of our intruding guest. It was morbid of us to be doing this while he was passed out but I didn't have it in me to push him off the side of the bed as I worshiped her cunt with everything I had.

My whispered name finally crested her lips and I was given a path to erasing everything that haunted her about Eliseo's appalling demise. A part of me knew he was right, that I had always laid in wait until I had good reason to usurp him. Another part of me warred, saying the exact opposite as it purred against Fitri's climax against my face. It was obvious which demon I let win. She grabbed the back of my head and let out a much different cry than the one I had come to expect these past few days.

When her cries of passion morphed back into sobs, my temper ignited. I bit her clit and licked the wound before forcing her onto her stomach, lifting her ass into the air.

"I hate you," she wept against the sheets as I ran my nails down the side of her hips, digging my fingers into her flesh.

"You're a fucking liar, *little iris*. But that's okay," I croaked. "I'll make you forget him." I plunged my aching cock, deeply inside of her inferno.

My eyes rolled to the back of my head as my body fell forward, covering hers. I didn't miss how her ass backed up and pulled me in deeper, silently communicating her real needs.

The bed shook as primal hunger overtook me —as her carnal desires reciprocated with a dangerous perilousness that rivaled all the near-death experiences of our past combined. A crimson haze shrouded both of us as the air in the room became thick and heavy, like the unconscious body beside us. Each thrust drove me toward a heaven I didn't deserve as she mewled like a kitten in heat beneath me, begging me to ruin her.

I gladly did.

She spasmed around my cock, clawing at the sheets but never pulling away. I bit down on her anyway, making sure she didn't change her mind as I drank from her sweetly right before she bedeviled me and milked everything I had to offer.

We both panted against one another as she wept louder beside my ear, shoving my face away from the torn flesh of her shoulder. As the high of my release died down, so did my soul. My heart stopped as I stared at her stricken face. It didn't matter that she healed exponentially.

What had I done?

THE CRACKLE OF FLAMES, THE SMELL OF COOKED FLESH and his final roar rang in my ear, mixing in with memories of rejection and burial, the smell of fresh dirt hitting the top of my coffin. I let out a stuttering breath, trying to regain control of a mind that was reconstructing itself before my mind's eyes.

When Gunner returned to the living room, face flush, my envy rivaled my self-hatred, fighting its way toward resentment. I wanted to strangle him.

I wanted to strangle her for letting him drink from her.

It didn't matter if I almost killed him in my rabid lunacy.

My animalistic urges told me otherwise, battling my human psyche. I ran my hands through my hair and pulled at my scalp, forcing my eyes away from the puncture wounds on his neck... slowly healing.

"You calm now?" Gunner asked cautiously as he came to sit on the opposite side of the couch.

I felt a growl rumble beneath my chest but I swallowed it back down, blinking a few times. I rubbed at my chest, feeling the smooth expanse of skin, reminiscing the pain from the clawing she gave me the day I locked her inside the house.

She didn't need to add any more bloodshed to her memory, she didn't need to see the way his skin melted off with fat, sizzling in the flames.

"She hates me," I deadpanned. My chest constricted and I wanted to peel my flesh off in self-punishment. She hated me and I claimed her. She hated me... and I loved every moment of it.

Leaning onto my elbows, I hung my head in my hands and struggled to breathe as my body and mind waged war.

"She doesn't fucking hate you. Stop being dramatic. But what the hell was going through your mind to do that while she's still broken over Eliseo, man? Get your head out of your ass," he growled, kicking me.

I snapped my head to him, my mouth watering, reminiscing the way he tasted in the heat of my anger. As if he knew, he straightened and glared in defiance.

"I fucking hate you too for almost turning me into a corpse," he gritted out.

"But did you die? No. You were breathing right beside us the whole time." I shot to my feet, pacing the room. "I wanted to watch your body fall off the bed while the little fox screamed my name. But because I fucking care, I kept you there. Don't forget it."

He shot to his feet too, the temperature in the room elevating, then burning at infernal heights when he shoved his finger in my chest. "You don't fix something broken by breaking it further, you asshole!"

Asshole.

She loved Eliseo for it and she'll love me for it.

I swatted his hand away and he threw a punch. I dodged and threw one back. The room began to spin as we both landed on the floor in hand-to-hand combat, battling for something bigger than what was in front of us. With snarls and growls, I felt his own inhuman strength grow as he kicked me against the couch. I slammed into it, rolled and landed on my hands and feet, watching him slowly get to his.

We slammed into each other as if it was the last fight we'd ever have. We didn't see her come in, but we felt her... right before she grabbed both of us and threw us against opposite walls. Groaning from the impact, I shook my head and glared at her.

She was hunched over, her arms wrapped around her stomach, her eyes full of animosity and coldness.

"How could you, Reed? They burned him," she sobbed, falling to her knees. "They always resort to fire. I should have known. I should have never led us here. It was better to die out there than to hear his cry."

I crawled to her and she hissed, making me jerk back. "And you! You did this! You let it happen! You took me away, separated us! I should have died with him!"

"The fuck you say?" I growled, straightening and looking down at her with disgust over her words. "How fucking dare you, threatened to take *my* life by taking yours!"

"Reed, calm the fuck down, you delusional bastard!"

Maybe I was. I watched with abject bitterness as she welcomed his touch and not mine. The darkness inside of me tore through my soul as if a living entity wanted to claw its way out into the surface to finally consume its host.

I should let it devour me. Because right now, nothing I said or did could fix anything...

I dropped to my knees and hung my head in my hands toward the floor, heaving in breath as the shadows of my mind swirled around me.

The sound of her sobs were the currency for the demons to torture me. My name cursed under her breath were stab sounds meant to chisel a deep void in my chest until nothing of me remained.

The rejected son. The cursed one. The one who was going to be everyone's downfall. I had been cast aside, buried, forsaken. The moment I stole a piece of heaven for myself, I should have known it would be my final downfall. As much as hate and self-loathing ran through my veins with each pump of my heart, I was too selfish to let go of what I took possession of.

I lowered myself, and gradually reached out. Hope was the most dangerous thing of all but I was desperate to make her see our connection. When she turned her face into Gunner's chest, I exploded. My vision blurred, cleared and blurred again as fists, snarls, bites, and blood splattered in the room.

I thought the pain was from me subduing my competition but the reality was, Gunner had me in a chokehold, his body forcing mine still beneath him. I didn't know what was real and what wasn't anymore, my entire being focused on the body lock, Gunner had me in. It was a move he never used in training. It was the only reason why I couldn't see it coming.

"I'm not going to tell you again," he gritted next to my ear right before the bedroom door slammed shut.

25

FITRI

Time moved slowly.

Samuel and Remi came back. They checked up on us but I didn't remember any of it afterward. I no longer had any desire to leave the house as I sat on the edge of the bed, staring out the window. Watching the windows move, my mind supplied that it was a breezy day, but I felt nothing.

And I felt everything.

I didn't realize my body shook until Gunner placed the bowl of food on the side table and wrapped a blanket around me. As much as it pained me, Reed had to take care of me while Gunner was at work and then vice versa.

At least I didn't have to face Reed the entire time.

Didn't he realize, guilt ate at me every time he looked into my eyes? Every time my body cried out for him knowing it was wrong. I didn't understand the changes in me and was afraid of what I would find out.

Night turned into days and days turned into nights.

I found myself sitting in the living room, staring at the picture on the wall when the cushions depressed beside me. His scent had changed and it wrapped itself around me like a caress when all I could do was cry because I didn't want to feel this way.

"Fitri, please," he begged quietly and I closed my eyes, afraid of seeing his.

When he nudged the spoon beside my lips, I automatically opened, accepting his offering. When he wiped the side of my lips with a napkin, they trembled. When he brushed my hair and braided it, I hung my head in my hands.

I sobbed harder when I felt his dejected forehead against my back. Nothing else. I berated myself for still wanting his arms around me, but they never came. No, instead he gathered the bowl and utensils, stood up quietly and left the house.

Time continued to move forward and it was as if the light switch in my mind turned on and I noticed Remi sitting beside me prattling on about Samuel and his annoying habits. My lips twitched when she told me about how hard she had to work to keep certain unsavory women away from him and she stopped mid-sentence to look at me.

"You're back," she whispered, and my eyes

burned with tears. She embraced me the same way I did her when her mother died and the irony burned itself in my mind. "We've missed you."

"I missed you too. I'm sorry."

"Why are you sorry?" she asked as she pulled back.

"I was supposed to be protecting you..." I trailed off, no longer sure of what I was supposed to be doing in this life anymore.

"We take care of each other. You taught me that. And the guys. Gunner's been pulling double shifts to cover for your absence when some of the community began coming around to ask about why you wouldn't leave the house."

"What?" How many weeks have passed?

Remi nodded. "And Reed's never left your side since."

"What do you mean? He always leaves," I told her, aware enough in my depressed mental state of his presence exiting the room after he completes the task of taking care of me.

She slowly shakes her head and wrinkles her brow. "He hasn't eaten. He's been so distracted while tracking, they relieved him of his duty. He sleeps against your closed bedroom door and Samuel has to force him to get cleaned up. And when he leaves the house... he sits beneath your bedroom window with his head hung in his hands as he listens to you cry..."

"I haven't been able to talk to him or get him to interact with me. He's been a shell of himself and the only thing he reacts to is your movements and needs."

I felt the breeze today, simply because it told me my face was wet with tears that had been running down without my notice. We were both suffering and I didn't know how to fix it. I didn't know what we were supposed to do.

"I'm sorry if what I told you is making you sad. I didn't mean for it to. I just didn't want you to think he was leaving you all the time," Remi admitted. "Some of the local women try to get his attention or feed him but all he does is slap the food away and gets to his feet, staring into your bedroom until they have no choice but to leave."

"W-where is he now?" Dared I ask?

Remi patted my knee and got to her feet. "Call to him, Fitri. It's all he's been waiting for."

How did she grow up so fast? I watched silently as she left me sitting on the couch, closing the door behind her. I took a stuttering breath and wrapped my arms around myself. The sick curl in my gut from so long ago returned and fear laced itself around me with thoughts of Reed.

When did it happen? The more I thought about it, the more I realized it wasn't fear but trepidation. I stared at the painting and wiped my face. After a few moments, I walked into the restroom and undressed. Stepping into the stall, I turned on the water and let it force me to feel. There was no going back. He was truly gone.

What would Eliseo have wanted for me? I

scoffed beneath the water. Eliseo never saw himself apart from me.

It left my lips in a guilty whisper before I knew it happened.

His shadow immediately appeared behind me right before he stepped into the shower close enough to touch. I was scared to turn and he never touched me. The only thing connecting us were the splashes of water that jumped from his body to mine.

I slowly began washing myself, wanting to feel a semblance of normalcy. Raising an arm, I rubbed my skin, down my sides, letting my other arm bend at the elbow and touch Reed with the tip of my fingers. Slowly, he raised his own to wash the side of my hips, never straying from the area.

With a deep breath, I guided him around my body, instructing him to help me as I turned around and stared into the dark fathom of his eyes. He dropped to his knees and wrapped his arms around me, burying his face against my stomach and my heart broke.

We both stood there, under the spray of water for an indeterminate amount of time before I began to wash his hair, noticing its length.

I tapped his shoulder when I was done and he stood up, turning off the water and like deja vu, wrapped me in a towel and began drying me off. He quietly placed the towel back on the rack and carried me to bed, tucking me away before leaving the room and shutting the door behind him.

The next few days felt stranger, but I was finally up for leaving the house. I stood beside the kitchen building and watched everyone as they came through. Gunner walked out with his apron with a smile, heading my way.

"Hey," I greeted him.

"Hey, you." He kept space between us as he scanned me with worry. "Everything okay? Do you need anything from the kitchen?" he asked over the chatter of the residents who were beginning to stare as they walked by.

I shook my head, trying to keep my smile but knew I was failing because he gave me a look that didn't need to be translated out loud.

"Reed, grab two bowls on your way back. Meet me in five minutes."

I looked around, confused at Gunner's instructions because Reed wasn't here... until the man in question turned the corner from the opposite side of the building and followed behind Gunner without looking my way.

Remi was right. He was always watching me. Overwhelmed from the stimulation of being out, I turned on my heel and made my way back home.

Someone spat at my feet as I made it toward the residential areas and I stopped to look.

"I know you're lying. You all are. Where there's one bloodsucker, there's more. I don't know how you're doing it, walking in the sun, but believe me, I made sure the Chieftain knows of my suspicion," said an old woman with an ugly sneer.

"I don't know what you're talking about," I feigned and she let out a humorless laugh.

"We'll get another fire show, soon enough."

The hairs on the back of my neck stood and I quickened my steps home. Before I could pass the next two houses, a hot hand grabbed me and I threw a punch. Reed's face snapped to the side and he took a few deep breaths, licking his lips, before turning back to me.

"What did she say," he gritted out, rolling his neck around.

"She's waiting for us to follow Eliseo," I whispered angrily, my blood boiling.

Without another word, he moved faster than I could see. I ran and caught up with him just as her neck audibly snapped and she sagged onto the ground.

"What did you do?" I hissed.

He nonchalantly straightened and walked back toward the kitchen without another word. I stood there fuming, unsure of whether I should get rid of the body or walk away so no one sees me next to it. I chose the latter, needing more time to mull over what occurred.

Slamming the door I growled and kicked the couch. What was he trying to do out in the open like that? What the hell was he thinking?

The door opened the next few minutes as he brought in two bowls and set them on a smaller table we accumulated to replace the last one we broke. My chest heaved as I turned to face him. "Reed? What is wrong with you?"

"A lot of things. Sit down and let me feed you," he replied calmly.

"You killed her! Anyone could have walked by!"

"I would have killed her regardless."

"Why, Reed?" Why was he acting like this?

"Because I protect what's mine!" he roared, the first time he let his temper out since... since... I shut out the world. It was as if our emotions were in sync and that kind of power terrified me. He grabbed the side of his head and growled, haunching over as if he was kicked. "What do you want from me, Fitri? Every time I'm with you..."

"I—Don't turn this around on me, Reed!"

He grimaced and turned his back to me, tilting his head back and running his hands down his face. "What do I need to do? Tell me."

"Stop trying to confuse me! What are you talking about?" I cried out, my pulse frantically trying to jump out of my skin.

He turned and lunged, grabbing my upper arms, forcing us to move until my back hit the wall that divided the living room and the bedroom. "Tell me what I need to do to make you forgive me!"

He punched a hole beside my head and my breath stuttered, the aura of his fury encompassing my senses.

"Tell me, Fitri. Tell me what I need to do. I'm dying a thousand deaths while I'm breathing in life only you can give me. Brought high... just to bury me alive."

I blinked back tears as my lips trembled. When he lifted his face toward mine, his broken expression eviscerated my soul. I opened my mouth to say something but a loud pounding came at our door.

"Open up! I know you're in there!" came an unfamiliar male voice.

Reed's pupils dilated before he broke away from me and jerked the door open.

"There was a witness to a murder and you're the only suspect. You're coming with us!" the guard threw out before grabbing Reed.

My heart leaped to my throat as I ran after him. A crowd was already forming and old trauma stress slammed into me, the sound of screams, Eliseo's roar and my mother jumping into the flames. No, no, no, not again!

A fight ensued as Reed flipped the guard onto his back, straddled him and began to pound his skull in. The force of each hit vibrated the ground until the nearby women screamed and the other guards tackled him.

"He's just like the other one!"

"I fucking knew it!"

"Where are the rest of them?"

Hands, hands all over me, pulling me away from where I needed to go. I felt Gunner before he appeared, shouldering his way through the crowd, pulling some of the men off Reed. The heat of bodies burned me as I pulled away from some of the hands and made a few steps before someone tripped me, slamming my face on the ground. Clawing forth, dirt broke under my nails as I made my way toward Reed.

"Grab him!"

"Get the wood!"

"NO!" was all I heard before my ears closed up and the world spun. It was his blood that burned my nares, his blood that called to a deeper part of me. The hands that pulled, slipped as everything around us turned red. The scent of metal, the scent of flames, the scent of released bowels mixed in the air as the screams became a low vibration hum beneath my skin with every step I took.

My own hand slipped as I threw the corpses aside on top of each other, my eyes trained on the last guard standing, his gun rattling in his hands. I wasn't sure if my lungs were pulling in air, not until I saw Reed's body, also covered in blood, contorting and convulsing. He spewed blood from his mouth all over the dead bodies beneath him right before he roared in anguish.

Gunner wiped his own mouth with the back of his hand before he twisted the last guard's neck from behind, dropping him to the ground. The Chieftain, who stood a few yards away, froze in place, his hands on the shoulder of one of their robed men from beyond the inner wall.

As clouds began to gather, the smell of impending rain filtered through the thick atmosphere as I dropped to my knees beside Reed who was still shaking.

"Reed...?" I wanted to sob, rebuking myself for my part in whatever happened between us. "Please."

I didn't know what I was asking for and I didn't wait for an answer as I covered his shaking, bloody form with my own tightly. He cried out again and shoved me aside. His arms were wrapped around himself as he fell forward right as the skin of his back began to peel.

I reacted without thought, biting my wrist and hands, slapping it all over him, trying to rub my life with his... the same way he'd been begging me to do when I spurned him.

It was the broken groan that had me grab his face and kiss him through his pain. I sat down and pulled him over me, wrapping my arms around his shoulder, pressing his head against the crook of my neck, offering him to drink.

He latched on immediately, pulling at my essence. The only footsteps that came behind me were Gunners, his own scent permeating the air around me as he crouched down and ran his hand through Reed's hair while his other hand landed on my shoulder.

We both gasped when bone emerged from his back and then plumes of black feathers. Reed's body shook violently until the rest of his wings finally emerged, spreading widely in all its dark glory.

"Fuck," Gunner whispered and I gently cupped Reed's bloodstained face to mine, peppering him with kisses, silently asking if he was okay.

A shuddering sigh was his only response. And that was when I realized... the entire community was deathly quiet.

26

"W-What are you?" the Chieftain whispered in horror.

I stood, bringing Reed to his feet beside me while Gunner stood on the opposite side. Staring at the man who most likely sentenced Eliseo to his grave, something inside of me broke free. The woman I was afraid of evolving into had found her place among her men.

"The harbinger of your death if you touch any one of mine," I hissed, still hungry for vengeance and retribution.

The Chieftain took a step back, caught himself and attempted to stand tall. No longer did he hold his false smiles. He stank of deceit. "You dare bring your wickedness here?"

With the massacre of his most loyal followers at my feet, I took a confident step over their bodies toward him. His eyes widened as mine sharpened.

It was his religious man who bravely spoke

next. "I-I never—He emerged like a—like an angel of death come to life, right before our eyes. Is this our divine punishment for past transgressions or is this... our new beginning?"

I didn't know who he was speaking to and at the moment, I didn't rightfully care. The only thing on my mind was protecting my men and making sure what happened to Eliseo never happened again— not while I was here. The sky darkened as additional storm clouds rolled in as if the world was finally angry on our behalf for all the shit we had been put through. My skin prickled as electricity began to weave its way through the air around us, a sign of the intensity of what was coming.

My men followed behind me, Reed to my right and Gunner to my left—the way it was almost meant to be. Denial was my human weakness and it had no place here. I finally understood why they all claimed themselves to be the elite in this existence.

"Have you come to save us from ourselves?" The religious man continued, standing his ground in what looked like humbleness while the Chieftain tensed, his body ready to flee at any moment.

"It's time to stop the madness and the pires," I said as I ran at inhuman speed, grasping the chieftain around the neck and lifting him right as the skies roared and rumbled.

My fragmented past, reflected against the lightning as if for all to see though I knew it was only in my mind. Flashes of my mother's face coming toward me as the crowd cursed her name for trying to save a bloodsucker. These very walls and perhaps with some of these very people. My childhood home no longer stood, but the scars this place carried never left with it. Beyond the farm lay a piece of me, the one Maverick tried to exploit in my youth, only to be warned of again back at Ashborne. How blind was I to not see everyone around me using me as a pawn in their wicked schemes? From the innocent farm boy in Silverforge to Queen Isabella of Clan Cirse. And yet without fully knowing it, I played my hand and won in the end.

From prisoner to the fissure in her plans of ruling as a deity, the world had a bigger role for me, one that may topple all she ever knew. I destroyed the boy who selfishly desired to defile the outcast and now it was time to destroy the very thing that threatened to haunt me here—because I was no longer the frightened girl, but reborn into something beyond any of their understanding.

"The cycles of history have taught us nothing, despite the constant wheel of death that continues to spin in an endless loop of insanity. Do you not all see the pointlessness of it all?" I gritted out with a hint of sorrow.

The Chieftain gasped for breath but I didn't wait for his answer as I tossed him aside with a flick of my wrist. Reed picked up where I left off and looked to me for my next order. His eagerness in showing me his support made me weak in the knees but I couldn't let the people here see that he had become one of my biggest vulnerabilities.

How often have our fears been the beacon to those who wish to exploit us? How often have we begged to be left alone in the name of peace, only to bring more predators in our wake? To have war brought to our doorsteps—the very thing we had been trying to avoid.

Thunder boomed in response and the skies lit up as if to show me the way.

Never again. Never again will I let them destroy everything I had, only to be brought back to life in pieces. I looked at the rest of the faces around us as the skies began to cry for our injustice. "Well? Is there anyone else here that needs to say something? I'm all ears and frankly, I'm about fucking tired, so speak your peace now because I'm not leaving. No longer will anyone have the power to make me do anything I don't wish to do."

The rain pelted down on us with increasing speeds as lighting ran across the skies, illuminating unsure faces laced with a hint of fear before concealing them again.

"Are-Are you going to kill us?"

My eyes darted toward the voice. It was the nurse who took care of Samuel so long ago, the girl Daniel flirted with by the kitchen. The human part of me reminded myself that they were not all this way—experience had taught me that alongside my traumas and no longer was I going to be played the fool.

"I don't want to. I never intended to. But I cannot be blamed for my self-defense. I want to live like everyone else... I just want to live." My voice softened at the end as my body vibrated with such hatred for all that had happened and with such awareness of what I was capable of. Looking at her face now, I wavered. Did Silverforge deserve mercy?

Light illuminated the sky again as if responding to my internal cries for clarity.

"Don't believe her! They're all the same! Just like those damn Lekim's that betrayed us!" the Chieftain accused, and we all turned to look at him. My anger twisted but Eliseo's face cut my rage before it could escalate. He was the one who made me believe that not everyone was out there to see my demise. He brought back hope when I had lost it.

I shook my head slowly, understanding dawning as another vein of lightning ran and struck a tree in the distance with a loud crackle of sparks. It was why Eliseo never could put his guard down here, no matter how calm our lives had been during that time. He had alway been my guide, even when I never asked him to be—even now. I sadly looked at Reed with my decision who responded accordingly to my request by ripping his head off his shoulders, pulling out his spine with it.

Blood bubbled from the wound as he dropped his body, and began making his way toward me.

I studied Reed's expression, taken by surprise when he got on one knee, presenting the chieftain's head like a gift. My heart skipped a beat at his actions, knowing we were both still walking on eggshells around each other in many ways. How much more did I need to make him suffer when he had done nothing but steadily stand beside me?

I took his offering and stared into the epitome of what ignorance and fear created. Tossing it aside, I stared at the robed man and thought of Gunner. Necessity fueled my every move before I tore his body in half, the long fabrics of his robes making him fall awkwardly to the ground.

I would make sure religion never hurt him again. No one heard his sigh but me and I held onto it like a treasure, burying it inside my heart.

The crowd skittered back and as a couple of the residents ran wildly toward us with their pitchforks only to have Gunner rip their limbs apart and drop them on the ground screaming in pain as their hearts continued to pulse blood out of their wounds. I watched with growing admiration as he casually grabbed their weapons and impaled their necks, ending their incessant noise. When he looked over at me, my heart skipped a beat as I let out a resounding sigh.

"I'm tired of lies," I whispered as the rain continued to pour down on us, washing away the evidence of all our sins for none of us were saints here. None of us could afford to be in order to survive. With the Chieftains' admission, it didn't escape my notice that not one of the residents balked at the admission as if it was something new —once again telling me, Eliseo had always been right. As these people needlessly added to the blood-soaked ground, I wondered if there truly was any hope for civilization and humanity in the future.

Perhaps, my former executioners were correct in their war toward making this world one dominated by vampires.

"He doesn't represent us all," the nurse spoke again, albeit a little shaky. Her courage in the moment shone like the lightning that continued to accompany nature's wrath. "We didn't all agree with his ways but had no other choice. This is our home."

Her words hit and my eyes burned with unshed tears. This was supposed to be our home... with Eliseo, and now he was gone.

"We couldn't do anything to stop him. I wanted to," she added as Reed tilted my head up and stared into my soul.

"What do you want me to do? Tell me what you need, *little iris* and I will burn the world down for you," he proclaimed only for my ears.

"Don't think you can get one up on me, Reed. I'm here for you too, Fitri. We'll follow you until the day we die."

I knew they would. It wasn't something that

didn't require verbal validation or reconfirmation but I appreciated them all the same. I could smell Samuel and Remi close by as well, though they chose to remain hidden behind the crowd. I understood why they chose their tactic. It was their way of letting me know they weren't going anywhere either.

I never set out to be the leader of anything, yet circumstance always threw me into the role anyway. Eliseo was my excuse to continue hiding, to pretend that I didn't have to worry with such an alpha making room for us no matter where we chose to go.

But life had other plans for me. As the thunder rolled and the weather threatened to physically drown us all in our follies, I tilted my head back and looked toward the sky. Was the religious man right? Was there something bigger at play, controlling our lives the way it was meant to go despite how much we thought we had free will this whole time?

Margaret's voice whispered in my mind.

"Things have changed, Faheema. I don't know what life has brought you but I know you never deserved what happened. But time can be a wondrous thing. Perhaps this was the ancestor's way of showing you the right path. One that will lead you to what you need to discover in order to finally find peace."

It was time to stop denying the truth that was in front of me.

"Things are about to change," I announced

without looking at anyone. "Silverforge is on the verge of its third rebirth and if you do not wish to follow me, now is the time to leave…" I brought my head down and looked at every one of the faces around me from young to old. "Or we'll make you."

Calmly, I walked back to my humble home with my men behind me. Thunder boomed and lightning struck, casting long shadows in front of us—painting us sentinels in this new world we were about to create.

When we reached our neighborhood, Maxwell's door swung open with wild abandon against the growing storm, his home empty. I didn't know what it meant, but I knew I would understand it in the by and by.

We entered our home and a different kind of electricity passed between us. Reed adjusted his wings around the furniture as Gunner stood at attention, waiting for my next command. I trusted my natural instincts, no longer willing to let the human side of me throw me into confusion.

I crooked my finger and slowly divested myself of my clothes along the way to the bedroom. My blood was rapidly twisting inside of me, the fight from earlier driving me toward a primal need to rid myself of the adrenaline. Before making it to the bed, Gunner wrapped his arms around me from behind, kissing along my neck and I sighed.

The shift and bristle of feathers circled the room as Reed stared at me with blatant hunger. It was said that newly made vampires thrived on blood and sex during their initial transition. But what of the ones that weren't created by a host? Would this appetite for destruction and carnality wade over time? Or would it forever bind us with its influence?

Was this how the first of the elites felt at the dawn of their new world?

I turned in Gunner's arms, kissing him slowly, exploring this new dynamic with caution. It was something none of us had experienced, and like my declaration to the people of Silverforge, I was going to take it by the horns.

Gunner lifted me onto the bed and let his weight down, forcing me to wrap my legs around him. Reed groaned from the far side of the room, forced to watch as Gunner finally let himself become one with me.

Skin to skin, I felt like we were on fire. The invisible flame that swirled around my soul, pulling him in to devour him too. Emotions collided like the shutters of Maxwell's house, the weather mimicking our inner storm. Gunner's brand of lovemaking differed in a delicious way as our bodies slid against one another. I licked up the cord of his neck, nipping at his skin, speeding up his pace. I gasped as lightning struck outside before cloaking us in shadows. As I fell over the cliff of ecstasy, Gunner's teeth sank into the top of my breast, throwing him over the edge of his own release.

A tortured growl came from the corner of the

room as Reed slammed his head against the wall behind him with the back of his head. I reached my arm out toward him and his wings flared like an ethereal sentinel sent from another world. With quick strides, he got on the bed as Gunner lifted us both toward the center in a seated position. Gunner stared at me as I stared at Reed who looked like he was currently battling inner demons, trying to decide which he would let win this time.

"Come here," was all I told him as he leaned in and stole a kiss.

My gut churned wickedly like those many weeks ago until trailed his kisses along the slope of my shoulder and he bit into my back the same time Gunner bit into my neck. Then and only then did the dark foreboding ominous presence that clouded my mind during Eliseo's distance dissipate with the rainstorm that blew in through our window.

Thunder boomed again as the men both gave in to their primal urges, alphas fighting for dominance over my body yet placing my needs and pleasure as priority. I relished it, finally understanding the power I held over them, the power I abused and didn't realize it... until now.

The abandoned hybrid child, flesh peddled into a community that sentenced her and led her on the path of constant fatality. As Reed turned me toward him, he sealed my thoughts with a passionate kiss right before he lifted my hips and united us as one. Wings as black as death flared before softly engulfing me in darkness.

I was never meant to be the abomination they made me out to be...

...but the queen they were all afraid I would become.

I am *Sili*, the hunted, the outlier, forging my destiny from the very darkness that sought to consume me.

PLAYLIST

    Dorothy - Rest in Peace

    Metallica - Don't Tread on Me

    The Pretty Reckless - Make Me Wanna Die

    Ledger - Not Dead Yet

    Fireflight - Unbreakable

    Amon Amarth - Find a Way or Make One

    Stray Kids - Venom

    Red - Release the Panic

    Lacey Sturm - Impossible

    Bad Wolves - Zombie

If you get your kicks in a magical manner, order toys from websites like bad dragon, and prefer your monsters *in* your bed instead of *under* them, then Y. D. is your girl.

Writing everything from spicy dark fantasy to fluffier-than-a-cool-marshmallow romance, Y.D. La Mar has her fingers in all sorts of man-meat pie, and the sky is the limit. Somehow, this magical mistress manages to balance her spicy author life with her responsibilities as a mom, a wife, and a resident of Sin City—*oh, irony, you've felled me.*

When the world is full of black-and-white, Y.D. plays in the grey zones, spending her time creating new ways to shock and awe her editor, as well as her readers.

Follow Me!

FLOWCODE
PRIVACY.FLOWCODE.COM

WANT UPDATES AND SNEAK PEEKS?

Sign up for my newsletter!

Also by YD La Mar

STREET ARRHYTHMIA TRILOGY

The Scent of Jasmine

For The Love of Import & Blood

To The Beat of The Streets

Spinoff

Arachnophilia

REVERSE HAREM

Warring Suns

The Truth Enslaved

SCI FI

The Essence of Esme

Deliverance (cowrite)

PARANORMAL

The Hunger of Thieves

Heart of The Reaper

Heart of the Reaper: Tales from the Underworld

Soul of The Reaper

Fate of The Reaper

Bury Me Alive

Lead Me Through The Fire

The Good Char

PSYCHOLOGICAL THRILLER

The Truth Enslaved

Actus Reus

CONTEMPORARY

The Formation of Us

The Conception of Us

The Revelation of Us

The House of Eden (cowrite)

When the Bloom Burns (cowrite)

OMEGAVERSE

Gero

Bernhard

Severin

DYSTOPIAN/POST APOCALYPTIC

We Are the Fallen

We Are the Guilty

The Executed

MONSTER SHORT STORIES

Sinful Attraction

The Sky Below

Maeonia

Between Heaven and Earth

Fantasies Inflamed

Her 13th Hour

Ignus Fatuus

Suckers

Crimson Salt

ANTHOLOGIES

Used and Bound

Captured by Darkness

Until the End

After the Rain

Into The Woods

A Foster Fling

Bound by Monsters

Once Upon a Nightmare

Monsters in Love: Lost in the Dark

Monsters in Love: Lost in the Forest

Monsters in Love: Monstrous Ever After

Monsters in Love: Lost in the Deeps

Monsters in Love: Aloha Nui Loa

Monsters in Love: Lost in the Fire

Pollinators

The Red Key Club: Valentines Day Edition

The Red Key Club: Halloween Edition

Creepy Court

Crimson Vendetta

For the Love of Villains

SHARED WORLDS

Inferno World

Games of the Underworld

Rise of the Dreads

Monsters Ball

Rescue Me: A Hero Romance Collection